THE WOLVES OF VENICE

THE WOLVES OF VENICE

Alex Connor

First published in the United Kingdom in 2020 by Aries,
an imprint of Head of Zeus Ltd

A CIP catalogue record for this book is available from the
British Library.

ISBN 9781838932978

Typeset by Siliconchips Services Ltd UK

Cover design © NAME

Aries
c/o Head of Zeus
First Floor East
5–8 Hardwick Street
London EC1R 4RG

www.headofzeus.com

BOOK ONE

THE PUPPET MASTER

‘Do not be afraid;
Our fate cannot be taken from us;
It is a gift.’

Dante

Life is a toy made of glass; it appears to be of inestimable price, but in reality it is very cheap.

Pietro Aretino

Prologue

Venice, Italy 1548

A whisper is as dangerous as a trumpet call, they say, and in Venice a whisper remains within the Republic – for eternity. It shifts amongst the wooden poles that hold our city afloat. It clings to the agued steps and laps its tongue against the wet stonework. Sssh, it says, speak nothing, only whisper. Whisper it into the ears of the fish and the carcasses of drowned men.

I didn't discover the truth until many years later; it was a matter about which my father never spoke. But I knew he hated me for it, for the scandal that clung to his heels, the murmurings that faded, but never completely ceased. My mother was eighteen when she gave birth to me and eighteen when she died. A week between giving birth and losing life. She was found hanged, her chemise stained with afterbirth blood. Her feet were only a hand span from the floor, the window open, church bells effusive in their Easter welcome as her eyes stared open, the whites blood spotted, her body swinging slightly in the draft. Milk that should have fed her son oozed through the cotton chemise, making plate sized orbs, and around her left wrist there was a bruise, indigo, darkening to the colour of molasses.

This is what they told me.

This is what I believed.

The physician said my mother had suffered a brain fever; 'milk fever,' some call it, a temporary madness. She had been so troubled that she had committed self murder and alienated herself from God whilst bringing disgrace on the Gianetti house. They said that she had regarded suicide as a blessing, a release from pain.

But in my dreams I hear her choking, see her hands scrabble at the cord around her neck, watch her feet jiggle and shudder, doggy-paddling in dry air, her bladder loosening as she suffocated.

It was my fault. Had she never given birth she would not have killed herself. I was the worm in her belly, the wasp in her head; I was the cause – and my father reminded me of it every day of my life.

Chapter One

St Mark's Basilica,

Venice, 1549

The rest of his relations with the great is mere beggary and vulgar extortion.

(Burckhart, on Pietro Aretino)

He was walking splay-footed, his gait typical of an obese man, his arms swinging at his sides like the oars of a boat, churning up the hot air as he crossed St Marks. Pietro Aretino, mountebank, confidante of Titian, whoremonger, literary pornographer and known across Europe as 'the Scourge of Kings.' As he entered the church he sensed someone behind him and, dipping his porcine fingers into the Holy Water, turned.

"Signor Baptista," Aretino greeted the man, making a

flamboyant show of crossing himself. "I heard you were away in Florence."

"It was a short visit."

"To see your family?"

"My family is Florentine, yes. But I was there on another matter."

Aretino glanced at Baptista's side, his sword's gilded pommel catching the light from the high windows above.

"Did you find use for your 'friend', Adamo?"

"My friend is seldom lazy for long." He replied, his oval face perfectly composed, clean shaven, the sloe eyes unreadable.

Cunning bastard, Aretino thought, waddling to his seat as the choir began singing. Immediately Aretino's gaze moved from Baptista to the young boy soloist, then his attention passed to a stern faced man in one of the front pews. Almost as though he was aware of being watched, Barent der Witt glanced up, curtly returning Aretino's effusive bow of the head.

"You said you had news for me?" Aretino whispered to Baptista as they took they seats at the head of the congregation.

Knowing that he could be seen by seen by everyone, Aretino's presence worked as a reminder to those who feared him, which numbered hundreds in Venice. Every lie, every secret, every insult, Aretino took care to hoard. He had made his own personal abacus of sin; rows of petty spites, their numbers increasing into slanders, crimes, depravity, even murder. Blackmail was his peculiar skill; holding knowledge that was so damaging – that a man, or woman – would pay to keep such matters quiet. With impunity he bled the coffers of the nobility. And those of kings.

But now Aretino was adjusting his clothes, the damson red of his cape voluminous against the black garments beneath. It irked the writer that Baptista was so well muscled and lean; seemingly incapable of gaining poundage from the sweetmeats and the glacied fruits that Aretino ate so greedily. He was envious of his imperviousness to heat too; in the midst of a Venetian summer Baptista remained composed, his clothes never marked by sweat patches. The same sweat patches Aretino would struggle to conceal under layers of the finest linens from Egyptian merchants.

People might go in fear of Pietro Aretino, but Mother Nature remained unimpressed.

"You have news for me?" Aretino repeated. "Is it concerning the Dutchman being back in Venice?"

"No, this is not about der Witt."

"Then whom?"

"Gilda Fasculo."

Aretino shrugged his thick shoulders, his head almost touching Baptista's otter sleek hair as he bent to reply. "Who is Gilda Fasculo?"

"A usurer in the Jewish Ghetto."

Aretino blew out his lips, his eyes fixing on the priest for an instant before moving back to the solo choirboy. "Usury is forbidden in Venice."

"She does not call it usury."

"A cat is a cat if it meows."

"Unless someone has taught it how to bark."

Aretino laughed, a low sound, at the back of his throat. "A woman, you say?" He thought for a moment; the ghetto – which had been established in 1512 – had not initially interested him, but as the Jews had become more established

Aretino was curious to know more about their legendary business acumen. "So have all the Jewish men suddenly become eunuchs to let some hag run their business?"

"Gilda Fasculo is very skilled and she has support."

"Not from the Republic—"

"The Republic, signor, is as supple as a new whore." Baptista replied.

"And this new whore, who are her protectors?"

"Her sons, Federico and Angelo—"

"Children!"

"Men in their twenties. Newly come from Florence with their mother..." Baptista's voice rumbled underneath the singing of the choir, Aretino following every word as he continued. "... Their father died and they came here – to the ghetto – for sanctuary."

"Was the father a usurer?"

"A merchant who died suddenly—"

"And left his family penniless?"

"He owed money and goods, that was why they fled Florence to escape their creditors."

Aretino tapped Baptista's knee; an action his knew the younger man detested. "And you, my dear Adamo, do you know who these creditors are?"

"I believe I do."

"And *I* believe you do." Aretino replied. "And naturally these poor creditors would be grateful to know where – and from whom – their money and goods might be recovered. Of course, if the lady – this Guida Fasculo – is so adept with money there's a possibility I might make an allowance. *Forget* my duty to the state in return for a little commission. After all, this poor family should be granted a new beginning."

Baptista shifted his position in the pew, brushing away Aretino's hand. But his dislike of the pederast was superseded by his liking of being Aretino's closest ally and spy. Besides, he was vaccinated against the writer's spite because of his usefulness; Aretino might hope to control him, but he was never sure of Baptista's loyalty, aware that the Florentine's skills might be employed elsewhere by a higher bidder.

"Perhaps I should speak with the lady?"

Aretino's eyebrows rose. "But not in the presence of her sons."

"No, a meeting alone would be better for all us." Baptista replied, inclining his head and sliding out of the pew.

"Oh, and one more thing," Aretino said softly, gripping the man's wrist with one beefy hand. "Find out why the Dutchman's back in Venice. I don't trust that dour apothecary."

Chapter Two

Venice had been the greatest trading power on the globe, their wealth accumulated by Venetians merchants who took advantages of the Crusades to increase their precedence. Politically adept, the Crusaders were persuaded to overthrow rivals merchants in Constantinople, and, as a reward for this ruthless attack, they were granted transportation to the Middle East and the Arab Empire.

The Venetians' wealth escalated, but their monopoly did not hold and when the Portuguese discovered the riches of the Indies the Venetians lost their stranglehold on the spice trade. And so the Republic's days of magnificence as a trading nation were curtailed, but the ever resourceful Venetians soon expanded their other methods of money making. Chemical industries were established to produce sugar and scented soap and despite the fame of Florence's silk trade, during the sixteenth century Venice's production increased six fold, together with their own manufacture of textiles. Developing secret – and infamous – methods of dyeing, the Republic's fame grew, especially as it was accompanied by the famed glass makers in Murano.

Yet for all the skilful advances in industry and despite their continued – if limited – overseas trade, the Venetians developed a reputation for opulence and brilliance. In a matter of a few years the shift had taken place and the Republic had compensated for their losses in goods, by asserting their supremacy in art.

Culture was the preferred trade. By the early sixteenth century Venice was famed for its books and printing works, Hebrew tomes published and distributed across Europe, some to the very places where the Jews had been forced to leave. Accepting their loss of power as a marine nation, Venice flourished in alternative ways, the government lifting the ban on theatre. Actors and musicians were suddenly free to perform for the nobility, and charge for their amusements, and before long patrons invested in plays and musical displays.

And, as ever, sex was a commodity, as valuable as spices or gold thread. Having always flourished in a city that enjoyed the flesh, the whores fell into distinct categories. The common street walker; the kept mistress of a merchant; and the upper echelon of the cultured whores. The women who counted musical talent, artistic appreciation and a brilliant wit as sidepieces to the banquet of their sexuality.

With the lavish and demanding appetite for beauty came the genius. Titian was already famed in Venice – as had been the Bellini brothers before him – but the younger painters were sensing an opportunity, and with that opportunity came the clash of the giants.

House of Tintoretto

'Fondamnta dei mon'

The torchlight reflected obliquely off the water as

Tintoretto pulled the door closed behind him and glanced down the side of the canal. He could smell the Adriatic, its sting of ozone strong, but better that than the stagnant water in the long summer swamp months. Raising the rush light higher he moved towards the bridge as the evening mist made curls against the stonework, the damp air creating an aureole around the torch. He was relieved that it was so quiet, long before Venice had warmed up, the sulky fogs reluctant to let go and keeping people indoors.

Above his head, coming from an apartment high up, he heard a sigh of music. Tintoretto didn't know what kind of music, fancied that it came from a lyre, but wasn't sure. He didn't really have time for music or the pleasures of Venice. And he knew that he would never be a favourite with the Doge or flattered in court circles. The nobility might one day favour him, but only by proxy, due to his having once been Titian's student. Titian's *temporary* student.

Tintoretto paused, listened, then crossed the bridge and headed for the hospital, taking a short cut to the back entrance. A woman glanced at him curiously as he passed, Tintoretto making a muted greeting and hurrying on.

"I was wondering if you were coming," a weary voice said as Tintoretto pushed open the double doors, the wood warped, riven with graffiti. "You are so very late."

"I forgot the time, caro dottore" the artist replied, placing his rush light into an empty wall bracket and glancing at the doctor.

His face was as dark as a mole's, engrained over eighty hot Venetian summers, his cheeks concave, his eyes drooping behind black rimmed glasses. Although dressed sombrely, he sported a ruff in the Spanish style, the white speckled with flecks of dried leaves, heavily scented with sandalwood. It was a legacy of the plague: when doctors had worn nosegays and masks to prevent infection – and in a vain hope of killing some of the stench.

"Medico Norillo," the artist began, keen to continue. "I have something for you—"

"In return for something *from* me?"

Tintoretto wasn't certain what the old man meant, and continued. "— I have the frame for the portrait of your wife."

"Which is not the same as money."

"You asked for a portrait!" Tintoretto replied, infuriated. He had known the old doctor for many years, but his increase in prestige made no impact on Norillo.

"But a portrait is not lira, is not a bag of gold."

"You will not be disappointed." Tintoretto replied, abashed.

"I am *already* disappointed. My life is a continual parade of disappointments." the doctor replied, taking hold of Tintoretto's rush light and passing it to him. "Come on, come with me. *Come on!*"

Moving behind the old man, Tintoretto replayed the conversation in his mind. Was the doctor teasing him? *Was* he serious? *Was* he disappointed?... Tintoretto found himself floundering – a feeling that was familiar to him and had been all his life. As usual, he was unable to decipher the doctor's real mood. He cursed his own stupidity, thinking of Titian and how he and his cronies were so socially adept, so skilful at reading between the words and picking out the kernel of truth.

Following the doctor, Tintoretto's thoughts returned

to the past, to the time of his apprenticeship. His father, although not an artistic man, had noted his son's talent and taken him to see Titian, the greatest painter in Venice. They had hurried through the Venetian streets, over camel-humped bridges and steaming summer canals until finally they reached an impressive villa in the Cannaregio district of the lagoon.

The gates had been manned by two black slaves dressed in startling yellow, an opulent fruit garden leading towards the studio. *Look* the building seemed to say, *see how rich I am, how successful my owner must be. And yet here you come, with your worn breeches and your dyer father, hoping to be accepted here...*

"You must be polite, my son, you hear? Titian is the greatest painter in Venice, in Italy even." His father had hissed into his ear, both of them staring at the figure which approached.

A little below six feet in height, Titian had been wearing breeches and a white shirt, the sleeves rolled up to the elbows. His burly arms were clean without the usual paint spots seen on most artists, his face refined, the short trimmed beard a dark auburn, his eyes unexpectedly blue. His appearance was a surprise to Tintoretto; he might have been a wealthy merchant, a banker at the Doge's palace, even an elegant cardinal. But not a painter. Not the usual kind of unkempt, pre-occupied artist that ran a frenzied studio and touted for business across Venice with their portfolio under one arm.

"Welcome," Titian said graciously, his voice autocratic as he explained that he was occupied with commissions for the Doge and for the court and he had no need for more apprentices.

"But, signor Titian, my son has talent—"

"I do not doubt it, but talent alone is not enough to succeed in Venice." The artist had replied, flicking through the drawings handed to him. "There are many competent painters in the city."

Tintoretto's father had not been willing to cow to anyone. Even the Republic's premier artist.

"He is very quick, we call him *Il Furioso* because of his speed. He can paint a wall in the time another man would struggle to reproduce a child's head. People come to watch him." he nudged his son, "Show the Maestro what you can do. Show him!"

"Show him?"

Sighing, Tintoretto's father handed his son a piece of charcoal and a sheet of paper. "Draw something boy!"

The apprenticeship which followed had been a matter of triumph for Tintoretto's father. He was a dyer and considered his son's success as a badge of honour for the family. But it didn't last, the association coming to a bizarre and sudden halt. And this time Tintoretto's drawings did *not* work in his favour.

He remembered the day, white and hot, the sea without its usual horizon marker. As ever he had arrived at Titian's studio soon after dawn, exchanging a greeting with the cook newly returned from the market. With his drawings under his arm, Tintoretto had glanced into the mirror in the hallway leading to the studio. His curly hair had looked dusty, his eyes challenging, almost hostile. Surprised, he had tempered his expression, then moved onto the courtyard, crossing the cool marble flags and pushing open the wrought iron doors to the studio.

The smell of paint had been strong, mixing with the odour of stale wine and perfume over laden with oleander and orange blossom. The previous night the scent would have been lyrical, but it had become jaded, almost sour. As his eyes had adjusted to the shuttered light, Tintoretto had tripped over a small dog, almost colliding with a black woman carrying a bowl of fruit. Keeping her eyes averted she had guided past him, the painter suddenly aware of laughter coming from a curtained alcove.

"How clumsy you are," a man said, pulling back the curtain and then opening the studio shutters to allow the daylight to enter.

Tintoretto had flushed, his awe of Titian obvious, his palms sweaty as he laid the drawings down on a table under the window, aware that there was someone else in the studio behind the alcove. A woman? Maybe, but not likely, Titian, unlike many of his Venetian cohorts, was faithful to his wife.

"I brought the drawings you asked for, maestro. And others, a number of others."

Titian had looked at the work, his shrewd blue eyes alert, his knife-shaped eyebrows rising. "So many? Why so many?"

"I wanted... I just..." Tintoretto had trailed off. Was quantity a sin? Were his master's words a comment or a rebuke?

"I was excited—"

"*Over* excited." Another voice had said suddenly, the barrel like figure of Aretino coming into the light. "How very busy you have been." He had looked over to his friend, Titian staring at the drawings in silence. "And how are they?

Is this avalanche of expression worthy of praise? Or has our little dyer been too busy and too fast for his own good?..."

Titian had said nothing, just continued to flick over the drawings, one by one, then once again. Tintoretto could see the charcoal images activated in front of him, women moving, embracing, men on horseback leaping and falling, and several shifting figures of Jesus swept up in the shuddering melee.

"... So is industry akin to talent?" Aretino had continued.

Still Titian had said nothing.

"... Or should talent be weighed and measured like a precious oil?" Smiling, Aretino had taken an orange off the fruit platter and begun to peel it, staring at Tintoretto. "Are you trying to impress your master, little dyer?"

"I was just drawing –"

"Just drawing?" Aretino had repeated, "Of course, I see that you wish to be as good as Titian."

"I could never be that—"

A sudden noise had made him jump as Titian slammed the leather portfolio closed, one corner of a drawing trapped like the broken wing of a bird.

"I can teach you nothing."

"But I am your apprentice!"

"No longer, Tintoretto," Titian replied, "There is nothing I can teach you. You are not in need of my tutoring."

Aretino had paused with the half eaten orange in his hand, his sly gaze moving from Tintoretto to his friend and back again.

"You think this little fellow has nothing to learn?" he asked mockingly. "Titian, you must show a little mercy, Venice will not support a painter you have dismissed as your apprentice." He had dropped the sucked orange onto the platter and wiped his hands on a serving cloth. Mischief had flickered like a light inside him. "Is Tintoretto an indifferent painter?... Or a great one?"

Titian had not answered. Not in words. He had simply turned his back to indicate that Tintoretto had been dismissed.

The doctor was losing his patience, his fretful voice dragging Tintoretto back to the present. "Are you coming? Come on!" Norillo whined, opening the metal studded door beside the anatomy theatre. It was a place well known to Tintoretto, a narrow ante room off the morgue in which was one central stone slab. At the base ran a trough to catch the blood, a table with old dissecting instruments set against the wall.

Fifteen years had passed since Titian had so summarily dismissed Tintoretto and, as Aretino had predicted, Venice had made its judgement. The Doge and the nobility had not welcomed the little dyer, his lack of polish and courtly manners had alienated him almost as much as his talent had ostracised him from his master. Titian had been Venice's glory; Tintoretto was merely the brilliant upstart. And so it remained; Tintoretto admiring Titian's genius, Titian wary of *Il Furioso* and determined – in collusion with his cohorts – to deny him access to the patrons and the court.

"Good God, what happened to her?" Tintoretto said, glancing over to the grotesque torso of a woman lying on the stone slab and putting a cloth up to his nose. "She has been dead a while."

The doctor shrugged. "I called you yesterday. If you had come, there would have been no smell then. This is summer, ice is expensive. Next time go to Padua." He moaned. "I do my best for you. If I was caught, I would be punished, I'm risking my reputation for you, Tintoretto, I have done for years." He mewled. "But do you thank me? And how do you repay me for my kindness? With a painting!"

"A painting of your *wife*." Tintoretto retorted, walking around the mutilated corpse. "Surely, Norillo, you are not disappointed with my work?"

"Nature didn't make her handsome, but you managed it." The doctor replied grudgingly. "The bitch let me into her bed last night for the first time in years." He looked at the corpse and then folded his arms. "It's a while since you've been here. I would have thought you knew enough about the human body by now. You're famous all over Venice now. Although some say that's only because Titian's away and you've got an advantage. Some say—"

"Some say anything," Tintoretto interrupted. "I need more light, hold that lamp up for me."

"Titian is in Germany now, working for the King—"

"He is a great painter."

"And he admires you," Norillo said, holding up the lamp. "Or he wouldn't have thrown you out all those years ago. Titian doesn't like competition."

Tintoretto turned back to the old doctor. "He has nothing to fear from me—"

"Liar!" Dr Norillo replied, rearranging his glasses and shrugging. "No one comes to Venice to fail."

"I didn't *come* here, I was born in Lombardy and that's part of the Republic."

"Then it's your *duty* to succeed!" The medic snapped, his tone softening. "I saw your painting of the *Miracle of the*

Slave in the Scuola di St Marco. There was quite a queue to see it. People were staring and wondering how you could paint the bodies to look so real, so solid."

"I use little figures, models," Tintoretto admitted, flattered despite himself. "You see, I make them from clay and position them to see how they would look in a painting..." He picked up a scalpel and drew it down the length of the woman's neck on the right side, from her ear to her collar bone. "... Then I put the little clay figures in a box and light them with candles to see how the finished picture would look–"

"Like a child playing."

Tintoretto nodded. "Yes, like a child playing." He bent further over the corpse and studied the exposed jugular vein, his forehead wrinkling. "But now and then I need to see a real body to remind myself, to *assure* myself that am right. There is always something more to learn." He stepped back. "How did she die?"

"Not of the plague." The doctor replied, mockingly. He gestured to the mutilated torso, minus its arms and legs. "She was murdered. Her corpse dismembered, God rest her soul."

"D'you know who she was?"

"Unknown to me and unclaimed by any family."

"And no one knows who killed her?"

"No one cares!" the medic replied. "The body was found in the water—"

"Like this?"

Norillo nodded. "Like that. Four days ago and brought to the hospital's anatomy room."

Tintoretto studied the torso. "The wounds where her

arms and legs were severed are old, there are no new cuts." He looked at the shoulders and thighs where the limbs had been removed, the muscles grey, the bones the colour of soured milk.

"No, no new wounds. Apart from the one you've just made," the medic agreed, nodding. "You know how it works. When a body's brought here I let the medics know it's available for dissection in the Anatomy Theatre—"

"For a fee?"

"Of course for a fee! Everything's for sale in Venice. I'm an old man, I need to provide for my family. If anything should happen to me they need to be safe. We all know how the poor live in Venice, I don't want them to suffer." Norillo whined on. "But I take a risk with you. The bodies are only supposed to be used by doctors, not fucking artists."

"You get more from me than the doctors. That painting I did of your wife is worth good money, so don't try and fool me, Norillo."

Wrong footed, the medic shrugged. "What's all the interest anyway? D'you know the woman?"

"She looks familiar," Tintoretto admitted. "I think – maybe – she sat for me a year ago. I can't be sure, she's different—"

"Everyone looks different without their arms and legs." Norillo said snidely. "I can tell you one thing for certain, she drowned. But she was cut up first. Whoever killed her tortured her before they tossed her into the water."

Tintoretto flinched, then looked back to the corpse. "And no one came to see her?"

"No one."

"In four days, *no one* came to claim her, or view the body?"

"I've told you, no one claimed her." Norillo hesitated, the rush light flaring as a draft entered the dank chamber.

The pause was enough. "*Who* came to see the body?"

"It's not my position to say." Norillo whinged, moving from foot to foot.

"*Who* came to see her?"

"Why does it matter—"

"*Who?*"

"He thought it was a woman he knew, but it wasn't—"

"*Who* thought?"

"Baptista. Adamo Baptista."

The name curdled in the damp air; it sent a shudder through the old medic and made Tintoretto pause. Adamo Baptista, artist, gambler and Pietro Aretino's spy; a Florentine who moved around Venice untouched. A man suspected of a dozen crimes, about whom rumours flourished in the dark like mushrooms; a man who escaped the authorities by stealth -shielded under the protection of the dissolute Behemoth, Aretino.

In silence Tintoretto took out a small vellum pad and sketched the woman's mutilated torso, then her face. He took great care over the details, making hurried notes about the colour of her lashes, the chip off one of her front teeth and the faint indentations on either side of the bridge of her nose. When he had finished he turned back to the medic, who was tapping his foot impatiently by the door.

"See to it that she gets a proper burial."

Norillo shrugged. "The girl's bound for the Autopsy theatre tonight—"

"Can you not stop it?" Tintoretto asked.

The doctor pulled down the corners of his mouth in a grimace. "No, I **cannot** stop it – and why should I? The doctors have to learn, you know that. Besides, you've never bothered about a corpse before—"

Tintoretto looked down at the disfigured girl.

"For pity's sake, don't let them cut her up. Hasn't she suffered enough?" he turned back to the old man. "You know what will happen, they will leave after they've finished with her and then talk about it, describe what she looked like, what had been done to her. They'll share the details all over Venice."

"That's not my concern." Norillo replied shortly, pulling the sheet over the corpse. "She's passed feeling anything."

Tintoretto shook his head. "If you can't stop the autopsy, promise me this. When they're done with her, see that she gets a proper funeral."

"That will cost—"

"I'll pay for it!" Tintoretto said shortly. "And if Adamo Baptista comes back—"

"Look, I don't want any trouble with that man." The medic retorted nervously. "No one does. I'm not getting involved."

Tintoretto tapped his arm. "Be calm, medico, I'm not asking anything of you. There is no danger. But should Adamo Baptista comes back, don't tell him I was here. You understand?..."

Norillo nodded.

"...don't tell him was ever here."

Chapter Three

Signora Castilano was watching a pair of men talking on the street outside. Even though she had come from Spain and been graciously assimilated into Venice's business life, she looked on all other foreigners as a lower class, fodder to her peculiarly luxurious mill. She could estimate from the opulence of the turbans and the silken flutter of the breeches that the merchants were Turkish and affluent; probably dealers in silks, tapestries and the gold threaded trimmings for which Venetian women had an insatiable appetite.

The courtesans would pay generously for such exclusive fripperies, decking themselves out like show horses as they glided across St Marks. Much business was undertaken in the time it took to cross the famous Square. A whore could ensnare a protector, a man could undertake a business deal, and an opportunistic woman could net herself many a glossy fish.

Hearing the door open, Marina Castilano turned to see a man enter. He was in his fifties, dressed in sombre, dusty black clothes and wearing a large brimmed hat in the Dutch style. His face, buckled with lines, had retained its Northern pallour, a great dark birthmark on his left cheek. From his neck hung a small glass vial full of liquid and round his left wrist was a bracelet of dark hair, intertwined with gold.

"Signor der Witt," Marina greeted him, smiling at one of her infrequent, but lucrative, clients. "How can I help you today?" she glanced at his dishevelled clothes. "You have been travelling?"

Der Witt took of his hat and turned the brim round in his hands. "You have many clients, Signora, I thought you might be the person best placed to help me."

"It's true, I rent clothes and embellishments to many in Venice."

She smiled, her fortune had been made over the years in the business of pretence. Venice was a city of pride; pride in beauty; pride in money and the *appearance* of money. A man needed to seem wealthy enough to own an extensive wardrobe, and to know of – and wear – all the royal fashions come from the courts of Spain, France and Germany. Very few could afford to endlessly replace their clothes to avoid the indignity of wearing a garment twice and so the trade of garment hiring flourished.

For the more adventurous young men of the nobility Marina was a willing and discreet supplier. Able to furbish them with more individual styles; transparent tunics and breeches for the homosexual partners of wealthy men: ribbons and gilded bells to tie around their genitals; and the open crotch silk pantaloons favoured by the courtesans. Venetians clerics favoured love making with a whore who pretended to be a boy, and a chemise that flattened the woman's breasts and yet left her genitals exposed was considered a delicious pretence.

All of Marina's elegant and expensive stock was delivered

by the merchants coming from Europe and the Far East, laden with goods for the prosperous and greedy Republic. China was a particularly inventive country for the sexually deviant. Marina had been doing business with a merchant from Hong Kong and another from Istanbul for many years, buying wares that she sold – not in the respectable shop with its refined and elegant outlook to the square – but in the atelier up the narrow back stairs.

Yet there was something Marina did not sell – sexual stimulants or *devices*, those she left to the old drabs hired by the courtesans. Although lucrative, such trading was always open to blackmail and the threat of the Inquisition. But the old whores, madams or apothecaries were not adverse to performing an abortion or pretending to cast a spell. In Venice it was part of life; an unwanted child, an unwanted lover, an unwanted rival – all and everyone was for sale, or for disposal. For a price.

Over the years Marina Castilano had become a skilled funambulist. Rivalry in Venice was frenetic; a whisper in the wrong ears could result in a shop closing and a business disappearing overnight. So she had learned discretion, working with her younger sister, Lucia. Speaking Italian in public, but Spanish in private. Keeping secrets, something natural to her. The dark guile of her home country running through her blood.

So now she was looking at the Dutch apothecary and wondering exactly what he wanted.

"Signor der Witt, please tell me how can I help you."

"Pietro Aretino is one of your customers."

She smiled, putting out her hands, palm upwards. "I cannot say. I never discuss—"

"I know he comes here, everyone knows." der Witt continued. "That is not the issue. I merely wondered if his... if his *colleague* Adamo Baptista came also."

Marina could sense a movement in the alcove behind and knew that her sister, Lucia, was listening. The thought comforted her, it was always imperative to have witnesses – especially with a man like Barent der Witt. And especially when he was asking after Adamo Baptista.

"I can deny or confirm, signor—"

"Signora," der Witt said, moving closer to her. "This is a matter of some importance. I assure you I understand your reluctance to break a confidence. I would not ask it of you if there was another way—"

"You are right, I *am* reluctant to break a confidence and so I must, sadly, ask that this conversation goes no further."

Der Witt fingered the glass vial around his neck; his thumb closing over its stopper like a lock.

"Surely there is no harm in asking if Signor Baptista is one of your clients? I could find out as much by asking one of your neighbours."

"I imagine you would already have done so," Marina replied calmly "and had no luck. Or you would not be asking me directly."

He sighed, his heavily lined face contemptuous. "Is everyone afraid of Adamo Baptista?"

The question hung in the air like a meat hook holding a dead carcass, Der Witt the first to speak again.

"I find it strange, signora, that you do not ask me *why* I have come to you, and what this matter of importance might be. And *why* I might be asking about Signor Baptista."

"It is not my concern."

He ignored the reply and continued.

"I will tell you anyway. You had a maid, signora, a woman called Gabriella Russo. She came to me afraid, very afraid. She said that she needed help and begged me to help her."

"I know nothing of this." Marina replied, watching out of the corner of her eye as her sister came into view. Lucia stood beside her sister, her stout form confronting the Dutchman.

"As my sister said, Signor der Witt, we know nothing. Gabriella did work for us and then she left abruptly, *sin explicación...*"

"Without explanation." Marina translated the Spanish into Italian as Lucia continued.

"...and we have not heard from Gabriella since. I think my sister would agree with me that we did not know of her being in any trouble."

Marina nodded, the Dutchman looking from one sister to the other. "But I didn't say she was in trouble."

"You said she was afraid and needed your help." Marina continued, her tone even. "*Did* you help her, Signor der Witt?"

"No." he said bitterly. "Not in time."

"*In time?* Why, what happened?"

"Gabriella has disappeared."

Marina sighed, glancing at her sister. "You say she disappeared before you had chance to help her and I've already explained that she left the shop without explanation. Causing us much inconvenience. If she has disappeared, maybe Gabriella chose to. Perhaps she does not wish to be found."

The Dutchman brushed away the explanation with one hand. "She was afraid, she needed help."

"And if she had come to us, we would have helped her, but she never confided in myself or my sister."

Marina was always discreet, but Lucia could not control her curiosity. "*¿A qué le tenía miedo?* Excuse me, signor, I asked 'what was she afraid of'?"

Der Witt paused, his expression unyielding. "As you say..." he replied, moving to the door "...it is not your concern."

Chapter Four

The Jewish Ghetto

Venice

Stepping over a pool of rain, Ira Tabat moved down the narrow alleyway towards his home, pushing open the doorway and climbing two flights of stairs. The rain had seeped through a crack in the roof, a sliver of water ribboning down the plaster. He consoled himself with the fact that it was worse for the Jews in Rome; their living quarters in the capital were flooded every year in the rainy season, and they were still forced to pay taxes for their board.

At least in Venice life was less Draconian; the Republic's Jews allowed to work in the city in daylight. But at night they were forced to obey the curfew, the gates locked at dusk. Since childhood Ira had hated the sound, the dull metallic thunk of the gates slammed shut, the realisation that he was imprisoned, jailed for nothing but an accident of birth that had created him a Jew.

He took off his jacket and glanced over to the bed against the wall. As usual, his mother was asleep, breathing rhythmically like a clock. Tick, tock, in, out, tick, tock, in, out. But no alteration, no chimes, no striking of some relieving bell. Her clock was uniform, a silent soldier stomping down the minutes to some unknown destination, in some unfamiliar time.

"She's resting well."

He turned to smile at his sister, Rosella, solemn faced, but undeniably handsome; with great dark eyes and a long fine nose over a wide mouth. Within the last year Ira had seen her mature, noticed how the ghetto boys stared after her and he had warned them off, proudly protective – as their late father would have been.

"Did she eat anything today?"

"A little, but mostly she sleeps." Rosella replied, setting out two places at the scrubbed table and then jerking her head towards the door. "Angelo Fasculo next door was caught by the shirri for not wearing his hat," Ira thought of the yellow cap all Jews were forced to wear, along with a small yellow wheel on their jacket. If they forgot, or lost the badge, it was sometimes overlooked – but not if they were caught without the cap. "He was fined 50 ducas and they said he was going to have to spend a month in jail."

Ira shook his head. "But he's new here—"

"Angelo told them that but they still want the 50 ducas." She sighed. "It's stupid, everyone knows some people are allowed to stay beyond the curfew. I heard the Corenelli family have their Jewish lawyer and banker at their parties, and no one objects. Instead, they show their cleverness off to their friends, like a couple of Jewish dancing bears." She cut some bread and cheese and laid it out on the table. "Someone else told me that Abel Solomon attended Mass at Chiesa di San Giacomo di Rialto with his employers. A Jew in a Catholic church—"

"He attended Mass, he didn't take Mass."

"Attend it, take it," she retorted heatedly, "what's the difference? It's still a betrayal of faith. If we don't defend who we are, we will become like everyone else."

"And have easier lives," Ira replied, smiling wryly as he began to eat.

"Easier lives, but false lives. We were born what we are and must remain true to it. We don't belong to Venice, or Rome, or any other city or country. We are complete in ourselves."

He smiled at her earnestness, her conviction. She was emphatic about everything. What was right, what was necessary, what must be fulfilled. All her life, Rosella had wanted to study music, but in a ghetto there was no money for tuition, so instead she worked as a maid for a Hyman Golletz, a Jewish piano teacher, and he had paid her in singing lessons. Her progress had been intermittent, his teaching uneven, but as she had grown and developed a strong contralto voice, Golletz's interest had increased. At weddings and feasts in the ghetto Rosella had been encouraged to perform, her voice intense and haunting as she sang the ancient Jewish songs.

There was even talk of her having a career outside the ghetto, so when Rosella suddenly announced that she was no longer working for Hyman Golletz, Ira stopped, bread on one hand, cheese in the other, his expression baffled.

"*What?*"

"It's selfish," she said emphatically, cutting into the cheese. "what this family needs is to make money, not waste time pursuing a pointless hobby—"

"Hyman thinks you could be a professional singer—"

"Only in the ghetto."

"Not necessarily," Ira persisted, "he said that your voice had improved so much he might be able to find work in the city for you—"

"And a fat fee for him," she retorted.

He studied his sister's face, her hands busy, breaking the bread, crumbs falling onto the scrubbed table like dry snow.

"Has Golletz behaved improperly towards you?"

Her dark eyes were scornful. "Hyman's seventy years old!"

"I just wondered, your decision seems very sudden."

"It's just that I feel..." Rosella ripped into the bread, "I feel guilty. I'm not earning much as a maid and I wondered if well... if there was *another* way to bring money in."

Ira laid down his knife and leaned back on his stool, his gaze moving over to where their mother was sleeping. "Why do we need more money? We can't do anything for our mother now. There is no more—"

"I know there's no medicine that can help her. You know that. You've tried everything, God knows. You're a doctor, Ira, you would know if you could do anything. You've even asked other doctors in the ghetto, but we all know our mother's slipping away, she's dying..." She baulked at the word, then moved on. "But if we had some more money we could get better lodgings, somewhere more comfortable for her, for all of us." She hurried on, seeing a look of irritation cross her brother's face. "You can't work any harder, no man could. Your patients have grown to trust you, they ask for you, they rely on you. Ira, everyone values you. Even the traders come to you for advice—"

"For the pox."

"Not always," she retorted, smiling. "You're known, people talk about you. They trust you—"

His tone was cold. "But I don't earn enough."

"Don't be offended! I didn't mean to hurt you, you've provided for us since I was a child, but now *I* can provide too. And what I'm saying is that working as Hyman Golletz's cleaner is not the way to a fortune."

"So you have found a way to make a fortune?" Ira asked, his eyebrows raised. "Tell me, Rosella, I'm fascinated as to how you are going to fill our coffers and put us all in a palace."

Angered, she pushed back her stool and rose.

"Don't mock me! I'm not a child, and perhaps it's time you realised that, Ira. I have a right to a say in this family – just as much as you do."

"I have never said otherwise!" He snapped, his tone softening. "So what's your idea?"

She turned to move away, then turned back, taking in a breath. "You know the painter, Tintoretto?"

"I know of him. Everyone in Venice knows of him. Why?"

"I was in the piazza last Wednesday afternoon, it was raining very hard—"

"I remember."

"—and he approached me. Very politely. He's rather a shy man, a little awkward. And he asked—"

"He approached you in the street?" Ira repeated, enraged. "And you spoke to him?"

"Tintoretto was very polite and begged me to forgive his presumption, but he wondered if—"

"If?"

"— I would sit for him."

Sighing, Ira leaned forwards with his elbows on the table, his head in his hands. "Sit down, Rosella." She could tell from the tone of his voice that he was angry and regained her seat as he continued. "You're seventeen years old, respectable young Venetian women of your age are kept in their homes and only enter the streets with a chaperone—"

"But we are *not* Venetians, we are Jews."

"We are no less than them! You are as respectable as the daughters of the Rannuccio family or the Colonia—"

"But I have to work for a living."

"Not as a whore!"

She flushed. "Is that what you think? That being a sitter for one of Venice's finest painters is being a *whore*?"

"Titian—"

"We are not talking about Titian! We are talking about Tintoretto, and he is an honourable man. I have asked around, spoken to Hyman Golletz and others in the ghetto and I've heard many good things about the artist. I admit that if it had been Titian I would have been nervous—"

"You would have had every right to be nervous. Titian may well be powerful and admired, but his circle is one of the most infamous in Venice. And most of his models are courtesans."

"But Tintoretto is not Titian."

Ira rolled his eyes Heavenwards. "It doesn't matter, Rosella, it's not what it is in reality, it's what it *appears* to be."

"That's a rabbi's argument. So we should go without because of people's opinion? In *reality* we're poor, and that's also what we *appear* to be. But this is a way for us to prosper." She took in a breath, her eyes fixed on her brother. "I went to temple, to ask advice..."

He realised then that his sister was serious. She had not said I went to the synagogue, but *I went to temple to ask advice*.

"...the rabbi said it was a matter for my own conscience."

Ira shook his head "The usual answer—"

"But it *is* a matter of my own conscience." Rosella replied, "and my conscience says that I wish to do this. I trust Signor Tintoretto, he said that if I preferred I could come with a companion."

"Would it be a waste of my breath to forbid you to do this?" She reached out towards her brother's hand, but Ira moved it away, his expression unyielding. "We do not need better lodgings, Rosella—"

"*You* do not need better lodgings," she replied. "Because you, brother, are not here for more than a few hours a day. You come in with the curfew, bone tried, and then you fall asleep. When they open the gates at sunrise, you leave. And sometimes before, because a doctor has a freedom to come and go when he is called for. You live here, but your life is beyond the ghetto, your thoughts far beyond this sticky cluster of houses crammed one on top of each other. You don't see that the sun has to fight to make any impression on the alleys, or that the weak plaster we pack into the holes in the roof when it rains never lasts and falls off again with the next storm. Your life – your *mind* – is out there." She gestured to the city beyond the ghetto walls. "And I don't blame you for that, Ira. You're building a reputation, something encouraged in Venice; it's a city of reputations. Any man without an idea or a dream wouldn't last a week. You *have* a dream, Ira," she leaned towards him. "It's a good dream, because you're a good man…And now you pull a face at me! But I've heard people talk about you 'Ira Tabat is a remarkable doctor. Amongst the finest in Venice.' Even the Dutch like you," she smiled, trying to coax him back into good humour. "and the Dutch seldom like anyone."

"They *are* surly." He agreed.

"But when Lijsbet comes to Venice, who does he seek out? You. You healed his leg when he could barely walk on it. Your reputation is known. Your name is spreading."

"As it should be. I'm thirty one, Rosella, not a boy."

"And most of the doctors in the ghetto are much older men—"

He brushed her words aside. "You're changing the subject, this has nothing to do with Tintoretto—"

"It has, because I've made up my mind." She said quietly. "I would never dishonour my name or my family, I am no whore, nor will I ever be. I have too much respect for myself. But I will sit for Tintoretto and you must trust me… You see, I want a life outside the ghetto too."

"It is not safe outside. Not for a young woman."

"I understand, but I will not take risks." She assured him. "You have ambition and I want to be something more. I can't marry a rich man, or parade like a Venetian Contessa, but I can live another way." She held his face with her hands and looked into her brother's eyes. "I want *my* escape. And Tintoretto is *my* escape. He is famous, his paintings are seen by thousands, people stand in awe of his work. Even if I live and die in the ghetto my life will mean something. If he paints me, I am someone. If he paints me, I exist."

Chapter Five

Walking silently over the bridge towards the alleyway, Adamo Baptista paused at the main entrance of the Jewish ghetto in Cannaregio, then walked in. The buildings were blank faced, unlike the Venetian opulence of their neighbours, several covered stone wells breaking up the bareness of the square, a few listless trees as dowdy as their surroundings.

He was aware that he was being watched, that a small clutch of people had gathered, standing under an awning at the doorway which lead to the Kosher butcher and the synagogue above. Venetian law forbade the building of free standing temples, so the synagogue was built over the shop, above the bones and offal of the dead animals below, crushed between a boarding house and a dressmaker's. Baptista checked the street signs, then moved towards a house with a green painted door. As he approached a man came out, glanced suspiciously at him, and then moved off. Unperturbed, Baptista pushed open the door and looked in.

A woman in her late sixties was seated at a table by a narrow arched window overlooking a weary courtyard. Her hair was grey and tied back from her face, her profile stern, and lined as tree bark. Without speaking, Baptista watched as she counted out money, gathering the coins in neat piles and laying them in a row in front of her. He waited patiently, looking about him. The room was furnished with a table, four chairs and a menorah, the seven branch Jewish candlestick, the chamber divided by a curtain. Behind which Baptista could not see.

"Why are you standing there?..."

He glanced at the woman, who had turned and was looking at him. "... Do you wish to speak to me?"

Nodding, he moved across to her. Now he could see her more clearly she had a resolute expression, her eyes stone grey. "What can I do for you, Signor Baptista?"

"You know me?"

"I know of you."

"As I know of you, Signora Fasculo." Baptista replied, taking a seat opposite her at the table. He glanced at the rows of coins, his head tilted to one side. "Usury is forbidden in Venice."

"And yet I hear of Christians offering credit with interest, which is apparently legal. The Venetian banks obscure it by claiming that a service is being provided with the loan." She held Baptista's stare. "We—"

"You."

She nodded. "*I* am useful because I am prepared to lend to the very poor, something the banks would not allow."

He nodded, then frowned. "But, Signora Fasculo, how is it that *you* have funds to lend?"

"They are not my funds."

"Ah," he said, his tone mocking. "So you loan in order to grant loans?"

The great pale eyes flickered. “May I ask what business this is of yours, Signor Baptista?”

“May I ask how you know me?”

“You are talked about.”

“For what reason?”

“Does there have to be a reason?”

He smiled, leaned back. “C’e sempre un motivo per tutto a Venezi.”

She frowned. “Forgive me, my Italian is not good.”

“‘*There is always a reason for everything in Venice.*’” He translated for her, looking around the room. “Of course you do not have to speak Italian with Jews, do you?”

“No. We speak Hebrew amongst ourselves.”

He nodded. “My employer—”

“You have an employer?”

“Indeed. If a man holds secrets it is useful to have an ally who shares them…Where did your money come from, Signora Fasculo?”

“From other Jews in the ghetto. People who appointed me to look after their funds. When we came here we were going to set up our own bank, but that was forbidden, so instead there was a vote and I was elected.”

“And you receive a wage, a fee, for this service?”

“A small one, yes.” She replied, her hands clasped together to prevent them shaking. “The people trust me.”

“Why would they do that?”

“*What?*”

“Trust you. Why would they do that?” Baptista repeated, his tone light. “Or were you better at handling money than your husband was?” He could see the shock register in her face and continued. “Signor Guido Fasculo was stupid with financial matters – he must have been, or he would never have left so many debts when he died."

She swallowed, but held his gaze. "*What are you talking about?*"

"Money, Signora Fasculo… and your debts."

"It's all lies!"

"No, it's not. It's the truth. And I find it fascinating that the widow of a man who fled angry creditors in Florence should be put in charge of the ghetto coffers in Venice... "he smiled without warmth. "You and your family left Florence and came to Venice to leave your past behind. Just as you left unfortunate creditors..."

Silent, Guida Fasculo watched him.

"...Naturally the people you cheated are angry. And, I imagine, they would be very grateful for someone to tell them the whereabouts of you – and your sons. So they can recover what is rightly theirs—"

She looked at him pleadingly: "I am working as hard as I can to gather together funds to pay off the debts. I intend to repay every lira—"

"But how long will that take, Signora Fasculo?"

"I don't know..."

"Well, I can tell you – a long time." He sighed, pretending regret. "We have two alternatives here. One," he tapped the index finger of his left hand. "I can – and should – tell the authorities about the criminals living in our city. Of which you are one. Or two" he tapped his index finger again. "I could suggest a way out of your troubles." He leaned towards her again. "Would you like to know a way out?"

"My sons—"

"Cannot protect you. Instead they will be disgraced with

you. Venice likes order, the Doge does not tolerate crime – which is why the prisons are busy. Of course you may only be flogged publicly and your head shaved—"

The colour had gone from Gilda Fasculo's face, her voice curt. "What do you want?"

"To help you."

"To ruin me!"

"It is all a matter of perception." Baptista replied phlegmatically. "Not all the Jewish in your ghetto are poor. I can see that. Some of the women are superbly dressed and the professional men have big bellies and jingling pockets. There are famous doctors and lawyers here who are paid handsomely for their skills. And I think you should use the trust that they have placed in you—"

"I only deal with the very poorest."

"Signora, do not fucking lie to me," he said quietly, "I am not a fool, neither is my employer. We know exactly to whom you lend money. And we know who your creditors are in Florence. We know all about you – and I'm offering you a chance to escape justice."

Her voice wavered. "You call this an escape?"

"You can sit in here like an old crone for years and pick off your debts until your body is ancient and you piss when you walk. But it will take too long—"

"I cannot cheat my own people." She replied, distraught.

"Your husband did in Florence."

"He was a bad businessman, not a criminal!"

"And yet here you are, left to carry the burden." Baptista retorted. "Perhaps you will reconsider the offer. In return for my silence, you will pay a fee that you can skim off the ghetto rich."

"They are not rich!"

"Are you *very* stupid, Signora Fasculo?" he asked, his tone contemptuous. "We have already surmised that there are many poor here – and as many rich."

"But none is as rich as Venetians!"

"Money is money, wherever it comes from," Baptista replied, standing up. "My employer is offering you a fair deal – I would take it, Signora Fasculo, the galleys are not a place for old women."

And here I am, entering the tale again. Not in chronological order, but as the story flows best. It was essential that I positioned most of the principal characters in place first; Pietro Aretino, Adamo Baptista, Barent der Witt and Ira and Rosella Tabat. Oh, and of course, Tintoretto. I have now set the skittles on the board and, in time, they will all begin to fall.

What you didn't know until now was that I, Marco Gianetti, am apprenticed to Signor Tintoretto, the contract drawn up six months ago by my father, Jacopo. Apparently he had almost begged Il Furioso to accept me as his apprentice as my talent is, at best, 'pedestrian'.

I could have had the talent of a flea, but the Gianetti family is one of the wealthiest in Venice and artists – even revered ones – always need money. Naturally, if my father had tried the same approach with Titian he would not have had the same result; Venice's premier painter is sleek with success and boasts full pockets. Kings and Doges fight to be subjects of Titian, Tintoretto having spent years growling and running behind for scraps.

No one disputes his genius, but Il Furioso is just that; furioso that his talent has been constantly undermined by Titian. But as Venice is a city of opportunists when Titian was called to Germany and France his absence left a sinkhole into which Tintoretto dived, head first.

And so it was in the winter of 1548, when Il Furioso was glossy with triumph, his reputation fixed by the four paintings had created for the Scuola di St Marco. In Titian's absence the little dyer had been seen stomping across the city, with me in attendance, often carrying small wooden boxes and a battered felt bag of paints and oils. My master had other assistants, but I made him laugh, so he favoured me.

The very thing my father loathed, made me popular with Tintoretto and one bitter February morning when Venice glowered like a sick cat, my master called for me, grabbing my arm as I entered.

"You are late! You are always late. Why?" he asked, pausing at the sound of the clock striking from St Marks. "We begin work at the same time every day, why can you not remember that?"

"'We are what we repeatedly do. Excellence then, is not an act, but a habit.'" I replied, smiling. "Aristotle."

"Aristotle was not a painter, Marco. You are. Only if you were learning to be a philosopher would quoting a dead Greek support your argument." He led me to a side table, pulling away a cloth. "Light the candles."

As he did many times before when he was planning a new work, Tintoretto had created a series of wax figures, in various attitudes, one suspended from the top of the box by a piece of string. An angel, I presumed. The box – a vegetable box I had fetched from the market the day before – was stained with tomato juice and measured no more than two feet in depth and four feet in width. In height it was around eighteen inches, the whole tableau crowded. His wax figures frantic, urgent. Furious with activity.

"An angel?..." I asked, pointing to the suspended figure.

He nodded brusquely.

"...... he has a tomato stain on his arse."

Tintoretto laughed, nudging me with his elbow and was about to respond when we heard footsteps approach.

A heavy footfall, accompanied by a hoarse cough, as a man entered. He came in from the bitter cold, his breath leaving his lips in a vapour, his weighty body covered in a white cloak, like a mountain under snow.

Of course I knew him, Pietro Aretino.

Dear God, it was such a cold day. The oil for the paint had begun to freeze so I had placed it close to the fire, and the linseed scent was rising. It contested the gardenia cologne Aretino had rubbed into his beard, his booted feet stomping over to the box of figures.

Now I look back – so many years later – I realise the appeal that coarse tableau had for him. Tintoretto made – and manipulated – his models to compose his paintings. They were aids to his genius; without life, and later to be melted and reformed. But when Aretino stared at the wax figures, those colourless clever forms like squirming embryos, he saw them as he saw people. Humanity he could manoeuvre, twist, contort into the shapes he chose. A man. A woman. An angel. As ripe for picking as tomatoes.

"Marco Gianetti, is it not?..."

I nodded.

"...I know your father." Aretino continued, circling the box like a hawk circles a stoat. "Do pass onto him my admiring regards. We are old, dear friends, as you must well know."

I wanted to reply that my father had never spoken of him, but then my father spoke little to me of anything. So instead I remained silent and watched the great white mass of this famous – and feared – man walk about Tintoretto's studio, his gardenia cologne pungent in the stinging air.

"How many apprentices have you killed, Il Furioso?"

Baffled, he glanced at his visitor. "What?"

"The cold!" Aretino mocked him. "Before long, you will not need your little boxes, you will have frozen humans to work with." He glanced over to me and smiled. "How would like to be a frozen statue, Marco? A beautiful young man for Tintoretto to put in a box and play with?"

Embarrassed I flushed, struggling for a retort. Impatiently Aretino walked away. He could hear him exchange a little conversation with Tintoretto and then he moved to the door.

He did not look at me.

He did not speak to me.

He did not acknowledge my existence.

He didn't have to.

I was already swinging, like the little wax angel with the tomato stain on its arse.

Chapter Six

Discomforted by the pomp of Venetian Catholicism, Barent der Witt hesitated at the entrance to the chapel, remembering the cool white interiors of the Dutch churches in his homeland. He longed for the cold North light that glowed on white alabaster pillars, for the azure blue of a silent morning and the first powdering of snow on the canals which promised a hard freeze. Nothing froze in Venice. Nothing burned the skin as savagely as when a man accidentally touched an Amsterdam railing on a winter's morning.

He fingered the vial around his neck, amused at the furtive attention it provoked. Of course it would have been self defeating to explain what the potion inside was; much better to allow people to imagine; to fret over supposed sorcery. Der Witt pushed back his rigid black hat – so popular in Amsterdam – and glanced at his watch. Perhaps he had missed her, but she had said that she would meet him at eleven. And it was only ten minutes passed.

Guilt had dried into his bones, into his blood, and even the nerves of his teeth. And there were only poor examples of those, his teeth blackened by years of chewing herbs, a broken canine kept numb by the application of tincture of cloves. No one realised his dental problems because Der Witt never smiled. In fact his embarrassment over his teeth had made him draw down his top lip slightly when he spoke, a mannerism that he had adopted as a child and was still using in his fifties.

But apothecaries were not obliged to be light hearted. People believed in a potion given by a dour man in dark clothes far more than they would in one provided by a smiling boy. Let others charm in Venice, allure was not der Witt's trade.

The touch on his arm startled him, a woman pulling him away from the church entrance towards an alleyway. He could hear her laughing. "How fearful you are!"

The Dutchman was not about to be amused. "Why did you call me out at this time of night?"

"Did I disturb you, Signor der Witt? Did I pull you from the Doge's dining table? Or a game of cards at the palace?"

She took off her hood, her hair piled high on her head to allow her neck to be seen to its best advantage. Blonde, of course. All Venetian courtesans were blonde, and if not, they wore wigs, or dyed their mouse-back tones with urine. He had seen them sitting at the windows in the backstreets letting the sun do what God had not. Later, they would gravitate to the front rooms of the palazzos that looked out over the Lagoon, or parade across St Marks Square on their vertiginous chopines. Glorious specimens, dressed like Contessas, although Venetian law forbade the whores to wear pearls. Jewels, certainly. Pearls, never.

A newcomer to Venice, on seeing these sumptuous creatures, would presume that their hold was complete. But the lure of women was equalled by the glistening appeal of young men, bardasses touting for business in the alleys or, for the more fortunate, in the reception rooms of the Doge's palace. It intrigued der Witt that sodomy was punishable by death as it was so rife and so flagrant. In a valiant attempt to guide the tributary of deviation back into the moral watercourse, whores had been hired to sit at the windows bare breasted to entice the passing men. It was a noble effort by the authorities, but young noblemen still took their pleasures with bardasses and, if they were not available, women dressed as boys. One of the particular specialities that Caterina Zucca offered.

But she wasn't thinking of sex, or money. Not at that moment. "You've been asking after a girl called Gabriella. A girl who used to work for the Castilano sisters, a girl who has gone missing."

"What's that to you?"

"You are very abrupt, Dutchman!" she teased him, flicking some imagined fluff off the brim of his hat. "I could ask the same. Why is it important to *you*?"

Without answering, he glanced away from her and looked down into the canal water below. He could see her image reflected, ghost pale dress under a sombre cloak, hair like a gilded ornament, and her face – with its skilful maquillage – lying adeptly about her age. From a distance of twelve feet Caterina Zucca could have been young, from a distance of twelve inches she was nearing forty. But beautiful, still beautiful. And as clever as the monkeys imported from Africa; quick learners, full of sly charm and pretty manners.

"Why are you being so unfriendly to me?"

He kept staring into the water. "I am unfriendly with everyone. I am a dour man."

"Not behind a closed *dour*," she replied wittily, remembering their infrequent, but lusty, encounters. "I am only asking a question."

"For whom?"

"For myself! Who else?"

"Caterina, you want to know something. So what is it?"

"What I said before. Why are you asking about a missing girl?" she paused, then added. "And why ask the Castilano sisters about Adamo Baptista?"

"Do all women talk!" he snapped. "Our conversation was in confidence."

"They told me in confidence," she replied. "And I told several others in that same confidence. I have every confidence in my confidences." She laughed and touched his sleeve. "Don't look so worried, of course I told no one else. But you would be wise not to ask anyone about Adamo Baptista. He's a man that makes people nervous."

She moved closer to him on the bridge her gilded head almost touching the matt black of his hat. Her voice was so low he had to strain to hear her.

"Do you think Baptista had something to do with Gabriella Russo's disappearance?"

"You are asking me questions I cannot answer."

"Oh, Dutchman, do you take me for a fool?" she said reproachfully. "There are several scenarios that could be possible. One, Gabriella was your lover and you sent her away. Two, she was your lover, you made her pregnant, and you botched her abortion. Three, she was not your lover and you botched the abortion. And four, she was Adamo Baptista's lover – and you botched the abortion." She clicked her tongue. "Which is it?"

"Gabriella was not my lover, she was a friend. And she came to me for help and I failed her."

"Why did she need help?"

"I don't know, she disappeared before I could find out." Der Witt said quietly. "Every day I go look at the bodies in the morgue, searching for her. I never find her."

"But she might have left Venice of her own choosing—"

"Rich women might have the chance to travel, with a chaperone and money to accompany them. But poor women don't leave Venice." der Witt retorted. "Gabrielle was a maid, she had no money, no family, she lived on her wage from the Castilano sisters, her life was simple, set to follow the way of every other woman."

Caterina tipped her head to one side. "So why is she missing, if her life was so 'simple'?"

"And why does it matter to you?" the Dutchman asked.

"You don't trust me and yet you expect me to trust you!" Caterina replied, sighing before she spoke again. "I need to tell you something, my friend. It might mean nothing, or it might be important, but you need to hear it. I saw Gabriella four days ago. She was crying, carrying clothes for the Castilano sisters, and I felt sorry for her. So I stopped and asked her what was wrong."

"And she told you?"

"No. But I knew she was afraid. Terribly afraid." Caterina continued hurriedly, "I was so worried that I said that if she was in danger she could stay at my house. She refused."

'How can I bring it to you?
Ask the Dutchman, he will explain.
I'm going to see him later to tell him
everything.

You must be careful...

I wasn't careful'

She was crying quietly, looking around her.

Rich clothes over her arms, the gilt buttons of a tunic catching the sunlight.

Looking round,

Ready to move on.

'The Wolves of Venice. Do you hear me?

There are four..

Don't let them tell you less.

Look for the four.'

Caterina repeated the girl's words carefully. "After she had told me that she hurried away, as though she regretted saying anything. Later I called by the Castilano shop, but Gabriella wasn't there and I never saw her again."

"I failed her."

"Gabriella said that she was going to meet up with you that night and tell you everything. Did she?"

"No..." he hung his head.

"She didn't keep to the meeting?"

His head bowed. "It wasn't her who failed, I did. You want to know why? I fell asleep, Caterina. *I fell asleep*. That's what you do when you age, you fall asleep like an old man, and fail someone who needs you."

She placed her hand on his shoulder. "So you never discovered what she was talking about? Never knew what, or who, are the four?"

"No." He coughed, took in a breath to cover the catch in his voice. "And I keep thinking that if I'd met her that night she might still be alive."

"But we don't know she isn't—"

"It's been five days now."

"Venice is a strange place, with many spies and many hiding places," Caterina said, pulling the hood over her head. "Don't give up hope, Dutchman. She might still come to you. Or to me."

He shook his head. "No, Gabriella was afraid. If she *is* still alive, she'll be hiding... And if she's dead the tide will carry her in."

Chapter Seven

It was a protracted winter, far too long for comfort, the Adriatic irritable with storms. Still in the long arms of February the days closed down around four, the chimes from St Marks and other Venetian churches a gloomy calling to prayer. Priests took to wearing shawls under their vestments, the congregation huddled together for warmth in the pews, even enemies, their shaking white hands extended for the communion wafers at the cold brass altar rail.

Above their heads the many Assumptions and Crucifixions retained their warm colours, whilst the drained faces of the worshippers looked to the paintings for comfort. In the pew nearest to the choir Jacopo Gianetti sat with his hands tucked into the sleeves of his fur doublet, his gaze averted from the man seated opposite.

He had spent a pleasing hour with Doge Francesco Donato, who had become Doge four years previously. If he was honest, Jacopo had little in common with the Doge, but he had been a long time friend of the Dogaressa, Alicia Giustiniani, a member of one of the most powerful families in Venice. There had even been a time, long ago, when a marriage between them had been suggested, but Jacopo's wealth – although more than enough for Alicia – had been insufficient to ensnare her family's approval.

Yet the fondness between them had endured. Alicia saw Jacopo as he had been as a youth; feckless, spontaneous, lively. Jacopo saw Alicia as *she* had been as a girl; sensual, flirtatious and superficial. But although the passing decades had all but obliterated Jacopo's liveliness and Alicia's flirtatiousness, in middle age they found a snug comfort in the memory of surriptious love. The girl who had enticed Jacopo Gianetti into dark corners now dedicated herself to the redecoration of the Doge's Place, and, like many a Dogaressa before her, became the formal protector of a guild, in Alicia's case, the glassmakers. The figure that had one been lithely alluring was now stout, her flippancy maturing into a radical protection of the workers. Their pleas and complaints she heard and bore enough influence on her husband to ensure that glass workers were able to travel abroad. She felt useful, resourceful, in control of herself. And her husband.

Fifteen years earlier the Doge of Venice had been quite a different calibre of man, immune to feminine interference. Andrea Gritti, distinguished diplomat and career soldier, had been a man Jacopo respected, but disliked, not least because Gritti was resistant to Aretino's charm and thereby Jacopo's influence. But when Donato was elected Doge and his wife Alicia became Dogaressa, Jacopo's leverage had increased expedientally.

It was simple to flatter an old lover into agreement and Alicia had been persuaded that Aretino, although at times an odious bombast, could also be a witty and famous asset to the court. Donato was not a man especially cultured, but

Alicia had an intense desire to make herself memorable. Redesigning the Doge's private apartments she had been grateful for Aretino's connections. His presenting of the finest merchants, most lavish traders in furniture and silver had been appreciated, his conversation outrageous and appealing. As a respectable matron, Alicia might feign disapproval, but she felt herself drawn to the literary letch and welcomed him at court. Before six months had passed Pietro Aretino had been firmly ensconced in the Doge's home and circle; an eagle amongst sparrows.

And *he* had made it happen, Jacopo thought resentfully. *He* had used Alicia's affection as Aretino's entrée, watching the bulbous writer outrage and flatter his way through the courtiers. Before long he was accompanied by the black crow, Adamo Baptista. A Florentine by birth, but by nature, who knew? One day he simply appeared; conjured himself from Aretino's shadow and remained, like a shadow, dark and inescapable.

Glancing up, Jacopo was aware of the confident stare of Aretino and the sidelong glance of Adamo Baptista; aware also that the latter was no follower of religion. As for Aretino, it had been said of him that '*the only person he had never criticised was God. But that was only because he hadn't met Him.*' Would God be afraid of the deviant author, blackmailer, liar? Jacopo wondered. Why not. Most were. There were hundreds in Venice who feared his tongue, his extraordinary knowledge of hidden scandals, personal foibles and long, dreadful secrets, all accumulated in the decades since he had arrived in the Republic.

His background depended on which version Aretino was relating, but most agreed that he had grown up in

Perugia, before falling under the protection of Agostino Chigi, the banker and Raphael's patron. Always ascorbic and witty, Aretino's poem *'The Last Will and Testament of the Elephant Hanno'* was written when Pope Leo X's pet died. Despite its lampooning of many leading figures in Rome, it had made Aretino's reputation as a satirist and his future was set. Spite was his main weapon. and sex, his Lust Sonnets written to accompany Giulio Romano's pornographic drawings, I Modi.

But I Modi caused a sensation so great that Aretino had to flee Rome, the Pope outraged by the obscenity, the introduction to the sonnets inflammable

Come view this you who like to fuck, without being Disturbed in that sweet enterprise… with all respect to hypocrities, I dedicate these lustful pieces to you, heedless of the … asinine laws which forbid the eyes to see the very things that delight them most.'

Later, when the Pope died, Aretino came under the protection of Cardinal Giulio de' Medici, but the writer only settled back in the capital when Pope Clement VII was elected. At that wasn't to last... Jacopo kept his gaze averted, his mother's sharp elbow pressed against his flesh like a dagger as he thought of the attempted assignation of Aretino, which – had it been successful – would have relieved many of the blackmailer's grip.

Instead the pederast had survived and left Rome to settle in Venice and develop his career as a blackmailer in the 'city of vices'. Vices he was personally committed to exploiting; so much so that 'he kept all that was famous in Italy in a kind of state of siege.' Not just Italy, Aretino's reach had also extended to Francis I of France and King Charles, both paying him to discover and reveal the other's weaknesses…

Jacopo winced as he felt his mother's elbow dig further into his flesh, his eyes moving upwards to the nave above the altar. So many years had passed since that night. So many Venetian summers and winters. Fifteen years, and all of them overhung by the threat of betrayal. Fifteen years of money exchanged at stone lintels; of favours extracted under duress. Fifteen years in which time Jacopo Gianetti, head of one of the wealthiest families in Venice, had been under the thumb of the corpulent, pustuler Aretino.

His gaze still fixed on the painted ceiling of the nave, Jacopo could feel the presence of the woman sitting beside him. His mother, Lavinia. Almost as critical as Aretino, certainly as proud. Defiantly protective of the Gianetti name and fortune.

"There need be no anxiety, my dear friend Jacopo" Aretino had said that night, fifteen years earlier. "I have no intention of exposing your secret –'

"I have no secret!" he had replied, sick to the soul, wondering how much – if anything – Aretino knew. He was a card player, almost as proficient as the incomparable Adamo Baptista – but he could be bluffing. He *could*.

Was he?

I am so cold, Jacopo had thought, standing by the canal, deep into midnight, thinking. His instinct had alerted him. *I am being watched.* Jacopo had sensed, glancing around him. For how long had he been watched? He had not noticed anyone. Heard no footsteps and a footfall always echoed in Venice in the night hours.

Yet he had heard nothing.

And Aretino had been leaning towards him, his bulk unpleasantly close. "You are safe, Jacopo, I will not betray you. You are a confidante of our wondrous Doge, a friend at court. How could I threaten the esteem of the Gianetti name?"

"I have done nothing." Jacopo had replied, but his voice – was that his voice? – was disentangled from his body; squirming like an eel at the end of rusty hook. "How dare you—"

"How dare I *what*?"

Jacopo paused, wrong footed. After all what *did* Aretino really know? And could he chance asking without giving himself away?... Jacopo had paused, wretched. Sick, so sick, stomach writhing, a bag of worms. Was he going to risk hanging the Gianetti name and reputation out like a banner at which the populace could throw their shit?

"Only you and I will ever know the truth of your dealings," Aretino had continued. "Your esteemed mother will not be troubled, nor the Doge. This is a simple matter of business between the two of us."

And then Jacopo had said. "I do not understand to what you are referring."

"I think..." Aretino had quoted an exorbitant sum. "... paid every month would be fair."

"For *what*?" Jacopo had replied. But that voice of his. That borrowed voice of his that did not work for him. *That* voice was lying. And they both knew it. "I am an innocent man."

"Of what have I accused you?" Aretino had responded, smiling like a gargoyle. "Tell me, Jacopo, what do you fear

I will expose? Have you so many secrets that I might be favoured with a choice?"

There had been no reply to the sleek question, to the damning question. To answer would have been to admit, to confess, to agree that a secret existed: that same secret which would cause the Gianetti coffers to be bled for as long as Jacopo or Aretino lived.

Above their heads Jacopo had heard pigeons scuffle for purchase on a window ledge, and wondered how. *How* Aretino had known. Or did he? And at the same precise moment realised that the knowing – or the *presumed* knowing – would be enough to buckle him. But he would not allow the truth breath; he would not allow vowels and consonants to be formed: he would not permit the empty alleyway or the dank canal to hear it.

And so a mental noose had wrapped itself around his neck and when he left Aretino that night it was etched into his skin like a brand. In the summer it would itch, chafe; in the winter it would burn like ice. But it would never leave him...

Drawing in a breath, Jacopo's gaze moved from the nave to the altar, to the choir stalls, then to the pew opposite. And he knew, before he saw looked, that Aretino's eyes were fixed on him.

Chapter Eight

"... **I don't want him in here!**" Jacopo shouted, pushing away his servant, sweat making the sheets damp. "Tell him to go away!" and then he grabbed at the man's arm and dropped his voice to a rasping whisper. "I don't want either of them, you understand. Keep them away from me. *Mi senti, tienili fuori! Tenerli lontano da me!*"

The servant turned to a stout maid who was staring at her master writhing in the bed. Usually such a proud man, but now ranging like a bull. She wiped Jacopo's narrow forehead with a cloth, his white hair – undressed and dishevelled – brittle and yellowing.

"Hush, signor—"

"He is a devil. *Lui e un diavolo!*" Jacopo's sunken eyes fixed on the maid, his head turning to one side as his confusion cleared. "*Why are you here?* Why are you in my room!"

"You have been taken ill suddenly. You are ill, signor—"

"**Get out!**" Jacopo ordered, throwing back the covers and attempting to rise.

But the action was too much for him, dizziness overwhelming his senses and making the furniture dance. The wooden chest and the carved bed were suddenly jiggling like peasants at a wedding, the scattered bed sheets a hurried fall of snow.

Gasping, Jacopo jerked his feet off the floor, leaping madly. "It is winter again! No, not so soon! Why did you not tell me it was snowing?" he asked the plump maid. "It should not snow in Venice. Snow brings the bears."

The maid turned to the manservant, staring with his mouth open. "Get the master's son and bring him here."

"No, not my son!" Jacopo shouted. "He is not to come near me. Keep him out."

Defiantly Cara Banti held her ground, but her master had slipped out of consciousness and was lying, spread eagled, on the carved bed. Covering him with a blanket, she thought of all the years she had seen Marco Gianetti ignored and reviled, Jacopo only speaking to his son to criticise or mock. A cruel, cold man, Cara had decided long ago, a man who had married again when Marco was seven, a man whose second wife had died of a fever. And why? No fever killed her, Cara would mutter under her breath. Neglect, lack of love, *mancanza di amore*, had killed the little one.

She had come into the Gianetti house like an offering; a sixteen year old daughter of a powerful Venetian family. *Sixteen*, Cara had remarked at the time, not enraged by the age – it was common for brides to marry young – but by the timidity of the second Signora Gianetti.

The life of the little sprat had been sudden and short; propelled from the chaperoned safety of her own family, she had been bartered and exported into the Gianetti palazzo, the carved doors closing behind her like a spring lock. Within a year she was dead, following the first wife into the Gianetti sarcophagus on the island where all the broken spouses came to land.

Jacopo had grieved for her loss. Or had appeared to. It was difficult to tell and besides, he was adept at hiding his feelings. Sparse in weight, thin featured, narrow shouldered, Jacopo Gianetti seemed slight, but he had been blessed with the constitution of a farm ram. She looked down at her felled master, a sweating effigy, so unlike he usual fastidious self. He took care of his appearance, but why she wasn't sure. Although Jacopo entertained as lavishly as a prince, there were few solo visitors, except for the occasional sighting of the gross toad Aretino. Yet as brilliant as he business dealings were reported to be, as opulent as his homes, as powerful as his name, Jacopo Gianetti was a hollow man.

"He has a fever." Cara told the servant. "Send for a doctor."

The man's eyebrows rose, his face slack. "I do not know where to find a medico—"

No, Cara thought, there had been little call for a doctor for Signor Gianetti, his health untroubled all the time she had served him. The old family doctor had died years earlier and there had been no replacement. And then she remembered what she had heard about the Jewish doctors.

"Find one in the ghetto! What a fool you are." Cara barked at the servant. "Fetch a medico from there."

"From the ghetto?"

She rolled her eyes in exasperation. "Yes, from the ghetto!"

"But it's after sunset."

"I have eyes, I can tell what time it is! The Jewish doctors are allowed to leave the ghetto if they are visiting their patients." she snorted. "When you get there, go to the double gates and ring the bell. Someone will come to you and then you ask for the medico."

"Do I wait for him?"

Cara stared into the dull face. "If you do not wait for him, how can he follow you back here?"

Half running, half walking, the servant made his reluctant way to the ghetto in the Cannaregio, the wealth of the Gianetti estate and gardens fading as he entered the industrial and utilitarian part of the city. The Cannaregio was situated an area of foundries, the fusing of metal being called 'getto', the term which was later bastardised into 'ghetto' when the area was segregated off from the rest of Venice in 1512. That was what the servant had heard, but what did it matter? If he was honest, the Republic was populated by every race and colour of man – merchants from Europe; traders from the Far East and slaves from Africa – no one was strange, no one was an outsider in a city of outsiders.

It was dark when he reached the iron gates of the ghetto, locked and bolted, a lamp lit above in the archway. Timidly he took hold of the chain and rang the bell, the sound resonating in the alleyway behind. No one came, the servant peering through the railings and catching sight of a square, flanked by cramped, high rising buildings; flat faced, blank, without charm.

"Hela?"

The servant jumped as a man appeared suddenly before him. His was bearded, but not like a Venetian, this was a full beard with ear locks. "Kenen ikh helfn ir?" the man paused, then spoke in Italian. "Can I assist you?"

"My master is ill. I've been sent for the medico."

"We have many doctors here. Do you have a name?"

The servant shook his head, confused. "I just need a doctor!"

"I understand." The man replied, "Ira Tabat is here—"

The servant nodded hurriedly. "Then fetch him, fetch Ira Tabat."

Chapter Nine

With the servant holding the candelabra high above his head, Ira followed the man up the echoing Carerra marble staircase towards the first floor of the palazzo. On the first landing a silk sofa languished under a Titian portrait of a nude, and on either side of the doors to the master suite were blackamoors holding torcheres aloft, the candlelight reflected on the black marble floor. The silence was depressing, only the sound of muted voices providing a solemn chorus below.

Aware of his shabbiness, Ira moved into a bedroom which could have housed five Jewish families in the ghetto, a fire banked high up the stone chimney, the curtains like closed eyes against the night outside. Placing his medical bag on the chair next to the bed, Ira stared at his patient, not for the first time wondering at the loss of power which came with sickness.

Jacopo Gianetti was breathing irregularly, his eyes moving under the lids, his hands clasping and unclasping rhythmically.

"Who found him like this?"

"I did, signor" Cara stammered, staring at the dark

haired, bearded man wearing a coarse woven tunic and breeches, his boots matt with dust. "He was rambling."

"I see."

"How long ago was this?"

"No more than an hour."

"I need some water and a bowl, please."

She nodded, bringing it over to Ira and laying it beside the bed. "Anything else you need, dottore?"

"I would like to speak to his relatives. Are his family here?"

A pause passed between them, Cara pulling an uncomfortable face. "Only his son, Marco."

"Then please bring him to me."

"He can't come here."

Ira paused. "Why not?"

"Signor Gianetti requested it."

"But you said the patient was rambling, delirious. He must not have meant to banish his son."

She folded her fleshy arms. "Oh, he will have meant it." Glancing over to check that her master was unconscious and could not hear what she was about to divulge, Cara continued. "They are apart... separate."

"Estranged?"

She nodded. *"Si, estraniato."*

"For how long?"

"Forever."

"Forever?"

"Since Marco was born. Since then."

Surprised, Ira looked back to the patient, checked his pulse and temperature, examined his skin, eyes and limbs, all of it overlooked by the stout maid. Ten minutes passed, then another, before Ira wiped Jacopo's face and then smelt the cloth.

"Good God!" Cara exclaimed, crossing herself.

"Some disease has a scent, signora, which will help me to make a diagnosis." he explained. "But there is no scent or odour on the cloth." He dropped it beside the basin, washed his hands and dried them on a towel. Finally, he shrugged. "If the mountain will not come to Mohammed, Mohammed must go to the mountain."

Later, when he thought back, Ira would remember his first impression of Marco Gianetti. Shown into a library on the ground floor, he found Jacopo's estranged heir feeding a macaw a sliver of black chocolate. He was so intent on the task that he had not heard Ira's entry and remained cooing like a child at the factitious bird.

"Signor Gianetti?"

Marco turned, smiled with all the humour of the world, and nodded. "Si, and you are Dottore Tabat?"

"Si." Ira agreed.

"How is my father?"

"He does not eat enough. He is malnourished, underweight and dry, he does not have enough liquid in his body." Ira watched Marco slide into a winged chair by the fire, his legs outstretched as Ira continued. "Does he have a poor appetite?"

"We do not eat together, I would not know."

The reply bewildered Ira. In Jewish families, however large, however small, meal times were communal, an opportunity to bond, to converse, sometimes to disagree. Conditions in the ghetto were cramped, but in summer time meals were eaten outdoors, long tables employed to handle the numbers as the women served the food. No one ate alone, unless they chose to, instead everyone was included, the breaking of bread sacrosanct. And yet, in the cadaverous Gianetti palazzo, two men ate apart, with a multitude of angry, empty rooms between them.

"Who cooks for you?"

"Cara cooks for me, has done since I was a child, but my father has a few chefs. And of course he often attends functions elsewhere in the city... I never suspected he would starve to death."

"Malnutrition is not the same as starvation." Ira replied, but he knew about both. "If you will allow me, I will write up a diet for him and maybe I should give it to your cook, Cara?"

Marco nodded, "She will help. She is a good cook, all good cooks are fat. The Doge says that no one should trust a thin cook... Why was my father confused?"

"Lack of fluid affects the brain, and the heat—"

"It's not hot!"

"—it is in his room," Ira replied, "I would advice you to have the fire dampened down, sweating causes more loss of fluid."

"So you don't intend to bleed my father?"

"Why would I bleed him?" Ira replied.

"Isn't that what medicos do?"

"Bleeding your father would only weaken him further."

"Oh, I see," Marco replied, thinking for a long instant. "Where did you train to become a doctor?"

"In Florence."

"Not Venice?"

"No," Ira replied, knowing that more information was

wanted. "We fled that city and came to Venice, to the ghetto. The Republic is tolerant of Jews."

"But they still lock you in at night."

Ira shrugged. "And yet here I am, I am free."

"Because you are a doctor, only because of that. You are not a free man." Marco replied, immediately flushing. "I had no intention of being rude, forgive me! I have never been to the ghetto or seen how you live." He was genuinely remorseful. "Is life... pleasant there?"

"We are safe."

"*We are safe...*'" Marco repeated, his expression shocked. "Were your lives in danger before?"

"Many countries fear the Jews. It has been this way for centuries. And for centuries we have settled in a city and then been moved on because of persecution. European Jewry is transient."

"My God, how little I know..." Marco remarked, then changed the subject. "They say that Jews make the best doctors."

"And the worst patients."

"But you," Marco paused, then carried on. "you are not like the usual Jewish doctors that have attended this family in the past. My grandparents favoured Isaac Schulman—"

"Who is now dead."

"I didn't know that," Marco replied, his eyebrows raised. "Are you replacing him?"

Ira shrugged. "I doubt it. There are many preferred doctors that would be favoured before me."

"Is that why you are......"

"Poor?"

Marco pulled a face. "Poor, but also much younger than

they are! And besides, many of them have come here with reputations, Venetians who will recommend them, advance their careers in the city."

"But they will still be Jews."

"And still richer than you."

Despite himself, Ira smiled. "I am not a politician. I cannot court people, I never could. I find socialising difficult. Not the work, I never find a moment of my work boring or tedious – but the flattery, the obsequious, the sycophantic cringing that takes place...I couldn't do that."

"It is a stiff neck that will not bend." Marco replied wryly, changing the subject. "Are you hungry?"

"I am working."

"I know, but are you hungry?" Marco repeated, "one thing does not exclude the other, does it? Dine with me, dottore, and be my guest." He urged him. "We cannot have another starving man on our hands."

Whether he was lonely or curious Ira wasn't sure, but Marco was a gracious host. Pressed into service, the weighty Cara prepared a light meal of sea food, the hard shelled and soft shelled crabs of the Lagoon cooked in butter, a dozen of the tiny octopus fried, their legs curled inwards, sepia brown. The scent was not like the fish in the ghetto; this sea food had an ozone taste and a sweet aroma, sea fresh, the Adriatic only giving up her spoils hours earlier.

Several times whilst his host was eating, Ira had snatched quick glances, judging Marco to be around twenty five, his face clean shaven, his mouth upturned at the corners. Good humour was evident from his open expression and soft eyes, and he spoke as a child would, without censoring himself. Ira imagined how attractive he would be to women, how his warmth would pull in admirers likes a tree pulls in the sun.

"That was excellent." Ira said, tearing into his bread and then wiping his plate clean, Marco watching.

"You enjoyed your meal?"

"How could I not?"

"Aren't Jews usually allowed to eat fish?"

He laughed. "We can eat fish, but we cannot afford delicacies like these." Embarrassed, Ira reached for his glass, Marco pushing away the water pitcher and holding out the wine carafe to him. "Water is for fish. Wine is for men."

"I do not drink."

"Everyone drinks in Venice."

"Except me."

"Because you are a Jew?"

"No. Because I chose not to drink."

"Sacrilegio!" Marco teased him. "You drink water, wine is only water from a grape."

Ira shook his head. "You make a very convincing argument."

"So you *will* have some wine?"

"No."

Laughing, Marco leaned back in his seat, the flames flaring up in the fire grate, a quick white curl of smoke leaping upwards like a dancer.

"Is the weather very different in Florence?"

"We have been here for a while now, I don't remember much about the weather where we lived before."

"But here the city can be cold in winter, and damp. Foggy."

Silently Marco gazed into his glass, watching Ira through

the wine, his dark face infused with unnatural colour. A Jew, Marco thought, he had never met a Jew before. He had known about the ghetto, but never been there, and had heard so many rumours that the residents were strange. Uncommunicative, taciturn. Foreign.

But then virtually everyone in Venice was a foreigner, unless you were born in the city. As he had been. As had all the Gianetti before him, generations going back centuries, powerful, prosperous, the friends and confidantes of the Doges. Just as his father was. Naturally with his inherited wealth Jacopo had had no need to work, but money was always a great enticement to a avaricious man, and for decades he had assiduously added to his portfolio of premises. In Venice and beyond.

"And yet he is starving." Marco said out loud.

Ira raised his eyebrows. "*What?*"

"I was thinking it seems strange that for all my father's wealth, for all his deals and schemes and riches, he is *hungry*. Perhaps it is not his body that is hungry, but his greed." Marco leaned over the supper table towards Ira. "Do you think there is an organ for greed? A little mean organ tucked behind the stomach? Perhaps it gurgles when it isn't fed, or farts when it's bloated." he pointed to his gut and put his head on one side. "An organ some men can never satisfy."

"You have a wondrous imagination." Ira replied, amused. "You should be a writer."

"No, no! I" he said with a flourish, "am a painter..."

Ira was caught by surprise. He had thought that the offspring of such a wealthy family would not have to work, especially as painters were regarded with little respect.

"… well, not a painter in reality. I am an eternal apprentice" Marco continued. "A little old to be one, I grant you, but although I entered my master's studio ten years ago it would seem I have advanced little. He allows me to paint a tree in the background and now and then a cloud!" He pretended to be dismayed then drained his glass, smiling at his own limitations. "My master is paid very well to keep me in permanent occupation and besides, he likes me, I amuse him, and so he has found other work for me to do. I have become *un cavallo da lavoro veneziano*."

"A *what*?"

"We are a very elegant breed of steed. We carry and fetch for our masters and wear the livery of the Gianetti household." He could see that Ira was still puzzled and explained. "I am a Venetian workhorse! I am not, nor ever will be, like the great bronze horses of St Marks."

Shaking his head, Ira laughed. "I never know when you are telling the truth or lying."

"You will learn to know." Marco replied, "Friends learn things from one another as their friendship progresses." He could see Ira's back straighten in the chair, a coolness emanating from him. "It seems that now I have insulted you—"

"On the contrary *I* have insulted you. You have given me a fine meal and I have—"

"Reacted like a bear poked with a needle." Marco replied bluntly. "But I said what I thought, as I always do. If you are truly discomforted, please make your leave. I offered friendship, but if the offer is rejected I bear you no malice."

Ira hesitated. "Your father would not like an association between his heir and a Jew."

"My father likes nothing I do, so it would make little difference. Before long he will find some girl for me to marry – she will, of necessity, have a fortune to feed that needy greed organ of his, but it will be merely a matter for politics, not love. Love I find elsewhere." He winked at Ira. "Have you ever been in love?"

He faltered, caught off guard. "I should see to your father—"

"You saw him only an hour ago and Cara is sitting with him, together with the nurse you sent for." Marco shrugged. "But if you wish to go, please do. I do not mean to detain you or make you uncomfortable—"

Wrong footed, Ira was on the defensive.

"Why are you speaking to me like this? Why the questions? Why the familiarity? Do you want to know something in particular? If so, please ask me, I will answer you as best I can, but we are not equals and that much we both know." He straightened up, anger barely controlled. Confusion made him irrational, hostile. "Seafood from the lagoon, finest wine, conversations that would be more in place between confidantes, why?"

"I am not a sodomite."

"Did I accuse you of such!"

Marco was imperturbable. "I thought perhaps you misread my actions. I merely wanted you to know that I like you – but not as a bedfellow." He put his head on one side. "Look how you scowl at me, suspecting manipulation where there is none."

But Ira was still wary.

"Maybe I am misjudging you. Or perhaps, like so many rich Venetians, you want to know more about the poor

Jews that you lock up at night? Does the Republic enjoy its human zoo? Do we amuse you like Pucchinello from the Commedia del Arte? With our ear locks, funny little hats and yellow patches on our clothes? Perhaps you are gathering details from me to pass on to your friends later? Poking fun at the ant hill of Jews in their midst—"

"I have no friends."

Ira paused, shaking his head. "I… I apologise. I was rude—"

"Yes, you were," Marco agreed, "and you were wrong. You will not believe me, but I will tell you again – I am not a man that plans. Plotting is alien to my nature, I merely respond. My father would say that is the mark of stupidity."

"Your father would be wrong."

"My father is never wrong. He is descended from a line of perfect Men, every one of them more cultured and more perfect than the last. Until myself," he smiled, Ira relaxing. "I did lie *un po* when I said I had no friends. I have many acquaintances and some beautiful female company when I need, but you are of particular interest to me. You and I are outcasts—"

"An outcast in a palace?"

"An outcast is an outcast despite his living quarters. Do not be surly, Ira, you have no enemy here."

For a moment Ira made no response, then moved to the door. "I will call tomorrow to see how your father is progressing. Please send for me if he worsens." He turned to go, then turned back. "You said you were a painter, who is your master? In whose studio do you work?"

Marco made a mock salute. "I am the brush washer and chief carrier of Tintoretto. *Il Furioso*, the glory of Venice."

BOOK TWO

And so the gods weave their tricks and follies around us. I'm thinking back and my hand is aching from writing. In the past it would have troubled me when I ground the paint for Tintoretto, or beat the oil – beat the oil! Titian would have none of that 'Only a fool beats oil, it breaks the soul inside.' I used to muse about that. Did the revered Supremo mean that stirring too quickly destroyed the soul of the oil, or the soul of the man who was doing the beating?

Titian would have been around fifty then, Pietro Aretino his closest confidante. Rumours circulated around Venice that the writer must have some hold on the artist, for, after all, Titian had no need for the likes of Aretino. But strangely they were friends, perhaps the painter liked the greasy dirt that flavoured Aretino's conversation.

Perhaps his wit and wickedness inspired his painting, certainly Titian had no fear of him and even employed him to act as his agent overseas. But then again, Titian had been born in Pieve di Cadore, a true Venetian, and so a master manipulator, perceptive enough to realise that even the most dangerous of men need one ally.

Ira was not a dangerous man, nor was I. Our friendship was new, unforced, as unexpected and simple as two lambs born to the same ewe. If I am honest – and I must be so, later it will become more difficult – but if I am honest now

I will say that I was fascinated by the whole allure of his being a Jew.

Venice was a magnificent aberration, blindingly beautiful, obscenely wealthy, full off the juiciest, carnal whores and the most villainous opportunists. As a Republic, entire of ourselves, we welcomed ambitious, scurrilous adventurers; we accepted merchants and traders of all nationalities and skin tone, bringing their skills and full pockets to sell or buy. No one cared with whom they traded. Just that trade was done. The day began with trade and the day ended with trade.

Yes, we were a city without prejudice – and yet the Republic feared the Jews. Admired their business acumen, their medical skill, their legal aptitude, but feared them none the less. So when my father – who had, of course, recovered – heard of my burgeoning friendship with Ira Tabat, Jew from the ghetto, I was summoned.

His study looked out over the Lagoon, a statue of a bronze warrior with a spear holding court in the square bay of the window. I used to fear it as a child, wonder if – one day – at my father's command – he would throw the spear at me.

"A matter has been brought to my attention which angers me." There had been no greeting, no tiny intimation of affection, his loathing was unwavering and constant. "I do not approve of your association with this Jew—"

"Ira," I said evenly. "His name is Ira Tabat."

My father swatted away the words. "— I expect little of you, but surely even you are aware of the importance of your position. You are my heir," he paused, the word was salt on his tongue. "... and as such, should choose your associates wisely."

"But you know him, father. Ira is the doctor who restored you to health. He is very well respected in Venice –

"— as a dottore I do not doubt his ability, but as a friend of the heir of one of the richest families in Venice, he is not suitable." He shook his head, his face was pinched with irritation, his eyes averted. My presence, as ever, was galling to him. "You are not a boy any longer, and a man must be more circumspect."

Behind the statue the clouds shifted, the sun obscured, a black shadow pooling over the marble floor. I glanced down, watching the shadow slide like a counter over the cold surface. The previous night I had dreamed of my mother for the first time in many years, had heard her choking in my room and seen her shadow swinging from the poster of my bed.

You cannot know someone you never knew.

Yet I knew her.

She visited me

When she wanted to see her child.

At night, without even one candle burning.

I would know her then.

"... Well, have you been to the ghetto?"

Snapped out of my memory, I gazed at my father in surprise. Who had told him I had even been there? Who had spied on me?

"Yes," I admitted finally. "I have been to visit Ira's family."

"Vergognoso!" he slammed his hands on the desk. "Disgraceful!"

His anger tempered mine, my voice composed. "How did you know I'd been to the ghetto, father? Have you set spies on me?"

"I do not wish to be made familiar with how you spend your time—"

"And yet you have me spied upon."

He ignored my interruption." – God knows, your life is not virtuous."

"How would you know that if you were not spying on me?"

"I do not have to answer to you! If I had a choice, I would limit speaking, thinking, or even seeing you. But you are my son and I prefer your visiting women – however dubious in character – to this ill judged company."

"So you would prefer my fucking a woman to eating with a Jew?"

"You have eaten with them!" he countered, raging.

"Yes, and they have welcomed me."

"I should think they would, the son of Jacopo Gianetti—"

"Should that impress them, father? Do you think the ghetto dwellers know the niceties of Venetian bloodlines?"

His mouth closed so tightly the lips became purple. I realised then how lonely my mother would have been – and how wretched the life of her short lived successor.

"If you continue this friendship I will be forced to keep you here until you come to your senses."

I laughed. Yes, laughed.

"You would imprison me, father? There would be little difference to my life. The Gianetti restraints would rival that of the Inquisition. I have been watched over and reported upon since birth – and the death of my mother"

He flinched, the reminder as savage as a razor cut.

"Your mother will not be mentioned it this house!" he

said, his tone dangerous. "I have warned you not speak of her—"

But I had the razor in my hand and I used it.

"Why can I not talk of my own mother?"

"Because you killed her."

"No," I said mercilessly, "she killed herself."

As I said it the sun glided out from behind the bronze warrior and loomed into the room. It threw an aura around my father's seated figure. Outlined his narrow head and counted out the fingers of his left hand. And under its heartless light I saw the fleck of spittle at the corner of his mouth and the vein thrumming at the left side of his neck.

If he could have died in that moment to punish me he would have done.

But he didn't.

And I wish he had.

For my father didn't know it then, but he would live to see me punish him far more.

Chapter Ten

Castilano shop

St Marks Square, Venice

The brocade was heavier than she had expected, lusciously embroidered with gold and silver thread, the trimming sable and at the back a lacing of ribbons intertwined with seed pearls. Absurdly opulent and difficult to wear, but then no Venetian matron would be renting such a gown; it was made for a courtesan to wear only temporarily.

She flipped up the skirt and examined the silk petticoats. In the past she had been fooled by a garment that appeared to be in pristine condition, only to find a blood stain, or a urine mark, underneath. Marina scowled, although not a judgemental woman, she despised slatternly people and had, on a few occasions, banned male customers from renting clothes. One instance still irked her, a pair of breeches returned with vomit in one of the pockets.

Shaking her head, Marina turned to her latest acquisition. She had bought a kimono from a Japanese merchant, a trader new to Venice, and had placed it in her window on display. Her rivals, she thought with satisfaction, would be outflanked and envious. And to guarantee that the salt was rubbed deep into the wound, she would ensure that the person who rented the garment was someone of importance. For in Venice, the garment was secondary to its wearer. The most exquisite gown or doublet would mean little on a porcine merchant, or a doughy faced Contessa.

Marina had always known this, just as she had always instinctively obtained the finest garments in the latest fashions. When she first came to Venice she had suffered from her rivals jealousy. Clothes were rented secretly by dealers' cohorts and returned soiled. Or she was outbid, gowns and trimmings meant for the Castilano shop being stolen, or redesigned. But Marina was a businesswoman and realised that the finest advert for her shop and the quickest way to her fortune was to choice her customers. She was the only one in Venice who would refuse to loan a garment to a person who would fail to do it justice. Every one of her clothes would find its ideal wearer, the stature and the personality dovetailing to make an entrance for the gossips to gawp at, whilst also bringing further clients to her shop.

As Marina had hoped the kimono had drawn immediate interest – but from the most unlikely source, Adamo Baptista. Confounded that the sombre Florentine would wish to rent the exotic garment, Marina had offered her professional advice.

"It is remarkable, Signor Baptista, but too small for a man of your impressive stature."

He regarded her without answering, then made a small

movement with his head. Immediately a youth had entered from the street and stood beside him.

"Signor Baptista?"

"I would like you to try this garment on." He had explained, then nodded to Marina. "If you wouldn't mind."

In contrast to Baptista's raven like attire, he was dressed in an azure blue doublet and hose, the sleeves ruched, the collar boasting an intricate, beaded ruff. And above the ruff an ivory, mask like visage gazed at her; its only animation a pair of densely black, oblique eyes.

"This is Signor Nikolas Volt," Baptista introduced the youth, "he has come from Germany to be my secretary." As Marina wondered at the young man's heritage, Baptista – in his usual manner of pre-empting a person's next thought – continued. "Signor Volt's mother was Japanese, and his father German. You see why this garment would be suitable for him?"

It was perfectly suitable, and it suited him perfectly, Volt's ivory hair and skin a startling contrast to the crimson of the kimono, his black eyes complimenting the ebony designs stitched onto the silk. He had slid into the garment like a child into a warm bath, and it had responded to his elegance. Baptista had then informed Marina that the kimono would be worn the following evening, when he and Nikolas Volt would be attending a concert at the Doge's Palace.

Marina smiled in anticipation of the coming triumph, dragging herself out of her daydream and bending down to gather up several pairs of shoes bound for the storage room below. The area was used to house the articles that were to be refashioned – or privately sold on – and also served as a makeshift bedroom for the maid. Indeed it had been where Gabriella Russo had slept.

Marina glanced over. The girl's straw palette was still by the wall, the cheap wooden cross hanging above it... Of course she and her sister and searched, but all Gabriella's belongings had disappeared with her and it seemed that despite Barent der Witt's anxiety to discover where she was, Gabriella had not been found...

That was the way with some young girls, Marina thought, there was little appeal in being a servant and small likelihood of catching the eye of a suitor in a shop run by two unmarried women. Moving past the bed, Marina headed for the shelving at the far end of the narrow room. There were already over five dozen pairs of shoes piled up, and she was adding the new ones to a high shelf when something caught her attention. Surprised, she pushed the nearest shoes aside to see more clearly, then paused.

They had been hidden well. Unseen in the days since Gabriella had disappeared.

Warily Marina drew out the shoes. Shoes she knew. Shoes familiar to her. Women's shoes, unadorned work shoes. The shoes she had seen Gabriella wear.

The tops were unmarked, but the soles were stiff with blood. No longer fresh, but the colour of dead meat.

Chapter Eleven

Adamo Baptista gestured for the man to come closer to the table, putting out his hands for the pack of cards. Taking them out of their silk wrapping, he then studied them at length, admiring the gilded round edges, the hand ornamented face cards and the extravagantly painted Pucchinello jokers.

With an expert's skill, he began to shuffle.

"S'il vous plaît, monsieur!" the merchant cried. "soyez prudent!"

Baptista paused and looked at the rotund little Frenchman.

"Lauret..." His expression was bland, but his eyes were hostile. "... are you telling me how to handle cards? A gambler used to most of the gaming houses in Europe."

"No, monsieur!" the short man blundered, his neck flushing. "I would not dare to give my opinion—"

"But you just have." Baptista replied, slowly shuffling again. "Who is your best customer?"

"You are, monsieur."

"And when you sold me a pack of cards that you swore were from Russia, did I pay well for them?" he paused, waited for the little Frenchman to answer.

"Oui..."

"Even when later you confessed they were faked in England?"

"*But I did not know they were forged!* I only discovered that later when the merchant was flogged and confessed. He was a villain, he fooled many, you must believe that I had no part of his villainy." He was sweating, a foot smaller than Baptista, his striped silk tunic marked under the arms. "You cannot trust some of the traders—"

"So it would seem."

"—on my life, I would never cheat you."

"You hold your existence cheap."

"If I was trying to trick you, monsieur, would I risk coming to you again?" Lauret wailed. "I wanted to bring you something unique. This is pack is magnificent!"

"But the last one proved fake. So how can I be sure you are telling me the truth now?"

Lauret was scared, and confused. "Because I am! Because I know, I know they are genuine. There is only one pack of their kind in Venice and it was painted by a pupil of Bellini. The gilding around the corners is perfectly uniform and the faces of the major cards are layered with lapis lazuli and onyx."

Baptista shrugged "Which would make them cumbersome to shuffle or deal."

"No, the layers are sliced finer than a bee's wing. No would know they were even there unless they examined the cards under a microscope..."

"A gambler would know. A cheat would know." Baptista replied, shuffling rhythmically. "An expert at gilet would feel the subtle difference, a cheat would sense the 'bee's wing'" he paused, fingering the cards. "... to him it would feel like a paving stone."

"Monsieur, please, no more shuffling." Lauret reached out for the cards but Baptista stepped back, still shuffling, the gilt edges blurring into a gold Catherine wheel as the Frenchman continued helplessly. "...They are very delicate and worth a duke's ransom."

"And worthless if damaged?"

Lauret nodded, unable to trust his voice. Then Baptista, in one quick movement, flung the entire deck into the little man's face.

Crying out, the Frenchman fell to his knees, scrabbling for the cards, his podgy hands grabbing at them as they scattered on the tiled floor.

"Don't ever..." Baptista said, lifting his foot and pushing the little man over. "...try to fool me again." His boot rested on the Frenchman's arse. "Or I will ruin your trade and have you imprisoned—"

"**But I have done nothing!** I'm not lying, I am innocent."

"Then you are the only man in Venice who is."

Lauret was close to tears, gathering the cards tenderly in his hands, mortally afraid of the Florentine and of his reputation. People spoke of Adamo Baptista's cruelty, but without citing events; they murmured about his spying for Aretino and how he kept the fat pornographer fed with scandal. But *what* scandal, no one knew. Venice buzzed with hearsay, Baptista a man feared by reputation. A thief, a murderer – who knew for sure?

And the mystery made him all the more dangerous.

With effort, Lauret struggled back to his feet. "How can I make this right, monsieur? Tell me, and I will do it."

"I heard that you sell goods to the Castilano shop."

He nodded. "Yes, yes! They have bought trimmings from me, and tassels from Seville—"

"There was a girl who worked there. A maid. Her name was Gabriella Russo. She's missing—"

"This has nothing to do with me, monsieur! I know nothing!—"

Baptista drew in a slow breath. "You must stop lying to me, Lauret, it becomes tedious. You say you know nothing, and yet you knew this girl, didn't you?" Baptista paused, watching the Frenchman squirm. "I heard that you took a liking to her. I heard you met with her after work, walked with her."

"It was innocent! There was nothing wrong in it... She reminded me of my daughter."

"And of course for a man so far from home a reminder of a loved one is priceless." Baptista's tone seemed almost sympathetic. "The authorities are not interested in a missing maid, but if she was known to be fucking a French trader, a proven thief, you could find yourself in jail, suspected of being involved with her disappearance—"

"But—"

"—and some might feel that justice had been served if I handed you over. The galleys would soon trim some of the grease fat of your fucking haunches."

"I beg you, monsieur!" Lauret pleaded, close to tears. "The girl meant nothing to me. We were friends, that was all."

"But you talked together?"

He nodded. "As father and daughter."

Baptista glanced away impatiently. "Get out of my sight. You are no help to me—"

"But maybe I *can* help!" Lauret pleaded, plucking at the Florentine's sleeve. "Tell me what you want. I will do anything you say."

Baptista turned back to him. "Of course you will, Lauret, we both know that."

"So what can I do?"

"Answer my questions, that's all. Now tell me every detail, Lauret, did this girl take you into her confidence?"

The Frenchman tilted his head to one side, his expression eager. "Her confidence? About what?"

"You tell me."

"She spoke of having no family. She said that her boyfriend worked at the foundry – no, I remember that wrong – it was at the tannery. Yes, he was a tanner working for Drago. But that doesn't matter because she would have nothing to do with him anymore—"

"*No, no piccolo chiacchierino!*" Baptista said impatiently. "What I want to know is this – did Gabriella take you into her confidence about a *secret*?"

"*Did* she have a secret?"

"I'm asking you, idiota!" Baptista replied coldly. "Did she tell you a secret? *Scandalo?* Something that was important, something that might be dangerous for her."

"Not that I remember." Lauret replied, regretfully. "But maybe if I thought about it again –"

Baptista drew in a breath, putting out his hand for the pack of cards.

"Yes, yes! Take them!" the Frenchman said eagerly, "Take the set. You can have them for nothing. No money, *jamais*. Take them as a token of my esteem for you, Monsieur

Baptista, and in the hope that there is no bad blood between us." He placed the cards in Baptista's hands and watched as the Florentine picked out the Joker.

Languidly he turned the card in his hand, examining the image.

"A little fat man, grinning like an ape... Does he remind of anyone, Lauret?" Deftly he tucked the card into the belt of the trader's breeches. "This is for you. For luck...Think carefully about what the little maid told you, go over every word she said and see if you don't remember something important. Something I need to know. Something you need to tell me." He shuffled the cards again languidly, his tone even. "And if you try to trick me, or lie to me, you will need more than a card to save you."

House of Tintoretto

'Fondamnta dei mon'

Making low grunting noises under his breath, Tintoretto shuffled through the drawings on his worktable. No one else was allowed to touch them, the irregular piles of sketches growing haphazardly. At times they overbalanced, pouring like an overflow from a weed-laden gutter, Tintoretto picking them up and studying them. Merciless, he threw away those he disliked, making a new pile of ones he considered useful and putting those he prized in a leather portfolio, its original green faded by sunlight, the suede dusty and spattered with pimples of hot wax.

He was thinking about a woman. A woman's face, a very particular face.

"What are you looking for?" Marco asked, glancing across the studio to his master. When there was no reply, he moved over to stand beside him. "What are you—"

"I heard you!" Tintoretto replied, still searching through the sheaves of drawings. "I am looking for someone I thought I knew."

"Who?"

"If I knew, I wouldn't be looking for her, Marco!" He said, pulling out two sketches, then dismissing them. "I have been looking for over an hour. This is a waste of time, a waste of time!" Agitated, he moved away, then turned back. "Forget it, *I* must forget all about it. I have work to do." Then turning to Marco, he added: "But there is something else, something I should have told you yesterday. We need a new model. And I have a girl in mind; she has a beauty that is unusual. Very dark, some *intelligenza* in her eyes—"

"And Florentina?" Marco asked, reminding him of the buxom whore he used often. "She is your muse. Or thinks she is."

"Florentina is a handsome woman," Tintoretto agreed, looking for a place to lay down the portfolio he was carrying. "but I need someone fresh, younger, with an innocence. I saw this girl in the piazza and approached her. She is a decent girl, anyone could see that, so I was reluctant – I have no skill with people, women in particular – but she had such a wonderful face I dared."

"Most women would be honoured to be painted by *Il Furioso*." Marco teased him.

"Most Venetian women, perhaps. A woman working in the wool factory or one of the glass blowers perhaps. Did you know that they say that some of the women are better than the men? Their creations are more delicate, the glassware fine as lace—"

"Florentina will be jealous," Marco teased again.

"Florentina is a whore. A lovely face, but so greedy. All the whores are greedy, they ask so much and all they do is pose. I pay them more than their customers – for much less exertion."

"I hear some work hard for their fee."

Tintoretto swivelled round, frowning. "You must be careful. Some of them are clean – but others, not so. Catch the pox and then what will you do, Marco? Treatment with holy wood, grinding up the herb from tree bark, will do nothing. The apothecaries are lying, within a year who would lose your nose and then" he tapped his forehead. "your mind. *Nothing* works on the pox. As for mercury, no, never! Mercury kills before it cures anything."

Marco sighed. "I haven't got the pox, master."

"Take care to stay that way! You are from a noble family and have to protect your reputation—"

"And the handsome fee my father pays you."

Tintoretto threw up his hands. "Your mouth will get you into trouble one day! I should dismiss you, throw you out like Titian did. He had more sense than I have. Keeping you on here when you learn little and are always late!" He snapped, taking the portfolio and slamming it back on the worktable before he spoke again. "I hope the girl sits for me. Such a wonderful face, sad and clever at the same time. She wore the yellow patch on her sleeve."

"She was Jewish?"

"Si."

"Does she have a name?"

"Of course she has a name!"

"What is it?"

Tintoretto shrugged. "I don't know! But I gave her *my* name and my address and told her to call. I would pay her, and I told her that, also assured her that she could bring a chaperone to the studio with her."

"What did she say to that?"

"She didn't remark about the chaperone, only explained her situation. That she already had a full time job working for some piano teacher" he pulled a face, "and so she could only sit for me until sundown, because afterwards it would be curfew and they lock up the ghetto." He thought about it, shaking his head. "It would give me little time in the winter when the days are so short, but in the summer it would be easier."

"But only if she agrees to model for you."

"She will," the artist said simply, "she has to. I know this, believe me, this girl is meant to come here."

Chapter Twelve

Pietro Aretino's bulk was planted firmly before the bronze statue in Jacopo's window, his girth blocking out the sculpture, leaving only the spear on show. A disembodied arrow head aiming for the skies.

"Aretino."

He turned at his name and inclined his head. "I believe you are to be honoured by our beloved Doge," Aretino said, his tone creamy. "How deserved, how right for such an honourable man." He moved to a large leather U shaped chair and sat down, the leather creaking under his weight. "I came to offer my congratulations, my dear friend. The Gianetti house is bearing yet another crown."

"What do you want?" Jacopo asked sharply, moving behind his desk and putting a yard of marble between them.

"*What do I want?* How unfriendly you are, Jacopo, one might think I had offended you in some way." He continued, Gianetti's rudeness intensifying his animosity. "You snubbed me at church the other day. That was unnecessary, and not something I would have done to you, friend."

"Unless the word friend has had its meaning changed in the lexicon I am not your friend." Jacopo replied, knowing full well it was the date that, exactly fifteen years earlier,

Aretino had first tied on the leash. "We could at least cease this pretence—"

"But I like pretence, it makes life so much more bearable. Surely you must agree with me, Jacopo? Truth, as we both know, is not always pretty."

"I'll ask you again, why are you here?"

"Your elevation will of course increase your influence, power – and finances." Aretino replied, his eyes bright with malice. "A little increase is justified, I feel. After all, I have not raised my fee in fifteen years."

"Get out!"

"Jacopo, we both know you don't mean that. If I did leave now I would got to the Doge and tell him – regretfully – what I know of your dealings. As a long time friend of yours (if 'friend' is being used in your preferred context here) the Doge would naturally insist I was mistaken. He would ask for proof. And I would be forced – *forced* – to provide it."

"You have no proof."

Aretino's smile puffed up his cheeks and made his eyes narrow. "Really? Then what have you being paying me for over the last fifteen years?"

Irritated, Jacopo reacted without thinking. "You're bluffing. You know nothing. You could have been bluffing all this time."

"Then ask to see my cards, Jacopo. I will display them gladly in front of yourself – and the Doge." Aretino's smile faded, his rage sleekly unpleasant. "Your attitude towards me has been increasingly hostile. In public you avoid me and people have noticed. If the Doge notices it will not be good for my status."

"Your status is only fit for the dung heap."

Aretino drew in a long, slow breath. He had thought to tighten the strings on his puppet, to jerk him into line. But the puppet was proving unwieldy, and dangerous to his ambitions.

"I hear you have been ill, and naturally I am enormously relieved to see you recovered." The threat made no impact, Aretino surprised by the lack of response, but ready with his next move. "No matter, despite your coldness towards me, I feel nothing but affection for you, Jacopo, and to prove the truth of my words I would like to share my knowledge, experience and courtly influence—"

"Which I made possible for you!"

"Indeed, your initial introduction to Andrea Gritti and your closeness to the present Doge was of great value, but it was my wit that cemented the association." Aretino replied, fingering the edge of his sleeve. "My power is such that now *I* can return the compliment that you once granted to me. I can advance your family name—"

"I am not interested."

"— not with you, dear friend! But with your son, Marco."

Jacopo tried to rise to his feet, but his legs failed him. **"Do not touch my son!"**

"Why are you worried? You have no great love for him, in fact it is common knowledge that you detest him. All Venice knows that you can barely endure being in the same room with your own flesh and blood." Aretino flipped back the sleeve of his doublet, a wide strip of black silk showing underneath. "But I can offer him—"

"Nothing! You are *un pederasta! Un omosessuale!*"

"— I can offer him a prosperous and pleasurable life at

court." Aretino said, his eyes flint. "You cannot offer him that. The Doge is your confidante true, but he finds you too dull for court life. Your son, however, is handsome and amusing. I have only met him once and he did not overly impress me then, but I hear from Tintoretto that he is a lively young man." Aretino clicked his tongue, the sound reverberating inside Jacopo's brain. "Court is the place for Marco—"

"I warn you—"

"No," Aretino said warningly. "*I warn you*. You have no say in the matter. I know your son, he would be an asset at the Doge's court. After all, my friend, how could you wish to impede Marco's progress? At court he would have access to culture and many influential contacts—"

"And whores."

Aretino shrugged. "He has access to whores on the streets, in the squares. If your son wants whores he does not need to go to the Doge's Palace to find them."

"He does not want whores!"

"Are you sure of that?" Aretino asked, walking around the study and pausing by the statue of a horse's head. "Ah, this is a copy of the Greek original. Very fine, very fine indeed... "he turned back to Jacopo. "You mustn't forbid me the chance to do something noble, my friend, I can make Marco into an important man. He is handsome, charming, a little flippant perhaps, but he is only young and has much to learn—"

"He is learning!"

"How to be a fucking dauber?" the writer snapped back. "Tintoretto is a genius, of that there is no doubt, but your son is an assistant, no more. He is wasted in *Il Furioso's* studio. Marco should be using his … other talents."

Jacopo's narrow face had flushed. "If you touch him—"

"You think I want to bugger your son?" Aretino asked, putting one finger to his mouth as though considering the suggestion. "That was not what I had in mind, Jacopo, how base of you to think it of me."

"Everyone knows you are a sodomiser. You brag of it."

"Everyone knows you are a liar and a crook. And yet you do *not* brag of your virtues, do you?" he parried, "I wonder, which of us would seem the most virtuous in God's eyes? A cheating coward, or a man who enjoys the flesh."

"A man lying with another man is a sin—"

Aretino waved aside the comment, his tone bored. "You and I have a deal, Jacopo. I have been very obliging for the last fifteen years. I have kept your secret safely, and thereby you have kept your status in Venice." He ran his left forefinger down the long marble nose of the horse sculpture. "One word from me and your family is destroyed. Your mother would die of shock, I fear. And all your business dealings would come to nothing." He sighed, as though regretful. "Of course the new prisons are an improvement on the Old Piombi. As you know, the Doge has kindly favoured Venice with a new gaol on the ground floor of the eastern wing of his palace. The Pozzi."

Jacopo flinched, his mouth cloth dry. The Pozzi were infamous, the isolated quarters notoriously damp and barely allowing any light to enter through the high, slit windows. Even in the demonic heat of summer the warmth never penetrated, and in winter the winds and chill from the Adriatic entered and never left. Men imprisoned there, even temporarily, suffered badly, and those held long term became old men in their thirties.

Jacopo thought of his mother, of the disgrace, of a trial at which all of Venice would attend to witness the demolition of a great name. Mockery, shame, obscene graffiti scrawled on the walls of the squares, and then – if he survived imprisonment – exile.

"So, Jacopo, we are agreed?"

He weighed his threatened disgrace against his son's possible degradation.

"Are we agreed?"

The loss of power and money, of status and respect, all to protect his son. A son who detested him. A son who had been a thorn in his side from the moment of his birth... Jacopo paused, calculating...What was one person against a legacy? One man set against the nobility and status of a great name? And why should he presume that his son would be harmed? Marco was a man, not a child... He gazed at the writer, his heart slowing like that of a snake.

Aretino saw the shift and prompted him: "So, *are* we agreed?"

"Yes," Jacopo said, finally. "we are agreed."

Chapter Thirteen

Intent and nervous, Marina Castilano entered the church of St Moise, taking a seat at the back of the pews and kneeling down. Her hands shook with cold, the Holy Water with which she had crossed herself dew on her fingers. Beside her lay her workbag, a soft beaded pouch marked with her initials. Initials she covered hurriedly with the edge of her cloak. Still keeping her eyes closed, she pulled the bag towards her, so closely she could feel the soft nudge against her thigh. Prayers made judders on her lips, scrambled, her attention wandering every time someone coughed, or footsteps sounded nearby. Finally Marina rose from her knees and took her seat in the pew, the bag on her lap, her gaze moving over the congregation.

The February cold had left many indoors, worshippers less devout when the chilled Adriatic wind bought fog and short days. Marina had intended to light a candle, but had forgotten in her haste, hurrying past the gridiron of flame that held up so many pleas and pledges to Heaven. And if she had lighted a candle for what would she wish?

You cannot unsee what you have seen, Marina thought, her grip tightening on the bag on her lap.

She had thought of confiding in her sister, but Lucia was

impractical and no keeper of secrets. But to who else could she turn, Marina had wondered. The Dutchman? She hardly knew him; he was just one of many customers. And besides, he might well have been asking after Gabriella – but for what reason? No, she decided, not the Dutchman.

Her gaze travelled along the pews, noting the hunched couple sitting together, the man with his head on his wife's shoulder. Hardly a man at all, mostly bone, his face cadaverous, hooded, illness corroding his features. She considered them for a long moment. Wondered about the woman, how she would fare when he died, if she had children to provide for. If she had money. They didn't look prosperous, but the wife – if that was who she was – appeared much younger than him, still able to make a life.

What did it matter about two people she didn't even know? Marina asked herself impatiently, turning her gaze away from the couple to a priest trimming the wicks of the altar candles. Perhaps she should ask advice from him. She could see his long nose, his jutting jaw, but it was a profile that offered no welcome. No, not him. No, not here.

Resigned, Marina rose to her feet, crossed herself and left the church, making her hurried way across the Bocca di Piazza heading for Calla de Carro. A mist was rising from the Lagoon, sneaking down the canals and making the buildings spectres. Within weeks Venice would begin to throw off her winter melancholy and from under scowling clouds and glowering tides would finally come the sun.

But not now, now the winter was intent on counting out every one of her long days, Marina finally arriving outside a narrow house with dark green shutters. The area was affluent, the door furnished with a knocker in the shape of a Medusa head, its hammer weighty in her hands as she rapped four times.

"*Ciao? Come va? Aspetta un attimo.*" A voice called out, a man opening the door seconds later. He was eating an apple, his eyebrows rising as he looked at Marina. "You are come to see Signora Zucca?"

Surprised, she nodded. "Si."

"You are very small."

"What?"

"And a woman. Can a woman really handle and shoe a horse of such size?"

Marina shook her head. "No, I'm not here about a horse!" She looked round, wondering if she should leave, then hurried on. "I wish to see Signora Zucca on a private matter."

He bit into the apple again, tilting his head to one side. "I see, well you better come in."

Nodding she followed the young man, the gloomy daylight replaced by dark narrow corridor which lead to a vaulted, curtained and candlelit interior where a fire smoked listlessly in a brass grate. Dirty plates and glasses were abandoned about the room, some disguarded on pieces of ebony furniture, a painted harpsichord by the window and a velvet shawl Marina recognised thrown over the carcass of a cooked chicken.

"Forgive this mess, there was a party here last night." A woman said behind her, Marina turning. "Oh, Signora Castilano! Did I order something and forget to collect it?"

Marina smiled apologetically.

"No, not at all. This has nothing to do with the shop.

And I apologise for arriving uninvited, Signora Zucca, but it is important that I speak with you."

The young man was still leaning against the harpsichord, eating his apple, his eyes fixed on their unexpected visitor.

"Alone..." Marina blundered on, glancing at him.

"Oh, very well." he said idly, tossing the apple core into the grate and moving into the back of the house.

Marina waited for a moment, wondering if she had made a foolish decision that she might well come to regret. Caterina Zucca was a known courtesan, and although she frequented Marina's shop it was quite another matter for a respectable matron to visit the home of a kept woman.

Uncomfortable, Marina hesitated, studying the handsome blonde standing in front of her. "This is a matter of some delicacy."

"I am an expert in dealing with matters of delicacy," Caterina replied lightly, gesturing for her visitor to sit down. Without making a comment, she then pushed aside the shawl, and the cooked chicken, and took a seat beside her. "Go on, please."

"It's difficult to know where to start."

"The beginning, perhaps?"

Marina nodded. "Perhaps you remember a maid we had at the shop?"

Interested, Caterina leaned forward in her seat. "Gabriella?"

"Si, Gabriella!" Marina agreed, footsteps overhead making her pause.

"It's only my son, don't worry."

"That was your *son?*"

In reply Caterina picked up a candlestick and held the

flame near to her face to illuminate her skin. Immediately the fine lines and wrinkles became apparent. "Candlelight is very forgiving – from a distance." She smiled. "Personally I seldom go out in daylight, so cruel to a face that is no longer young."

"Yet you are still beautiful."

Caterina laughed. "I am a skilful and an amusing companion. I believe my cerebral wit will long outlive my bodily wiles." She put down the candle on the table beside them and turned back to her guest. "I heard a rumour that Gabriella was missing."

Marina nodded. "She has been missing five days now. We don't know where she's gone, or why. When she was at the shop she seemed happy. She never said she wasn't content..." Marina trailed off, staring at Caterina's face, her instinct heightened. "How did you hear that Gabriella was missing?"

"Venice has few secrets."

"Forgive me, but that's something of a surprise. Gabriella Russo was a maid, she had no family, and in all the months she was with us she has few visitors at the shop. And yet apparently her absence has been noted by people such as yourself." Marina paused, feeling her way along. "I wonder *why* it would be of interest to you, Signora Zucca?"

"Or you."

"She was my maid."

"And you seem very concerned about a maid. Almost afraid, if you don't mind my saying." Caterina replied, "Have you reported her absence to the authorities?"

Marina made a clicking sound with her tongue. "The authorities! No, I haven't reported it to the authorities. It would be a useless exercise. Who would care for a missing maid?"

"You do." Caterina replied, curious to know more. "Which means that Gabriella meant something to you. Or her disappearance does." She could see Marina flinch and pressed on. "Please confide in me. You have chosen to talk to me, so there is little reason to hold back anything, Signora Castilano, I am well used to keeping secrets."

Marina's hesitation was brief.

"Do you know the Dutchman, Barent der Witt?"

"Yes."

"Do you know him well?"

"I know him intimately," Caterina replied, amused to see the shopkeeper blush. "But I also know him as a friend."

"I've heard strange things about him. Of course everyone knows he's an apothecary, but some say he makes cures and others say poisons." Marina was uncomfortable. If the Inquisition discovered she was even talking about such things she would be watched, perhaps interrogated... The room was closing about her, the scented candles overwhelming as she gripped the bag on her lap. "Der Witt came to my shop and asked about Gabriella. He said she was afraid of something and he had wanted to help her. He seemed frightened."

Caterina leaned back in her seat, her arms folded. She was suspicious and took no care to disguise the fact.

"May I ask why you are *really* here, Signora Castilano?

"I am here about Gabriella!"

"*What* about her?"

"Do you know what happened to her?"

"Do you?"

"*Do I?* My interest is genuine. Forgive me for troubling you, Signora."

Angered, Marina stood up to leave, Caterina catching hold of her wrist.

"Excuse me for doubting you, but I am wary. It pays to be so in Venice. Gossip can cause tragedy, or so I've found. Yes, I know the Dutchman, as I say, we are old friends. And yes, he also asked me about Gabriella. He said he had failed her."

"How had he failed her?"

"They were due to meet and she was going to tell him something, but the meeting never took place. He never saw Gabriella again." She watched Marina retake her seat, noticing how she gripped the bag on her bag. "It tortures him that he let her down… He thinks she is dead."

"Dead?"

Caterina nodded. "He visits the morgue every day to look for her body. I try to convince him that Gabriella could still be alive, that she could simply return after some indiscreet dalliance with a man. But Der Witt is sure she is dead." Caterina could see Marina pale. "Are you ill?"

She shook her head, then reached into her bag and pulled out a package wrapped in a soft cloth. After pausing for a moment, she passed it to Caterina, watching as she opened it.

"Dear God…" she said, turning over the shoes and seeing the dried blood on the soles. "Are these Gabriella's?"

"Yes."

"Are you sure?"

"Yes, I remember them well. She replaced the pink ribbons for pale blue ones... I found them in my shop, hidden amongst all the other shoes I store there." Marina replied, whispering. "Why?"

"Why what?"

"If she was hurt, surely Gabriella would have come to us for help. Or gone to the hospital. We would have known she was injured. But if she was… if she was killed, *who hid the shoes?* She can't have done. It would not be humanly possible." Marina glanced around, her voice faltering. "So who killed her? And who came into my shop and hid the shoes after her death? And why?"

'You must be careful…

I wasn't careful'

She was crying quietly, looking around her.

Rich clothes over her arms, the gilt buttons of a tunic catching the sunlight.

'There are four of them. The Wolves of Venice.'

Looking round, listening

Ready to move on

'Four. You hear me?

Four. Don't let them tell you less'.

In silence, Caterina re-wrapped the shoes then repeated, word for word, what Gabriella had told her.

Marina stared at her. "But what does it mean? *Wolves of Venice?*" she said, unnerved. "What was she talking about?"

"I don't know. And I've told no one about it other than Barent der Witt – and now you."

Marina stared at the parcel in Caterina's hands. "Only you know about the shoes."

"Good." Caterina said crisply. "Signora Castilano, no one else must know about any of this..."

She noticed the shopkeeper flinch.

"... you've told someone?"

"No, but when der Witt came to my shop he asked me about Pietro Aretino and Adamo Baptista, just before he asked about Gabriella. I kept wondering why. And now I'm wondering how much they knew; if they're involved in some way...I asked der Witt, but he wouldn't say anymore."

Caterina looked away, remembering. Adamo Baptista. Yes, she knew him. She had been hired by him as a courtesan, asked to remain dressed but to lift her skirts and walk around the room in front of him, her genitals exposed. Amused, she had done so, smiling. But he had reacted with irritation, instructing her to remain silent, her expression blank. After a little while of her parading he had suddenly uttered a loud whistle. Curious, Caterina had wondered if he wanted her to act like a dog – such play acting was not unknown to her – but instead the door of Baptista's study had opened and the exotic Nikolas Volt had entered.

The youth had walked over to Baptista, allowing the older man to whisper in his ear. Nodding, Volt then moved to Caterina and kneeled down, instructing her to ride him like a horse. Well used to the sexual proclivities of men, Caterina obeyed, Baptista taking out a small, ivory handled whip. At first she had thought it was for her to use on Volt. Nothing too perverse, nothing too unusual, nothing she had not done before. But instead Baptista had taken off his own doublet and began to flagellate himself, coming to a climax as he whipped his back and shoulders, his impenetrable gaze never leaving Caterina's face.

When he had finished, Baptista had dismissed Volt and handed her a purse of money. An ornate, black mesh purse, tightly woven. A purse she had emptied of its contents and then thrown into the Lagoon, watching as it had twisted and writhed, jerking on the tide before finally descending like a dead bird.

"You must be very careful," she said, looking intently into Marina's face. "And you must say **nothing** to either of those men about this. Not one word." she pressed the shoes into Marina's hands. "Take these and destroy them—"

"But they might be important!"

"To whom? To Gabriella?" Caterina waved the suggestion aside. "She needs them no longer. If she does, she will return for them. But I doubt it. You – and I – must pretend ignorance. The maid is missing, we know no more."

"But she confided in you—"

"Yes, and I wish she had not!" Caterina said bluntly. "I have had enough trouble in my life not to want more. Listen carefully to me, please. Avoid Aretino and Baptista. They are wolves. I've thought about what Gabriella said to me many times and I think she was referring to *them* when she spoke about The Wolves of Venice."

Marina frowned. "But she said there were **four**. *'Four, don't let them tell you less...'*"

"All the more reason for us to forget everything we have seen or heard. Two wolves are dangerous, four would be lethal." She dropped her voice. "Men like that come on the tide to scavenge. Aretino is clever and ruthless, but beware Baptista. For all of Aretino's reputation, the Florentine is the more dangerous of the two. Aretino fears a loss of power. Baptista fears nothing."

Chapter Fourteen

Venetian noble women were virtual prisoners, kept in *clausura*, their homes – however sumptuous – their gaols. Their identity was dictated by their male relatives; a woman was a mother, a wife, a daughter, even short undertakings outside the home watched and restricted. If a woman travelled in Venice, she travelled by private gondola to attend church or social events, always chaperoned and always heavily veiled. So confining was their existence that unless they had female relatives they could soon find themselves trapped in a male orientated world that had little time, or interest, in the female life.

A woman's duty was to domestically manage her family and her home, which she left infrequently. Her outfits were extravagant, gloriously detailed, often imported, her jewels magnificently rich. Her home was also extravagant; decorated with Turkish carpets, Italian marble, French fabrics and a plethora of Dutch still lives, in the newest fashion. Hog-tied in luxury, many Venetian noble women relished their existence; others rebelled, envying the freedom of the whores.

The very whores who could walk about Venice alone. Dressed exquisitely, they were on a par with the noblewomen, except for the fact that they were free. A courtesan with beauty, wit and learning could enchant the most influential minds in Venice. These were no slatternly whores, but elegant women debating with scholars and academicians, their salons attended by the richest men in Venice.

Barent der Witt had access to noblewomen *and* courtesans. Although against the laws of the Republic he undertook abortions, unwanted foetuses left to the crabs at the bottom of the Lagoon. His secret entree to the highest in society had been forged by apothecary skills imported from the lowlands of Holland. Exiled from Amsterdam, der Witt had found a niche in the island city and a number of noblewomen had sought out his services via their maids.

"Signor der Witt?" He turned at the voice, tipping his black hat to the slight figure approaching him. He knew the girl, delicate, with red hair and skin the colour of sea ivory. A maid who worked for one of Venice's most neurotic Contessas and also for Caterina Zucca. Something he knew Paolo kept secret. A maid who worked for a Contessa *and* a whore? *Che scandalo...*

"My mistress would ask a favour of you."

A favour. The word often used. And abused.

"What favour would that be, Paola Larioni?" he asked.

"The Contessa requests a little of your tincture. The tincture you gave to her last week."

"Surely she cannot need more so soon?" he asked, taking off his hat and feeling the damp mist settle on his hair. "I cannot—"

She smiled, heart shaped face surrounded by the blazing hair. Not beautiful, but sweetly appealing. "The Contessa insists."

"The Dutchman refuses," he replied, his tone brusque as he moved away from her.

She ran after him. "Please, signor, my mistress is suffering."

"No, Paola, she is not suffering." He stopped walking and looked at her. "The glass workers are suffering in crowded rooms, in dim light, in heat that would suffocate a bull. They do not have workbenches, but create their marvels sitting on the floor, their backs bent over double. In winter these women appreciate the warmth that the glass making affords them. In summer, they sweat with the inescapable heat, their skin breaking out in sores." Sighing, he turned his hat around in his large hands, a habit he had brought with him from Amsterdam. "No, your mistress does not suffer… Tell her I will come to see her in a few days." He touched the girl's shoulder briefly. "And you. Are you recovered?..."

She nodded, flushed.

"… Call by to see me again soon, Paola, I will give you something the Dutch whores use to prevent pregnancy. Sometimes that works well. But being careful works better." He turned to move away, then turned back to her. "Your mistress uses the Castilano shop, does she not?"

"Often. There are always new clothes and fashions coming into Venice" Paola's face dimpled with amusement. "and she is very vain."

"And you always go with her to the shop?"

"Of course. The Contessa cannot go alone."

He hesitated for a moment: "Do you know the maid who works at the Castilano shop? A girl called Gabriella?"

Paola thought a moment longer, then shook her head. "No. I never saw a maid there. There was never one in the shop. Perhaps in the house behind... Is it important?"

"No, no. It is of no consequence, it counts for nothing." Der Witt replied, preparing to move away. "Remember to visit me, Paola. Do not forget."

The girl watched him go, wondering how she would communicate his refusal – and how much her mistress would then rail at her. Without the tincture the Contessa would feign illness, lie down in her bedchamber and Paola would have to bathe her feet, massaging the hooked toes until her mistress's breathing altered and she fell asleep.

Paola was still watching the Dutchman as he crossed the bridge, heading for... Where she could not guess, but rumours about his dealings always accompanied him. Like the glass vial around his neck; the hair bracelet, and the U shaped mark on the inside of his elbow which Paola had glimpsed once when his sleeve had been rolled up. People also gossiped about garden he had created seemingly overnight. Rows of potent herbs, low growing fruit and pungently scented flowers unlike any seen in Venice before. He would – so the story went – pick the blossoms at night and take them back into his house, the house which always had its shutters closed.

Paola didn't know if the Dutchman was a poisoner. If he had added to the Italian skills by bringing toxins from his homeland. She didn't know if he was an occultist, although many claimed knowledge of it. She didn't know if he was a killer, or if the Inquisition would follow on the heels of the rumours and seek him out. Paola Larioni only knew that in amongst his affluent clients the Dutchman treated the wretched; that as he entered the back gateways of the rich he also attended the dank dwellings of the sick: people to whom he showed kindness without seeking – or accepting – any reward.

Slowly she moved on, thinking. Some claimed Barent der Witt was evil. But if that was evil, Paola thought to herself, it was better than any kindness she had ever known.

I never knew about the deal between my father and Aretino. Not until years later, and by then it was too late. It was all too late.

What I did know was that I had been singled out by one of the most powerful men in Venice, a writer who scandalised and intrigued society at the same time. A man with unlimited ambition and a ferocious appetite for money and depravity. Did I wonder why he had selected me to mentor? I presumed it was to feed his homosexuality, but I risked his displeasure at once by saying I was a lover of women. He replied mockingly, promising me the most infamous whores in Venice instead of shop girls or kitchen maids.

I could have told him then that I had lost my virginity to Cara, my father's housekeeper. Yes, that Cara. She had been much younger, and not so fat, but lusty, my fourteen year old head resting between her full breasts after she had seduced me. Her love making had been all soft, moist flesh and kisses like a mother hen pecking a chick. For several months I worshipped her, until she left my bed for that of the coachman.

We never spoke of it again...

So I didn't tell Aretino about Cara and instead I fell under his bewitchment. My father – I see now that his conscience had been temporarily pricked – warned me to keep my distance, but that only increased my interest, and having no other men in the family to advice me I fell under that rancid, sexual, deviant spell that so many courted. Because, you see, in being Aretino's protégé my elevation would be meteoric.

Only one person tried to intervene, my grandmother, Lavinia. She had me brought to her room by a servant and then rapped her stick on the table in front of her twice, making the dogs bark below.

"You are behaving like a fool, and you will regret it."

"But was it not you, Contessa, who said only recently that the young should be allowed to be foolish—"

"Foolish, but not reckless," she retorted, white hair frothed around her face, her eyebrows faded away with age, her stick – ebony, with a sculptured silver head of a crown – striking the table. Again, the dogs barked below, and inside I was laughing at her, because she was very old and very angry and besides, she had been so disinterested in me before she could hardly demand obedience now.

So I accepted Aretino's next invitation to a gathering he was holding on the Grand Canal outside his palazzo. There were ten, maybe twelve gondolas, full of dazzling women and young boys, naked from the waist up. The youths were lying with the women and then with each other, the music of Andrea Gabrieli played by the orchestra on shore, dancers performing beside them. Mesmerised – yes, that is the word – I watched the parade, Aretino seated on the first gondola, myself beside him. At his feet, like a lap dog.

But what a lap dog, what a pampered, indulged, spoiled pet.

My wit flashed like a struck match, the clothes given to me creating a little prince, and the wine offered making the night float, the boats suspended under clouds as the moon seemed planted, fixed, in that indigo sky above us. A man does not need sex to be seduced. A man does not need an orgasm to feel elated… There were many hundred of petals thrown on the water that night. Where they floated near the lights you could see their colours, where they were sinking, or beached, they were in the darkness, their colour bled out.

He bled us all, that weighty potentate who patted my shoulder and applauded my wit, signalling for Adamo Baptista to come over to him. A whisper passed between them and then I was summarily dismissed, taken from the vessel and abandoned on the side of the Grand Canal, watching the lighted boats, the whores, and the bare chested boys as they floated away.

Chapter Fifteen

Tintoretto's studio,

May 1548

"Where have you been?" Tintoretto said, confronting Marco as he walked in. "I have seen nothing of you for days, and you sent no word. Were you ill?"

He shuffled his feet, his tone flat. "Yes, I was ill—"

"That is not what I was told when I sent for word at your home!" Tintoretto raged. "This is not good enough, you cannot treat me like this." Grabbing Marco by the sleeve he hauled him to the back of the studio and into a closeted office, slamming the door behind them. The walls were slatted with shelves, small wooden boxes of wax figures, statues, a piece of armour jostling for space next to rolls of canvas and bottles of wine. Pushing Marco into a seat Tintoretto glowered at him.

"What is the matter with you?" he asked, slapping him on the shoulder. "Why are you whoring with Aretino?"

"He is a friend of yours!"

"He is an acquaintance! He commissions paintings from me, he does not invite me into his home or to his orgies."

"But he champions you. The four paintings you did for the Scuola di St Marco he applauded publicly—"

"No doubt he realised that his praise would reach Titian's ears abroad and cause further coolness between us."

Marco was not backing down. "Aretino commissioned you to paint the ceiling in his house, and then to paint his portrait."

Tintoretto smiled to himself. Yes, the writer *had* hired him to paint his portrait, but Tintoretto had never been gulled by Aretino, or cowed by him. When he had taken his subject's measurements he had not used a tape measure, but a stiletto. A subtle reminder of Aretino's previous hostility.

"You must stay away from him, Marco—"

"Aretino is cultured. Well read, he can speak on any topic with confidence. As for orgies" Marco replied drily. "I have seen no orgies."

"You will. And you will see dwarves set to fight with animals and the most famous whores in Venice tie ribbons and bells around little boys' cocks. So Aretino can hear them – even if they are out of his sight. Hear them and salivate as they approach."

Marco shifted in his seat. "This is all hearsay. You are jealous because Aretino and Titian have never included you in their circle."

Stung, Tintoretto shook his head. "So now you insult me? Idiota! Do you know *nothing*? Do you hear *nothing*? Aretino is a blackmailer, a pederast—"

"As are many in Venice."

"You are defending him!" the painter replied, slapping Marco on the shoulder again. "You are the son of Jacopo

Gianetti, of one of the most honoured families in Venice, and you chose to mix with this mountebank?"

"Titian is his friend, the Doge is his friend, Aretino is invited to every palazzo in Venice – and beyond – his talent applauded, his wit quoted endlessly—"

"And his *merda*? Do people celebrate his taking a shit? Is it gold? Does it smell like fresh linen?" Tintoretto stared at his apprenticeship. "You are a fool! You are *intossicato*, drunk with him. You think he will raise you up for nothing? No, there will be a price—"

"He has asked nothing of me."

"**Yet.**" Tintoretto snapped. "Yet. But he will, Aretino does nothing for nothing. He will bleed you like a calf, he will pull on the string he has woven around you and then cut you loose." Marco thought of his humiliating dismissal the previous night and looked away as Tintoretto continued. "It is a game for him. He will entice and repel, entice and repel, until you are only able to think of one thing – how to please him."

"I am not an idiot!"

"Neither are the Kings that Aretino has enthralled. Neither are the boys he corrupts, the men he blackmails, the women he debases." Tintoretto leaned towards him; although there was only ten years in difference in their age, the painter's tone was paternal. "These are deep waters, Marco, too deep for you. You want to bask in his power? Become a fixture at the Doge's palace? Take a seat beside him whilst Ludivco Agostino plays? I understand, who would *not* want such luxury, such glamour – but it is false." He pointed to one of the cardboard boxes, with its little wax figures arranged inside. "*This* is what you are to Aretino," he grabbed one of the figures and crushed it in his hand. "A toy. And all children grow tired of their toys in time."

Gilda Fasculo took a seat at the table, her two sons sitting opposite. Federico and Angelo, both heavily built, wide shouldered, with the fairer eyes and hair colour of the Russian Jews. Inherited from their late father. And both quick to anger, another legacy he had passed on. Since their arrival in Venice, Fredrico had worked on the boats, unpacking the goods brought in by the merchants, lifting carpets and furniture and the occasional bronze figure brought from Persia and beyond. All bound for the Rialto, the economic heart of Venice. The work was gruelling, but away from the industrial factories, it was at least clean.

At first his brother Angelo had wanted to train as a tanner, but the conditions of the trade had proved brutal. The exhausting scraping of the skins by hand, with knives that quickly blunted. And then there was the stink of the fetid water in which the leather was softened; an acrid stench that burned the mouth and throat and blistered the skin. Tanner's throat had caused the premature death of many men, the bronchia and lungs affected, the stomach lining ulcerated.

So Angelo had left the tannery and joined his brother on the boats, working together and obeying the laws of the ghetto. Neither of them intelligent, neither gifted. Both – even in their early twenties – under their mother's control.

"I will say this again," Gilda said warningly, "let me handle the situation with Adamo Baptista."

"He threatened you," Angelo interrupted, "I should challenge the bastard—"

"No, you will not!" Gilda snapped. "You are to do as I say, do you understand? I have kept this family together, despite your stupid actions, despite your determination to start a fight with virtually anyone."

"If we are insulted—"

"You *look* for insults!" Gilda replied, her tone hardening. "You look and you find. And God knows, there is always something to be insulted about. But that is our life, and violence will not help our cause." She unclenched her hands, spreading them, palms down, on the scrubbed table. "I have this matter under control—"

"How?" Federico snapped. "You're being blackmailed."

"Be quiet and listen!" she hissed. "Baptista is working for that pig Aretino. We are forced into giving them money – that much we cannot change or we'll be exposed and hunted down like animals. How Baptista found out about our past I don't know. He comes from Florence, maybe he heard it on one of his trips." She laughed coldly. "What I can give him is nothing in comparison to what Aretino is worth, but he would still squeeze me dry, make me a liar, a cheat, make me betray my own people. If you had seen Baptista; he had no mercy, just a relentless fixation on his goal. That bastard would see me in the galleys." Her tone was bitter. "But I don't intend to let him win."

Angelo leaned forward, aware of his mother's cunning. "What are you going to do?"

"What does anyone know about Adamo Baptista?"

"He's a mediocre painter, who goes from one artist's studio to another, never stays long anywhere."

"They say he's a spy," Fredrico contributed. "and a gambler."

Angelo nodded, interrupting him. "Apparently a very

good gambler. People say he cheats, but no one can prove it. And no one dares challenge him. He learnt to play in his home city, Florence."

"Why did he leave Florence?"

Angelo shrugged. "No one knows."

"At the moment," Gilda corrected him. "But that can change. Baptista is very confident because knows people are afraid of him. There are rumours all the time about his violence. But there are just that, *rumours*. Who truly knows what this man has done? And yet people avoid him because of his reputation."

Angelo folded his arms. "It works, no one will challenge him."

"But what crimes has he committed? A man like Baptista must have a past. Things he hides—"

"And how are we going to find out what he's hiding?"

Gilda paused, thinking. "He has no family in Venice?"

"He has no one but Aretino, and I doubt they are friends. Baptista is in Aretino's pay."

"Exclusively?" Gilda asked. "No, I doubt it. He travels too much to be merely Aretino's dog. And what of this young man who has suddenly emerged?"

Angelo shrugged. "I don't know about him—"

"I do." Gilda replied, leaning across the table towards her two sons. "News travels speedily across the islands and it all ends up in St Marks. Remember, some of our more prosperous Jews attend functions in the city and there they hear the gossip. The gossip they then pass onto me." She smiled craftily. "The young man is Nikolas Volt, a German youth of nineteen. His appearance is strange, half Germanic, half Japanese. But the question is – *where* did this creature come from? And what is he to Adamo Baptista?"

"His lover?"

She shook her head. "No, Baptista only sleeps with women. He has a horror of homosexuality."

"But he works for Aretino."

"But doesn't sleep with the fat *maiale*." She retorted sharply. "In the past Baptista was always alone. No one ever saw him with anyone – apart from Aretino. So this Nikolas Volt must be important to Baptista for him to suddenly become his companion. That's a very public statement, and Baptista doesn't like anything in his life to be public – unless it suits him in some way."

Angelo was losing interest. "Well, what good is it to us? What does it all mean?"

Impatiently Gilda tapped her fingers on the table, her eyes shrewd.

"It means that Adamo Baptista is not the only one who can root out secrets. He would see me in the galleys, would he? We'll see who ends up there." Her gaze moved back to her sons. "You must listen to everything and everyone. Whilst you work, you listen to people gossip. Because people gossip in Venice all the time. People coming from different countries, with their stories, with titbits of news that might prove valuable. Do not ask questions, that would be too obvious, but *listen*." She banged her hands down on the table, making her sons jump. "As for me, I have my own methods... We must find out about Nikolas Volt and about Baptista's life in Florence. Something that we could use in *our* favour." She explained coldly. "If Adamo Baptista has an Achilles heel, I want to find it. I want to find it and sever it. And I want to cripple him."

Chapter Sixteen

The Rialto

Venice

The tumblers were performing their routines, four Spanish jugglers working on the lush grass of the square, the crowd pushing forwards and applauding as one of the tumblers completed a double summersault and landed perfectly, with his arms outstretched in triumph. Having bought a selection of seafood in paper wrappers, Marco handed one to Ira, then sat on the stone wall beside him.

"Feast days," he said, his fingers picking into the food. "The players always come out on feast days. And night." He frowned. "I only like the soft shelled crabs, not the ones with hard shells."

Ira was eating both, swallowing as he looked at his friend. "Who is the feast day in honour of?"

"I don't know," Marco replied, picking out the hard

shelled crabs and throwing them over his shoulder. "There are too many to remember. Do Jews have many saints?"

"We don't have any."

"How sensible," Marco replied, pointing over to where a girl was entering the garden with a bear and two handlers. The animal was not yet fully grown, jerking its head against the ring through his nose. "Caterina Zucca has a new slave."

Ira was surprised at the comparison which had occurred to his companion. "You look at a performing bear—"

"It hasn't done anything yet."

"— and think of a woman and her slave?"

"Have you met Caterina Zucca?"

"Don't be stupid, Marco, you know I haven't."

He looked crestfallen. "I only asked—"

"I know she's a whore."

"*Courtesan.*"

"There's a difference?"

"Indeed there is!" Marco replied. "A Venetian courtesan is welcomed in high places and courted by intellectuals—"

"And bedded by them too."

"— naturally. You cannot judge her, she is remarkable. Very lovely, of course, but beauty is not her only gift, she would impress you with her knowledge." He sneaked a look over to Ira. "You must love women."

"I admire them."

"But you must have loved a woman once. Surely?"

Ira stared ahead, watching the woman and the bear, the handlers keeping close to the animal as it resisted performing. On his right he could see that the tumblers had finished and were collected in a group, their costumes stained with sweat, one wiping his face with the back of his sleeve.

"I did love someone very much. A long time ago, in Florence."

"What was her name?"

"That's not important."

Marco sighed, lying back against the stone wall. "If you must be mysterious, very well. But answer me this – what was she like?"

"Like land to a drowning man."

Marco had not expected such a response and was unsure how to reply. Normally he would have made a joke, teased Ira, but something warned him against levity. "What happened to her?"

"Nothing happened."

"But you lost her?"

"Do you see her with me?" Ira countered bitterly, finishing the seafood and screwing up the paper into a compressed ball. "She had a great heart, she was kind, loving. Generous with everyone, but she developed tuberculosis and died... I didn't expect it, no one did. But she was weaker than we thought and..." he stared ahead, trailing into silence. "I would have married her if she had lived."

Marco nudged his shoulder. "You will find someone else."

"I don't want to."

"You must! You're a man, you need someone to—"

"To fuck?" Ira queried. "No, I don't need a woman just for that. Not any woman. But you do, and that's your choice, Marco. And anyway you have more opportunities than I do to find such company." He had been wondering for weeks how to put his doubts into words and continued carefully:

"You were telling me about Caterina Zucca. I suppose you met her through Pietro Aretino?"

"No, they are not friends. But we all attended the same concert and he introduced me... You don't like Aretino, do you?"

"I don't know him." Ira replied, clapping as the juggler began again. "But what I've heard of him he's hated. Many people – including some in the ghetto – speak of his many cruelties."

"He has been kind to me."

"I'm sure he has."

"What do you mean by that?" Marco countered, noticing the chill in Ira's tone. "You've changed since I've been fortunate enough to become a friend of Pietro Aretino's—"

"A friend?"

Marco nodded. "Yes, a *friend* and since he has become a friend of mine you've become cold with me."

"You imagine it."

"I do not imagine it!" Marco retorted heatedly. "When I mention what I have been doing, or where I have been invited, you say little. Even concerts at the Doge's palace do not impress you. I am becoming known—"

"You were *already* known as the son of Jacopo Gianetti, you already had honours and a reputation – which you could now lose because of your new acquaintances."

A roar went up from the crowd, the jugglers working together, four men in a line, tossing metallic balls in spirals, the colours blurring and spinning against the sun. The heat had risen, trees with their leaves only half opened making limited shade, a drowsy, soporific breeze coming in from the Adriatic.

"You are jealous," Marco said, his tone sullen.

"No, I am concerned." Ira replied.

"You *are* jealous! And I understand why." Marco continued. "But you *can't* begrudge me my good fortune. Aretino had chosen me to mentor, to present to influential people at court. He is wealthy, clever, a word from him can make or ruin a reputation and he wishes to further my career and make me prominent in Venice."

"Like Caterina Zucca?"

Marco jumped off the wall, his expression defiant. "I do not want to argue with you, Ira. We are friends and I want us to remain so—"

"It is *because* we are friends that I risk saying this. You have changed, Marco. Not just the clothes," he gestured to the extravagant outfit he was wearing, "but your manner. You ignore your work, you disrespect Tintoretto, for what? To be flattered by a blackmailer? Corrupted by a man whom people fear but no one loves?"

"You have no right to say all this—"

"But I dare say it, Marco, and risk your anger." He persisted. "Be careful that you are not developing the one thing of which you accused your father – greed. Greed for power, status, approval—"

"*You cannot tell me what to do!* You cannot advise me. You are not my father—"

"And neither is Pietro Aretino! If you are looking to him for paternal guidance you are looking in the wrong place." He caught hold of Marco's arm. "Please, be careful of this man. And of his associates, like Adamo Baptista. Aretino may have the admiration of the Doge, but Baptista does not, and no good can come of any association with him."

"I don't associate with Baptista!" Marco snapped, shaking off Ira's grip. "You tell me the motives of others, you warn me of their intentions – but what do *you* want from me, Ira? When we met you were just one more Jew doctor from the ghetto—" he stopped, immediately regretting his words. "I didn't mean, Oh God, I'm sorry—"

Stunned, Ira shook his head and stood up. "I have given you my opinion, but what do I know? Your city and your culture is not mine, Marco, I have no right to comment, but I will say just this and then no more on the subject. Remove yourself from Aretino's influence. If you do not, you may find yourself having to pay a price even you cannot afford."

Chapter Seventeen

Rosella had tied the scarf around her hair several times, but was still not satisfied, finally discarding it and tying her hair back instead with a strip of blue lace. Asleep in her bed by the wall, her mother lay motionless, Rosella glancing over to Ira, her concern obvious.

"Is she worse?"

"No," he shook his head. "Not worse."

"She hardly moves now, I don't think she even knows we are here." Rosella said quietly. "Will you sit with her until I return?"

"Yes, I said I would. But don't be late and miss the curfew."

"Angelo Fasculo nearly missed the curfew again the other night. He thought he was going to be fined, but he was just given a warning." Her face had flushed slightly, Ira noticing.

"D'you like him?"

"Angelo is … nice."

"A hard worker." Ira said, thinking of the usurer's son. Not ambitious, but steady, handsome, and although at times volatile, a kind man. "Has he asked you to go out with him?"

"Yes… but I haven't agreed to meet him yet."

"But you would like to?"

"If you approve, yes, I would like to." Rosella replied, keeping her flushed face averted and changing the subject. "I don't understand why you are still worried about my going to the studio. Marco will be at there whilst I pose for *Il Furioso*" she pulled a comical face. "and you know Marco. He's like a brother to me. He fusses and treats me as you do."

"You don't think he's changed?" Ira asked, "that he's not as he was?"

"He's quieter. I've noticed that."

"Moody." Ira added. "He is not falling in love with you, is he?"

She laughed. "No! And I would *never* fall in love with Marco Gianetti. Angelo Fasculo, maybe," she teased her brother. "But Marco? No."

For four months the two men had been close. In that time Marco had often visited the ghetto, but since Jacopo's recovery Ira had been banned from the Gianetti palazzo. The boycott had irked Marco, but Ira had expected it and, as such, accepted his exile. Their very differences had proved to bond them. Marco was easily bored, a poor timekeeper, indifferent to responsibility and frivolous with money. By contrast, Ira was devoted to his profession and his family, deeply aware of his obligation to them.

Yet each complimented the other. Marco found in Ira and Rosella the siblings he had never had; Ira found in Marco a freedom, an artlessness he envied. And when Rosella began to pose for Tintoretto Marco had immediately offered to chaperone her.

"*Il Furioso* is not a satyr" he had told Ira. "As for Titian, if you sister was sitting for him, then I would worry."

Despite his reassurances, on the first visits Ira had accompanied Rosella to Tintoretto's studio and Marco had taken her home to the ghetto, doffing his cap in mock service at the gates. As for Rosella, she enjoyed his company and found him amusing, but her affections were growing for Angelo Fasculo, her life expanding as the studio was. Having hired four more apprentices, *Il Furioso's* workload ran with the same efficiency as a factory. The drawings were made, copied, then the master would create his wax figures. Only then would Tintoretto begin to paint. Frantically, covering yards of canvas as he repeatedly checked his models to ascertain that he was following the configuration. Often he was so intent on what he was doing, he would move without looking, assistants pushed out of the way roughly.

After a couple of weeks Rosella felt confident to attend the studio alone, Marco walking her home later. But over the past month Marco had been intermittently absent, Tintoretto infuriated, and Rosella deciding to keep the upheaval a secret from her brother in case Ira prevented further visits.

"He is a fool!" *Il Furioso* had snorted as Rosella posed for him. "Marco does have some talent, but he is so lazy, so so feckless." He had thrown up his hands in irritation. "He thinks I am not good enough—"

"No, that's not true."

"Keep your head still! How can I draw you if you jiggle about like a puppet." He had moved over to the raised dais and turned Rosella's head an inch to the left. "Good, yes, hold the pose."

She had done so, still managing to talk. "Why would Marco think you were not good enough?"

"Titian dismissed me when I was his apprentice. Some say because he disliked me, others that I was too much competition for him." He had paused, stared at Rosella's profile. "Titian's father was a distinguished soldier and his family boasted many notaries. My father was a dyer," he had laughed, the hazel eyes mischievous. "I was not born for court and palaces. Nor for courting Contessas and the nobility – but Titian was made for such things. A courtier, a lover of women, a genius."

"No more than you."

"You are kind. **But you keeping moving!**" he had snapped, then continued more calmly. "Marco is impressed by Titian and by Pietro Aretino, the writer. You know of this man?"

"No," she admitted, "who is he?"

"A lying, blackmailing, braggart with a clever tongue." Tintoretto had replied, "A very gifted writer, a very amusing conversationalist, but depraved."

"*Depravato?*"

"I have said too much—"

"But why would Marco admire such a man?"

"He has wealth—"

"The Gianetti are rich!"

"— but Aretino has connections to the nobility, to the Doge's palace, to beautiful women, and all the best this city can offer. Which is temptation of the highest order." The painter had replied, "If he champions Marco, he will become famous in Venice. After all, the boy has the beauty and the wit, Marco Gianetti also has an honourable name, something Aretino prizes."

"But he could have fame *here,* as a painter, taught by you."

"Art is struggle, suffering, toil. An artist has to fight for commissions, for public notice. There is no ice slick to the top – and Marco does not like hard work. A painter spends much of his life alone, in a world with the population of one." He had pointed to the box on the table beside him. "Why would he make little wax images, when he could have breathing bodies to play with?"

Suddenly Ira tapped his sister's hand, bringing her thoughts back to the present. "You had better go now, Rosella, or you will be late."

Nodding, she left the house and crossed the main square of the ghetto and was just exiting the gates when a man stepped out. The sun was behind the figure and for an instant Rosella didn't recognise him.

"Marco? Is it you?"

He nodded, moving to her side. "Have you said anything to Ira?"

"About your absences?" she replied, pulling her shawl around her shoulders as the daylight faded and a chill came down. "No, I've said nothing. But the master has said a great deal."

"Tintoretto is angry with me."

"He thinks you are a fool." She said simply, glancing over to Marco and risking the next words. "Why *are* you mixing with Pietro Aretino?"

"So he's been talking about me! Discussing my business with strangers."

She stopped walking. "With *strangers*? I am a stranger to you now, Marco? I wasn't a stranger when you came to our house and I fed you. I wasn't a stranger then—"

"I didn't mean it." He replied, falling into step with her as she walked on. "I meant … things have changed."

"*You* have changed."

"Why is that such a terrible thing?" he countered. "I am allowed freedom to do what I want. To live as a choose."

"No one has ever questioned that. But perhaps too much freedom has been bad for you."

"You sound like my grandmother!"

"If your grandmother knew how you were behaving she would be less kind than I am." Rosella stopped walking and faced him. He was wearing a fitted black velvet doublet with brocade edging, a trim white ruff around his neck. The beginnings of a beard and moustache were starting to change his appearance; no longer the amiable young man, but a male with some hauteur about him.

"You *have* changed," she said, with a sadness in her voice. "I liked the old Marco."

"I had no finesse."

"You had no conceit." She replied, walking on, Marco following.

"I wouldn't allow any other woman to speak to me as you do." He said sharply. "You are not my sister—"

"No, I am not your sister, your mother or your grandmother. I am the sister of your closest friend, with whom you have shared a very deep friendship. Have you visited Ira lately?"

"We argued."

She looked at him curiously. "My brother said nothing about an argument."

"I said something unforgivable."

"I see, so that is why you have neglected him as you have neglected your work and your mentor," She moved away, Marco running to keep up with her. "and you would mistreat them both? Two of the best men in Venice! You should be ashamed to ignore them for the likes of Pietro Aretino."

"Hoow can you judge him! You do not even know him."

"I have been told what he is, and I worry for you." She hurled back. "He uses people, he has favourites and keeps them like pets, then dismisses them. He plays cruel games, and you are not cruel. You would find such treatment painful."

Marco looked away from her, surprised by the accuracy of her words. He had sent word to Aretino after his abrupt dismissal, asking if he had offended his host in some unknown – and regretted – manner. But there had been no response and the silence had added to his discomfort.

"... If your morals don't matter to you, what of your family name?"

Angered, Marco moved in front of her, blocking her way. "My family name means nothing! My father would not care if I were alive or dead. If this Aretino is the monster everyone thinks, then why has my 'good' parent not warned me? Only once he muttered something vague, but nothing of any note. My father, the estimable Jacopo Gianetti, has been an acquaintance of his for years and I have never heard him utter one word of criticism about Aretino."

Rosella glanced away.

"I have no right to speak as I did, I apologise. As you say, your father has no issue with this friendship, so what right have I to judge. I know your father was lacking in many ways, but you cannot hope to find a substitute in this man," She stared into his face. "Just answer me this, Marco – what do you want from Aretino? Tintoretto says you want fame, you want to be at court, with the most brilliant and most beautiful people in Venice. I understand, it is something many desire. But when you have that, Marco, then what? What will you do with it?"

He looked at her, bewildered. "What will I do with it? … I will be happy."

"Are you sure? It is not within any man's remit to offer – or withhold – another man's happiness." She said gently, taking his arm. "Come with me now, Tintoretto will be so happy to see you—"

He baulked, like a horse fighting the bit. "Tell him I'll come along later."

"And Ira? What do I tell him?"

"That I'll call by tomorrow."

"Of course you will." She said sadly and walked on.

Chapter Eighteen

His first impression of Venice was one of noise. Noise and more noise, hundreds of men milling about a square, chattering in different languages and dressed in a variety of styles in every colour, material and design imaginable. Turks in turbans and Chinese with queues jostled amongst merchants doing deals whilst sitting on bales of carpets, parrots and monkeys in gilt cages squawking and rattling their bars.

June had kept her promise and the heat had returned in full measure, the Adriatic setting aside her grey and making the Lagoon turquoise again. And under the sun stood twenty men, shipped from Africa as slaves. Bakita was one of them, taken from his home and transported on a ship that had heaved and battered against the waves, many of the slaves vomiting in the hold below deck, the stink of urine, faeces and vomit unbearable as the heat rose. A storm had caused damage, the cover of the hold ripped away, the rain pelting in and washing the filth around the chained feet of the men below. But the water brought life and only two of the twenty men died, the others arriving at the Venetian Lagoon and standing, naked except for a loincloth, whilst the hammering, yammering throng heaved around them.

Their arrival caused much interest, merchants and nobility coming to view them as they were paraded on the steps, bidding started by a corpulent German in a military uniform that had seen many battles. Bakita was the third to be offered for sale, his muscular frame pointed out by the bellowing German, a stick pointed at his arms and calves to prove their strength. Unable to understand a word of what the man was saying, Bakita's gaze moved over the crowd and came to rest on two women. One a tall blonde woman, the other a slight, dark haired woman around twenty, both of them pausing to look at him.

The German was shouting and losing control, as another man pushed his way to the front and made a grab for Bakita's arm. Two other men, dressed in some form of guard like costume, pushed him aside, but the German had lost his hat and his footing as Caterina Zucca spoke up, her voice carrying over the crowd.

"I will buy him." She said, the German scrabbling to his feet and nodding as she repeated the words in German. 'Ich werde ihn kaufen.'

A further altercation followed between the German and a Turk, but Caterina held her ground, finally paying the German and turning to the African.

"Do you speak English?"

He shook his head, guessing at the question as Caterina turned to the young woman beside her. "He will learn, and he will be ideal."

Since her visit from Marina Castilano, Caterina's unease had grown, and when her son had left Venice her vulnerability had become obvious. There were some kitchen staff in the house, and Caterina had her own private maid, but no confidante, and the memory of the bloodied shoes had disturbed her sleep incessantly. So when she had been approached by a young woman called Tita Boldini she was suspicious.

"I have been sent to you by Madame Dinette in Paris," Tita had told her. "My mother was French and my father was Italian. When they died I was left alone and followed my mother's profession." Her Italian was exceptional, but underneath was a nuance of a French accent, her inflexion rising on certain words. It gave her voice a lilting quality that was compelling.

"You were sent to me by Madame Dinette?" Caterina asked with interest. Dinette was an aged hag, a woman of grotesque appearance and unfathomably wealthy. A madam on the grand scale: not discreet like Caterina, but bold and infamous. "And what did the lady tell you about me?"

"That you were one of the finest courtesans in Venice. Not young any more, but still famous and popular."

"You insult me."

Tita had opened her serious grey eyes. "I did not mean to."

"You have inferred that I am old."

"No, that you are not young anymore. But still beautiful." Tita had answered. "I was told that you spoke six languages and composed music, that you had lovers in the nobility and were a friend of the Doge. Also that you had a speciality."

"And all this is should share with you?" Caterina had replied, studying the girl carefully; the long limbs and narrow head, the curiously feline appearance. "You are unremarkable."

"Et je suis remarquable quand j'ai besoin d'être."

Caterina had smiled. "Indeed. I imagine that you *are* remarkable when you need to be."

Yes, she had thought, to a man you could be very remarkable indeed. Especially if trained by the harpy Dinette who had studied the infamous tricks of Chinese love making and added some perverse quirks of her own. From India, or so the rumour went, and Turkey, and beyond. With clients in the clergy, the nobility and many in French politics, Dinette had proved herself above the law. Her girls were never imprisoned or even charged, their loyalty unquestioned – because Dinette understood how life functioned. That the highest payer secured the greatest devotion.

"May I ask why you left Madame Dinette?"

"I wished to return to my father's homeland."

"He was a Venetian?"

"No, he came from Rome."

"But you did not choose to find a home there?"

"I was recommended to you, Signora, and you are in Venice."

She smiled, her face softening, the feline features becoming flirtatious. "I will not disappoint you."

"I have only two other girls." Caterina replied, warming to the newcomer. "I do not run a brothel here, I offer extraordinary women with extraordinary gifts." She had studied the girl again. "Your clothes are not good. I'm surprised that Madame Dinette did not present you more elegantly."

"Madame requested that I leave behind the clothes she had provided for me." Tita explained. "Madame is generous when you are working for her, but not when you chose to leave."

Caterina raised her eyebrows. "You need new clothes—"

"I have little money."

"That won't be a problem for long. Soon you will have plenty," Caterina had reassured her. "But in order to look like a Contessa you have to dress like one. Your clients know they will fuck you, but they do not wish to be reminded of your profession. If you cannot buy your clothes, you can rent from the Castilano sisters."

"I understand."

"There are men who asked for specialities, some require beatings or other humiliations." Caterina said, pausing and re-reading the letter from Madame Dinette recommending Tita, before tossing it to one side. "She says that you are very adventurous."

"I am also very strong and no man has ever hurt me, physically or mentally." Tita replied. "Madame might have also remarked that I am seldom afraid. I do not think any man or woman is above me. Even in this profession, I have pride in myself." She smiled with unexpected sweetness. "A young woman alone either is used, or learns to use others."

"Tita, *il mio bambino*—"

"I am not a child."

"— do not try to use me. If you do, I promise you will live to regret it." Caterina said firmly, gesturing to the letter. "Of course, I have only your word to say that it is from Madame Dinette. It could be fake."

Tita smiled again. "And *I* could be a fake."

"If you are, you will do well in Venice. It is all fakery here."

Unlike the other girls, Tita had moved into Caterina's house, the other courtesans having apartments of their own and the little redheaded maid, Paola, living at her parents' home. Usually Caterina would have resented having to share her space, but she had been nervous and was relieved to have company of a redoubtable woman. She had also checked the reference from Madame Dinette and discovered that Tita was exactly what she claimed to be and was pleased to have her living in the house. But now Caterina thought, glancing over her shoulder at the tall African following them, now I will be truly safe.

In silence, Bakita walked behind. He was aware of the people staring at him, and fixed his eyes on the glowing crown of Caterina's hair, following it as though following a torchlight. His instinct told him he could trust her, but the younger woman made him anxious. Tita Boldini had a ruthlessness he recognised, some inkling of a hard past. But there was something else that troubled him – an undercurrent of aggression. Another person might not have noticed it, but it was evident to Bakita, and it made him wary of her.

He did not realise then how accurate his instinct would prove to be.

Chapter Nineteen

Aretino was sucking his fingers, one by one, the cream sauce sticking to the beard hairs round his mouth, his bulging stomach covered by a white napkin the size of a tablecloth. Sighing, he pushed aside the bowl of mussel shells, dabbed at his lips, and glanced at his visitor.

The beard and moustache that Marco had decided to grow had proved luscious, his mouth framed like a split peach.

"It has been a while since we met, my dear Marco."

"I sent a note—"

"Ah yes, I have been busy. So very occupied with matters that take my attention more than I would like." He dipped his fingers into the bowl beside him and idly flicked a little water at Marco. It spotted the pale silk of his doublet. "Why so serious, my friend? You seem to have lost your wit. I hear that *Il Furioso* is very angry with you, so I thought it expedient that I did not occupy too much of your valuable time..."

"But I—"

"... I have been selfish, monopolising you." He could see the hunger in Marco's eyes, the desperation for approval, and jerked the strings. "But then perhaps we could come to some sort of an agreement?"

"Yes," Marco said, clearing his throat. "Yes, I would like that."

"I will make time for you from now on... Do you visit Caterina Zucca?"

"No, I only met her once when you introduced us."

"She does not like me."

Marco shrugged. "I would not know if that was true, or not."

"She has been a famous courtesan for a number of years, but time is beginning to ravage her." He wiped his face with a napkin. "Soon she will be unable to set her fees so high, even for her 'unusual' gifts. However, she now has a new girl in her stable..." Aretino turned his gaze from Marco onto the plate of fruit bedside him. For several seconds, he rummaged through the assortment, then beckoned for his servant to take it away. "... a French girl. Do you speak French?..."

Marco nodded.

"... Excellent. I feel I owe you for my rudeness. But I acted in good faith, Marco. Your master was very angry, accused me of leading you astray." He shrugged his fleshy shoulders, lying sleekly. "What could I say? But now I can make up for it. An introduction to this new girl is very apt. Whether you fuck her or not is up to you."

Marco hesitated, unsure of what to say, as Aretino continued. "You must attend to your painting lessons, like a good boy. Keep the artist happy, although I hear he has a woman who is keeping him content at present."

"Tintoretto?" Marco asked, surprised.

"Why not? Apparently she is a decent girl and no doubt the little dyer will do the decent thing and marry her." Aretino said, drawing in a long breath. "Decency is so very dull, don't you think? A decent man is a bore, or so I find... how is your dear father?"

Marco nodded. "He is well."

"'He is well'... how would you know, poor lad? Jacopo has no time for you, does he? Cruelty is unforgivable. I have often wondered why he is so remote from his only son." Aretino tapped the seat beside him. "Here, sit by me, we have to talk. You must tell me your secrets."

Unsure, Marco hesitated, then took the seat offered. "I have no secrets."

"Of course you do. Even when I was your age I had secrets. Well, to be honest, at your age I had many perverse secrets." Aretino tapped his thigh. "You did not answer my question."

"What was the question?"

"I asked why your father was so indifferent to you."

The question was a barb, poison on the tip, and it stuck in Marco's gut.

"My mother died giving birth to me."

Aretino raised his eyebrows. "Friends should not lie to one another."

"I'm not lying!"

He waggled his finger in front of Marco. "You and I both know the real tragedy, that your mother – God rest her immortal soul – killed herself." He looked around as though anxious someone might over hear. "I understand that your father would not wish this to commonly known, but it is a long time ago and, as the Doge says, it is very doubtful that your father drove your mother to her death."

"What!" Marco retorted. "The Doge said *what?*"

"That your father was not responsible for your mother committing suicide."

"That wasn't what you said."

"It was exactly what I said, dear Marco."

"You spoke of my father driving my mother to suicide—"

Aretino sighed expansively. "Marco, do not let your own suspicions cloud your judgement—"

"I never said my father was the cause of my mother's unhappiness and suicide!"

"Of course you didn't." Aretino assured him, taking a glance at him out of the corner of his eye and smiling inwardly. It was so easy to manipulate the Gianetti men. Two generations of dupes. "Before I forget, there was something else I wanted to speak to you about, Marco. You have a Jewish friend, a doctor called Ira Tabat."

"Yes, that's true."

"I suppose your father does not approve of the association?"

"Ira is a good friend."

"And a Jew."

Marco stiffened in his seat, Aretino making a mental note of the response.

"Yes, he is Jewish. He is also a fine doctor and has treated my father."

"Well, now here is a question for you. This friend of yours, this noble doctor, has a sister, I believe?"

Marco's chest tightened. He didn't understand why, just that he felt threatened.

"Yes, her name is Rosella."

"And Tintoretto tells me she is very beautiful."

Relaxing, Marco nodded. If Tintoretto was involved it was safe. "She is, yes."

"Are you in love with her?" he asked, nudging Marco. "Come now, we talk of fucking whores, but love is a different matter. You can trust me, Marco, do you love this pretty Jewess?"

"No," he said honestly, wondering if it was the right answer; if saying she was his amorata would have protected her more. He was feeling increasing hot, his thoughts unsteady as he reached for the glass of wine at his elbow.

"I ask for a friend, Marco. I have a dear friend who would like to meet this lovely girl. His intentions are perfectly honourable, you will be relieved to hear, it is just that he has noticed her and is" he laughed hoarsely, "most keen to have her acquaintance."

Marco drained his glass, the wine taking effect and making him relax. Rosella was in no danger, he told himself, indeed, she might have caught the attention of a wealthy man. He pushed down the knowledge that few noble Venetians would marry a Jewess and asked: "You said he was honourable?"

Aretino nodded. "Indeed, and wealthy in his own right. A very singular person, very private and many talented. A man who travels a great deal. Handsome, or some say."

"I should talk to Ira before I offer up an introduction," Marco said evenly. "He is the head of the Tabat household."

"Ah, but would the doctor agree?" Aretino asked, looking regretful. "I understand he is a very stern character, very honourable and very much in control of his family."

"He cares for them—"

"But sometimes a brother can be too protective and scupper a sister's chances."

"He is a reasonable man."

"And a reasonable man can be obstructive." Aretino replied, his tone cooling. "Surely this would be better kept between ourselves?"

"I wouldn't feel comfortable doing that." Marco replied, "Ira trusts me."

"So did I." Aretino said, using the past tense, something Marco picked up on immediately. "But apparently you do not trust my judgement, and that saddens me. I have grown to think of you as a surrogate son. Forgive me, I know it is wrong, but I do have affection for you and understand the injury your father has done you." He glanced away, looking out over the water. "Perhaps, in my small way, I wanted to give you the opportunities and pleasures that this great city offers. Opportunities which have been withheld from you through no fault of your own." He could sense Marco wavering. "But I will not pursue the matter and perhaps my initial – reluctant – desire to curtail our friendship would be the honourable course of action."

"No." Marco said, more sharply than he meant. "Our friendship matters a great deal to me."

"All my friendships matter. I wish nothing more than to see the people I love get what they deserve. Which is why I presumed to make an enquiry on behalf on my dear friend who wishes only to meet Signora Rosella Tabat. But if you do not trust me—"

"I will speak to Rosella myself." Marco replied, his hand shaking as he laid down the wine glass. "What harm is there in an introduction?"

Aretino smiled benignly. “Indeed. What harm?”

“May I ask the name of your friend?”

“You know him, Marco. His name is Adamo, Adamo Baptista.”

Chapter Twenty

Summoned, the Dutchman made his way to Caterina Zucca's house, taking the water entrance and skirting the main reception rooms, heading instead for the narrow steps which lead directly to Caterina's bedroom. In the passageway outside stood the African, Bakita, who nodded and held open the door for the Dutchman to enter.

Obviously waiting for him, Caterina approached with a lamp in her hand, then locked the door behind them. Still silent, she checked that the shutters were bolted and finally beckoned for him to take a seat. He did so, noticing a stranger sitting in a chair by the wall.

"This is Tita Boldini," Caterina explained. "She is now one of my girls."

He was expecting her to leave immediately, but instead she waited until Caterina dismissed her, Tita staring at him as she passed, her gaze holding his as she left.

"Thank you so coming so promptly," Caterina said, "I need your help..."

He watched her: a weighty, unsmiling man sitting at the edge of a chaise longue, his hat in his hands.

"... Did anyone follow you?"

Surprised, he shook his head. "I don't think so. Why would they?"

She was walking up and down in front of him, her dress brushing the carpet, the silk pile bending one way, then another. Obviously anxious, she fiddled with a chain around her wrist and then turned to him, her voice low.

"A while ago we spoke of the girl Gabriella, the missing maid—"

"I remember."

"— from the Castilano shop. You said you were looking for her and I told you about the conversation she and I had in the square." She quoted Gabriella, word for word.

'... The Wolves of Venice.

Four. You hear me?

Four. Don't let them tell you less.'

"I remember." The Dutchman said, listening as she continued.

"A month ago Marina Castilano came to see me. She had found Gabriella's shoes. They were covered in blood and had been hidden in her shop."

Der Witt reacted fiercely. "*Why didn't you tell me!*"

"I thought it better not to." Caterina replied, unnerved. "As you said, the authorities would never be interested in a missing maid and her body has never been recovered." She hurried on. "I hoped that Gabriella had left Venice. I knew that it was unlikely, but as time passed and she wasn't found, I wanted to believe it. Besides, I was frightened. Venice is full of shadows, illusions. The girl's disappearance, the shoes, it was all strange. Almost unearthly."

His eyes widened. "You suspect the occult?"

"No. I don't even believe in it! I believe in man and what man is capable of. And that's enough."

The Dutchman shook his head. "If you wanted to keep it secret, why are you telling me now?"

"Because of the shoes. I told Marina Castilano to get rid of them."

"Why?"

"Why keep them!" Caterina countered. "The woman had frightened me, talking about how she had come to realise that if Gabriella was dead *she* couldn't have hidden them. And if she had merely been injured *why* would she have hidden them?" Caterina sat down, facing the Dutchman. "However much I've tried I can't stop thinking about it. *Who* had been in the Castilano shop? *Who* had hidden those shoes? And *why* had they hidden them?"

Der Witt was smoothing the nap of his hat with one hand. "They must have known that they'd be found—"

"Exactly."

"— perhaps that's why they did it." He replied, his forehead ridged with lines. "Someone was trying to frighten Marina Castilano. Or…"

"Or what?"

"They *wanted* the shoes found."

"By the woman who owes the shop? What good would that do?"

"Perhaps they thought she would go to the authorities with them."

"But Marina didn't."

"No."

Caterina rose to her feet, pacing again. "After a while they would have known that she didn't report finding the shoes. Which means that they would either think she *hadn't* found them. Or that she had destroyed them."

Der Witt nodded. "Or, as I said before, they were deliberately frightening her."

"Yes!" Caterina snapped. "And I'm involved. Marina Castilano came to *me*. You told *me* what you thought. Gabriella confided in *me*. I am tied up in this and I'm scared. God, I'm so scared."

Der Witte gestured to the door. "You have a guard now."

"The African?" Caterina asked, "yes, I trust him."

"To protect you?"

"Of course to protect me! This morning I had another visit from Marina Castilano. She had come to tell me that she had **never** destroyed the shoes, that she had felt it was wrong to get rid of them. So she had hidden them, without telling anyone, not even her sister. In an entirely different place in the shop."

The Dutchman looked up. "And?"

"They're gone."

"*What?*"

"Someone entered the shop and took them—"

He shook his head. "Perhaps she forgot where she had put them? Or mislaid them."

"She says not. She was certain, and I believed her. The shoes are gone." Caterina repeated. "Now you tell me, my friend, who knew they were there? Who took them?"

He glanced at his hat, turning it in his big hands, his head bowed. "Perhaps the more important question is *why?*"

Chapter Twenty One

Tintoretto's studio,

June 1548

Tintoretto was not about to show his pleasure and ignored Marco when he walked in, directing his conversation to one of his other assistants. Softened by pleas from Rosella, he had decided not to dismiss Marco, but he was reluctant to welcome him back like the prodigal son. Instead he ignored him, walked past him holding a canvas and then nudged him out of the way twice before he spoke to him directly.

"Marco, pass me that portfolio. That one! Yes, that one!" he said, rubbing his face with the palm of his left hand. "I dreamt of her again last night. I had thought I was cured."

"Who did you dream of?"

"An absent apprentice." He said sarcastically, then shrugged. "No, I dreamed of a model I once had. I can remember her and I cannot remember her, at the same time. So strange. Her face troubles me. I am in love with her face."

"I heard you were in love with someone else entirely."

The painter turned to face Marco. "Little pigs with their big ears. I suppose that fat oaf Aretino told you? You shouldn't believe all you hear from that source. He lies from his mouth and his arse."

Marco bit his tongue, unwilling to contradict. "So, who is this woman you dream of?"

"A face from a while ago. I drew her, I know I did, and I would not have destroyed the sketches. She was fascinating. I wanted to use her in a painting." He put aside several studies and continued to search through the portfolio. "She's in here somewhere. I have to find her."

"Does it matter?"

"Does it matter?" Tintoretto repeated. "You ask if my interrupted sleep, my delay in my deliveries, my assistants working non stop to fill in for me – you ask if it matters? Yes, it matters! And I will not rest until I find her!" Tintoretto replied, moving towards the back door of the studio. "I am taking the drawings into the garden—"

"But it's raining."

Exasperated, he blew out his cheeks. "Rain, why today? Why now? This is impossible! I *have* to find her."

"What does she look like?" Marco asked, eager to help, to dampen the guilt he was feeling.

His argument with Ira and his exchange with Rosella had flustered him, but the task Aretino had set for him was proving impossible. Several times he had considered telling Aretino that he was unable to carry out his wishes, but always decided against it. He would lie awake staring up at the ceiling and see, in amongst the painted panels and carved finials, faces which grimaced at him. Goblin night gargoyles; ghosts a bad conscience had conjured up. And he wondered if he would dream of his mother again. If she would come to rebuke him, to swing beside his bed, her nightgown white against the dark window behind.

In the morning Marco depressed any thought of refusal. Too afraid of displeasing Aretino, too scared of the humiliation, the revenge the writer would be sure to publicly claim.

"Maybe I can help?" Marco said, putting aside all thought of Aretino and glancing over to Tintoretto. "If you describe this girl, I could look through the drawings with you."

"She was" the artist thought for a long moment, "very young, her face a little too wide, if I am being critical, her nose had a tiny – *minuscola* – bump, but her eyes were large, like a beautiful fish..."

In the past Marco would have laughed, comfortable in the secure atmosphere of the studio. But he now felt panicked, out of place, a horse underwater.

"...She had a strange quality about her. She was like a creature from the lagoon itself." Impatiently Tintoretto began to look through the sketches again, studying them, then passing them over to Marco. "I would *not* have thrown her image away. I know that much for certain ..." Finally he jabbed his finger down on a small sepia drawing of a girl's head.

Marco glanced at him, "Is that her?"

Tintoretto sat down heavily. "It *was* her."

"*Was?*"

"I had hoped I was wrong." He felt tears prick behind his eyes, his hand shaking as he laid down the drawing. "I saw her only a while ago, Marco, but she didn't look like this. Not any more." Tintoretto crossed the studio and returned a few moments later with another drawing, a very meticulous, detailed sketch. His hand still shaking, he laid it beside the first.

"Gabriella. Her name was Gabriella Russo." He pointed to the sketch. "This is the one I drew of her in the Morgue."

Marco stared at the drawing, "Jesus Christ..."

"She was murdered. Her body dismembered then thrown into a canal." Tintoretto studied the two drawings of the same face, one beautiful, one destroyed. "I remember Gabriella very well, she was quiet, reserved, but once, when I was drawing her, she smiled at me. The light was coming in from the window and I noticed her front tooth was chipped. She told me she had run away from home, and that her father had chipped her tooth when he hit her..."

Marco kept staring the macabre sketch. "I don't remember her."

"No, you wouldn't. She only came here twice. On both occasions you were absent. The first time you were ill and stayed at home, the second... oh, I don't remember, there was a reason you didn't come. But then you're lazy, sometimes you just can't make yourself move!... When I paid her she promised to come back, but she never did. If I remember rightly, she worked as a maid for the Cabriole sisters." he sighed, genuinely moved. "I'm sorry, Gabriella. So sorry it was you."

"Did she have family in Venice?"

"No," Tintoretto replied. "But I should tell her employers what happened to her. And then go to the authorities. Gabriella is dead and buried, but they will want to have her formally identified for the files—"

"Do you need to do that?"

"No, I do not *need* to do it, Marco, but I will. In the same way I did not *need* to pay for her funeral, but I did."

Rebuked, Marco changed tack. "You said that her father hit her. Do you think he killed her?"

"She was raped before she died," Tintoretto replied. "The doctor told me that when I went back to arrange the funeral. The bastard had let them do a full post mortem on her, even though I had tried to prevent it. Money, you see, as always. Everything is for sale in Venice." He shook his head. "It was because of the post mortem that they discovered the rape."

"But" Marco persisted, "do you think her father killed her?"

"He can't have done, because he died ten years ago. And ghosts don't kill..." Tintoretto glanced at the gruesome drawing again. "... only men do that."

BOOK THREE

That summer Baldassare Donato began his career and was feted as a singer at St Marks, his tenor voice as mellifluous as a lute, whilst Venetian music formed its own style to suit the interior of the Basilica San Marco, with its opposing choir stalls that made notes hover like moths. They say that the Venetian polychoral style was created to allow singers and instruments to perform together, or in opposition, harmonised by the great machinery of the organ. Then something else caught the interest; rumours coming from Rome that there was a miraculous castrato performing in St Marks; Giovanni Spolatti, a castrated youth whose voice was unearthly.

Are you impressed by my knowledge?

Of course not, it is common to Venetians. We all appreciated music and art, Titian returning from his travels to find my master his rival, the little dyer flexing his muscles with his four paintings in the church of Scuola Grande di San Marco. I imagine Aretino's public praising of his work would have irked Titian, but the older master was soon back at his tricks, making his canvases sigh and dance for the nobility. I will say that he had aged from his sojourn abroad, his beard longer, grey interruptions in his hair: but his ego was intact, his promenades across St Marks slow and mannered, like a sleek cat lifting his tail to re-mark his territory.

Only a week after Aretino had asked the favour of me, my father was taken ill, my absence from the writer's company a blessing. People may well have wondered at my sudden compassion for a parent who despised me, but my father's illness gave me a blessed respite. I had toiled over the question of Rosella – how could I sanction an association with the likes of Adamo Baptista? And at other times I would look to excuse my anxiety. Rosella was a grown woman and besides, what was an introduction? Merely the means of one person meeting another, via a mutual acquaintance. My mind see-sawed like the Spanish tumblers in the park: up and down, up and down. Always knowing that, at any time, there could be a fall from grace.

With my father's sickness came the need for Ira. He might reject my personal summons, but he could not reject a patient.

Have I mentioned how hot it was that August? Abnormally hot, as though we had fallen from a usual summer heat into a glassworker's furnace. Even the stonework was hot to the touch, the fruit ripening early and rotting before it hit the ground. Normally we would have left Venice for our home in the countryside, but my father's sickness marooned us. Like the merchants, we remained, and, like the merchants, we sweated.

Aretino did not send word, or request my presence. At first relieved, I became anxious by the silence, then relaxed as a further week passed without communication. Another followed. News had travelled of my father's illness and we were left alone, only Cara and I in attendance, and Ira visiting the sickroom daily. I was assured that my parent's illness was not life threatening, but that his convalescence would be protracted.

My relief was shameful.

And then, as the third week of August exited, I woke to hear the rain beating on the shutters. It was fearsome in its attack, hailstones the size of grapes storming the canals and bouncing off the roof tiles. Under the thundering noise the church bells marked out the hour of seven as I hurried towards my father's bedroom.

Cara was asleep on the settle at the foot of his bed, her plump body partially uncovered, the pink flesh of her dimpled knees peeking from under the cover. She slept with her mouth open, her muffled snores suppressed by the noise of the falling hailstones, her left hand clutching a rosary. I didn't wake her, even though I was aware that something very terrible was going to happen.

I realise what you're thinking, that my father had died. But you're wrong. The storm seemed to rejuvenate him, break his fever, the shutter banging to the rhythm of the church bell striking. And I knew what my father's recovery meant – I was released, forced to respond to Aretino. If I had hoped the writer had left Venice I was disappointed. The wolf was just waiting for my reaction. To see how greedy I was, how ambitious. To see if I would chose him over my friends; treachery over loyalty; innocence over corruption.

I was juggling with my soul.

And knew it.

Chapter Twenty Two

Barent der Witt closed the front door of his house and slid the bolt. For several moments he waited, listening with his ear against the wood, straining for footsteps. There were none, merely the sound of a dog barking, the noise echoing down the alleyway which lead to the Dutchman's home. He waited a little longer, thinking of something he had overheard earlier – that the Inquisition were interested in him.

Fingering the glass vial around his neck, der Witt moved through the back kitchen and into the yard beyond. Quickly he uprooted several plants and, placing them in a bowl of water to prevent them drying out, hid them under a grid. He then hurried back into the house. Abortion was illegal, but the authorities often turned a blind eye, a favour they did not extend to sorcery... The Dutchman glanced around his study, judging it as a stranger would. The desk was under the shuttered window and covered with paperwork, maps and drawings. Beside it was a mounted skeleton of a monkey and a snake in a glass jar, yellowing with age. Compasses, a pair of callipers and a globe professed intellectual interests, but at the base of the desk, half hidden under the knee space, was a Ouija board.

Fuji, as it was known in China, had travelled to India and Europe, used as a form of necromancy and communication with the spirit world. As it became wildly used, the practice was condemned and regarded by the Catholic authorities as a form of divination. Fearful of all devilry, the Inquisition had ruled that the use of Ouija boards was against God; that it was blasphemous, a means to conjure up demons. They were not the only authorities to fear the practice. Even in der Witt's homeland the Dutch church had banned the board and declared it a means of occultism.

Der Witt was still listening, straining for sounds outside and imaging at any moment the door being broken open. Nothing happened. Footsteps passed by, then seemed to retrace their steps, the Dutchman scarcely breathing. Had someone informed on him? His heart pounded, sweat running down the small of his back. Venice was open to many different nationalities and religions, but sorcery was forbidden by visitor and resident alike. His gaze moved back to the Ouija board – should he gamble on moving, on trying to hide it? Or would such an attempt alert them to his presence?

The Dutchman moved against the wall, away from the window, waiting. Silence outside. Had they gone? He kept waiting. Silence. But an instant later the footsteps sounded again, running *towards* the entrance. Out of the corner of Der Witt's eye he could see the edge of the Ouija board and flinched as he heard a fist slam against the locked door.

"Signora Castilano?"

Marina nodded, flattered as the famous – if unkempt

– Tintoretto entered her shop. Uncharacteristically flirtatious, she twittered like a canary, already imagining the kudos of his patronage. Il Furioso knew a great many influential people and powerful patrons. If he was not fashionable himself – she tried to ignore the worn boots he was wearing and the paint spotted breeches – his sitters most certainly were.

"What can I do for you, Signor?"

Tintoretto looked about him – reeling from the plethora of dummies, clothes, ornamentation and fabric on every available space within the confines of the shop.

"I have some unfortunate news..."

Marina said nothing and waited for him to continue.

"... you had a maid called Gabriella..." Her face was no more than a stiff mask as he went on. "It is my sad duty to report that she is dead."

He had expected some response, perhaps even a sob. But instead the woman continued to stare at him blankly.

"... Signor Castilano—"

"You are wrong, Gabriella left Venice."

He shook his head. "I wish with all my heart it was so, but I have seen her body with my own eyes. Poor Gabriella—"

"We have had news of her in Rome."

The lie was so obvious he almost smiled. "No, that is not possible. As I say, I saw her, I drew her corpse when she was found—"

Marina sat down heavily, her legs failing.

"May I get you a glass of water, signora?" Tintoretto asked. "Are you alone here?"

"Why does that matter!"

Her response alarmed him. "It does not, I was merely asking—"

"I do not believe what you have told me, Signor. I think you are lying."

"Why would I?" he said firmly. "What would I have to gain from such a cruel trick? I came here only to tell you what had happened to your maid and to try and set your mind at rest—"

She laughed harshly. "**At rest!** You want to set my mind at rest?" Her voice plummeted. "If this is true—"

"It is."

"— you are not setting my mind at rest."

"Forgive me, signora, I do not understand."

"— was her death an accident?"

He paused, unwilling to reveal the full details. "No, it was not an accident."

"So Gabriella drowned herself?"

"She drowned, yes."

Marina's eyes flickered. "Someone else drowned her?"

He nodded. "Yes, I am sorry to tell you that they did."

Her voice was strained. "She was murdered?..." He nodded. "...Have you have reported this to the authorities?"

"I have just done so."

Her mouth opened and closed, but she said nothing, Tintoretto speaking again. "Gabriella is now laid to rest—"

She interrupted him. "Who killed her?"

"Who knows?"

"And naturally the authorities do not care about a maid! They will not seek out the man who did this." Marina snapped, her face waxen. "So her killer is free?"

"Signora," the artist said kindly, "I believe that Gabriella's death was committed in a moment of madness. I do not think it was in any way planned."

Her gaze turned on him fiercely. "How do you know? I think you're wrong, signor. I think Gabriella's murder *was* planned. Too many strange things, too many people have been involved for it to be random—" she stopped talking, her eyes averted.

"*You already knew she was dead?*"

"How could I? You've just told me."

"But you said that there were 'too many people involved.'"

Flustered, she blundered on. "I want you to leave my shop—"

"Who else has been involved in this?"

"I want you to leave—"

Tintoretto shook his head. "No, I am not leaving until you explain. Please, tell me who else has knowledge of her death."

"No one knew of her *death*, we suspected it, that was all."

"*Who* suspected it?"

"Does it matter?"

"Yes." Tintoretto replied. "So I'll ask you again, *who* suspected that Gabriella was dead?"

"What is the point of this conversation?" she countered. "Do you even know Caterina Zucca or the Dutchman, Barent der Witt?"

Wrong footed, Tintoretto took a seat opposite hers. "Why is the Dutchman involved?"

"He is a customer of mine, he knew Gabriella and was naturally concerned when she was missing."

"Was he a relative? A lover?"

"No!" she retorted impatiently. "The girl asked for his help and they were supposed to have a meeting but he missed it. His guilt is driving his concern, he's tormented by it—"

"And he knows Caterina Zucca?"

"They are friends," Marina admitted. "and Gabriella had confided in Caterina. Why don't you ask her? Ask Caterina Zucca what she said. As for Barent der Witt, he warned me not speak to anyone about the girl."

"But you spoke to Caterina Zucca?"

Marina nodded. "I went to see her. I was afraid because der Witt had mentioned Pietro Aretino and Adamo Baptista—"

"*Baptista?*" the painter repeated, concerned. "What about Adamo Baptista?"

"That I should not talk to him."

"Wise advice. Did you obey him?"

"Yes." She shuddered. "I want nothing to do with such a man."

Tintoretto remembered his conversation with Dr Norillo, how he had forced the medic into admitting that Baptista had visited Gabriella's body. And how he had insisted that his own visit should not be mentioned.

"Did Gabriella know Baptista?"

"I don't know! But I doubt it, she was a respectable girl." Marina said firmly. "Whilst she lived here she seldom had any visitors, and hardly left the shop. Why she would know someone like Adamo Baptista, I can't imagine." She looked at him. Suddenly suspicious. "How did *you* know Gabriella?"

"She sat for me... She was always patient, but rather sad...

Forgive my being blunt, Signora Castilano, I do not mean to shock you, but artists study anatomy to learn how the body functions and how to recreate it in paintings. Although I have much experience, on occasion I still attend the autopsy rooms to further my knowledge or refine it," he took a quick glance at her face. "And that was how I discovered Gabriella was dead. I saw her body in the morgue."

It seemed to take a while for her to understand. "*When* was this?"

"Nearly four months ago."

"*Four months!*" she snapped. "Why did you not tell me sooner?"

"Because I did not recognise her at first," he said gently. "It was only when I found an old drawing of Gabriella and compared the details that I was certain. She had a certain shape to her upper jaw and a chip in her front tooth."

Marina's lips parted, her head bowed, a hand going over her mouth.

"And this killer, Gabriella's killer, knows where she worked. Where she lived… he knows *this* place."

"He might not have done. Her killer might have met Gabriella elsewhere."

"No, Signor, *he knows this place,*" Marina said helplessly. "You see, he comes and goes as he pleases. He takes and returns what he wants, when he wants. He plays games, torments me. He could be here now and we would never know it."

"I don't understand." Tintoretto replied, unsettled. "I don't know what you mean."

"No, you do *not* understand." she said, rising to her feet.

"And neither do I. Nothing of this matter makes any sense and I am tired of it."

"Signora, let me help you. I will go the authorities again and speak to them."

She shook her head. "No, I am done with it! It is your problem now, talk to Caterina Zucca and the Dutchman if you wish, but I will say no more."

"You cared about Gabriella—"

"I did, but not enough when she was alive and I cannot change that now she is dead. I will be leaving the city tomorrow. I am taking my sister and we are moving away from Venice. There is nothing in this world – or the next – that would make me stay here another day."

Chapter Twenty Three

Beautiful colours can be bought in the shops on the
Rialto, but good
drawing can only be bought from the cabinet of the
artist and talent with
patient study and nights without sleep

Having just secured a portrait commission from a relation of the influential Graduccio family, Tintoretto was occupied in the back workshop, Marco watching him from the main studio. He could see that his master was preparing a batch of clay and knew that he would soon be busy making his models for the painting of the family group. Twisting the anonymous lumps of clay into presentations of his sitters, a major Crucifixion temporarily relegated to a back wall.

The family portrait was a commission that would usually have gone to Titian, but as *Il Furioso's* star was on the rise he had secured the prize with all the glee of a fisherman finding a mermaid in his net.

Nodding to an apprentice who was winching an easel upright, Marco moved through the studio, two other painters priming a massive canvas for the master, another grinding paint with a pestle and mortar. The June day was nowhere near its ending, the light still intense at seven in the evening as Marco approached Rosella and tapped her on the shoulder.

She spun round, smiling when she saw him. "The master has a new commission—"

"I heard. He stole it from under Titian's nose."

"I'm glad" she replied, tying up her hair, the skin on her arms lightly tanned. Venetian women avoided the sun, their pale skin prized, but in the ghetto people escaped their crowded houses to eat in the square, even in the middle of summer, taking what shade they could from the mean planting of trees. "Did you see Ira today?"

Marco wavered, glancing over to Tintoretto. But his master was concentrating, certain to remain in the workshop for hours.

"No, not today... Are you ready to go home?" Marco asked. His voice sounded distorted in his ears, but she did not seem to notice, just gestured to the drawings on the table. "Tintoretto drew these today. *Il Furioso* imagines me far more beautiful than I am, but I do not tell him so." She was in high spirits, "A muse, he called me. His Muse. He even said I could take one of the drawings! Can you imagine?... I was thinking to give to Angelo Fasculo."

"Who?"

"Oh, just a friend," she said lightly, but her eyes were brilliant. "*A Muse.* Have you ever heard anything so absurd?" she laughed.

"I was going to walk you home tonight," Marco said quietly. "but I can't—"

"Marco, how do you think I get home when you are not here?" she asked, the great dark eyes questioning. "I do not need a chaperone anymore."

Her words took him unawares. "But tonight you do need a chaperone, Rosella." He insisted. "There has been some trouble in the streets. Some fighting—"

"So tell me where and I will avoid it."

He was adamant. "I would feel better if you were accompanied home." Marco continued, staring at the mass of dark hair tied back, fine strands sticking to the damp nape of her neck. He could also catch a scent of ripe tomatoes clinging to her skin. A wholesome smell of high summer. "I have asked someone to accompany you. He will be here very soon."

She sighed, amused. "If you insist, but it isn't necessary."

"I must go now." Marco said, unable to stay and witness what he had done. "Until tomorrow."

As he moved off she caught his arm, then smiled. "You are so kind to me, Marco. Always so kind."

Angelo Fasculo waited at the doorway for his mother, watching as she drew up a contract with one of her customers, the dancing master, Hyman Golletz. He signed first, then her hand moved over the paper in a confident sweep, the F of Fasculo elongated. Dapper in his pleated doublet and slashed breeches, the old man fingered his groomed beard and nodded at Angelo.

"Rosella Tabat is looking very well lately." He teased him, Angelo flushing. "Such a lovely girl and with a beautiful singing voice. I could have found her work but now

I hear she prefers sitting for *Il Furioso*. Such a waste of talent."

Folding the contract, Gilda passed a copy over to him.

"Thank you, signora." He said, turning back to Angelo. "You should engage Rosella Tabat's affections, my boy. And I would do it soon, before someone else does."

When the old man left, Gilda turned to her son. "So, what have you found out?"

"Nothing."

"Nothing!" she replied, "There must be something to discover about Nikolas Volt."

"No one has any information."

She pushed back her seat, irritated. "Nothing at all?"

"Only that he is a friend of Adamo Baptista—"

"*I know that already!* Two weeks, and this is all you discover! If I had hired a fish in the Lagoon it would have uncovered more."

"There is nothing *to* uncover!" Angelo retorted, stung.

"You are very sullen today."

"I have every right to be." He retorted, "I have just seen something I did not expect."

She paused. "Are you going to tell me?"

"Adamo Baptista was accompanying Rosella home." His mouth made an angry dismissive noise. "*Rosella!* With Adamo Baptista! Rosella—"

His mother cut him off, leaning over the table towards him. "As you say, this is unexpected. Why would Rosella Tabat go with him? She knows his reputation, I can't believe she would be seen with him by choice."

"She certainly didn't seem at ease."

"Were they talking?"

"He was." Angelo said bitterly. "Rosella kept her head bowed, looking at the ground."

"Was he familiar with her?"

"*What?*"

"— did he touch her, take her arm?—"

"No, he didn't. And if he had, I'd have struck him."

Gilda waved the words aside. "How many times do I have to tell you that violence is pointless? *Guile* is all that matters, especially when dealing with the likes of Adamo Baptista. Guile and patience." She thought for a long moment. "You are fond of Rosella Tabat, aren't you?"

"She's a neighbour."

"People fall in love with their neighbours all the time, it's not against the law, Angelo... I'm old, but I remember being in love..." Her tone softened. "*Are* you in love with her?"

"I think so... Yes."

"And you talk? I know you do, I have seen you, and others have commented on your friendship. It's no secret in the ghetto. Nothing is." Gilda smiled and tapped the back of her son's hand. "She's a beautiful girl, she observes the faith, cares for her mother and her brother and works hard...But if you are serious about her we should find out why she is walking with the likes of Adamo Baptista."

"I couldn't believe what I was seeing—"

"Angelo, listen to me. This may well be of importance." Her tone hardened. "Baptista is our enemy, it would be unfortunate if your romance was hindered by such a rival."

"I should confront him—"

"No. You will confront *her*." Gilda advised. "See what

she says and then we will know where we stand." Her hand rested on her son's. "And whilst you are talking to Rosella about that wolf Baptista, see if she knows anything about his lap dog, Volt."

"Why should she?" Angelo asked, taken aback. "She was just walking with Baptista, nothing more."

"Nothing that we know of. Don't be foolish, Angelo, you know that in this city reputation is all. A single woman seen with that black crow will incite interest. People will gossip, and when they gossip we may learn something valuable."

Abruptly he withdrew his hand. "You are asking me to use her."

"Only to safeguard us!" Gilda hurled back. "If Rosella is innocent, she has nothing to fear. She might have simply been accompanied by the man and unable to refuse his companionship. But if she is involved with Adamo Baptista, then we *have* something to fear. As you said, Rosella is a neighbour of ours, and if someone – who is not Jewish – wants access to the secrets of the ghetto he requires a spy *in* the ghetto."

"That's ridiculous! Rosella is not a spy. She would never betray us."

"You may well be right. It may all amount to nothing, but I must be sure." Gilda replied, "Remember the situation we are in. Are we to be blackmailed until we are bled white? Until I've been forced to cheat and thieve from everyone in the ghetto? And then what is to follow for me, the galleys? Your scruples do you justice, Angelo, but perhaps your first duty should be to your mother and your family before Rosella Tabat."

He shook his head. "But I know Rosella, she is honourable. She would never betray us—"

"All to the good," Gilda replied. "If you are right then perhaps if she will not betray us – but she might be willing to betray her new friends."

Chapter Twenty Four

His breathing steadying, Barent der Witt opened the door to her urgent knocking.

"Thank God it's you." he said, standing back to let Marina Castilano enter. "Are you alone?"

"Quite alone."

"Why are you here?"

"To say goodbye and to tell you something," Marina replied. "I'm leaving Venice with my sister this afternoon and I wanted to tell you that Gabriella's body was found and identified. The painter found her—"

"*Who?*"

"Tintoretto, *Il Furioso*."

"What has he to do with Gabriella?"

"It was a fluke," Marina explained, "he saw her corpse when it was brought to the morgue. He recognised her and came to tell me because she had been my maid and disappeared from my shop and he thought – quite rightly – that I would want to know..." She shrugged. "I thought you would too."

He pushed the door closed with his foot. "Why are you leaving Venice?"

"You know why." She chastised him. "Whether you believe it or not, I'm not safe if I stay in that shop—"

"You can't be certain of that."

"I can be certain enough to leave."

"But what of your business?"

"I'm closing it. When I return to Spain I will send for my things and start again in Madrid. My losses will be great, as you may well imagine, but I will be alive and will have kept my sister safe." She paused, then spoke again. "There's more I have to tell you and I'm sorry but it is not pleasant..."

"You have started, you cannot draw back now."

"Gabriella was murdered. Tintoretto said that her body and face were destroyed."

Der Witt leaned against the desk for support. "It's my fault."

"No."

"It's my fault," he repeated. "If I had met her that night, I could have prevented her death."

"You don't know that, no one does." Marina replied, "You could just as easily say that Caterina Zucca failed her, that she should have insisted Gabriella stay at her house. Or you could accuse me. Why did I not notice she was afraid? You did, but I didn't. I saw Gabriella every day, I talked to her, gave her instructions, ate the food she prepared and lay in the bed she made for me, but I didn't really care about her. I didn't *see* her." Her voice wavered. "If you have a cross to bear, I have one also."

"You are leaving Venice, but I am not." Der Witt replied. "Nor will I, until I have found Gabriella's killer."

"May I ask why her death means so much to you?"

"You have asked me before, Signora Castilano, and again I decline to answer. Let me just reassure you that my motives are sincere." He hurried on. "However there is something I would like to ask you – did Caterina Zucca tell you what Gabriella said to her?"

Marina nodded. "About the four? *The Wolves of Venice.* Yes, she told me."

"Did it mean anything to you?"

"No, nothing." Marina admitted. "Does it mean anything to you?"

"Nothing."

"It has no code, no magic in it?"

"None that I have found."

"What a shame," she said almost bitterly, "I had hoped that it was something a man like you could solve." She studied the sombre figure in black, the heavy featured face. "I imagine Caterina Zucca told you that I had kept Gabriella's shoes? That I brought them back to the shop and hid them in another place. And yet they are gone."

"Yes, she told me. I found it hard to believe. I thought you might have been mistaken. That being so afraid you had put them somewhere and forgotten where." He shrugged his shoulders. "How else could they be gone?"

"Some people say that you are not merely an apothecary. That you also practice black magic, sorcery," she looked around the study, her gaze coming to rest on the Ouija board half hidden under the desk. Gingerly she nudged it with the toe of her shoe. "You should be careful, Signor der Witt, the Inquisition will root you out. Perhaps you, like myself, should leave this city."

"I have business here."

"Everyone has business in Venice." She replied, walking about his room and studying the maps. "I dressed the most beautiful whores, most brilliant nobility and the richest

Contessas in Venice. Everyone of note came to my shop. The merchants knew me by name, called out to me when I visited the ships newly arrived from Paris and the Far East. They let me walk about the bales and boxes freshly unloaded, even allowed me to put my mark on the silks before anyone else had seen them. Yes, it's true, I had all the fashions from the French and Russian courts... Everyone knew my shop. Everyone was envious of my wares and my clientele. Even Adamo Baptista bought from me." her gaze turned back to the Dutchman. "You flinched. Are you afraid of him?"

"I am afraid of everything I do not understand."

"Then you must be afraid a great deal of the time," Marina replied. "I know I am." She pointed to a map on the wall over the fireplace. "Where is this?"

"The Hague."

"Is that where you came from?"

"Once."

"Perhaps we should all stay where we are born, in our own countries. Perhaps we would all be safer if we did." Sighing to herself, Marina picked up her bag and moved towards the door, then turned back to the Dutchman. "May I ask *you* a question?"

"You may ask."

"And you will not lie to me?"

"How will you know?"

She smiled wistfully. "A Venetian answer from a Dutch apothecary. Only in Venice..." Her voice became serious again, her gaze fixed on his face. "Who are *The Wolves of Venice*?"

He didn't reply.

And, after another moment, she left.

Chapter Twenty Five

Jacopo Gianetti sat upright in his bed, his sleep disturbed, old dreams returning, dreams he had thought long dead. People were so real in dreams, speaking and moving as they had done in life, then leaning towards him, whispering, whispering words he could not hear and knew he should hear. Consonants and syllables that were imperative, but without proper form. The whispering he could sense, but the words alluded him and he awoke with a sensation of encroaching dread.

Having heard his footsteps pacing around, Cara tapped on the bedroom door. "You are awake, Signor Gianetti? It's not yet five."

He wondered if the time was supposed to matter and moved over to the water basin.

"Signor Gianetti—"

"*Lasciami! Lasciami solo!*" he snarled, hoping the servant would walk away, then he glanced into the mirror hanging above the basin. There had been a fleeting intention to rinse his face, but instead Jacopo found himself staring at a reflection of his dead wife suspended from a rope behind him... Startled, he stepped back, knocking over the basin.

Hearing the crash, Cara ran in. "What happened,

signor?" Surprised, she stared at the broken bowl and the spilled water splashed across the wooden floor.

White faced, Jacopo pointed to the image over the bed. But in the instant it took for Cara to turn, it disappeared.

"Are you ill, signor?"

He shook his head dumbly. "No……"

"Do you need a dottore?"

"No, no. But I did not sleep well," Jacopo replied, in that dusk voice of his, which always lied. "I had a nightmare."

She was bending down, picking up the pieces of broken china, her hair greying at the crown. Was she getting old? He thought, yes, of course she was. Cara had worked for him for many years. But if she was old, he must be old too.

"Am I sick?" he asked, his usual coolness replaced by a helpless pleading. "Am I sick again?" He touched his forehead, "I think maybe I am. I need a doctor, get Ira Tabat—"

"You said that you didn't want him here again."

"Are you telling me what to do? Are you my master now?" he snapped, skirting round the bed, his left hand timidly lifting the covers to see if there was anything underneath.

Horrified, Cara watched him. "Is there something wrong with your bedding, signor?"

"There are things in this bed that should not be here!" He wailed, pulling back the covers and then relaxing as he saw the empty expanse of white sheet. It had been a dream, nothing more. Nothing over which to lose his composure. "Forget what I said, Cara, I was half asleep."

"So you *don't* wish me to call dottore Tabat?"

"I do not think—" His equilibrium deserted him.

Suddenly he could smell perfume, a particular scent from Naples which his first wife had always worn.

Cara stared at him, watching his gaze flicker backwards and forwards from the bed.

"Yes, I think you *should* call Tabat. Yes, call him! Tell him I want to see him, that I am not myself." Trembling, Jacopo slumped into a chair beside the unmade bed. "Tell him I would be grateful if he would hurry. Yes, yes, tell him to hurry."

Troubled, Rosella moved around the room, laying the table for the evening meal. In her bed behind the curtain, her mother moaned softly in her sleep, as she often did, but she did not wake. She never awoke anymore... Rosella stood over her mother, looking at the face she remembered. Yet it bore no resemblance to the parent she had once known, and she envied her peace. Felt an inappropriate jealousy because sickness had abandoned her mother in some place free of emotion, responsibility or confusion. Where she had nothing asked of her, nothing expected; a place of inertia.

Without wishing to, Rosella conjured up an image of Adamo Baptista's face, the smell of wood smoke on his clothes, the fine hairs on the back his hands, and the voice that had been courteous and yet sensual. She flushed, uncomfortable, wondering how she could have found any part of him appealing. No, not appealing, *desirable*. Her throat dried, her mouth sticky with shame. But she had done *nothing*, nothing at all. Nothing that would dishonour her, or her family.

But she had wanted to.

And the thought left her limp, a dull ache in the pit of her belly. She had never felt such a pain before, certainly not with Angelo Fasculo. And yet she had imagined herself falling a little in love with him. Had even pictured a life with him. Would it be so very bad to love him? Rosella asked herself. Angelo was attentive, a hard worker, and a Jew; they were from the same culture, they understood the ghetto life. It was true he was not cultured, but culture a person could teach themselves. *She* could teach him... Rosella closed her eyes, trying to coax her thoughts away from Baptista and return them to Angelo.

Ira walked in unexpectedly, startling her. "Rosella, I have to go out again on a visit to Jacopo Gianetti."

Jacopo Gianetti... The surname echoed around her brain. Gianetti. *Marco* Gianetti, her friend who had arranged for Adamo Baptista to accompany her home. She felt anger and at the same moment gratitude. Another thought followed on immediately. *Why* had Marco introduced them? Was he presenting her as he would a plate of food? An offering?... She shook her head against the thought, no, Marco was simply being kind, ensuring that she returned home in safety. But to pick Adamo Baptista to act as chaperone...

"Can I take this with me?"

Nodding, Rosella turned her attention back to her brother. "Yes, of course, I'll wrap it for you," she said, putting the bread and cheese into a cotton pouch and handing it back to her brother. "Be careful tonight. There was some street fighting earlier on."

"Fighting?" Ira queried, tucking the package into his pocket. "You weren't caught up in it, were you?"

"No, no, I wasn't anywhere near..." She said, adding. "... Marco warned me."

She could sense Ira's disapproval and wondered what would happen if he discovered her stroll with Baptista. But how could he *not* find out? People always gossiped and they had been seen in the streets and at the entrance of the ghetto. She had even noted Solomon Isaacs pause at his doorway to stare, pointing them out to Hyman Golletz. And if he had seen them, the news would have been spread within the hour.

"... I saw Rosella Tabat walking with that bastard Adamo Baptista. I would not have thought a respectable woman would want to consort with the likes of him."

And soon others would have joined in.

"Perhaps Rosella is not as innocent as she seems. She poses for that painter, after all, what kind of girl does such things? I heard Il Furioso used whores in his paintings. All of them nude...Of course her mother can't advice her, and her brother's too busy to see what's going on..."

"And to think that Angelo Fasculo is in love with her. I can't see Gilda approving any match now..."

"Rosella?"

She jumped, Ira looking at her. "Is everything alright with you?"

"Yes. Why wouldn't it be?"

"It's just that you seem different."

Was she different? Rosella wondered. Was it obvious on her face that her body had changed, become moist and willing. Could people tell by just looking at her? Could her brother tell? She didn't want it to show, but she didn't want to stop the sensation either; that carnal, hypnotic response of the body.

"Different?" she repeated. "How?"

"You look tired," Ira said, kissing her on her forehead. "I may be late, don't wait up for me, will you? And if I see Marco I'll thank him."

"For what?" she asked breathlessly.

"For warning you about the fighting on the streets. What else?"

The brawl that had taken place in the afternoon had quickly died out, leaving St Marks hazy in the late summer evening. Birds, listless in the heat, dozed on the unpacked tea chests and bails of cargo unloaded onto the quayside. Delicate porcelain imported from the Far East, safe in its straw filled boxes, dozed indolently on a muted tide and in the distance the horizon began the slow dampening down of the sun.

Apparently the fight had begun because of a theft, some man being relieved of his wallet by a French pickpocket, the thief taken to the prison – where he had immediately sent for Adamo Baptista.

"Lauret, do you never learn?"

The corpulent little merchant put his hands together pleadingly. "I am not guilty. It was all a misunderstanding, I swear."

Waving for the guard to leave the cell, Baptista stared at the frightened man. "Those cards you gave to me—"

"They were the best, monsieur."

"They were indeed." Baptista agreed, smiling coldly. "I have no complaints there."

"Did you win much?"

"Is that any interest of yours?"

The little man shook his head. "No, monsieur, forgive my impertinence."

"As for the other matter I set for you, did you manage to remember anything important that Gabriella Russo told you?"

Lauret was shaking so much that he could hardly gather his thoughts. "Please, can you get me out of here? I have never been in jail before. My health is not good. Despite appearances, I am not a well man."

"You should have thought of that before you stole—"

"I stole nothing! It was the girl."

Baptista looked at him with a disbelieving expression. "A girl? What girl?"

"That's was the strangest thing, I saw her in the crowd and I recognised her. I knew her from the past, I can't remember where or when, but it will come back to me." He looked round the damp cell and coughed unconvincingly. "I swear, Monsieur Baptista, *she* was the thief, not me. I saw her with my own eyes—"

"This girl?"

"Yes!" he agreed "and I was so surprised to see her in Venice. She was walking about in the crowds. Her dress was expensive, but she had very drab cloak over the top and it almost covered her costume, so that I only caught a glimpse of the fabric when she turned—"

"I'm not interested in fabric, Lauret. Or a fantasy girl."

"*But she wasn't a fantasy!*" the squat little man retorted. "And whilst I was trying to remember where I had seen her before she moved further into the crowd, where it was the most dense – I think there were some musicians playing. A lute, I think, yes, I'm sure it was a lute. You know how it is sometimes in the square, you can't tell a lute from a lyre…?" he looked into Baptista's bored face and hurried on. "Anyway, this girl – young woman really – she slid over to an elderly man in a quilted doublet—"

"*Get on with it!* I am not interested in his attire!"

"— and then I saw her cut the strap of the purse on his belt. As quick as that! So fast you couldn't see her hand move. The old man must have felt something because he turned. The girl had gone. But he saw me. And I panicked. I ran..."

"How far and how fast can you run on those stunted little legs of yours?"

Lauret flushed. "Not far... The crowd caught me and they didn't believe a word I said. Even after I told them to search me and they found nothing. They just said that I must have had an accomplice."

"Did you?"

"I swear on my life I didn't take the purse! *She did!*" the Frenchman paused, breathless and sweating profusely. "You have to get me out of this place."

Baptista leaned against the wall. "You ask me to help you and I come here, leaving Signor Aretino and a fine dinner, but what do I get in return? Nothing. I have been waiting for days, but you haven't even answered my question, Lauret. Did you think over what you and Gabriella Russo had talked about?"

"If you get me out of this place—"

Baptista leaned down towards him, his voice ominous.

"I swear I will leave you here until the greasy flesh drops

off your pig bones. These are the new prisons, but they are still overcrowded. And soft, feminine looking prisoners, or prisoners who dabble in the occult—"

"I don't have anything to do with the occult!"

"The Inquisition would disagree, Lauret, and I would have to give evidence that you do trade in cards. Of course, you could be lucky and they might merely give you a warning, or they could examine the cards you gave to me – with their unusual *patterning*." He paused. "All those tiny indentations that a clever gambler could use to his advantage. If the Inquisition didn't punish you for dealing in the occult, the authorities certainly would for cheating at cards. It would mean a heavy fine."

Lauret could see the trap opening up before him and stepped back from the edge.

"There's no reason to do anything hastily, monsieur! I have not been idle." He stammered. "As you asked, I went over everything I could remember, everything Gabriella and I talked about. Believe me, there was nothing important, just conversation. Jokes, gossip, some of it foolish."

"Nothing that struck you as strange or uncommon?"

"Well, maybe one thing..."

"Go on."

"Gabriella told me that she wanted to leave Venice, but she didn't have enough money and I told her that if she waited until I returned on my next trip I would lend her some." Lauret shrugged. "I'd done some good trading, but reinvested everything and had no money left to lend anyone, even Gabriella."

"So what happened then?"

"She said she'd wait for me. But she wasn't happy, I could

see that. Not angry with me, just sad... When we parted that night Gabriella hugged me and I told her to take care of herself and then she said something strange. She said that Venice had its own wolves."

"Wolves in Venice?" Baptista repeated.

"That's right. That's what she called them."

"It makes no sense. Did she not explain what she meant?"

Concentrating, Lauret thought back. Then he repeated, word for word, what Gabriella had said the last time he saw her. "...'*Four. Don't let them tell you less. Look for the four.*'"

Baptista considered the words, Lauret looking at him imploringly. "Is it important?"

"Maybe."

"Please," Lauret begged. "I've told you all I know. Get me out of here, I'm a sick man, I won't survive. Please, make them release me."

"I suppose I could..." Baptista said, smoothing down his doublet and straightening his white cuffs. "but then again, a little more time thinking might encourage you to dredge up some more information."

"I've told you all I know!"

"Well, that's very unfortunate, Lauret." He said, moving to the door. "However I feel it's my duty to speak to the Inquisition about your dealings—"

At once, Lauret blurted out: "There's something hidden in the Castilano shop."

Baptista's eyes flickered. "*What?*"

"If I tell you, don't say you heard it from my lips. It would be the end for me. I'll tell you everything I know if you get me out of here and keep me safe." Lauret begged. "I have a family, I have to get back to France, they need me—"

"They also needed you when you were fucking Gabriella Russo—"

"I was her *friend!*" the little man retorted. "Only her friend—"

"A friend who let her down." Baptista replied. "But before I give you any promises, I need to hear what you have to say, Lauret. And don't try to fucking dupe me, I'll know, and you will spend the rest of your life here, whilst I go to France and visit your family... So, now that we understand each other, tell me – what exactly is in the Castilano shop?"

Chapter Twenty Six

He had never expected to enter the Gianetti palazzo again, Ira passing between the two guards at the front entrance and following a morose servant up the grandiose staircase, along the same vaulted passageway and on into Jacopo Gianetti's capacious bedchamber. Although it was mid summer, the shutters were still bolted, the first of a hot day's sun worming itself through the cracks.

In the dim light, Ira paused. The bed was pulled away from the wall at an angle, the mattress turned over, half on, half off, the base, Cara stepping forward when she saw Ira at the doorway.

"Thank the Holy Mother, dottore, that you come so quickly."

Her gaze moved over to the far corner of the room. There was only one candle burning, Ira barely able to make out a crouched shape in a white nightshirt. It was Jacopo Gianetti. But he did not move, instead, as Ira's eyes became used to the lack of light, he could see another figure sitting beside him.

"Is that you, Marco?" he asked, moving forwards.

As the man rose from his seat Ira could see he had been mistaken. With an expression of extravagant compassion,

Pietro Aretino gestured to Jacopo, still huddled in his chair. His legs were drawn up to his chin, her arms wrapped around his calves, the whites of his eyes glowing in the dim light.

"My dear friend is not well, dottore. We must do something to ease his anguish."

Without answering, Ira turned to Cara, standing behind him. "Some more light, please, I cannot see." Still ignoring the writer, Ira moved over to Jacopo just as Cara set a candle stick on the table beside the bed.

His face now illuminated, Aretino stared at the sick man and made a clucking sound with his tongue. "See how Jacopo stares? And such high colour, surely this is not good. But you are the expert, dottore, I am only a concerned friend." Aretino sighed. "Is this a recurrence of the fever he had before?"

"May I ask if you would be so kind as to leave, signor? I need to examine my patient."

Aretino's eyebrows rose, and he was just preparing a reply when Marco entered.

"A servant came for me..." He had obviously been running and was out of breath. "What happened?"

Aretino's voice was silken. "My dear boy, your beloved father has been taken ill—"

At once, Ira interrupted him. "Please Marco, if you and Signor Aretino would wait outside I would be most grateful. I need to treat your father alone."

He expected immediate agreement, but instead he caught Marco's sidelong glance to Aretino and was reminded of a soldier, looking to his sergeant for instructions. He also noticed a large signet ring on his friend's left hand and a faceted gold chain lying like a dead snake on the black velvet of his doublet.

"Marco, please."

"But Marco is Jacopo's son," Aretino said, interrupting. "and, as his son, he has every right to be here."

"He does – but you don't," Ira replied, more sharply than he had intended.

"You are impertinent, dottore Tabat."

"I do not mean to be. I merely wish to attend my patient as speedily as I am able. In my own time and on my own terms."

Awed, Marco was watching the altercation between the two men. Aretino, immense in his silk cape, his stomach distended, his manicured hands fluttering like a pair of white doves. Be-ringed, white doves, Ira thought. Tagged and tamed, like you are, Marco. With your great, new ring on your little finger. And how long before you have another? A steel ring welded around your neck.

"My services were called for, Marco. Do you wish me to treat your father, or not? It is *your* choice."

"Come now, let us leave the good dottore alone," Aretino smiled slyly, taking hold of Marco's forearm and steering him to the door. Once there, he turned back to Ira. "My dear old friend is delirious, his words are nonsense—"

Ira listened.

"— therefore I would put no credence on anything poor Jacopo says in his condition." Aretino continued. "His father was taken this way, quite insane at the end. So distressing for the family."

Waiting until the door closed behind them, Ira turned to the maid, his voice lowered. "Is it true about his father?"

"I wasn't here then, dottore, but there were rumours that Leonardo Gianetti became strange as he aged. He was a recluse certainly, and had a violent temper, with fits of crying. You could ask his wife about his illness, dottore, the old lady is still very much alive. But I know one thing for certain, Leonardo Gianetti was much older than my master when he lost his mind. He was in his seventies."

"And how long has Signor Gianetti been confused?"

"Only a few hours." She replied, "At first he said he had had a nightmare and that he didn't need a medic, but then he seemed afraid of something and panicky, and then he told me to get you."

"How was he last night?"

"As he always was."

Ira nodded. "What has he eaten today?"

"Nothing. He was awake early and then became *agitato*. He pulled the sheets off and said there were things in the bed that shouldn't be there." She stared at Jacopo, who had relaxed his grip around his knees and was sitting quietly in his seat, his expression normal again.

"Signor Gianetti," Ira addressed him, his voice calm as he moved back to his patient. "How are you feeling?"

"I am troubled." The words were emotive, but his manner was characteristically cold. "I am troubled by those I once knew."

Ira drew up a chair beside him. The one Aretino had just vacated. "Your servant said you had a nightmare."

"I did, but then it was real. In the mirror."

"What was?"

Jacopo looked at Ira, his eyes moist. "Do you know my wife?"

"No, signor."

"She loved me. I think so."

"I am sure she did."

"Why are you sure!" Jacopo responded. "What do you know of my life? My family? You are not welcome here! You are the one who has tried to take my son away from me—"

Ira laid his hand on Jacopo's arm, soothing him and changing the subject. "What was your nightmare about?"

"The Gianetti family is one of the richest in Venice." Jacopo carolled to himself. "The Doges have always been our friends and confidantes. I was close to Andrea Gritti." he nodded. "Yes, it's true and he was a great warrior… but of late I have been troubled."

"By whom?"

"People are jealous of our wealth," he leaned towards Ira, his skin sticky with sweat. "And I don't blame them. But they want my riches. My palazzos, my horses, my money. Money I – and my family – have inherited. Not like the greedy merchants. Turks, Jews, Arabs, men without a good name and no status, but they come to Venice to sell their rank perfumes and spices and make their fortunes to spend on whores," he waved his hand around the room. "I have Titian's paintings on my walls, and Bellini. My father collected gold and silverware that the Pope in Rome envied." He stopped suddenly, staring at the bed, his eyes widening again. "I didn't cause her death, she chose it. May God forgive her. I do not!" He snatched his arm away from Ira's touch. "You are one of those Jews, stealing from us!" His voice had become high pitched, the words jumbled, his hands banging on the arms of the chair as his feet struck the floor at the same time.

In silence, Ira walked over to his medicine bag, taking out a glass vial and turning to Cara. "Please can you bring me some water?"

She nodded, returning moments later, Ira mixing nine drops into the water and moving back to Jacopo.

No longer raging, he was composed. Proud again, his voice defiant. "What are you doing in my room!"

"I have something for you—"

"I want nothing from you, Jew."

"It is not from me," Ira replied calmly, "it is from your wife, she is worried about you and said that you should drink this."

The words had a becalming effect, Jacopo looking at the glass, his fingers reaching for it, then hesitating. "I wasn't always a bad man, whatever some say. I have responsibilities, a family name to live up to. People have called me cruel, but I have to be firm at times. In truth, it was not my nature to be so taxed with work and properties, boats, staff, so many staff, and people thought me aloof. It was hard, so hard in business. But I had no love to temper me..." His bottom lip slackened, his head drooping.

"Your wife is worried about you, signor. Take the medicine she sent."

He leaned towards Ira, his head inches away. "Do you understand? I must *make* you understand. He poisons people."

"Who does?"

"That fat toad Aretino. He poisoned me."

"He put something in your food?"

Jacopo laughed, covering his mouth with his free hand. "No, not in my food! Not even my wine!" he became serious again and pointed to his head. "In here. All those years, poisoning me. He put worms in my brain. He keeps them in his garden, in a thousand glass jars. He breeds them, then lets them go free in summer. I've seen them crawling through the crack in the shutters... But I understand now. I have his measure. Oh yes, I have the bastard's measure. I thought my wife was dead. But I only dreamed it. *I only dreamed it...*" Jacopo fell silent and he took the glass from Ira.

"Please drink it, Signor Gianetti."

"You said my wife sent this?.."

Ira nodded.

"... Will it kill them? Will it kill the worms?"

"Yes. It will kill every one of them." Ira replied, watching as he tipped back the glass and drank.

Cara had remade the bed whilst Ira was tending to his patient. For fifteen minutes both of them had listened to a litany of maudlin self pity, rage and vicious insults. Yet as the sedative began to take effect, Jacopo allowed himself to be lead back to bed, his eyes fixed on the canopy overhead.

"Will you tell her that I drank it?"

"Yes, I will tell her."

"And tell her that I forgive her," Jacopo whispered, "tell my wife I forgive her..." his eyes snapped open. "But don't tell Aretino! The pig will kill us all if he can. **Marco must not be with the writer**. My son is in danger, do you know? *Do you know?*" he was beginning to lose consciousness, his voice failing. "You must get him away from Aretino. I beg you. Do this for me. For him."

Chapter Twenty Seven

Under the scorching sky the rain plummeted down like someone emptying a basin out of an upper window. It fell on St Marks Square, the tiles soon marbled, the boats jerking like caught fish on the Adriatic's moody tide. Carpets and rugs that had been unloaded onto the quayside, were hastily covered, silk bales water-spotted like a toad's back. A Turkish merchant, turbaned and sporting an ivory whip, rallied his slaves; a trading boat almost overturned; a gondola carrying two veiled women was buffeted on the Lagoon; and a man in opulent striped breeches skipped between the puddles, as nimble as a goat.

Pulling his hat down over his forehead, Barent der Witt hurried over a bridge, narrowly avoiding a collision with a dog looking for shelter. The Dutchman was glad of the rain; it would keep most people indoors, and those still outside preoccupied and unlikely to notice what was going on around them.

He had wondered if Marina Castilano and her sister had truly left Venice and had decided to visit Caterina Zucca. As usual, Bakita, her guard, was stationed outside her door, dressed in yellow waistcoat and breeches, the silk material vibrant against the dark skin. He was, as ever, silent. Der

Witt didn't know if it was because he knew no Italian, or if he was instructed to say nothing.

Quietly, der Witt knocked on the door.

"Who's is that?"

He called out to her. "Your friend, Barent der Witt."

"Then come in, friend!"

The courtesan was alone in her bedroom. Usually Caterina would receive visitors sitting on her day bed or a couch, but this time she was in her main bed, and obviously sick.

"Signora," the Dutchman said, doffing his hat. "You are ill?"

Her face was florid, her blonde hair without its shine, her face without its maquillage. "As you see, my friend, I am not working. A summer cold, delivered via the Adriatic or some merchant selling his wares *and* his infection." She patted the bed beside her, then shook her head. "No, not there. You must not sit close to me, I do not want to give you anything to make you suffer."

"Have you been ill for long?"

"Four days. It not all bad however, on hearing of my incapacitation one of my clients requested my dirty handkerchiefs. Men can be so … bizarre." She shrugged. "I am setting my newest girl to tend to my favourites. Tita Boldini, I introduced you last time you were here."

"I remember." He said, turning his hat in his hands and moving on hurriedly. "Have you seen Marina Castilano?"

"She has left Venice." Caterina replied, frowning. "Marina said she had told you."

He nodded. "Indeed she did, but I wondered if she had truly left."

"You could have visited the shop to find out." Caterina teased him, "and yet you came to see me. As you have a reason for everything, good der Witt, why are you here?"

He hesitated before answering. "Do you think she was involved in Gabriella Russo's death?"

Surprised, Caterina leaned back against her pillows, her left hand stroking a large white cat. "Why would you say that?"

"Marina Castilano was trying to get information from me. The last thing she said was about Gabriella and *The Wolves of Venice*."

Sighing, Caterina held the cat against her bosom and stroked it. "No, I do not think Marina was involved. I think she was frightened, terrified that someone might come back to the shop and hurt her. I understand. The business with the shoes was unnerving." She sneezed, dabbing at her nose, the nostrils reddened.

"May God bless you."

"He blesses me with friends like you," she replied sweetly. "I wonder if tomorrow I could go out. Wearing a veil, of course."

"It is raining heavily and might rain again tomorrow. Why would you risk it?" der Witt countered. "Anything you need, you staff will get for you. Or do you want me to give you some medication?"

"No, no, do not fuss!" she replied, querulously. "I am just bored. I am tired of being a hermit."

"Your clients will wait, Caterina. Anticipation is a powerful aphrodisiac."

"It depends how *long* you make a man wait." She replied. "They are very fickle, always ready to find new breasts, a new arse, a new adventure... Did you hear that the Doge is planning an event for September? Fireworks and Donato singing. I suppose Titian will attend, he is involved in everything that happens in Venice."

"Not everything. It was Tintoretto who paid for Gabriella's funeral."

"But that was because she sat for him."

"As you have done in the past."

"As I have done," she agreed, nodding. Setting aside the cat, Caterina leaned towards der Witt, her expression serious. "We will never know the truth, my friend. What Gabriella meant will never be explained and you have nothing for which to reproach yourself." She patted the back of his hand. "It is necessary to let tragedy go. Let the mystery stay buried with Gabriella. She can do no more... And neither can you."

When he left the rain was still falling, the sky Giotto blue, the sun flickering like a humming bird between the clouds. His head bowed he walked on, his left hand holding the glass vial he always wore around his neck, his fingers taking comfort from it. No one noticed him: in a city of a million strangers of every description, nationality and religion, der Witt went unseen.

Which was just what he wanted, arriving at the back entrance of the Castilano shop and checking the door. It was locked, he then moved into the narrow alleyway between the shop and the next building and found the side exit. The door was warped, the wood splintered and the handle broken off. Tipping back his hat, der Witt looked round, then took a small instrument out of his pocket. Seconds later, he entered the Castilano shop.

Before Marina had left she had packed up much of the merchandise, boxes piled on top of other boxes, rugs rolled and contained with leather straps and stacked like logs. She had been serious, after all, he thought, looking round. Where once there had been activity, splendour and colour, there was only an abandoned husk. Her name was still on the window, but nothing else of her remained.

Pushing open the cellar door, der Witt took one of the candles off a shelf at the top of the stairs, lit it, and began to descend. It place was damp and he wondered how practical it had been for storage, then remembered that Marina had kept most of the fabrics in an upper room. At the bottom of the stairs he placed the candle in a disguarded holder and then continued with it, walking towards the far end of the long, narrow chamber. He passed the bed where Gabriella had slept, holding the candle high and then seeing the rows of shoe racks facing him.

They were all empty. Not even a lace, or a button remained. He remembered Marina telling him about hiding Gabriella's bloodied shoes, then moving them, then finding them in another place. She hadn't said where, just insisted that someone had moved them. Someone with access to the shop... Der Witt paused, Marina had assured him that her sister had been ignorant of the whole affair, and had been equally certain that she had not forgotten where she had put the shoes.

So where were they now?

Der Witt glanced around him, ducked down to look under the worktable and beneath the bed. He even tapped the back of the wall where the shelves were stacked, to see if there was a hidden alcove behind. He found nothing. The

Dutchman was of an age to resent mysteries and long for solutions. Already he had considered a dozen explanations, even allowing himself to meditate on the supernatural. But a man seeped in secrets and well versed in the art of suggestion, knew that there was always a human explanation.

Someone had terrified Gabriella. Someone had killed her. People killed for money, lust, or jealousy. Der Witt leaned against the worktable. Gabriella had had no money, and no means to steal a fortune. So was it lust? It was true that Gabriella had been raped, so had it been a crime of passion? He dismissed the idea. Rape was power; he knew that, he had aborted many unwanted foetuses which had been conceived in violence. He had seen women made sterile, their attacker raping them with a poker or a broom handle. Once he had tended a child of twelve who had been sodomised by a nobleman, a scion of one of the most famous Venetian families. He had seen lust perpetrated on the street whores of Venice; the women who went with the slaves and sailors off the ships, men who had been celibate for months and hungry for sex. And the whores served them. Women who had once been pretty, or wives, or mothers. Some widowed, some drunks, some who would fight another woman naked in an alley for a bet. Yes, der Witt thought to himself, he had seen enough of lust.

Tired, he sighed, thinking of Gabriella's grotesque death. Her face had been disfigured, her limbs removed, her killer obviously wishing her to remain anonymous for as long as possible. He had wanted to destroy her, pull her apart. It had only been by a fluke that Tintoretto had recognised her. That wasn't lust, der Witt decided, that had been hatred.

Der Witt took off his hat, rolling the brim around in

his hands as he always did when he was thinking. So had the motive been jealousy? Had Gabriella stolen another woman's husband or lover? Unlikely, she had been a reserved, respectable girl, diffident almost. Then perhaps she had rejected someone? A man who could not accept her rebuttal. A man who had hated her for it. His thoughts moved onto another consideration. Gabriella had been a maid, with little or no important connections, but what if she had accidentally uncovered something that had put her in danger?

'*... You must be careful, I wasn't careful...*'

The Dutchman stared ahead, thinking. Was Gabriella killed because of something she knew? *The Wolves of Venice... the four* – were they real? So important that they would have killed to protect their identity?

A loud noise sounded overhead, Der Witt startled, but keeping silent; unwilling to let anyone know he had entered the shop illegally. Perhaps someone had seen him and notified the authorities. Which would mean trouble, imprisonment, questions asked which he did not want to answer. Questions finally answered that would keep him in blistering Venice, far away from the Hague and the cold Northern light.

Still silent, the Dutchman listened to the noises overhead. Someone was walking about. A thief? Or a member of the Inquisition who had followed him? His heart rate accelerated. He had known they had been making enquires about him for a while. Might they have finally decided to make their move... Uncertain, he considered what to do. Should he call out, explain to who ever it was that he had been a friend of Marina Castilano and was looking after the shop for her? Or hold his tongue and wait until the person left?

When there had been no sounds overhead for several minutes the Dutchman approached the steps, ready to ascend. But although there was silence from above, it seemed as though the person hadn't left, or even moved; that they were standing directly above him.

Knowing he was there.

Chapter Twenty Eight

When Ira finally left Jacopo Gianetti's bed chamber he paused on the corridor outside to fasten his medical bag, Cara's footsteps still faintly audible from the room he had just exited. Thoughtful, Ira ran his hand over the leather of the bag, his initials braded on it – **I G** – some fancy of Rosella's who had taken such pride in his qualifying as a doctor. He thought that even if he became as wealthy as Jacopo Gianetti he would never use another bag, he would ask Solomon Taborski to mend the worn leather instead, patching it up, letting it age as he did.

Not that he would ever become as rich as Jacopo Gianetti, or Marco, set to inherit a great fortune when his father died. Frowning, Ira thought of the ridiculous signet ring he had seen Marco wearing, too large for his fine hands, too much a show. All the months Ira had known Marco, he had never seen him wear jewellery, but now he was decked out like a carnival float. One of Aretino's bejewelled, twinkling gondolas with their decadent nymphs and rancid shepherds.

His anger surprised him, especially when Ira realised that it wasn't just anger. That he was also jealous of Marco Gianetti; of the indolence, the wealth, the lazy entitlement to a luxurious life that was his without effort. Ashamed,

Ira tried to justify his feelings, but they stuck in his craw like dry bread. Marco had been a good friend for months, they had been comfortable in each other's company – after Ira's initial suspicion. And in the ghetto Marco had been welcomed, Rosella accepting him without question. His charm cajoled people into liking him, his good humour welcomed. But not by all; many had asked why the heir to a dynasty would mix with those of another race and religion.

Ira knew why; Marco needed the surrogate family he and Rosella offered. He had *welcomed* the differences of the ghetto, the parsimonious surroundings in direct contrast to his own extraordinary, cold abundance. But over the last month Ira had watched his friend alter, the corrupting influence of Pietro Aretino casting its putrid shadow. There had been times Ira had seen Marco drunk in the middle of the day, walking with Aretino and his coterie, a gaggle of courtesans following. Patiently he had listened to his friend's reports of musical concerts or influential parties at the Doge's palace, later Marco had even regaled him with the sexual exploits Aretino had provided for his amusement. He knew all the whores in Venice, Marco told him, although he only used boys.

He only used boys... Marco had said the words as though they meant nothing. As though Aretino's voracious sexual appetite had left none injured, which was not true. It was common knowledge that the writer visited the prison, choosing desperate boys and offering them freedom in return for sexual favours. His contacts at the gaol were like his connections everywhere; pernicious and malevolent. And no one could challenge him. It was not for nothing that Aretino's sobriquet was *the scourge of kings*.

Yet Ira still could not understand *why* Marco had come so completely under Aretino's influence. He had more wealth that the writer could ever accumulate and a respected name: he was, without any doubt, superior, safely elevated amongst an elite Aretino could only terrorise and blackmail into subservience. But for how long would his power go unchallenged? There had already been one assassin attempt on the writer, there were sure to be others. Men with grievances willing to kill the biggest, most hated toad in Venice. And yet, despite everything despicable about him, the power Aretino possessed had been like a whirlpool to Marco Gianetti, sucking him in to drown.

Uneasy, Ira glanced down the hallway. On either side of stood servants in full livery, silent, staring ahead, as immobile as caryatids, a row of gilded torcheres still lit although morning had already made its entrance. At the head of the staircase Ira glanced down the stairwell, at the yard after yard of exquisite Carerra marble, the central portion in the entrance a mosaic of Bacchus and Adriane. Glorious, imperious. Soulless.

"My dear dottore," a voice said, Ira turning to find Aretino approaching. "You see how we left you to your ministrations? How is my dear friend?"

"I am returning this evening to check on Signor Gianetti's progress. At the moment he is sleeping soundly." Ira made a move to go, but Aretino stopped him, putting his hand in the crook of his arm.

"Are you sufficiently qualified to attend him?" he asked, his small dark eyes amused. "There are many finer – more experienced – medico in the ghetto. I have wondered often why it was that you were called to attend."

"I was recommended."

"By whom?"

"No one you would know," Ira replied, removing his arm from Aretino's grip. "If you would excuse me, I have other patients—"

"In the ghetto? Or in Venice? If the latter, I do hope that you wash your hands before you treat any Venetians, dottore, they say there are many rats in the ghetto."

"There are biggest, fatter rats out of it." Ira replied curtly.

"It would seem that there is some animosity between us," Aretino said, his manicured fingers stroking his beard indolently. "...which is unfortunate. I have many contacts and could recommend you to the most influential people in Venice. People Marco knows. In fact, I believe your friend would approve of my advancing you."

"Why?"

"*Why?*" Aretino repeated. "Because Marco has affection for you."

"But he does not respect my advice."

"Advice is something that demands disrespect."

"Even when it is in his own best interests?" Ira countered. "Marco would be better served if you encouraged him to concentrate on working with Tintoretto—"

"Marco will never be a great painter!"

"He is not without talent."

"Being 'without talent' does not impress anyone." Aretino replied, his tone silken. "Marco is a young man, with a young man's appetites."

"Which is natural, but should take up only a part of his life, not all of it."

"I merely spoil him – to make up for his father's lack of affection for the boy."

"Why?"

"Does there always have to be a why?"

"For a man like you, yes." Ira replied, seeing with satisfaction that he had scored a direct hit.

Aretino's eyes narrowed, but he said nothing for an instant, his voice placating when he spoke again. "And what *precisely* is a man like me?"

"I do not know you personally, Signor Aretino, but I know of people who have had dealings with you. And suffered for it. There are rumours in Venice—"

"Ah, rumours!"

"Attempted assassination is not a rumour."

"All famous men inspire envy and hatred."

"All wicked men deserve it." Ira replied.

He had wanted to avoid a confrontation, but having entered into an exchange with the writer he could not walk away. All his resentment and anxiety for Marco had come to the fore, together with his dislike of the corpulent rake in front of him.

"You should be careful," Aretino said, his tone warning. "I am not a man to challenge. And I am not a man who is devoted to his countrymen and the needs of others. I am content to be devoid of any humanitarian feelings. My desires are for my own advancement and pleasure—"

"So your mentoring of Marco is not for his good, merely to give you pleasure?"

"The two are not mutually exclusive," Aretino replied, "A charming young man is introduced and accepted by

Venetian society – his rightful place. Naturally it counts as a triumph for Marco, and for myself."

"Jacopo Gianetti is not a fit man," Ira said shortly. "I have asked a colleague of mine to see him and we both agree that he will not live much longer. I do not know when he will die, that I cannot predict, but in God's time he *will* die and then Marco will inherit a vast fortune." His tone became sarcastic. "Which, naturally, is something you would advice him upon?"

"I know the right people—"

"No, you know the *wrong* people, Signor Aretino, and your manipulation is obvious." Ira struggled to keep his temper. "But I will say this here and now – to your face – that I will do anything in my ability to break the hold you have over Marco Gianetti. I will use whatever means at my disposal to rid him off your perverted influence. And I swear if it is within my power, I will destroy you."

Aretino smiled, watching as Ira moved away. "Please give my regards to your beautiful sister, dottore. I believe we have friends in common."

Ira snapped round. "We have no mutual friends!"

"But we are both are fond of Marco," Aretino continued his eyes flint hard. "Indeed it was he who made the introduction—"

"What introduction?"

"—that of your lovely sister to my good and noble friend. Adamo Baptista."

Chapter Twenty Nine

The Dutchman glanced around, looking for another door, another exit. But the only exit was at the top of the staircase, and someone had locked that door. Someone who had watched der Witt walk into the ambush that had been so carefully prepared. Someone who knew the layout of the Castilano shop well; someone with enough knowledge to search, or hide things on the premises. The same someone who had taunted Marina Castilano and driven her out of Venice.

The Dutchman was no longer young, but he was thick set and resolute. If he was attacked, he would fight – unwilling to face Italian justice, which seldom came down in favour of a foreigner. But in the meantime, he would wait... Taking a seat on the narrow bed, der Witt turned the hat brim in his hands, thinking. Marina Castilano had been desperate to discover what he knew. Indeed her last words had been Gabriella's. So had she been convinced by his apparent ignorance? Or had she sent someone to confront him directly? ... Thoughtful, der Witt glanced up the steps towards the bolted door. If he kicked it hard enough he could break the lock and free himself.

But who was waiting outside?

His hand closed around the glass vial hanging from his neck. Its coolness calmed him. Out of the corner of his eye he could see the candle flickering slightly. Had someone caused a draft by opening the outside door on the floor above him? He listened, hopeful. Several moments passed. Then the candle regained its calm, the flame a little oasis in the cellar's gloom.

Fondamenta dei Mori,

Studio of Tintoretto.

"Where is he? Where is the bastard?" Ira shouted, entering the studio and overturning an easel as he looked around. "Come out, you craven pig! Come out and face me!"

Hearing the outburst, Tintoretto hurried in from the back room, his sleeves rolled up, his smock splattered with paint and freckles of hot wax. Baffled by the sight of the usually reserved Ira Tabat shouting at the top of his voice, he confronted him.

"What is the matter here?"

"Where's Marco?"

"He was here a little while ago, then he left," he painter replied. "What's he done?"

"You ask him." Ira replied, brushing past the apprentices who had gathered to witness the scene. Enraged, he ran to the back of the studio and into the workshop beyond. *"Marco! I know you're here—"*

"But he is not." Tintoretto replied, following him.

Ira turned. "Give him up! Wherever you're hiding him, give him up. I should never have let my sister come here.

I should have forbidden it! Everyone knows what these places are like—"

"This is a studio," Tintoretto replied calmly. "Everyone is busy, pre-occupied with work—"

"Like Marco?" Ira snapped, pointing his forefinger at the artist. "Give him up or I swear I will rip this place to shreds to find him."

"You will find little if you rip this place to shreds. Only insects and mice hiding in their nooks and crannies. No Venetian nobility, of that I can assure you." Tintoretto said calmly, leading Ira into the small workshop and closing the door behind them. "Sit down, my friend, take a moment to compose yourself."

He poured a glass of wine, but Ira brushed it aside. "I don't drink."

"Luckily, I do," Tintoretto replied, downing the wine in one swallow. "Perhaps you should tell me what all this is about."

"Marco Gianetti."

"That much I worked out for myself," Tintoretto said drily, "he's very foolish, you know. A character that is pleasing, but unfortunately also easy to lead and impress, but he's good at heart."

"Hah!"

"I take it you have reason to think otherwise. So what has he done?" Tintoretto repeated, Ira looking at him with suspicion.

"*You're defending him*! Even before you know what he's capable of, you're telling me he's a good man. Why is that?"

"It's what I believe."

"Or maybe it's because you want to minimise his actions?"

"For pity's sake, Ira, I am not a carnival fortune teller! Just tell me what has happened."

"He introduced my sister to Adamo Baptista, and she has apparently made a friend of him."

"Baptista!" Tintoretto snapped, pouring himself some more wine. "But Marco would never—"

"Marco *has*."

"But why? He must surely know the kind of man Baptista is. Even Marco wouldn't be that stupid." Tintoretto walked to the door and called to one of his assistants. *"Se vedi Marco, portamelo subito!"* then moved back to Ira. "I don't understand *why* he would do such a thing."

"Because he was ordered to. He's under Aretino's thumb. He's a lap dog, running around, doing tricks to please his master. You must see how he's changed—"

"I haven't see very much of him at all lately," Tintoretto replied, "but I find it hard to believe what you're telling me. Marco thinks of Rosella as a sister, he wouldn't put her in any kind of danger or do anything to taint her reputation. He cares for her too much—"

"Oh, he cares for her," Ira said bitterly, "but he cares of Aretino more. For what that sodden bastard can do for him. Marco has fallen in love with the reflected glory of being the writer's protégé, he relishes the whores and the Doge's coterie, and, God help him, he sees Aretino as replacement father."

"His own parent cares little for him."

"That's no excuse!" Ira replied, "Marco has betrayed Rosella and he has betrayed me. I don't doubt it was done indirectly, that Aretino forced Marco's hand somehow, but he still allowed himself to be manipulated. He put a debauched swindler before our friendship and before Rosella's welfare." Ira glanced fiercely at the painter. "And d'you know why I'm so certain of what Marco has done? *Because Aretino told me*. And he told me with such pleasure. He made sure I knew that it was all was Marco's doing."

Tintoretto was still trying to calm the situation. "Ira, I understand your feelings, but think about it, please. You are assuming the worst and Rosella is a good girl—"

"**I know that!** She would never shame her family or do anything to embarrass herself. Not from choice – so she must have been trapped into it."

"You are supposing," the artist said carefully, "that something has happened, whereas she may merely have met Baptista."

Ira shook his head.

"No. There is more to it than that." His voice was hoarse with emotion. "I've seen a difference in Rosella over the last week. I thought it was tiredness – she has a job and she's been coming here more often to sit for you – but now I think about it, she's been avoiding me." He tightened his hands into fists. "Has she met Baptista here?"

"**No.**" Tintoretto replied sharply. "And you would do well not to suggest such a thing again. I am fond of you Ira because you are Rosella's brother, but you will *not* come here and infer that I was involved in anything underhand, or in anything that would injure your sister. Adamo Baptista is no friend of mine and I have my own reasons to hate him."

"Forgive me," Ira said, shame-faced. "I shouldn't have said such a thing."

"You're right, you shouldn't."

Embarrassed, Ira glanced over his shoulder into the studio beyond. The apprentices had returned to work, two of them fastening a mammoth sheet of canvas onto its wooden frame, another mixing some pigment, adding in the linseed oil droplet by measured droplet.

"Will he come back?"

"Marco? Oh, he will come back some time. Maybe in an hour, maybe in a week, but he always comes back. But by now he will have heard that you are looking for him, so he'll—"

"Hide?"

"Yes," Tintoretto agreed. "He will hide, because he will feel guilty. If he didn't realise what he had done, he will now. And if he was fully aware of his actions he will be afraid to meet up with you. Marco has money, but you have friends. Many people respect you, and not just in the ghetto."

Ira shrugged. "People there been looking at me strangely, or evading me. I thought I was imagining it, but obviously I wasn't. Last night Hyman Golletz seemed about to say something, then thought better of it. Now I know what he wanted to talk to me about."

"Rosella is a decent girl—"

"**Stop saying that!**" Ira shouted. "It doesn't matter, don't you understand? It not what it is, it's how it looks. The damage was done as soon as she was seen with Adamo Baptista – however innocent. A decent woman would not mingle with the likes of him. We both know that. And worse, *Marco* knew that. He knew it, and he led her into a trap. Whatever happened, or didn't happen, my sister is ruined. And I'm going to kill him for it—"

"Be calm, Ira, be calm," the artist urged him. "Talk to Rosella first, let her explain. Behaving like this will only frighten her away. Let her talk to you—"

"I'll talk to her, but first I'll find Marco." Ira got to his feet, his tone dismissive. "If you see the bastard tell him I'm looking for him. And tell him that wherever he goes and however long he hides, he won't escape."

Surprised by his confrontation with Ira and the reckless threat levelled at him, Aretino smiled to himself remembering how quickly the impertinent Jew had been corralled; his expression shifting from menacing to distressed. Immensely gratified by the way his plan had worked out, Aretino lingered in the water of the deep marble bath, capacious enough to hold himself and the two young men he had taken from the prison. The gaoler was a greedy man with enough secrets to make him malleable to the writer's wishes, and so he had accepted Aretino's heavy purse and freed the duo.

Water, Aretino decided, was a most comfortable medium. His bulk could relax on a bed or settle banked with cushions, bolsters and those tapestried pillows from Northern Holland, but his flesh revelled in being weightless, the water buoying him up so that he could fully appreciate the clever fingers and tongues of the youthful bardasses.

"I have often wondered, my dear Adamo, about your little companion, Signor Nikolas Volt."

Baptista was sitting on the other side of a screen, always an unwilling voyeur, a man who appreciated privacy in his seductions and abhorred the writer's exhibitionism.

And that day he had found Aretino even more loathsome, his bulbous, white body odious in comparison to his companions.

"*What* have you wondered?" Baptista asked, putting his finger to his lips as Volt himself entered and took a seat behind the screen.

"Are you lovers? He is a very pretty boy, so unusual with those slanting eyes and that rosebud mouth."

"I don't bugger boys."

"Girls perhaps?"

Volt tilted his head to one side, his sloe eyes watchful as Baptista replied. "Why are so interested in my private life, Aretino?"

"You know why. Have you fucked Rosella Tabat yet?"

Volt's gaze moved over to Baptista, his expression bland. "Is that what you want?"

He could hear water splashing, the writer's sexual diversion interrupted. "Don't torment me, Baptista, you know what we planned."

"We planned a seduction."

"So did you fuck her, seduce her, or whatever you chose to call it?"

"She rejected me."

"Hah!" Aretino snorted. Baptista could hear him heaving himself out of the bath and pad over to the screen. Wrapping a towel around his gut, he peered round, amused to see Nikolas Volt there. "Ah, you have your pretty baby with you. I see you would not want to commit yourself in front of your amor."

Volt was composed, shuffling a pack of cards, the pack that Lauret had given to Baptista. His slight hands moved in a rhythm, the coloured backs of the card flickering like sunlight through a stained glass window.

"Do you play as well as you shuffle?"

Volt paused, looking at the writer. "Do you wish a game, signor?"

"Certainly, but not of cards," Aretino replied, his attention returning to Baptista. "If the girl rejected you, force her."

"No."

"*No?*" Aretino replied, fascinated. "Since when were you so moral?"

"If I raped Rosella Tabat the whole ghetto would be up in arms. The part Marco Gianetti played in it would be exposed, as well as your own involvement."

"That would be a storm I could easily weather," Aretino said dismissively, "but I don't want Marco exposed just yet. I have other plans for him."

"Also remember that falling out with the ghetto would threaten our contract with Gilda Fasculo."

"She would not dare to speak out, knowing it would expose her and bring her creditors down on her."

Baptista shrugged. "Maybe you're right. But perhaps there is someone else who might be more of an adversary. Ira Tabat is a respected doctor who carries some influence. If I raped his sister, he might take me take me to court—"

"The case would be dismissed," Aretino said blithely." I would see to it."

Baptista smiled, "But not before Venice bathed in the details of your blackmail of Jacopo and manipulation of Marco Gianetti—"

"You are becoming nervous, Baptista. You well know that Jacopo would not dare expose me and ruin himself. I have him under my control, as he has been for many years and will continue for many more. He's my puppet. I can do with Jacopo Gianetti as I chose."

Baptista's expression was amused as he answered. "Perhaps if you did spend so long in the bath with your boys you would know more... *Jacopo Gianetti died an hour ago*. And his son has gone into hiding."

I heard that Ira was looking for me and I made my way home.

Like a weakling, I told the guards on duty at the door to prevent his entry – only to be told that Ira was already inside, attending to my father. Irony in all its perfection. Unable to return to the palazzo, I headed for Burano, a north eastern suburb of Venice, and a forty minutes journey by boat.

To this day, I'm not certain why I picked that island, it was so quiet, famous for its lace making. Only a month earlier I remember admiring a collar that the Doge's wife was wearing and she said it had been Venetian point lace, Punto di Burano, a speciality of the island's, the lace complicated and ornamental, its openwork fabric formed by looping, interlacing and twisting threads.

Naturally there was also some fishing in Burano, flimsy weathered boats bobbing like ducks on the late tide, a few fishermen staring at me as I docked. I understood why. I was a stranger, elaborately dressed, as out of place as an elephant caught in their nets. But it was lace that was the main talent of the island. As glass was to Murano, lace was to Burano.

Where was I headed? Where every coward heads, a church. The Church of St Martin of Tours, to be exact, a saint who watches over drinkers and the poor. I was no drinker, but my soul was poverty stricken. I was emptied of morals, a sickness inside which had made me vomit on the boat. Not sea sickness, conscience sickness. I knew the whole enormity of what I had been coerced into doing. But I had done anyway. I knew what the outcome would be when I introduced Rosella to Adamo Baptista. But I did it anyway.

To my shame, Aretino's approval mattered so much that for days after the fateful meeting I would not let myself think of my betrayal and instead glowed in the writer's approbation. He sent me his most carnal whores, I was welcomed at the Doge's Palace by people of immense influence in Venice and the merchants begged for my custom. With his puppet in place, Aretino declared me the most glittering member of the Gianetti history. And, when I inherited, the richest.

But that was then.

Never once did I think of seeking refuge with Pietro Aretino. My senses came back to me like a man recovered from fever, the memories of what I had done seeming more delirium than reality. But it was reality, I knew that when Aretino refused me admittance to his home, when my days became a void and the invitations ceased. I would like to assure you otherwise, but my Epiphany was not sought, but forced upon me.

I went to church in Burano.

I did not pray.

I did not dare.

I thought of my father, of Ira and Rosella, of the friendship offered so readily and abused so completely.

As I say, Burano was forty minutes away from the Gianetti palazzo, from the bronze statue of the warrior in my father's study, from Cara, who had once loved me, and the ghetto where I had been accepted. I could look across the water and see St Marks, could watch the same birds fly over my head that flew over the Lagoon. It was the same sea that was under my feet and the same sky over my head.

I was forty minutes away from everything I had once loved. And I had estranged myself.

Chapter Thirty

Der Witt tensed as he heard the key turned in the lock, the cellar door swinging open, light pooling down the steps towards him. Squinting against the sudden illumination, he could just make out the figure in the doorway. A woman, tall and slightly built.

"Signor der Witt?"

He rose from the bed where he had been sitting, picked up his hat, and answered. "Yes. Who are you?"

"Oh, you know me. It's Tita Boldini, I work for your friend, Caterina Zucca."

Without showing any surprise, the Dutchman moved over to the steps, recognising her as he began to ascend. Smiling, Tita watched him, standing on the top step, blocking his exit.

"The door was locked."

He nodded. "And I was locked in. Did you lock it?"

Her eyes were challenging and he noticed that her clothes had transformed from the simple attire in which she had arrived in Venice. Although her figure lacked the opulent bosom and small waist favoured by the Republic, her skin was luminous, with a faint sheen around her shoulders, her dark hair woven with gold thread and seed pearls. Yet the feminine clothing did not completely hide a robustness he found daunting.

"Why would *I* lock you in a cellar?"

"Why, Signora Boldini, would *you* be here at all?"

She laughed. "The Castilano sisters asked me to take care of the shop for them."

"That's strange, Marina never mentioned it to me." Der Witt replied, noticing that Tita did not step to one side and was still blocking his exit. Instinctively, he felt for the handrail and gripped it.

"Why would she tell you what her arrangements were, Signor der Witt?"

"We were friends—"

"Really?" Tita replied, her tone doubtful. "Did you treat Marina Castilano? Give her an abortion, perhaps?" The Dutchman tried to pass her, but she held her ground. "I've heard a great deal about you and how the Inquisition are asking questions. Caterina seems very fond of you, but she has a sweet nature, don't you think? Or is it false? Do tell me, you've known her much longer than I have and I'm new to Venice and eager to make the right impression."

He had mistrusted Tita Boldini the instant they had met and his instinct had been right. "I am sure you will leave a lasting impression here."

"But not all young woman do." She shook her head sadly. "Like that poor girl who was murdered. Gabriella Russo, wasn't that her name?"

Moving abruptly, der Witt pushed her aside, Tita laughing. "Do I make you nervous, Dutchman?"

"Did Marina give you a key?"

"How else would I have gained access? Or perhaps

I could have broken in, as you did." She smiled, her tone lilting. "We were talking about vulnerable young women, were we not? Poor Caterina is very nervous since the girl's murder. She hired Bakita for that very reason, although I mistrust him."

"Why would you mistrust him? He seems devoted to his mistress and Caterina speak well of him."

"She speaks well of a savage that speaks only a few words of Italian?" Tita replied scornfully. "How would she know what he is really like with so little information to go on? She bought Bakita off a slave ship, was told that he came from Africa, and nothing else. It seems very … unwise… to trust a man of whom you know so little."

"And how much does she know of you?"

"I came with references from France, from a woman Caterina knows."

"References can be bought or faked."

She slid her hand between his legs. "My references cannot be faked, Dutchman." Laughing, she moved her hand away, pleased to see his embarrassment. "What is that around your neck?" she asked, pointing to the glass vial.

His hand closed over it. "It is something that matters a great deal to me."

"Oh, like the snake in the bottle in your study."

Wrong footed, he reacted sharply. "How d'you know about that?"

"I know many things, that is my skill. At this precise moment I would like to know why you left The Hague so suddenly and why you are now in Venice."

"Forgive me, but my life should be of no interest to you." He moved towards the door, Tita calling after him.

"Very well, you keep your secrets, Dutchman, and I will keep mine. It's true I am new to Venice, but I have much experience of the world and its villains."

"I will take your advice to heart."

"Please do. The Wolves of Venice are circling—"

He turned abruptly. "*What?*"

"—and you would be best served by becoming part of the pack, not part of the prey."

BOOK FOUR

Chapter Thirty One

A month passed, taking July with it. Then August slung, low hipped, into the steamy Lagoon. Marco Gianetti did not return to Venice. In his absence, Jacopo Gianetti's funeral took place, his redoubtable mother, Lavinia, attending as the head of the family, cousins coming in from Rome and Naples. Relatives of which she had seen little and heard less, the majority of the Gianetti fortune having always been controlled by her late son, Jacopo.

The Gianetti fortune that would now pass to his only child, his son, Marco... Lavinia had received no explanation as to her grandson's absence. Despite her many attempts to discover his whereabouts, she had failed, except for one report that Marco had been seen in Sicily. Why Sicily she could not understand, the family had no contact with the island, but she did send men to search for her grandson and expected to hear that he had been kidnapped. Or murdered. Or with a woman. God knows, he was fool enough.

Marco had proved his lack of judgement by becoming Aretino's pet, Lavinia thought disapprovingly, when all Venice knew about the writer. But her grandson had been lured in by the power, the opulence of the court, and by believing himself accepted – when he was obviously being used. Just as her son had been.

On numerous occasions Lavinia had tried to reason with Jacopo, advising him to distance himself from Aretino. But despite everything she said, and the evidence she presented, Jacopo had remained stuck to the man like shit to a blanket... She had often wondered why Jacopo hadn't come to her and asked for her help. It would have been given; theirs was not a close relationship, but honour was as important as blood. Yet Jacopo had died with his secret and although Lavinia had searched all his papers she had uncovered nothing that would account for the hold Aretino had had over her son.

Lavinia had always been a clever woman, and a shrewd one. Jacopo had patently disliked Aretino, yet he had kept company with him and had advanced his cause with not one, but two, Doges. There was only one reason why he would have done so. Her son, like so many others, had been one of Aretino's victims.

Lavinia stood up. Age, and a rheumatic hip, made walking tortuous. Having suffered little ill health in her youth she found being elderly a toil and had even wondered about the enigmatic Barent der Witt. It was common gossip that the man was an abortionist, but he was also a great apothecary, or so she had heard, an acquaintance having been cured of a skin complaint. Slowly Lavinia moved to the window and looked out over the Lagoon, thinking.

What had made her grandson leave Venice? Was Aretino blackmailing him? Or punishing Jacopo by befriending his neglected son? Oh yes, Lavinia thought, that would be a spiteful trick, worthy of the writer. Or perhaps Marco had been driven away from Venice for some other reason? Aretino was seldom apart from Adamo Baptista and the Florentine's reputation was alarming. While Aretino used his tongue and pen to destroy lives, Baptista used a knife.

But what had been so important, or so shaming, that Marco had walked away from the wealth, the Gianetti name and the lifestyle? Her grandson, Lavinia decided, might have been a fool, but he was not that much of a fool. She cursed her own pride at having been remote from Marco, but reserve was her nature and she abhorred displays of affection. The child had not been at fault, but his mother's suicide had caused a scandal which had intrigued Venice for too long, one which had made Lavinia retreat further into the endless corridors and reception rooms of the palazzo. In a home so capacious she could be sure of avoiding her son and grandson and devoting her time to her own interests.

How foolish she had been, Lavinia realised, now seeing that her avoidance had merely resulted in ignorance. The reluctance to share family ties leaving her unbound and adrift, divorced from the intimacies and familial gossip which would have proved so useful. Unsettled, Lavinia thought back, remembering an argument she had overheard between Jacopo and his son. To Jacopo's – and her own amazement – Marco had formed a close friendship with Ira Tabat, the doctor who had treated Jacopo. Apparently the relationship had even extended to Marco visiting the Jewish ghetto... Lavinia winced, shifting her weight onto her other hip to relive the pain...It might mean little, but it was a something to investigate whilst she was waiting for Marco – or his body – to return to Venice. There was the Gianetti fortune at stake and the heir was missing. So if her grandson had ties with the Jews, perhaps there was an answer there.

She could hardly send men in to ask awkward questions, and Lavinia did not trust anyone else to ask them for her. There was only one solution: if the answer to her grandson's disappearance was in the ghetto, then that was where she would go.

A swift deterioration in her mother's condition called Rosella home to find her brother sitting at the kitchen table with his head in his hands. Panicked, she hurried into the small bedroom beyond and stopped in the doorway. The body of her mother was covered with a sheet, the outline of her profile like a stone effigy.

For years her presence had been that of a visitor, someone who might leave at any time. But the leaving, the final departure, was still a shock, Rosella sitting beside her mother's narrow bed and staring at the objects on the table. A small pitcher of water and a squat glass, a china bowl with a flannel wrung out and lying over the rim. Once blue, now faded to the colour of a rheumy eye. How many times had she dipped that cloth in water and wiped her mother's face and hands. How many times had she talked to her about work at the Golletz household. How many times had she thought – stupidly and pointlessly – that there had been a scintilla of response.

For so long suspended, her mother had slipped away, almost like a person eager to catch the curfew. And death *was* a curfew. Not like the ghetto's, but a curfew everyone was bound to obey.

"She didn't suffer..." Ira said, pausing beside his sister's chair. "It was very fast, she just slipped away."

In time for the curfew, Rosella thought dumbly. "Why don't you say what you've been meaning to say for weeks?"

"What does that mean?"

"You know what it means, Ira." She swivelled round in her seat to look up at him. "Marco."

"This is not the time!" He replied, moving to the door.

She followed him. "But this **is** the time, don't you see that? This is the exactly the time—"

"Our mother is dead!"

"I know! I feel her loss as much as you do. I feel the shock, believe me, perhaps even more than you. I was the one who spent the most time with her, I was the one who looked after her, Ira, when you were working. When you were away from the ghetto—"

"I never knew you resented it so much."

"Don't you dare say that!" she snapped, her voice breaking. "I *wanted* to do everything to help her, to make her life as comfortable as it could be, but she wasn't here. Her body was in this place; her breathing, her sleeping, was here, but what else of her was here? I always wondered how much she could understand, if she could hear, if she laughed with us when we were joking, or saw the people who visited us. She would have been so proud of you—"

"Is this where I say *'she would have been proud of you?'*"

"Oh, Ira, if you want to insult me, do it directly." She said coldly. "You've avoided me for weeks. You've come in and out without barely uttering a word. And I hate you for what you've done—"

He turned on her. "*'You hate me!'* What have I done to

you that's so shameful? What about your actions? You're right I don't look you in the face, Rosella, and do you want to know why? Because I can't bear to think of you with Adamo Baptista."

"It's taken you seven weeks to speak to me about this!" she shouted. "*Seven weeks*. In which time people have gossiped and blackened my reputation. I am a pariah now, a woman without a good name. I have been tried and convicted without being invited to give evidence in my own defence—"

"There is **no** defence! You knew well enough the type of man that Adamo Baptista is. You knew his reputation, his association with Pietro Aretino, and yet you consorted with him—"

"*'Consorted with him?'*"

"Yes, and you kept it a secret. Of course you did, you knew I would never approve. But if you'd come to me and talked to me—"

"*When*, Ira? When are you not busy? Not looking after your patients? Not caring for everyone – outside your own family." She said bitterly. "I was trapped into it. Marco—"

"*Marco!*"

"—yes, you can hate him for it. Blame Marco Gianetti, it was all his fault. None of it was my doing." She stood up to him. "But that wouldn't be true, Ira. Yes, you're right, I knew about Adamo Baptista, but I didn't seek him out. You want the truth? Are you sure? Are you *really* sure, Ira?"

He stared at her defiantly. "You want to confess? Now our mother is dead—"

She interrupted him. "Do not use her death as your excuse. Our mother was dying for years. My existence revolved around our mother—"

"Not entirely," he snapped.

"— that's right, not entirely. I loved her, but I was tired of my life. Tired of working for Hyman Golletz and listening to him endlessly berate me for not pursuing a career." She shook her head. "'*...you could have been famous...*' he would say. '*...Known all over Venice...* No, I **couldn't** have been, because singing lessons were a ridiculous waste of money, money we needed for living. For our mother, for our food."

"So this is all because of your lost musical career?"

"Why don't you ever listen!" she hurled back at him. "You are so stiff necked, so proud, so willing to judge and believe you are right. Singing was not important to me, but sitting for Tintoretto was." Her voice softened. "He made me important, he was interested in *my* face – in Venice, where there are so many beautiful women, he picked *me*. That was how much I pleased him and when I sat for him I was another, better, woman... Did you know that his studio always smells of linseed oil and smoke in the winter? Tintoretto makes his little charcoal sticks on the hearth and mumbles under his breath when he draws. I watched him once shout at his apprentices who were priming a canvas. "*Sbrigati! Sbrigati!* Be quick, be quick, I don't pay you to dawdle!" and then he would be sorry and send out for pastries from Signor Masaccio on the square." She drew in a slow breath. "Our mother was dying, I was unable to reach her, to talk to her. Signor Golletz is old – but the studio was full of life."

"And Marco." Ira said bitterly.

"Yes... We played tricks on Tintoretto sometimes. Like a brother and sister who provoke an elder sibling. Marco would draw crude outlines on the canvas *Il Furioso* was preparing for a religious scene, and Tintoretto would curse him to hell, tell him that he was the worst apprentice he had ever hired and that Titian was well rid of him." She was smiling at the memory. "Many times I was late and we had to run all the way home to avoid missing the curfew... Don't you understand, you *must* understand! *I trusted Marco.*"

"Enough to agree to go with Adamo Baptista?"

"There was no agreement! I was at the studio and suddenly it was time to leave. Marco came in and I thought *he* was going to walk me back to the ghetto, but he said he was busy. I told him I didn't need a chaperone anymore and that I would go home alone. That was when he told me about the street fighting and said it wasn't safe." She glanced way. Outside someone was chasing a chicken down the alleyway, the squawking and frenzied fluttering of feathers audible through the open window. "That was when Marco said he had arranged for someone else to see me home. The 'someone' was Adamo Baptista."

"And you went with him?"

"How could I refuse?" she countered. "Marco had left. I murmured something about being able to find my own way home. But Baptista wouldn't hear of it, he said the streets were dangerous. Repeating the same story Marco had told me. And so we walked together. I kept my head down, knowing what people would think – what *I* would have thought about a woman in the company of Adamo Baptista. In those thirty minutes – the time it took for the church clock of St Marks to cover half its dial – my reputation was ruined."

Ira's voice was damming. "Believe me, Marco will pay for this."

"For what? For sending Adamo Baptista to walk me home? How should he pay for that?" she glanced away, her face flushed.

"There is more?"

She stayed silent, Ira pressing her. "*Is* there more? You kept all this a secret for seven weeks, have you been seeing him all that time?" he moved towards her, Rosella stepping back. **"Have you been sneaking behind my back for seven weeks?"**

"Yes."

Shaken, Ira slumped into a chair. "You know what Baptista is? Dear God, how could you?" He thought rapidly before speaking again. "We will have to find you a husband, although I doubt even Angelo Fasculo would agree to marry you now."

"I doubt he would."

"We will find you a husband" Ira repeated, "Someone older, a widower perhaps. I will ask the rabbi to intercede—"

"The rabbi can do nothing. The only person who can help me now is Barent der Witt."

Ira looked at her, bemused, then realised what his sister was saying.

"You are having a child? *You are having Adamo Baptista's child?*"

She watched him falter, his usual composure upturned, his orderly life disordered, his family disgraced. She could imagine him thinking of Adamo Baptista, the black crow of Venice, and the Dutchman brought into the mess to abort an unwanted child. She could see in her brother's expression the thoughts scatter like fireworks. Exploding, imploding, then disappearing into nothingness; his plans no more solid that Tintoretto's little wax figures.

"Rosella, for God's Sake, tell me it isn't true."

"It isn't true..." She admitted. "...the child isn't Baptista's. It's Marco's."

Chapter Thirty Two

His paunch barely encased by the velvet doublet, Lauret hurried over the bridge and then paused, panting for breath. Fear and obesity were a dangerous combination, the little man leaning against the stonework to compose himself. It had been a mistake to tell Adamo Baptista about the Castilano shop, but his hand had been forced and now he was hurrying to the quayside and the boat leaving for France. Within hours he would be away from Venice and would never return whilst Adamo Baptista remained in the Republic.

"Lauret."

He swung round at his name, Baptista standing in the archway on the other side of the bridge. "There was nothing there."

"*What?*" Lauret croaked.

"There was nothing hidden at the Castilano shop. You cringing turd, you were lying—"

"No, monsieur! No, I was not! There *is* something in the Castilano shop. Something valuable, something important—"

"What exactly?" Baptista asked, moving towards the

merchant. "Please tell me, because I could find nothing. But then again you told me to look for a notepad – "

"A list."

"Very well, a list! But you didn't say *where* to look."

"Because I didn't know where! I just heard about some list." Lauret blundered.

"And then – after I have been treated like a fucking clown – I hear that you are trying to sneak off and leave Venice." Baptista walked over to Lauret, prodding him in his belly. "All dressed up, like a big fat beetle. You do realise how ridiculous you look? Those bowed legs of yours and that bald head make you look like a pair of nutcrackers." He reached into his pocket, Lauret flinching. "You think I'm going to cut your throat? No, runt, not yet anyway."

Sweating, Lauret blundered on. "I was told the list was in the shop and that it was the names of the people who were involved—"

"*In what?*"

"I don't know!" Lauret said desperately. "Some crime, perhaps? I don't know what! I've told you everything I know, monsieur," he stopped talking suddenly, his panic subsiding as he remembered something. "No! No, there *is* a little something I have for you. Something that you will like—"

"That I will like?"

"Yes. No... Maybe," Lauret was moving from foot to foot, his bladder leaking. "I remembered who the girl was and where I'd seen her before."

"*Which* girl?"

"The girl that stole the old man's purse in the market."

"The imaginary girl?

"She is **not** imaginary," Lauret replied, his tone pleading. "I knew of her in Paris. Her name's Tita Boldini. She looked different when she was in France, I think she has darkened her hair, dressed it differently – but it's definitely her. I would swear it on my life."

"There you go again, holding your life so cheaply." Baptista replied, but Lauret could see he was interested, his mocking tone had a curiosity to it. "Tita Boldini is one of Caterina Zucca's whores."

Lauret nodded. "And in Paris she worked for Madame Dinette."

"And why did she leave Paris?"

"I don't know—"

"That is not the answer I was looking for, Lauret."

"—but I can find out!"

"Much better. But there is still the matter of the elusive list, and your sneaking departure." He tapped the Frenchman on his bald head. "What would I have done without you, Lauret? You can't leave Venice. You stay here as long as I tell you to. As long as I need you." He tapped his head again, this time so hard it made the man wince. "Do I not pay you well enough to serve me?"

Lauret stammered. "Monsieur, you do... you do... not pay me."

"You're alive, aren't you?" Baptista replied smiling. "Now let's go over this again. You told me about a list which had important information which could be valuable for me to have... Surely you must know more about it?"

"Only that it was dangerous if it got into the wrong hands."

Baptista folded his arms. "So we have a dangerous list. Why? Are the page poisoned?"

"Not dangerous like that."

"Ah, so you *do* know more about it."

Lauret could feel a trickle of urine run down his leg, his voice shaking. "No one said anything about poison, it's more the names on the list, that's what's dangerous."

"So why would anyone hide this lethal list in a dress shop?" Baptista enquired dryly. "Or was Signora Castilano involved?"

"No, no." Lauret replied, shaking his head. "She left Venice because she was frightened. You know all about it, her maid was killed. My beautiful Gabriella had no arms or legs, they were cut off and her face disfigured—"

"And you still insist that have no idea who killed her?"

"Why *would* I know?" Lauret replied, stricken.

"Because you seem to know so much about it. Perhaps it was *you*? After all, with your podgy fingers and your bald head, you are no Adonis. Did you try to seduce Gabriella and she laughed at you?"

"No!"

"A man doesn't like to be mocked, and there is..." he looked him up and down, "... a lot of you to mock."

"I would never have hurt Gabriella," Lauret said helplessly. "she was like a daughter to me."

Baptista feigned ignorance. "So how did they know it was her?"

"What?"

"If her face was disfigured how could they be sure it was Gabriella Russo?"

"The painter Tintoretto identified her ..."

"Ah, Tintoretto."

"... Gabriella used to sit for him and he saw her body in the morgue." Lauret could tell that he had Baptista's interest and hurried on. "The painter went to the authorities to tell them who she was, and then he went to see Marina Castilano—"

"Why would he do that?"

"To tell her what had happened to her maid."

Baptista's eyebrows rose. "And Marina Castilano left Venice because of this?"

Lauret nodded. "She was scared away. Returned to Spain."

"And who were Marina Castilano's friends in Venice?"

The urine had soaked into the left leg of Lauret's breeches, the silk sticking to his thigh as he continued. "She knew many people and had customers who only wanted the best available in Venice. She was very well respected. I sold her some of my finest linens—"

"Get on with it!" Baptista snapped.

"—she knew Caterina Zucca quite well and I know she visited Barent der Witt."

"The Dutchman..." Baptista said, musing. "Now there is a man who moves around Venice like a lizard, getting in all the nooks and crannies, the intriguing glass vial always around his neck. I hardly think that dour creature is attempting to be fashionable. Tell me, Lauret" Baptista said, "what do you suppose is in that vial?"

"A potion?"

"'*A potion?*'" Baptista repeated. "And what would this potion be used for?"

Lauret was sweating. He had been relieved to slide off

the subject of the list, but now he was being interrogated about the inscrutable der Witt he wavered.

"Perhaps for... There are rumours about the Dutchman everywhere. He's from The Hague –"

"Hence he's called 'The Dutchman'" Baptista replied sarcastically.

"—yes, but he had to leave there because his daughter died."

Baptista whistled between his teeth. "Do you see how helpful you can be, Lauret, when you try? Like telling me about The Wolves of Venice, as Gabriella called them. Perhaps, do you think, that Barent der Witt might be one of these Wolves?" Lauret stared at him, not knowing how to reply as Baptista continued. "And perhaps this list, the one in the shop – that wasn't in the shop – contains the names of all these legendary Wolves. Would that make sense?"

Cautiously, Lauret answered: "I don't know."

"That's right, you don't. But you said something when we last spoke which I've been thinking about. You said '... *If I tell you, don't say you heard it from my lips. It would be the end for me...*' Now, explain something, will you? If you are just sharing with me the existence of this list, how would that be dangerous for you?" he put his forefinger over Lauret's lips to silence him and then continued. "In itself, it wouldn't be. But it would be very dangerous if you knew *who* was listed. And that makes me wonder if your sudden desire to leave Venice was not merely due to my presence – but to what you know."

Lauret was breathing rapidly, leaning against the stonework and trying to get his breath. His face was flushed, one puffy hand wiping the sweat off his forehead.

"I swear to God I don't know who they are."

"Did Gabriella Russo?"

He shook his head wearily. "How would I know?"

"But it was her who told you about the list?"

"Yes, but—"

"Did she confide in you before she was killed? Did she tell you who was on that list?"

"No, no—"

"Seems odd that the girl who was murdered was the same girl who knew about these 'Wolves of Venice' and this dangerous list. Perhaps she was killed because of what she knew?..."

Lauret could feel his pulse thundering in his ears, his heartbeat unnaturally loud, and thought he might pass out, even die on a stone bridge over a grimy canal.

"... It would seem that you have two choices." Baptista continued. "You can try to leave Venice again, but that would fail as I have spies along the quayside who would stop you. Or you could think about Gabriella Russo. How she ended up without her arms and legs and her face slashed. And then you could imagine *your* fat little torso tossed into the Adriatic, bopping about for the fish to nibble at, your eyes open to the beaks of the sea birds—"

"I can't help you!" Lauret wailed, his voice barely audible.

"But you must. Because by helping me you would be helping yourself. To be truthful, you have no other choice. And you realise that too, Lauret... Let me know what you 'remember' as soon as you can." He looked down at the merchant's feet. "You've pissed yourself. If I were you, I'd make up my mind whilst I still had a bladder."

Chapter Thirty Three

The door was slightly ajar as Bakita looked through the crack into Caterina's bedroom. He knew his mistress was at a concert, Leonardo Donato, the Doge, holding a lavish banquet after a recital in honour of the Spanish ambassador, a man known for his culture and also for his politicking. In order to continue the good relations between the countries, the Ambassador had brought with him a gift, a painting by Jan Gossaert, a Dutch artist of considerable repute, and after the feast there was to be a firework exhibition in St Marks.

Such a display had never been seen in Venice before and there was intense excitement, even some anxiety. Would the fireworks burn people? Or set fire to the houses? Would they destroy Venice and why would the Doge risk such destruction?

Years earlier, Lev Izmailov, ambassador to Peter the Great, had reported from China that they made *'such fireworks that no one in Europe has ever seen'*. But now they *would* see them, the Spanish Ambassador had declared boastfully, and marvel.

Bakita listened at the door, then moved his position slightly to see into the room from a better angle. What he had expected to see was his employer, Caterina Zucca, making an early return. Perhaps she had become tired, he reasoned, or brought back a client. But the woman Bakita caught sight of was not Caterina, it was Tita Boldini. Alone, carrying only one candle and bent over her mistress's dressing table.

He wondered at her recklessness and then realised that Tita would have expected him to accompany Caterina to the palazzo, as he usually accompanied her everywhere. Silent, his powerful form and ornate costume making his presence unmissable. But that evening Caterina had been collected by a lover and had needed no guard on the outing.

Bakita watched as Tita opened the middle drawer of the dressing table, easing it out with both hands. She was very quiet, he thought, adept, moving without making noise. A practised thief – because he was certain stealing was not something new to her. She was also careful to keep the candle away from the window, where it might be seen through the crack in the shutters. He presumed that she would also have some explanation prepared; that it had not been her, but one of the other girls. Or that she had forgotten her mistress was out and had come to bid her goodnight.

Abruptly, Tita turned round. Bakita knew she could not see him through the crack in the door, but she seemed to be looking straight at him, her pupils dilating like those of a cat. He felt a chill go through him but stayed motionless; expecting the woman to sense she was being watched and hurriedly leave the room. But she didn't, instead she moved *towards* the door.

"Who's there?"

He remained silent, startled when Tita snatched open

the door. Her expression was challenging. "The great black knight, what are you doing here?" she asked, tilting her head to one side. "Oh, I remember, your Italian is poor, I will speak slowly. What – are – you – doing?"

"You steal." He said flatly, taking her wrist and shaking her arm until she dropped the jewelled bracelet she had been holding. It fell onto the rug, the rubies glowing in the candlelight.

"I borrowed it—"

"You steal." He repeated. "I tell mistress."

"You tell your mistress?" Tita said mockingly. "I don't think so." She moved over to him and ran her hand down his chest, lingering over his crotch. "You stay quiet and will make you happy." Her hand moved expertly, her lips parting as she dropped to her knees.

"No." Bakita said, stepping back. "You steal, I tell mistress."

"I wouldn't do that," Tita replied, standing up and speaking very slowly so he would understand the import of what she said. "Just go back to your room and forget what you saw... You like it here, don't you, Bakita? You like your mistress?" she fingered the braided epaulette on his left shoulder. "You like your costume, with all its fripperies..."

He couldn't understand all of what she said, but he could see the threat in her eyes. "You are no good."

"Go back to your pen, African, or I will destroy you. Make sure your black arse is returned to a slave ship with the recommendation that your next owner should be a man, someone who uses strict discipline." She stooped to pick up the bracelet, but he put his foot over it.

"No."

"Yes," she replied, clawing at his leg, her nails leaving long scratches down his calf. Then before Bakita had time to react, she lunged at his face and scratched his cheek, her other hand ripping the fabric of her chemise, her hair unfastening. He reached out to catch hold of her, but she was fast and ducked out his way, running down the stairs and into the kitchen. A moment later he could hear hysterical sobbing, the coachman rushing upstairs carrying a sciopetta pistol.

"Move and I'll shoot." The man commanded.

Bakita put up his hands. "I did nothing, nothing—"

"You attacked that girl, bastardo, the mistress will deal with you."

"No, no," Bakita pleaded. "she lies –"

"**You** lie, pig. Look at your face – you're covered in scratches where she tried to fight you off," he gestured to the stairs. "Move! Go on, get a move on. And be grateful I don't shoot and say you tried to run." He forced Bakita downstairs and then locked him in the cellar. "You've run out of luck. It's going to be bad for you now," the coachman shouted through the door, "you're headed for the fucking galleys again. Bastard."

Pietro Aretino glanced around the drawing room of the Gianetti palazzo, noticing that he had been put into one of the less impressive chambers and not the most palatial. He found the thought irksome, a pinch to his pride, but showed nothing in his face when Lavinia Gianetti entered. She came accompanied with a slight, squirrel faced man who was holding a sheaf papers, a pen in his left hand.

"My dear Contessa –"

Lavinia waved aside the words, gesturing for the writer to take a seat. With some annoyance Aretino noted that the offered chairs were narrow and found himself sitting perched on the edge of the seat, the wood creaking under him.

"Why did you wish to see me, Signor Aretino?

"I wanted to offer my condolences on the death of your esteemed son –"

"You already sent your compliments when Jacopo died."

"—and I am most concerned about your grandson's whereabouts."

"Marco has been missing for four months. Since June, in fact, and now we are in October."

"Time does not stop for any of us, Contessa."

"Do you expect it to?" she replied tartly, gesturing to the squirrel like man. "This is my lawyer, Ranuccio Ferriti."

"Surely there is no need for lawyers –"

"I invited him here as a witness."

Aretino's smile turned to a grimace, then he recovered himself. "I mean only to offer my help in any way—"

"Then I could help me by telling me why you were blackmailing my son." Lavinia replied, glancing over to Ferriti who was taking notes, before turning back to Aretino. "This gentleman is my confidante, a man in whom I place absolute trust. You may speak freely in front of him, Signor Aretino. Now, I will ask you again, why were you blackmailing my son?"

"*Blackmail?*"

"Don't feign indignation, that is only for the innocent," she responded. "You relish in your reputation. You love your hold over the many puppets you control. So let us be frank – what is – *was* – your hold over Jacopo? Or was your interest in my grandson – of which neither of us approved – was *that* what gave you pleasure?" she gazed at him, her eyes penetrating. "No, that would not be enough. Jacopo would have paid you to stay away from Marco, and you would have agreed to the arrangement. So, obviously there was something else that you used as your weapon."

"Contessa, if anyone else had spoken to me as you have done today –"

"Hold your tongue! I am not afraid of you. I am old and disinclined to be threatened by a bully." Lavinia retorted. "I am also very rich, and not without my own power."

"Your power is over, Contessa," he replied with a thin film of contempt. "You are, as you rightly say, old, and you are not the heir to the Gianetti fortune. Once you had great power, but no longer. This is not the Venice it used to be."

"That is true, but there were crimes and villains before. There were thieves and charlatans and the worst of whores, but the city could manage them. But your kind of criminal – with your cohorts like Adamo Baptista and your secrets and threats – your sort gets fatter and fatter on other peoples' money and misery." She glanced over to Ferriti. "Are you writing this down?"

"Si, Contessa."

"*Eccellente*. I want every word to be accurately recorded." Her attention moved back to Aretino. "And please don't threaten me with a court case, signor. You can hardly claim slander."

"Despite your hostility towards me, Contessa, I would like to help you to find Marco."

"So you can fleece my grandson of his inheritance?"

"You think me capable of that, Contessa?" Aretino replied smoothly. "But how? The law is on his side, the side of inheritance. Of course, should your beloved grandson remain missing in time he would – forgive me – be declared dead. And then naturally there would be questions as to the Gianetti legacy. I believe you have male relatives, Contessa?"

Buffoons, Lavinia thought, incompetent men who would mishandle or waste the Gianetti inheritance. Males who had succeeded in life due to their genealogy, rather than their skill or courage. Over the months Lavinia had reluctantly considered the possibility that Marco might never return, but she doubted it. He had been forced to leave Venice, or gone of his own accord, *for a reason*. And if she discovered the reason she was convinced she would find Marco. Then, with the heir back in Venice, she could guide her grandson, advice him, and keep some control.

"I do not wish to discuss the Gianetti legacy with you, Signor Aretino. What I would like to know is this – what did Jacopo have, or do, that he needed to keep a secret? What secret was then discovered by you and used against him? You are a blackmailer by profession –"

"An author, Contessa."

"—of obscene literature."

He inclined his head. "The Church has declared it so. But Venice has been generous to my talents and rewarded me for my wit."

"Venice is generous to all manner of vagabonds. But she is equally dismissive of those who fall from grace, or lose the favour of the Doge." She sighed. "Your rise to prominence was affected largely by my son. His recommendations allowed you entry into the highest echelons of Venetian society and the Doge's Palace itself – places that would otherwise have been off limits."

"I disagree, Contessa, my literary works have made my name—"

"In Rome, not in Venice. In the Republic it was *Jacopo Gianetti* who made your name – after you had been dismissed from Rome." Lavinia paused, moving her position on her seat, her hip paining her.

"You are suffering, Contessa?"

"As you will, when – or *if* – you reach my age, signor."

"You lost your husband whilst you were young and now – at the end of your life – your dear son, Jacopo, has died." He shook his head in mock pity. "Your life has been full of tragedy, Contessa, the suicide of Marco's mother a great scandal and then the untimely death of Jacopo's second wife following on... I often wondered why Jacopo did not marry again. But then perhaps he did not wish to suffer any further losses."

Lavinia's expression remained calm. "Are you implying something?"

"About what?"

"The deaths of my daughters in law."

"We are all mortal, Contessa, it is up to the good Lord to decide when He calls us."

Slowly, she smiled. "Now I understand more clearly why Jacopo despised you. He did not fear you, but he was wary of what you could do to harm him." She glanced over to her lawyer. "Signor Ferriti and I would like to know if you are in any way involved with the disappearance of my grandson."

"Me?" Aretino replied, his forefinger pointing to his own chest. "Why would I be involved?"

"Marco was fascinated by you, and stupidly impressed. I blame his father because he had lived too isolated a life for a rich young man. In that respect, Marco was perfectly positioned for your manipulative attentions. I do not doubt that you flattered him by your interest and mesmerised him by your decadence. Your tastes are abnormal, but I presume you provided my grandson with women and the finest wines. Oh, and also a *gondola*. I heard you had provided one hand painted and decorated with Marco's own initials in gold." She sighed. "Your courting would have been manna to a boy who had been repeatedly dismissed by his father."

"Your grandson has great charm, it was a pleasure—"

"The pleasure was purely yours. You are not a man of kindness, Marco was serving a purpose for you or you would not have pretended to be his friend. The question I am asking is simple – what is my grandson's purpose?"

Aretino struggled to his feet, heaving his vast bulk out of the chair with difficulty and aware that the lawyer was surreptitiously laughing at him.

"I came here in good faith, Contessa, but I have been insulted. I do not know anything of Marco's disappearance or his whereabouts. Whether you believe it or not, I was very fond of him—"

"You use the past tense, signor." Lavinia remarked. "Is that a subtle hint?"

"An error in my grammar, no more," he replied, nettled. "If you would excuse me, Contessa, I must take my leave. Rest assured, despite your hostility, I will endeavour to find your grandson with all the means at my disposal. And should you require my help, you have only to ask."

Lavinia looked up at him from her seat, her expression dismissive. "I will ask nothing from you, and I have nothing *for* you, Signor. There are no secrets in my life to pad out your pockets."

Aretino bowed smoothly. "Can you be sure, Contessa? Can you really be *so* sure?"

Chapter Thirty Four

That October – the autumn of 1548 – the city was plagued by fog. It would descend at dawn and linger, grey and listless, around the great, dank bulk of St Marks and the sullen Lagoon. With the fog came the wind, brisk and persistent, making loading and unloading difficult for the boatmen. Many of the most violent gusts capsized the smaller vessels, merchants desperately trying to retrieve their spilled goods before they fell down to the sea's end. And under the wooden posts that held the city afloat, sank silver from Holland and spices from the Far East. The Lagoon grabbed at its bounty and the silt below welcomed its unaccustomed wealth.

The cold brought sickness as the damp swung up from the canals and from the cellars of palazzos. Starved of its summer heat, the walls grew chilled, fires making little impression, beds heaped with furs and tapestries. In the poorer areas of Venice the tanners, the dressmakers and the inhabitants of the ghetto looked to each other for comfort, keeping together, huddled like calves to a cow.

Only the glassworkers found enough warmth, the cramped conditions and the unending fires holding the damp at bay. In front of the great mouths of the furnaces, men sweated whilst their arms ached supporting the iron rods which – at their ends – carried the molten glass droplets. Against the darkening light the infernal ovens blazed like the mouth of Hades. With speed and skill the men fashioned the molten glass then dipped it into buckets of water, a hissing coming up like the warning from a snake pit.

Yet on the streets and bridges the weather had its way, Barent der Witt walking with his head bowed against a push of wind. Dishevelled and irritable, he entered Caterina's sitting room, took off his coat and hat and allowed her to lead him over to the fireplace.

"Come, my friend, you must be cold. A little Cognac, perhaps? I have some come from France, and it is quite superb."

He sat down in the seat next to hers in front of the fire.

"A little would be good. Thank you."

"You sound morose, Dutchman," she teased him.

"I would have thought to find you the same." He replied, "That is why I came here today, to talk to you about this business with your guard."

Caterina clicked her fingers in a gesture of annoyance. "Bakita attacked Tita. If she hadn't have got away from him God knows what might have happened. The poor girl was shaken, she didn't stop crying for an hour. And he denied it!" she said incredulously. "Can you imagine? With scratches all over his face and poor Tita with her chemise ripped—"

"You are wrong."

She blinked, confused, then waved aside the maid who had brought in the cognac on a tray. When they were alone again, Caterina turned to her visitor,

"I am wrong?" she repeated, pouring two glasses and handing one to der Witt. "But I have seen the evidence with my own eyes."

"No, you have seen the evidence you were *supposed* to see, and you have drawn the conclusion you were *supposed* to draw." Der Witt paused, sipped the cognac and felt the warmth flood his gut. "Tell me, Caterina, did Bakita ever – by a look or a word – make you feel threatened?"

"No…"

"Did any of the your girls complain about his behaviour?"

"They teased him for being shy!" She sipped at her drink. "But that does not mean anything—"

"Did they complain about him?"

"No."

"And although Bakita went with you everywhere, he never did anything to displease you, did he?..."

"No, he didn't." she agreed, "but that does not absolve him of guilt."

"...and the only time he *allegedly* did anything wrong was the one night you did not require his services?"

She nodded, but was unconvinced. "He could have been waiting for when I was absent and then took his chance."

The Dutchman shook his head. "Then let me ask you something else, Caterina. Did Bakita show any particular interest in Tita Boldini?"

She thought for a moment, then shook her head. "No. No, he didn't."

"In fact, he avoided her, didn't he?"

Caterina drained her cognac before replying. "Perhaps he *did* avoid her..."

"He did, I saw him. I also noticed that if Tita Boldini

approached him, or passed by him, he would avert his eyes and step away from her."

"Shyness makes men act strangely at times."

"It wasn't shyness," der Witt replied, "your guard was *afraid* of her. He always has been. Surely you noticed, Caterina? He would never look at her directly—"

"This is not proof of anything! But the scratches *are* proof—"

"Proof of what?" The Dutchman took hold of her hand and examined the nails. "*You* could reproduce the scratches on Bakita or on Tita Boldini. Any woman could inflict those injuries to make it look as though they were done in self defence. Any woman could rip her clothes and say she was attacked... Has Tita Boldini any scratches, any bruises?"

Caterina frowned. "No... no, nothing."

"Bakita is a big man, if he had attacked her she would have some injury on her body. Yet she has none. She is lying, I do not believe that your guard harmed her in any way. It was a lie."

"But why would she do that?"

"She wanted to have you to herself, to have power—"

Caterina shook her head. "The girl is a whore, like the rest of us – what power could she wield over me?"

"You are not thinking clearly." Der Witt replied, "Bakita is your guard, the person who keeps you safe. You brought him here because you were afraid, remember? You told me how much safer you felt with him in the house and how much it pleased you that he remained outside your door, day and night, even sleeping on a bench there."

"That's true, I was reassured by his presence."

"Naturally. The death of Gabriella, and Marina Castilano's

visits, had terrified you. You forget how you were, Caterina, but I don't. You could not sleep, could not stop thinking of what Gabriella had told you – and her murder." He paused before continuing. "Then Bakita came here as your guard, shortly after you had taken on Tita Boldini..."

She was listening intently. "Go on."

"How did she react to his arrival?"

"She was dismissive."

"Cruel?"

"At first she would taunt him, yes. I heard her a couple of times mocking him for his uniform. She said that in France only a eunuch would wear such silliness. I admonished her for it and told her to—"

"To what?"

"Apologise."

Der Witt grimaced. "My dearest Caterina, even a whore would resist apologising to a slave. I imagine the animosity she felt for Bakita intensified then."

"I still don't understand why Tita would want to get rid of him. We are women, we need each other for support and company, she should have been pleased to have a man guarding us."

Der Witt clicked his tongue.

"How do you survive in this city, Caterina?" he asked, irritated. "So clever between the sheets, so naïve with people. Tita Boldini has presented one face to you and you have taken it for reality. Whereas I have seen her other face. I have seen who she really is ..."

The Dutchman paused, listening, then quickly rose to his feet and opened the door. Tita had been eavesdropping, and although at first startled, soon recovered her composure.

"I apologise, Caterina, I did not know you had a guest."

"Tita, what a surprise." Der Witt studied the girl. "Do you need any treatment for your injuries after the brutal attack on your person?"

Her gaze held his. "You are very kind, but no, thank you."

"Bakita has been taken to the new prison, did you know?"

She glanced over to Caterina, then looked back at der Witt. "What of it?"

"Earlier today I visited him. He had a story to tell. One which bore no resemblance to yours, Signora Boldini. In fact, Bakita told me that he had caught you in your mistress's bedroom whilst she was out—"

"Is this true?" Caterina asked, getting to her feet and facing Tita.

"— and that you were stealing."

"You little whore!" Caterina snapped, lunching towards the younger woman.

But Tita ducked behind the Dutchman and held her ground. "How could you believe that slave over me? It's not true! He's lying! Everything Bakita said is a lie! I wasn't even in your bedroom. He's jealous, he wants you to himself. He told me so. And the only way he could do that was to get rid of me." Her voice wavered. "Bakita attacked me and I defended myself. How could you even suggest that I would make up such a story?"

"Perhaps it was not your story at all, Tita," the Dutchman replied, "Perhaps you merely performed this fiasco on the orders of someone else—"

"What are you talking about!"

"— there are many spies in this city, many informants. It

is often difficult to know who is in whose pocket. Villains work for their paymasters but their allegiance changes like the wind outside." His voice hardened. "I saw you, Tita."

She hesitated before answering.

"I told you, Marina Castilano asked me to look after her shop."

"*What has Marina Castilano got to do with any of this?*" Caterina asked dumbfounded, der Witt silencing her and turning back to the girl.

"I'm not talking about our 'meeting' at the shop. I'm talking about *your* meeting with Adamo Baptista."

Defiant, she threw back her head. "What of it? He hired me. I'm a whore and he paid me for my time."

"You were arguing, not having sex."

"Perhaps you're too old to remember passion." She replied slyly.

"Are you working for him?"

"He fucks me!"

"Apart from that. Are you spying for Adamo Baptista? Is that why you came to work here, to spy on Caterina Zucca?"

She sighed, putting her hands on her hips. "This is insanity. *Folie!*"

"Adamo Baptista lived in Paris for while, didn't he?"

"How would I know?"

"Because he used to frequent Madame Dinette's whorehouse and that was where you two became acquainted. You were one of Dinette's whores." Der Witt glanced over to Caterina, "You have a cuckoo in your nest, a very dangerous one, who wants to isolate you and will do everything in her power to make that happen."

Caterina stared at him, baffled. "But *why?*"

"I think she's been hired to do so." He glanced over to Tita. "What is your purpose here?"

"I've told you, old man, Adamo Baptista is just a customer—"

Impatient, Der Witt turned back to Caterina. "Where do you keep your jewellery?"

"In my dressing table."

"You have a key?"

"Naturally," she replied, moving into another room and returning a moment later with a key. "Here you are."

"Is this the only key?"

"Yes."

"And is it always hidden?"

"Always."

"But someone could search and find it, couldn't they? Someone with access to the house, someone free to look around when you aren't here."

Tita interrupted them. "Why would you immediately think that it was *me* who took the key! Bakita must have stolen it when he tried to steal your ruby bracelet—"

Der Witt sighed. *"Why would this woman know about a ruby bracelet" he asked Caterina, "... if she hadn't been the one stealing it?"*

Wrong footed, Tita started to bluster. "Everyone knows you had that bracelet!"

"No, they didn't. I was given that piece just before I went out." Caterina replied coldly. "In fact, I was going to wear it, but decided not to and locked it in the middle drawer of my dressing table. Where only **we** knew about it... *You lying bitch!*" she hissed at the girl, hurrying over to the drawer and then looking back to der Witt, her voice relieved. "The bracelet's still here."

He nodded. "I know. Bakita said Tita had dropped it when he confronted her. When she ran off he put it back in the drawer. Meanwhile she had alerted the coachman and he came up here, armed, to challenge Bakita—"

"Lies!"

"No, Tita. You knew that by charging him with assault he would be put in gaol, most likely shipped out of Venice. You got rid of him to protect yourself."

"I could report you to the authorities," Caterina said, her voice icy. "I could have you flogged—"

Hesitant, Tita looked at der Witt and then turned to Caterina. Her uncertainty had gone, replaced by a chilling poise.

"*You could have me flogged?* I could do a lot worse to you," she said unpleasantly. "You do well to be afraid, Signora Zucca, you are *not* safe, and never will be again."

Unnerved, Caterina took a moment to answer. "What are you talking about?"

"*The Wolves of Venice*. Sound familiar to you, Caterina? And to you, der Witt?" Tita asked.

Cautious. the Dutchman nodded. "Yes, I've heard the phrase before. But I don't know what it meant. I wondered if it was just a sobriquet for the vagabonds in Venice, or if it referred to anyone in particular."

"You think yourself so clever, don't you?"

"On the contrary, I am floundering." He admitted. "Then remain that way," she replied, moving towards the door. "I'm leaving now. Both of you stay where you are, and let me go. If you do not, Dutchman, I will personally see to it that the Inquisition know of the abortions you perform and the black magic—"

"Rumours, nothing more."

"Like the rumour concerning your daughter's death?"

He flinched, Caterina staring at Tita. "*What rumour?*"

"Ask der Witt what I mean – when you're next fucking him." She paused, opening the door. "I tried to warn you, Dutchman, but you wouldn't listen. And as for you, Caterina, I would keep very quiet about Gabriella Russo. Forget everything she said, everything she so unwisely confided in you. She had a bad death, one you would not wish to suffer yourself—"

Der Witt moved towards her, but she put up her hands.

"No further, or I will keep good my threat. *The Wolves of Venice* are real. All four of them. You have no power against them, no protection—"

"You think you can frighten anyone with fairytales?" der Witt said, his tone dismissive. "Stories to scare children, nothing more."

She shook her head, pointing to the window. "You see the mist outside? How it gets into everything, unseen and unheard? How it moves where it wishes and hides wherever – and whatever – it chooses?" She paused, glancing at the Dutchman. "As you well know, Marina Castilano was afraid. So afraid that she has now left Venice."

"And why were you in her shop?" der Witt asked.

"I am looking after the premises."

"No," he said flatly, "you were *searching* them. Did you find it?"

"Find what?"

"Whatever you were searching for." Der Witt replied,

"The shoes perhaps?" he said, moving towards her. "They aren't there, I've looked. Did you steal them, then return them later? It would have been easy for you, being a clever thief. Did you do it on someone's orders? To scare away the woman who owned the shop and leave the place empty and available to search?"

She sighed extravagantly. "You are old, and your mind is wandering."

"No, Gabriella worked there and she was afraid – just as Marina Castilano was."

"I wonder if she has returned safely to Spain..." Tita replied coolly. "... Or maybe her trip was interrupted."

"Dear God—"

She smiled at Caterina, her tone harsh. "God will not help you, but I can – if you listen to me. Say nothing. Do nothing. Remember nothing. And forget everything that has passed here tonight."

Caterina glanced at der Witt and then looked back to Tita Boldini. "And if we don't?"

"If you do not follow my instructions it would be a pity, and you may find yourself following in Marina Castilano's footsteps."

I had moved from Sicily to Naples, then on to Rome.

The Gianetti name – and the fortune that was mine for the claiming – was enough to grant me entry into the most affluent and influential of circles. A fugitive I was not; I ran only from myself. And I wondered daily what had happened back in Venice. If Rosella had been seduced by Adamo Baptista, or if she had managed her escape.

It would not have been possible, I knew that, however much I lied to myself. Aretino wanted his sport and would not have been denied his trophy. At times I convinced myself that it was not just my fault, that it was due, in part, to Ira's hatred of the writer; he had insulted him and Aretino would never forget a slight. But in reality I knew his ploy had been a three pronged attack; to revenge himself on Ira, corrupt me, and dishonour Rosella. How better to punish Ira than by smearing his sister's reputation. Reputation was all in Venice, in any Italian city, her association with Baptista – however innocent – would have dishonoured her and severely lessened her marital chances.

Would Angelo Fasculo still drop flowers outside her door? Would the badly written notes with the fingerprint smudges on them still slide under the Tabat entry? Or had the flowers died on the step and the paper withered, blown away by a push of wind? Did Rosella attend the synagogue with Ira, or speak in private to her rabbi? She had always been devout, was she still? And did she sit for Tintoretto and perhaps, once in a while, did they talk of me?

They should have cursed me, but their hatred would have been nothing to my self loathing. My cowardice bewildered me, my stupidity unbelievable. Such had been my devotion to Aretino I had betrayed my friends and failed to attend the funeral of my own father. Truly I can say that not one day passed without a sickening regret, without seeing myself as the writer's puppet, played to perfection by a master's hand.

"Hide it, quick, quick," Rosella had commanded me once in the studio, and I had bundled up Tintoretto's smock and hidden under his portfolio.

We watched like children as he roared and cursed, tipping over a small table and declaring that he would dismiss me and never paint Rosella again... Looking back, I believe he was entering into the game with us, as willing to be duped as we were to dupe. Then later I would walk Rosella home and she would stare at the courtesans in their extravagant gowns, believing that I did not notice her envy.

But what was I but envious?

Even with my gilded name, the Gianetti fortune and the ridiculous, absurd, frigidly glorious legacy, what was I but envious of others' influence and power? And hadn't I proved the depth of my envy by betraying those I loved in return for the favour of a charlatan?

I make no excuses for what I did, there are no excuses, and I swore I would make amends. But it took two weeks for me to find the courage. Finally I went to see Rosella, but she would not open the door to me. I waited outside, but she never left the house that night, or the next. At dawn on the third day, I returned, seeing her make her way to the market. Her eyes were swollen from crying and I ached – ached – with remorse. I called her name and she ignored me, and Hyman Golletz saw us, looking down as he turned away.

Only the previous week he had invited me to his home to eat with his family but in the ghetto everyone saw and knew everything. And he had known – even hours after the event – that Rosella Tabat had been out walking with Adamo Baptista. And before long he would know that I had plotted the whole wretched scenario.

"What do you want?" Rosella asked finally, turning to me. "Do you want to know what happened with Adamo Baptista?" her voice wavered, "What did you want to happen, Marco?"

"I didn't mean –"

"'Mean what!'" she hurled back. "Why did you trick me? Why would you do that?"

"I did not think –"

"No, you did not." She agreed, her tone bitter. "You would you do anything to please Aretino and his ilk. You are no better than a pack of dogs."

She cried again, walking on, and I ran after her. I cajoled her, begged her to forgive me. Knew that she had not slept with Baptista – just as I knew people would believe she had. I touched her arm and she brushed me away and walked on faster over a bridge. We passed many people and saw the Dutchman, Barent der Witt, and moments later she entered the Basilica di Santa Maris Gloriosa dei Frari. Together we took Mass and I prayed under Titian's swooping Assumption that we could be close again.

I missed her even then.

And knew, too late

I could have loved her.

But we were no longer engaged in one of Aretino's puppet shows; and I was no longer at the end of his string. We turned to each other for comfort. I, in my guilt, she, in her shame. When she cried, I held her to me and rocked her. I don't understand how, I had never been rocked as a child. But we were both lost children. The lost cling to each other and we did.

And so I betrayed her twice. Once with Baptista and secondly by my own actions. Afterwards we drew back from each other after that one helpless and desperate coming together; we parted without either of us explaining, but mutually letting go.

And then I ran.

Yes, that is how it was...

What I expected to happen afterwards I do not know.

It was months later when I finally turned myself homeward to Venice.

And The Wolves were waiting for me.

Chapter Thirty Five

"Ah, Signor Tintoretto, *Il Furioso*," Lavinia said by way of greeting. "Please come in and sit by the fire, this is most dreadful weather. Such damp I have not known for many years and there is nothing to lessen it. Or maybe that is merely my old bones." She watched as the painter took a seat, his curly hair long at the nape of his neck, his beard trimmed unevenly. So unlike the elegant Titian, Lavinia thought, and so much more likeable. "I would like to commission you for a portrait."

He smiled. "For yourself, Contessa?"

"No, no, I have too many portraits of myself! Titian painted the last one, he made me look like an old nanny goat."

"You are very cruel—" he teased her.

"No, no, *he* was the one who was cruel!" she replied, laughing, amused by his teasing. "No, this time I would to commission a portrait of my grandson, Marco." She tilted her head to one side. "Have you heard from him?"

Tintoretto shook his head.

"Sadly no, Contessa. And as he is no longer my apprentice, naturally your son's generous payment for his tutoring will cease—"

She tapped the floor with her stick irritably.

"Do not be foolish! All artists are poor, unless they are Titian, who is as rich as four kings. How such a genius can have a confidante like Aretino, I will never understand. No, no you must keep the money and keep working. You have such talent and Titian needs a rival. Your painting of *Esther before Ahasuerus* is magnificent. I believe you wish to combine the drawing of Michelangelo with the colouring of Titian. Is that not what the esteemed Paolo Pino claimed?"

Tintoretto flushed. "I have the quote upon my studio wall, Contessa. *'Il disegno di Michelangelo ed il colorito di Titian.'*"

"And you have succeeded, the four paintings for Scuola di St Marco are remarkable."

He inclined his head, always uncertain how to react to flattery. "You are most kind—"

"A moment ago I was cruel!" she replied, laughing again, Tintoretto relaxing. "Tell me something..." she leaned towards him, the stiff black bodice of her gown pressed against the white, paper-thin skin. "Is it true that you make little wax figures?"

"Sometime they are clay."

"And you place them in boxes to make your compositions?"

He nodded. "Yes, it's true."

"So that great swooping angel of yours began as just a little clay figure on the end of a piece of string?"

Tintoretto smiled. "It is strange you should mention that, Contessa. Marco had just begun his apprenticeship when I made that angel. I remember that he was also fascinated by it and by the tableaux I was working on...He was so light hearted then, happy to run errands like a grocer's boy, coming back laden with wooden boxes from the quayside."

"You miss him."

"Yes." Tintoretto agreed. "As must you, Contessa."

"Not so much." She admitted. "I am a frigid, unfeeling woman, with little affection in me. Which is why my son was a cold man and neither of us were as interested in Marco as we should have been. We neglected him."

"Neglect is a brutal word."

"But an honest one. You must understand something, my son detested Marco because he held him responsible for his mother's suicide. Which is absurd, but the mind is not logical, much like the emotions. The woman was *pazza*. She was unstable." Her honesty surprised him as she continued. "You looked shocked by my bluntness, signor, of course you are. Why, you are thinking, does this grim harpy confide in me? Why does she talk of an old scandal, why confess to such an unforgivable lack of love for her grandson?"

Tintoretto was unable to think of a suitable response. "Contessa I am in no position—"

"Hear me out, please. I am not losing my mind, Tintoretto, if that is what you suspect. My body is falling to pieces, but my brain is fresh, surprisingly so. Which is why I asked you to come here. Yes, I do want to commission a portrait of my grandson from you, that it true, but I also need an ally."

"An ally?"

She tapped the floor with her shoe. It reminded Tintoretto of a bejewelled black beetle scuttling out from under the skirt of her mourning dress, the jet beads blinking like scales.

"I have no time for games, signor! My son is dead and

the Gianetti inheritance is set to go to fools unless I secure it with the rightful heir. Who, as all of Venice knows, is at present missing. Please, if you would be so kind, tell me why my grandson left Venice."

He hesitated and she urged him to continue.

"Has it something to do with that reprobate, Aretino?" she tapped her stick on the floor again. "Come, come, we must trust each other! I put no duty on you, signor. I request nothing that will be against your principals or empty your coffers. I ask only for your honesty."

"Honesty is often dangerous –"

"Forget how I look, forget I am very old! I am also very strong." she snapped, "Whatever you say I will not die from shock, believe me. Too much has happened in my life for me to succumb until I have completed what needs to be done. *Was* Aretino blackmailing my grandson?"

Tintoretto stared at her, dumbfounded. "I do not know."

"The fat oaf was blackmailing my *son*," Lavinia confided. "I do not know what hold he had over Jacopo, but my son championed his career at court and with the Doges personally. He hated Aretino, and yet he endured him. He would visit the palazzo and Jacopo would feed him – the finest food always, delicacies that the gross pig feasted on – and my son would watch him with such loathing. I never knew what the control was, only that there had to be one. Perhaps Jacopo had cheated Aretino over property, or business? He was a greedy man, a great lover of money, acquisitive, always desiring more and more, but never fulfilled."

"I do not believe that I can help you, Contessa. Marco did not confide in me."

She frowned, leaning on the arm of her seat, her chin cupped in hand. "Maybe Aretino pricked my son's conscience over his wife's death." Her gaze fixed on the artist, "In case you are wondering, it was *not* murder, signor, but I know that Aretino would imply that Jacopo's behaviour was the cause of his wife's misery. Maybe he was right... Unfortunately my son's second wife died only a few years after they married. That was not murder either, she died of a chill. The weather was much like this and she was very delicate."

"You do not have to tell me these things, Contessa –"

"It is a relief to speak of them." she said honesty. "Secrets did not grow lighter with age, they weigh heavier and heavier until they force you into the grave beneath them." She hurried on, "I suspect that Aretino's interest in my grandson was to provoke Jacopo and add extra pressure, but, as I say, I cannot prove any of this."

Tintoretto stared at the old woman, wondering how much she really wanted the truth and what affect the revelation would have on her. To confide would be to destroy the image of her grandson, to transform him from a neglected boy into a cowardly man. And when she *did* know the truth, he wondered, would she still think Marco the rightful heir to the Gianetti fortune?

Because he didn't.

"The doctor who attended your son is Ira Tabat."

"Yes, yes, I know."

"Ira has a sister, Rosella, who works in the ghetto but also sits to me as a model." He smiled wistfully. "She and Marco were like brother and sister, always playing tricks on me, but when Aretino took Marco as his protégé your grandson changed, fell completely under the writer's thumb, impressed by his coterie and his way of life."

"His whores?"

"Yes," Tintoretto agreed. "Soon Marco's apprenticeship meant nothing to him. He would go missing for days. Although we all warned him of his association with Aretino, he was blinded, bewitched by him. He would do whatever the writer wanted and made him into a god."

Lavinia was listening intently, a pulse beating at her right temple. "Please, continue."

"You have heard of a man called Adamo Baptista?..."

She nodded. "Who has not? I believe he is dangerous and disreputable."

"... Marco would walk Rosella home before the curfew. As time passed, she didn't need a chaperone. But one night there had been fighting in the streets and Marco insisted that she was accompanied home." Tintoretto paused. "But he said he was busy and could not accompany her. So he had arranged for someone else to take her home—"

The old woman's eyes widened. "No."

"Sadly, yes."

"*Baptista?* My grandson arranged for that dark hearted man to act as chaperone?" she asked, shaken.

He nodded. "Of course Aretino was testing Marco, seeing where his loyalties lay. Would he endanger Rosella's reputation for him? Betray friendship for obsession?"

"And he did?"

"Yes... So Adamo Baptista walked Rosella home and people saw them and they talked. We all know how the city works. Reputation is everything for a woman, and she lost hers then."

"I cannot believe that Marco would do this!" Lavinia snapped. "It's so callous. So cowardly. I would never have thought it of him, Marco was always caring, always pleasing people. He was the only one of us who was kind," she said regretfully. "I can hardly believe it—"

"He had a good teacher. Aretino is a dangerous puppet master who plays with peoples' lives." Tintoretto paused, looked at his hands and at the fingers stained with paint, his thumbnail bruised. "Rosella is now carrying a child."

Lavinia leaned back in her chair, her face waxen. "She is pregnant with Adamo Baptista's child?"

Tintoretto shook his head regretfully. "No, Contessa," he said at last. "the baby is your grandson's."

Fidgeting in his seat, Aretino nodded graciously to the Doge's wife and then turned his attention back to the stage. The performers were acting out a new play along the lines of the Commedia del'Arte, but casting contemporary Venetians in the famous roles. It did not escape the writer that this new, hooked nosed, barrel gutted Pucchinello was based on him. How amusing, Aretino thought, making a mental note of the author as he applauded his apparent approval.

The chair beside him was abruptly taken, Adamo Baptista's bass voice low, but audible under the soprano's sweeping aria.

"I have some news that may interest you."

"News about Marco Gianetti's whereabouts?"

"No, news about Barent der Witt."

Aretino turned his feral eyes on Baptista. "*What* about the Dutchman?"

"His daughter died in mysterious circumstances, after which he left The Hague."

"What *kind* of mysterious circumstances?"

"She drowned."

"Hardly surprising..." Aretino said, applauding again and smiling at the Doge on the other side of the theatre. "... The Hague is full of fucking canals, what do you expect?"

"But a sixteen year old girl drowning in a canal is not usually *disfigured*."

Aretino turned his head to look at his companion. "Disfigured? How?"

"She was found without her limbs and her face slashed."

"Just like—"

"Yes. Marina Castilano's maid, Gabriella Russo." Baptista interrupted. "You remember Gabriella, don't you?"

"Don't be a turd, Adamo... When did this happen?"

"Four years ago."

"And was Barent der Witt suspected of being his daughter's killer?"

Baptista glanced at the stage, his gaze fixing on the Pucchinello figure. "You are being immortalised..." he said, amused. "...have you noticed how similar that actor's appearance is to yours?"

Aretino ignored the bait.

"You didn't answer my question, was the Dutchman suspected of his daughter's murder?"

"He was when he left The Hague."

Aretino considered the information. "But not *before* he left?"

"No, there had been no ill feeling, no trouble. There were just the two of them, Barent der Witt and his daughter. I think the authorities only suspected the apothecary when he left the country."

"How clever you are, finding out all this information." Aretino looked around the audience, craning his thick neck. "But where is your little friend, the luscious Volt? You should have brought him to the performance, he would have enjoyed it, I fancy the lad would do well following a theatrical career."

"He has no interest in the theatre."

"Do confide, what *are* his interests?"

"He listens. As I do."

"A spy in the making, you would do well to teach him all the tricks, Baptista, spies are in great demand in Venice."

"As they are in all great cities," Baptista replied deftly, Aretino's attention diverted back to their earlier conversation.

"Tell me, did the Netherland authorities continue to look for the girl's murderer after der Witt had left?"

"For a while, but it was soon forgotten. The family was not rich and had no power and the authorities let the matter drop. But then I discovered something else...." Baptista paused, the scene had ended and the audience was applauding vigorously, the opulent rococo ceiling of the theatre echoing with the sound, Baptista waiting for the noise to subside. When it finally did, he continued. "...another girl had been found in similar circumstances four months earlier in Paris..."

Aretino was listening avidly.

"... And at that time the Dutchman was in France. Although only for a short while before he moved on to Rome."

"Quite the traveller," Aretino commented. "but abortionists and quacks do have a varied and disparate clientele and tend to move from city to city." He gave Baptista a sidelong glance. "So our apothecary was in Paris when another girl was murdered?"

"It's possible, but my investigations suggest that he could have just left—"

"So it's not definitive either way?"

Baptista shook his head. "No one was looking for der Witt, so the people I talked to weren't emphatic about the dates."

"This is intriguing," Aretino continued. "So it's possible der Witt killed the girl in Paris? Murdered her in the same way as his daughter and Gabriella Russo. Most fascinating. But then again, it is of little interest to me at the moment, my mind is elsewhere. I asked you to find the whereabouts of Marco Gianetti."

"I have nothing to report yet."

"This is rather sad... Are you losing your considerable skill?"

"No more than you are losing yours," Baptista replied, "I do know that the Contessa has sent people to find her grandson. Without success."

Aretino stretched his legs out in front of him, his feet swollen, his ankles bulging over the edges of their embroidered velvet slippers.

"The old woman can't inherit the Gianetti fortune," he said. "and she won't want it to go to any of the fucking imbecile cousins – which it will do if Marco doesn't return to Venice and claim it. Of course, if he never returns the Republic could declare him dead."

"Perhaps he *is* dead."

"No, just hiding." Aretino shook his head. "And even though he knows that the insufferable Tabat will be waiting for him, Marco will return. Either to assuage his conscience or inherit." His gaze rested on Baptista. "I do wonder why Ira Tabat never went after you. Certainly it was Marco who set the play in motion, but you were the one who fucked his sister."

Baptista ignored the comment and continued with his previous thought. "Of course if any of the cousins *do* inherit the Gianetti fortune you won't get any of the money. You have no power over them: they are all God fearing and dull to a man. Jacopo was your fatted calf, Aretino, with his death and Marco's disappearance your lucrative association with the family is over." He stood up to leave, then bent down to Aretino, his voice lowered. "You never told me what your hold was on Jacopo Gianetti..."

"No, I didn't."

Baptista shrugged. "... It seems a pity that you have nothing with which to blackmail his son."

Laughing, Aretino touched Baptista on the cheek, an intimate action he knew would irritate him.

"My dear friend, my patronage of Marco was not merely to annoy his father. It is true that Jacopo is dead, but his valuable secret lives on. As potent and damning as it ever was. When the Prodigal returns I will visit the young heir and then – slowly, drop by drop – bleed Marco Gianetti dry." He chuckled, his belly jiggling. "Jacopo's secret is just another part of his legacy, that's all. And all legacies – like sins – pass down from father to son."

Chapter Thirty Six

Accompanied by her male servant and with her lawyer, Signor Ferriti walking alongside, Lavinia Gianetti was taken by sedan chair to the ghetto. Heavily veiled, she supported her body with cushions and rapped on the side of the chair when it jerked on uneven ground. The damp weather had affected her hip, pain making her irascible, her servant having to lift her out of her seat when they reached the entrance of the ghetto.

"*Non sono uno storpio!*" she snapped, poking the tip of her walking stick into the calf of one of her attendants. "I can walk!" Gesturing for her lawyer to approach, Signor Ferriti bowed and extended his arm.

"Thank you, I need to lean a little on you."

"A pleasure, Contessa," he replied as Lavinia righted herself and looked around.

The old woman was feisty today, he thought. He had tried to dissuade her, but she had insisted on visiting the ghetto, her mind fixed on a plan of action. One she had yet to share with him.

There was a sudden tug on his arm as they walked.

"*Idiota!* Slow down, you are here to help me, Ferriti, not to pull me over."

Slowly, they made their dilatory way under the arch at the entrance to the ghetto. Her face veiled, Lavinia pointed out a man exiting a doorway. A man who had already noticed her and was staring curiously.

"Tell him that I am visiting someone," Lavinia explained to her bemused lawyer, "and that I wish to call on the Tabat family."

Ferriti turned back to Hyman Golletz, who had overheard and was ready with his own question. "You are visiting the Tabats?"

"Did he not just say that?" Lavinia retorted impatiently. "Would you be so kind as to point out where they live?"

"You are come to see *Ira Tabat*?"

"Signor, forgive my candour..." Ferriti intervened, feeling Lavinia's grip on his arm tighten. "… but whom the Contessa has come to see is no business of yours."

"*Contessa?*" Hyman raised his eyebrows. The nobility coming to the ghetto, unheard of. And to see the Tabats. This was information he would be sharing later. "Contessa," he said, making a stiff bow, "sadly Ira is not here. He is a doctor—"

"I know, he attended my late son," she replied, brittle with pain and leaning heavily on her lawyer's arm. "I am very weary, and would like to sit down."

"Please, signor, where do the Tabat family live?" Ferriti asked. "If you would direct me."

But Hyman was not going to be excluded from the event and, at the head of the small party, he lead them towards a narrow house with a warped wooden door at the end of a terrace. With a flourish he moved to lift the knocker, only for Lavinia to push him delicately aside with her walking stick.

"Thank you, signor, we need no further help." She said, then nodded to her servant. "Knock!"

He did so.

Nothing happened, Hyman Golletz watching from the end of the street and wondering why Contessa Lavinia Gianetti was visiting the shamed girl who was now pregnant. The entire ghetto had been scandalised by the situation, Ira eager to share Marco's involvement in his sister's disgrace. His usual reserve was gone; instead he was brittle, scandal making him withdraw from his sister and spend as much time as he could away from the ghetto. Rosella continued to work for Hyman Golletz, but the walk from her home to his and the return journey – although short – was agonising for her. People whispered behind their hands and others turned their backs on her. Adamo Baptista had been hated by many; for one of their own to be associated with him was shameful.

Rosella had only one ally; Angelo Fasculo, her neighbour, encouraged by his mother to discover if Rosella was spying for Baptista. But Angelo realised quickly that she was no spy and although Rosella did not explain her situation it was clear that she had no affection for Adamo Baptista. Her humility and her gratitude for Angelo's kindness touched him and as the weeks passed his feelings intensified, her disgrace minimised. He even fantasised, in secret, of their eloping, leaving the ghetto and going some place where he could have Rosella as his wife and the child as his own.

But now Angelo was standing at his doorway with Hyman Golletz, watching the unexpected strangers.

"Knock again, more loudly!" Lavinia ordered, the servant repeating the action whilst the damp mist closed in on the narrow street.

Again there was no response, Ferriti stepping forwards and rapping impatiently on the door.

"*Ciao? Chi è la?*" came a female voice from inside.

"Signora Tabat?"

"Si."

"Please open the door, you have a visitor."

"But I am expecting no one." Rosella replied.

"Tell the girl to let us in!" Lavinia snorted, calling out. "I am the grandmother of Marco Gianetti and I would speak with you."

A moment passed then the bolt was drawn back, Rosella's head peering round the door. "Contessa, I am not—"

Pushing her way forward, Lavinia advanced into the shady hall, a narrow window at the far end illuminating a makeshift kitchen.

"Signora Tabat, I am very tired—"

"Forgive me, Contessa, but I did not ask you to come here." Rosella replied, moving out from behind the door.

Defiantly she stood in the hall, her belly slightly rounded, her face tense. The large dark eyes that Tintoretto had painted were suspicious, her manner confrontational.

"I need a chair." Lavinia said, "Whatever you think of my grandson, or of myself, it is only courtesy to an old woman to offer her a seat."

Reluctantly, Rosella lead Lavinia and Ferriti into a small sitting room. Against the wall was the bed where Livia Tabat had died, now empty and sporting a pile of blankets and washed linen. On the window ledge was a menorah and several lighted candles, one spluttering as Rosella pulled out a couple of wooden seats.

"Grazie." The Countess said, gesturing for Rosella to take the other chair.

"No, I will stand. That seat is for your companion."

"Signor Ferriti does not need to be seated, but you do – in your condition." Lavinia replied, impressed by Rosella's appearance and pugnacity. "I understand your anger—"

"No, Contessa, you do not."

"— very well, I will rephrase that. I would *like* to understand your anger. Tintoretto has explained what occurred; how my grandson manoeuvred a situation between yourself and Adamo Baptista..." Rosella said nothing and waited for the old woman to continue. "Naturally when I was told you were with child I thought the child was his—"

"*Naturally?*" Rosella repeated, "You *naturally* thought I was a whore? That I would sleep with, and carry the child, of a known thug?"

"Signora Tabat, I spoke without thinking—"

"Your grandson inherited the same failing."

Ferriti, sensing the animosity between the two women, stepped forwards. "The Contessa finds leaving the palazzo difficult—"

"Marco did not. He found leaving a very simple matter. But then he responded as all cowards do, he ran. Before you ask me, Contessa – because I am sure that is the reason for your visit – no, I have no information as to the whereabouts of your grandson. He has not contacted me or sent word—"

"Perhaps he would if you told him that the child you are carrying is his." Wrong footed, Rosella stared at her, but said nothing as Lavinia continued. "Tintoretto is very fond of you and it was he who told me what had taken place. I have said nothing to anyone else, but as time goes on and your condition becomes more and more obvious—"

"*Quanto?* How much?"

The old woman blinked and put up her hand to prevent Ferriti speaking.

"*You want me to give you money?* A payment to ensure that you will not divulge the parentage of your child?" she glanced at her lawyer before continuing. "Please let me understand what you are proposing, signora. For a sum of money you will protect Marco and allow people to think that you are going to have Adamo Baptista's child?"

Rosella folded her arms defiantly. "Isn't that what you came here to offer?"

"If it was, I would ask you to leave now, Contessa." A voice said as Ira entered, catching them all unawares. He did not look at his sister, but stood facing the unexpected visitor.

"Rosella has been badly used, and it was your grandson who organised it for the amusement of Pietro Aretino. And yet, despite Marco's guilt and his cowardice, you are bargaining for his honour – "

Lavinia rapped her stick on the floor. "*Silenzio!* I came here to assure your sister that my grandson will not be absolved of his responsibility." She replied, regarding Rosella with astonishment. "*You thought I would attempt to buy your silence?*"

"Is that not how it is done in a situation like this?" Ira interrupted, answering for his sister, his tone bitter. "You do not wish the embarrassment to you family—"

The Contessa looked away from him, her penetrating gaze fixing on Rosella. "I will be honest with you, Signora, you are not what I would have chosen for my grandson. And I doubt, in light of his actions, that Marco would have fulfilled your hopes either, but there is a child involved and so the matter must be rectified."

"How *can* it be rectified?" Ira replied. "Rosella is my responsibility—"

"Not entirely."

"When she decided to keep the child," Ira continued, his tone icy. "I told her I would support her decision. However difficult it will become, which it will, Rosella will be protected by me."

"You are not the father of her child." The Contessa replied, her tone as brittle as his. "It is the father who should be held accountable—"

"My sister is a Jew, Marco is a Catholic, there could be no talk of marriage between them and marriage would be the only way to prevent the child being brought into this world as a bastard."

Lavinia turned to her lawyer, "Is it possible that Rosella could convert?"

He was about to answer when Rosella interrupted. "I do not want to convert! My religion is important to me."

"More important than a child's future?" Lavinia queried. "Be reasonable, you cannot continue as you are, an unmarried woman is viewed harshly—"

"We do not need to be reminded of the shame," Ira replied, "But I have spoken to the rabbi and I am hoping to arrange a marriage for Rosella in another city where she is not known and where the child's past will be hidden."

"How proud you are," Lavinia said, her tone musing. "And what a burden you place on your sister to fulfil that pride. You do realise that you haven't look at her once? It is *so* difficult to look at her?"

He bridled. "Am I suppose to approve of what she has done?"

"Of what *they* have done." Lavinia corrected him, looking towards Rosella. "How old are you?"

"Seventeen."

"At seventeen I was married with a son of four. I had no say in the matter as to whom I would marry, or if I wanted children," she paused, her gaze piercing as she looked back to Ira. "It is very easy to condemn people for their actions where no emotions are involved. Have you never acted foolishly?"

"My actions are not the issue here."

"Have you never been in love?" she paused, studying his face. "Ah, I see I have hit a nerve, forgive me. And yet you are not married—"

"She died."

Lavinia shook her head. "There is so much tragedy in this world, isn't there? So much loss, and you are now looking at me and thinking *'Why is this old crone interfering in our affairs? Why is she even still alive? All dried up and bent over*," she smiled wryly. "But you must forgive me, in this situation I have to interfere."

"No, you do not."

"Your anger is like a heat coming from you. Such rage comes with great grief." Lavinia replied, "You are a young man, you will love someone again no matter how deeply you feel the loss now. We are all replaceable."

"Contessa, your visit—"

She cut him off.

"I have a confession to make; I do not know about love. Like all Venetian wives I was cocooned and expected to be an obedient brood mare. After Jacopo was born, my husband became ill and as he aged his condition worsened, until he was very unstable." she nodded at Ira. "Yes, Leonardo passed down his illness to Jacopo, my son—"

"And Marco?"

"No, there has never been any sign of emotional disturbance."

"He is young."

"Ah, that may be so, but with Jacopo and Leonardo there were early warnings. Intimations in childhood and youth. Believe me, I may well have been distant with my affection, but I have watched my grandson's health intently." She sighed, returning to her previous theme. "When my husband died I was left a young widow… Love is no acquaintance of mine. I read of it and hear the songs, but I have no understanding of the passion that can make a woman act foolishly."

"I accept what I did." Rosella whispered. "It was madness."

"*'Do not be afraid; our fate cannot to taken from us; it is a gift.'*" Lavinia smiled, quoting Dante. "Do you love my grandson?"

"I care for him, but do I love him? I do not know..." her voice was low, almost as though she didn't want Ira to hear what she was saying.

"How *could* she love a man like your grandson?" Ira asked, his tone incredulous. "Love has nothing to do with this."

"I was not talking to you," Lavinia retorted, looking back to Rosella. "Do you love Marco?"

"I… I don't know…"

"Many a marriage has succeeded on less," Lavinia replied, turning to Ira. "I know little of your sister, but much of you. I believe you a man of integrity and a gifted doctor. You would not be a liability but an asset to our family."

Uncertain, he asked: "What are you offering, Contessa?"

"A father for Rosella's child."

"A marriage?" Ira replied, his tone mocking. "If this some kind of trick—"

"Whatever made you so cynical?"

"Life, Contessa, life made me that way. You come here with your opinions, but you don't know what we are, where we came from, what struggles we have had. You cannot be expected to. I am respected as a doctor, but locked up at night. My sister, who can sing like an angel, works as a maid in the ghetto. We do not have courtly manners, because we are not of the court. We do not have a gracious home or elegant clothes, because we are not wealthy. You and I, Contessa, inhabit the same city, certainly, but you wear no leash or answer to any curfew bell."

"You are bitter."

"I am," Ira agreed.

"And aggrieved."

"Yes, that my sister should ruin herself in this way. Marco set a trap for her, but she could have freed herself, instead she rewarded her betrayer—"

Lavinia tilted her head to one side. "I do not think, Ira Tabat, that I have ever met such an angry man. You are unforgiving and cruel."

"You are right. But I make no excuse for my feelings."

"And you think yourself an honourable man." Lavinia

replied, shaking her head. "No, you are not. You are judgemental and heartless." She put up her hands to prevent his interruption. "Hear me out. Marco has acted without honour. He has been foolish and cowardly and must be made to atone for what he has done. Furthermore my grandson has no siblings and I would welcome a man of integrity – like yourself, Ira Tabat – to guide him."

"I thought I was angry, judgemental and heartless?"

"You are, but you are also a fine doctor and a man who stands by his family. A coward you are not." She replied, "we must give this child its rightful name—"

"Excuse me," Stepping forwards, Ferriti looked at the old woman with anxiety. "Perhaps we should discuss this a little more, Contessa? There is no immediacy to the matter—"

"And besides Marco is still missing." Ira added coldly. "Your plan will fail without your grandson. There is a chance that he will never return to Venice."

"Knowing you are waiting for him?" Lavinia countered. "Oh, he *will* come back. Venice is Marco's home, now he is lonely, uprooted. His flight will gradually seem less and less like an answer and more like an exile."

"Men live out their lives in exile."

She nodded sagely. "This is true. But my grandson is not a man for solitude. Loneliness will drive him home – and the child will keep him here."

Chapter Thirty Seven

The wind had disturbed the sea, sending foamy waves over the quayside and into St Marks Square. The few people who had been outdoors hurried for shelter, the mist coming down hard with the darkness. It was the 1st November and in the churches Mass was being held to anxious congregations crouched together against the gale gusting outside.

Tita Boldini had not been seen since she had left Caterina's apartment the day she had been confronted. She disappeared into the mist like vapour, taking all her possessions with her and leaving no trace. Cleared of all charges, Bakita had returned to his duties, always within sight or sound of his mistress, another guard employed to stand watch at the water entrance. From her window on the first floor Caterina could see anyone coming to her door or anyone approaching by boat, and all visitors were to declare their presence before entry. For a whore it was bad business.

She had not seen the Dutchman for several days and was wondering if he, like Tita, had evaporated. But finally he emerged, as solemn as ever, allowed entry to her bedroom and taking the window seat.

"You have been a stranger, Dutchman."

He nodded, took off his hat and tried to smooth his hair. "I have been kept busy with little free time." He jerked his head towards the window. "I noticed you have an additional guard."

"Thanks to you, I have learned to trust Bakita. The other man I hired as an added precaution."

"Has there been any trouble?"

"What kind of trouble should there be?" Caterina replied, her tone sharp. "Should I expect trouble? I thought that if we obeyed that little thief's instructions we would be safe." When he said nothing, she continued. "Forgive me, if I appear to be prying into your past, but I have to know. What happened to your daughter?"

"Why do you ask?"

"*Why do I ask?*" she repeated, "because the whore threw a mention of her at you and you flinched as though you had been struck. *'Ask the Dutchman about it.'* Those were her words. Oh, of course she did add *'when you next fuck him'* but at the moment that is not likely." Caterina took a seat, folding her arms as she stared at him. "I thought we were friends—"

"We *are* friends."

"— friends should trust each other."

"My daughter was murdered."

Shocked, Caterina unfolded her arms, one hand extended to touch him. "*Murdered?*"

"Murdered and mutilated, just as Gabriella Russo was." He looked up, flesh slack under his eyes, the frown lines deepened. "*Now* do you realise why I did not tell you?"

"So what was the rumour that little whore spoke of?"

"Word was that I had killed my own daughter." Der Witt

shook his head. "I could never have hurt her, and never, never cut up her body."

Caterina could see him trembling. A big, heavily built man, shaking like an aspen. "Did they find her killer?"

"No. And soon after she was murdered I left The Hague. I had some information from a source I trusted that I might find her killer in Paris."

"But you didn't?"

"No. But there was another girl killed just before I left Paris for Rome..." he looked her directly in her eyes. "It had nothing to do with me."

"I know you are not capable of such things."

"You may know it, but others thought me perfectly capable. Look at my reputation. I'm an abortionist – but I make made no excuse for that – the women I helped needed me. Some were rape victims, wives of brutal husbands, girls who had been seduced and abandoned." He shrugged his bulky shoulders. "But soon other rumours began, I am not certain how, but I was no longer a simple apothecary, but a man with other skills, sorcery, witchcraft."

"These are only rumours?" Caterina asked, pointing to the glass vial around his neck. "Rumours you encourage by wearing such things, that hair bracelet and the tattoo on your arm. I thought it was an affectation, a way to make it *seem* that you had magical powers."

"Without actually possessing them?" Der Witt asked. "Perhaps I did encourage it, at first. But before long people would avoid me, whisper behind my back, nudge each other as I passed – and I admit, here and now, that accepted the part I was given. What people fear, they avoid."

"You are not wicked, Dutchman, no one would be hurt by knowing you."

He rubbed his eyes, the whites reddened. "Maybe... All I wanted was to discover who had killed my daughter, my whole life was devoted to it. It was easier to travel alone and make no friends. Easier to travel when you settle nowhere. So I went from The Hague to Germany and then to Paris – where, as I've just said, another girl was murdered."

Caterina leaned towards him. "Was it meant to look as though you were involved? Did someone plan it that way?"

He nodded. "Yes, I believe so."

"Who?"

"I've made enemies."

"There is no way you can pass through this life without them." She thought of Tita Boldini then spoke again. "You mentioned Adamo Baptista, said you had seen that whore with him. You asked if she was working for him."

"I think she is." Der Witt replied, "I never told her what Gabriella had said, but she knew about *The Wolves of Venice*."

"She frightened me. That was why I hired another guard."

"But *how* did she know about what Gabriella had told us if she had been away from Venice and living in France? Tita could only have known through Baptista when he was in Paris."

"Were you in Paris at the same time they were?"

"No." he said emphatically.

A moment passed, Caterina shivering.

"Someone has just walked over my grave."

"What?"

She moved over to the fire to warm herself. "A while ago

I had an English girl working for me and that was what she used to say when she felt a chill run down her back." Wrapping her arms around her body, Caterina looked into the fire and watched the flames. "Is your daughter's death connected to *The Wolves of Venice?*"

Der Witt gestured for her to drop her voice and moved over to stand beside her.

"We must not be overheard, Caterina, we must be careful when we speak of this. There are spies everywhere, Aretino has many informers, spread over Venice like a fisherman's net." He paused for a moment, then continued. "I don't know if there is a connection between my daughter's death and *The Wolves of Venice*, because I don't know if these Wolves are a faction or a fantasy—"

"They did not seem like a fantasy to Gabriella."

He shook his head, exasperated. "If only I had met with her that night—"

"We cannot change what happened, however much we might want to." Caterina said firmly. "We must think of the present now. What we know for fact."

"Gabriella worked for Marina Castilano. Gabriella was afraid, so was Marina. And almost as soon as Marina had been scared away, Tita Boldini came to Venice." He looked at Caterina. "She was lying, she wasn't looking after the shop, she was searching it."

"For what? You think Adamo Baptista hired her to look for something?"

Der Witt nodded.

"Baptista seems to follow me wherever I go. He was in Paris, he knew Tita Boldini, and he *could* have been in The Hague—"

"*What?*"

"I only thought about it last night, then I had to confirm the facts. Titian is now in Augsburg, working on a commission for the Emperor, and Aretino is his agent, as everyone knows. Apparently Aretino went to Augsburg four years ago to visit the Emperor and settle the terms, and dates, of Titian's stay." He looked at Caterina. "And who accompanies Aretino everywhere?"

"Adamo Baptista?"

"Yes. It's a long journey from Augsburg to The Hague, but he could easily have done it, the man travels all the time, all over Europe. When – *if* – he was in The Hague four years ago it was the time my daughter was murdered." Der Witt kept his voice low. "Baptista was in Paris when another girl was killed, and now Gabriella has been murdered here, in Venice, where Baptista is at present residing."

Caterina glanced behind her, almost as though she suspected someone had entered. "Did these girls have anything in common?"

"Only their deaths. My daughter was seventeen, fair haired with green eyes, the French woman was forty, with red hair and blue eyes, and Gabriella—"

"Was dark haired and dark eyed."

He nodded. "Why would anyone want to kill four dissimilar woman in four different countries? Aretino is a blackmailer and a swindler, but a murderer? I doubt it. He likes to torture people mentally, not physically. But Adamo Baptista – who is *he*? We hear rumours about him, hints and innuendos, but nothing substantial. No one comes forwards and says *'he stabbed me,'* or *'he raped my daughter.'* His reputation is all. And he carries it like a banner before him so that people see it and are afraid, without even being able to read what is written on it." He paused, struggled to control his emotions. "If Adamo Baptista killed my child I will kill him. I swear it, as God is my judge."

Caterina laid her head on his shoulder, her voice a whisper. "Are we in danger, Dutchman?"

"I think we may well be."

"Then what are we to do?"

"I give my word that I will let nothing harm you, Caterina."

"You might be able to stop a man. You might be able to challenge Baptista, if it came to that. But what of the rest? Is he one of *The Wolves*, one of *The Four* Gabriella spoke about? And if so, who are the others?" she watched the flames splutter in the grate. "Aretino? Tita Boldini? Marina Castilano? It seems ridiculous, but how do we know who they are? Remember what that whore said? '... *The Wolves of Venice are real. You have no power against them, no protection... You see the mist outside? How it gets into everything, unseen and unheard...*'" She continued to stare into the flames. "What weapon is there that can kill an unseen opponent?"

"There is none."

"There is one." She corrected him. "Our protection is silence. To forget everything we know."

"I cannot..."

Her gaze was still fixed on the flames and she nodded.

"... I am being manoeuvred, Caterina. Whenever I believe I am coming closer to the truth someone tugs an invisible rope, pulling me into a different direction. One day I am facing ahead, then looking behind, then to the right, then the left. And always there is the threat that I will be found responsible for these murders. That someone will come after me. Or kill me."

"Then leave Venice." She said urgently. "Save yourself."

"I cannot save myself, I have no right. I made a promise to the memory of my child and I will honour it—"

"You death will not bring her back."

"I know." He said, resigned. "But if the answer is here, then here I must stay."

The quick tempered cousin of Hyman Golletz had been working all day, with little result because of the bad weather. Being a burly man, used to hostile conditions, he had continued on the quayside until the gale became too much and he was forced to leave. Grumbling under his breath, his head down, he hurried along the dock, a man unexpectedly emerging through the mist in front of him.

"God, you scared me!" he said, staring into the stranger's face. But it wasn't a stranger, it was a someone he had seen in the ghetto, someone who had been welcomed at his cousin's house. "It's Mario Gianetti, isn't it?..."

He nodded.

"... Come back home, have you? You fucking coward. I'd be careful you don't run into Ira Tabat or you're likely to find your teeth shoved down your throat." He spat, a glob of spittle landing at Marco's feet. "That fat pig Aretino and the black crow Baptista will be glad to see you, but they'll be the only ones." Marco tried to move away, but the man put a hand on his arm to detain him. "What's it like to have everything and be despised? Well, go on, answer me! You're shit, nothing more. Just a lap dog doing everyone's dirty work, betraying Rosella and setting her up to be used like a common whore." He grabbed Marco's collar and twisted it, staring into his face. "You're not even worth giving a beating to. Get back home, Gianetti, and claim your money. Your father's dead, it's all yours." Roughly he pushed him, Marco falling back against a low stone wall as the man shouted his final words. "And another thing – don't you dare to come near the ghetto again. If you do, God help you."

"Have you ever seen weather like this before?" Struggling to her feet, Lavinia glanced over to lawyer, then moved back to the window, trying to see through the fog. "You say Marco has returned?"

Ferriti nodded. "He has been seen—"

"By whom?"

"A relative of someone who lives in the ghetto. He's been going around talking about how he gave your grandson a beating and how he told him to leave Venice because no one wanted him." Ferriti paused, "I wouldn't believe his story, the man's a drunk and a braggart. He probably did see your grandson, but as to the rest—"

"So where is Marco now?" Lavinia snapped, reaching for her stick. "How long is it since this man saw him?"

"Only a hour or so—"

"An hour or so!"

"I have just been told, Contessa, and went to the quayside myself to look for your grandson, but it's deserted. The boats are tied up in this gale and there are no sailors or merchants working. The weather has driven everyone indoors." He hurried to pass Lavinia her walking stick, watching her regain her balance. "I have organised a group of men to look for him."

"With the reception he received, Marco might have left Venice again, taken the first boat away from here."

Ferriti was firm. "No, Contessa, the boats are not sailing tonight, not even to the other islands. Marco is in Venice, we just have to find him."

She leaned against a chair, thinking and rapping her stick on the floor. "Why did he not come here? Why did he not come back to his home?... Have you checked every entrance?"

"Yes, Contessa."

"Not just the main gates, but the water entrance? The door by the bridge?"

"All of them."

"He has keys, Marco can gain entry and be here without our knowing. There are so many rooms, so many unoccupied rooms."

"All have been searched, Contessa."

"When?"

"I set the servants to it as soon as I arrived, I wanted to check for myself if he was here, or not."

"So where *is* my grandson?" Lavinia replied, her tone querulous. "If he's not here, he must have gone elsewhere. But where?... He knows he will not be welcomed, he has already experienced one hostile reception, but he must want to make amends or he would not have returned... So if Marco chose not to come here for safety, where would my grandson go?" She looked over to the lawyer again. "Stop the search, cancel the men! I want you – and only you – to do what I ask."

Chapter Thirty Eight

His fingers were cold and therefore clumsy, snapping off the head of little wax figure he had made earlier in the day. Infuriated, Tintoretto swore and threw it across the studio, then placed some more wax onto the top of the stove to melt. The gale had tossed much of the water from the canal onto the walkway outside, some of it sneaking under the studio door, a little pool gathering under a new portrait of the Virgin and Christ Child.

As Tintoretto's apprentices had already left, the studio was deserted, candles and the light from the stove providing limited illumination. Rubbing his hands together to warm them, he waited until he could feel the prickle of some feeling return, before tossing a piece of bread onto the top of stove next to the pot of melting wax. Hunger was no way to work well, he told himself. If Titian was working tonight his belly would be full of delicacies, the fat oaf Aretino beside him, making his acerbic and witty comments.

Pre-occupied, Tintoretto flipped over the bread to toast the other side, looking around for the cheese he had set aside earlier.

"You are late. Very late, but then you always were." He said, without turning.

"How did you know it was me?" Marco asked, stepping out of the shadows.

"I have been expecting you," the artist replied, finding the cheese and setting out a plate with the bread halved and the cheese sliced beside it. "Eat."

"The wax is getting too hot."

Tintoretto took it off the stove and turned back to his food making no comment as Marco sat down beside him.

"I am sorry—"

"Yes, that is right, you should be," Tintoretto replied, wiping his mouth with the back of his hand. "I have become an unlikely confidante of your grandmother's. She had commissioned a portrait of you. Or I should say, she *did* commission a portrait, but when she discovered the reason for your leaving Venice I think the commission may well have been cancelled."

"You told her what I did?" Marco asked, his tone muted.

"It was not a secret for many in Venice, but the Contessa does not hear gossip so it was a revelation to her ears. She called you a fool – and I agreed with her," Tintoretto chewed another hunk of bread and cheese. "She called you a coward too, and I agreed with that," he said, the words muffled in the mouthful of food.

"I'm so ashamed." Marco said dumbly, "I am so ashamed for what I did to Rosella."

Tintoretto swallowed, glancing over to him. "What exactly *did* you do?"

"You know what I did!" Marco said angrily. "Ira will have told you, or Rosella."

"It was Ira. I have not spoken to Rosella for a while."

"She does not sit for you anymore?" Marco asked,

surprised. "I don't understand, she loved being here. Nothing would have stopped her coming to you... Did you tell her not to come?"

"No, I would always welcome Rosella, but I don't paint woman who are with child." Stunned, Marco watched him as he continued to talk. "...... they say the paint smells are bad for a baby. I don't know about that, but it is better to be safe. And of course there is the old wives tale about—"

"Rosella is pregnant?"

"I just said that," Tintoretto replied, tearing off another piece of bread. "... and as she did not allow herself to be seduced by Adamo Baptista, he is not the father." Carefully, he cut into the cheese with a knife, the blade catching the light from the stove. "And even as a good Catholic I do not believe in virgin births for those other than Our Lady. So..." he looked at Marco.

"It's mine."

"Yes, it is. And I am very pleased that you did not lie, or accuse Rosella of going with another man. If you had of done, Marco, I would have stuck this knife in your gut." He turned back to his meal, pushing some food over to his visitor. "I would eat, if I were you."

Listlessly, Marco cut into the cheese. "I didn't know."

"How would you? Rosella might not have got pregnant – but she did."

"What does she think of me? What *can* she think of me?" Marco asked. "Dear God, what have I done?"

"What men have done since time began—"

"I don't mean that," Marco replied, "I have to see her. I have to make this right—"

"Do you love her?"

"I … I don't know."

Tintoretto's eyebrows rose. "So it was merely passion?"

"No, it was something else entirely," Marco replied, "a kind of pity. I had pity for her and she had pity for me—"

"After what you had done?"

"She knew how ashamed I was, how regretful."

"And yet you lay together." Tintoretto said wistfully. "For comfort, I suppose. Like a couple of little, lost animals, scared of what they had done, scared of what was to come." He wiped his hands on a piece of cloth. "As soon as he hears you're back, Ira will come after you."

"I know."

"You should be careful, Marco, he is not merely angry, he is enraged. A man like that could do something he would live to regret."

"You think Ira would kill me?" Marco replied, his tone incredulous. "We were friends—"

"All the more reason for him to feel deceived. Perhaps if you wrote a letter to him first and then made an arrangement to meet, choosing somewhere where you would not be alone."

"This is Ira we are talking about."

"You are so foolish, Marco, like a child who has behaved badly but relies on his charm to be forgiven. But we are *not* children and this world is not a nursery." Tintoretto's tone was uncompromising. "If you wish, I will talk to him—"

"No! I am not afraid of Ira Tabat."

"Then why did you run away!" Tintoretto exclaimed. "You were afraid of him before, and that when you didn't know you had made his sister pregnant. Ira has every right to hate you, Marco, you have to realise that. He

will not be reasonable. I know his kind of man. They are judicious, patient, forgiving – until they are not. Until they feel betrayed, and then they are vengeful." He sighed. "I warn you, Marco, and you must listen to me – be very wary of Ira. Do not rely on old friendships or old memories. He has already forgotten those."

With only one man to accompany him, Ferriti left the palazzo and headed across Venice. The gale had not lessened, the wind force increasing, the flags of the Republic lashing against the flagpoles, or wrapping themselves as tight as winding sheets. Their clothes already soaked, the two men struggled on, the servant holding a covered lamp aloft to help them see their way. But the fog was so dense there was nothing to be seen more than a foot ahead, and they had to struggle to keep sight of each other as they hurried on.

Calling out, Ferriti's voice was drowned by the wind and he caught hold of the servant's sleeve to get his attention.

"That way!" Ferriti shouted, "it's that way."

The man nodded and together they moved on, the lawyer ducking into an archway with the servant following. Together they stood in the shelter, both breathing heavily from exertion, the rain pelting down on the canal in front of them and vibrating on the walls of the stone bridge.

"We have to cross." Ferriti told the man. "Stay close by me."

"Hold onto my coat, signor" the servant replied, "while I try to keep the lamp alight."

"Keep by me!" Ferriti commanded, and together they headed over the bridge, the servant losing his footing once on the slippery stonework, the candle's light flickering but still alight inside the glass cover.

The gale was howling in their ears, Ferriti alarmed at the noise, an eerie sound that he had never heard before in Venice. It seemed to take a shape, to expand in the fog, to scuttle about the passageways and follow them over the bridge. An unimaginative man, Ferriti still felt the urge to cross himself, the servant calling out over his shoulder.

"I see it! Just a little further."

"Thank God," Ferriti replied, moving on a few yards, the gate finally coming into clear sight. Urgently, he rang the bell, an aged man wearing the forelocks of an orthodox Hasidic Jew, coming over to them.

"What are you wanting here?"

"I am come on vital business," Ferriti replied.

"It is past the curfew."

"I understand, but I must speak to Ira Tabat." The lawyer explained, "it is of the utmost urgency."

The old man looked at him with an expression he did not understand, Ferriti repeating himself.

"It is urgent—"

"I heard you, signor."

"Then please let me speak with Ira Tabat."

"I cannot," the old man replied.

"*Be you must!*" Ferriti insisted. "I have news of which he needs to be informed, signor. It is a matter of the greatest importance –"

"You cannot see him because Ira is not here." The man explained. "He left just before you arrived when news came that Marco Gianetti had returned to Venice."

BOOK FIVE

I am writing this recollection many years later, almost forty years, in fact.

So much was to change so quickly that it is difficult to associate that young man with the person I am now. The man I became. You will meet me in the years that follow, and I will tell you everything. You see, a promise was made at the beginning that I would not lie to you, and I have not.

I am aware that my character will now seem shabby, not at all like the elegant costumes that could be rented from the Castilano sisters. They had also left Venice, but – unlike me – they did not return. Theirs is another story. They are not gone, just gone for now. They will reappear, as will many, as this history unfolds. Remember we are not yet at the end, not even the end of the beginning.

Looking back to the day I returned to Venice I was still young, and still naïve, thinking I could undo the malice I had created. Perhaps, if only for one instant, I even considered pleading with Aretino, but that thought was only ever half formed. My exile had finally given me insight; Aretino was now to me as he had seemed to others. Loathsome, greedy, amoral, cruel and pitiless. The game in which I had played a minor role had succeeded beyond his wildest expectations. His revenge on Ira was fulfilled two fold; Rosella's reputation was destroyed and she was pregnant.

At first Aretino did not know about the child, but when

the ghetto discovered how Rosella had been used they swore revenge on Aretino, Baptista, and myself. Although I had not plotted the scheme, my part in it was considered greater because of my betrayal of the Tabats and the ghetto itself; the place which had accepted me. The place and people I had chosen to abuse.

The reaction on the quayside from Hyman Golletz's cousin set the template for everyone's response. And rightly so, I deserved it. But I was still too young to realise that stupidity and impulsiveness can be forgiven, treachery can not. A plan has a mapping out, it is made with forethought, aimed to one specific conclusion. A plot is brooded over, thought about, perfected, each move considered, every flick and twist of the puppeteer's hands conceived in advance. Malice is a patient man's game.

And Aretino was a patient man.

He could plot and wait, and then hold a person to ransom for year after buckling year... Then I did not know he had been blackmailing my father, but I was soon to find out. And if, on that foggy night when I returned home to Venice, I believed I could make recompense to the Tabats, recover my life and inherit my legacy ... Well, does that not prove how great a fool I was?

My return was not just awaited by Rosella and Ira, but by the ghetto and all its residents. My return was also anticipated by Pietro Aretino and Adamo Baptista, whose plans for me were hardly begun. Unexpected and vigilant enemies were gathering in ranks against me, and yet I blundered home like a Prodigal without realising some outcasts are fated to remain in exile.

Yes, I came home that foggy night. But it was not the

home I remembered... Forty years later a chill goes through me as I look back.

Outside I can hear the guards changing their watch, the lights at the water entrance of the palazzo always lit, from the moment of dusk until dawn has come into her own. In my father's study – which is now used as my own – and in all the rooms I knew as a solitary child, there are always lighted candles, the corridors also, and when the fog comes down and I remember the night of my return I send for a priest and ask him to hold Mass.

He is searched on entry as is everyone and as the bells from St Marks sound the hour of four on a winter's afternoon I know that they are preparing the curfew in the ghetto.

I have my own curfew here.
My own, private, ghetto
Where I live alone.
And some nights my mother comes to visit.
I hear her and see her shadow on the wall
Swinging like a pendulum.

Chapter Thirty Nine

"For the love of Christ, stop them!" Tintoretto cried out, running towards the fighting men. Marco was on his knees, Ira striking him in the face repeatedly with his fist, the lawyer Ferriti running towards them and Tintoretto behind him. Still following the lawyer, the servant held the lantern aloft illuminating the two bloodied men. Although the fog was dense, Tintoretto could just make out another figure moving towards them, Rosella shouting at the top of her voice.

"Stop him! Please, do something!" she was running directly at the fighters, Tintoretto catching hold of her arm and pulling her back.

"No!" he said, signalling for Ferriti to hold her, then running towards the men.

"Ira, Marco! Enough!"

"Stop, please stop!" Rosella screamed, Ira's voice replying, his tone hard.

"Be quiet, Rosella!" He snapped, "I am doing what you should have done, I am going to kill this bastard." He was walking around Marco, both of them upright, shadow boxing. "I am going to kill him for disgracing you. For making you into a whore."

Marco lunged forwards. "It's not her fault—"

"But she went with you anyway." Ira replied, ducking out of the way of the punch and landing a fist on his opponent's chin. It was only a glancing blow and Marco rocked on his heels but stayed upright.

"It's my fault, not hers."

"Let him be!" Rosella shouted. "Please, Ira—"

Her brother's voice was hoarse with fury. "You want to save your lover, do you? Isn't that what a whore usually does? You should be working for Aretino now, Rosella, you've been broken in."

"You bastard!" Marco snapped, landing one punch on Ira's cheek, but missing the next.

Pushed to the sidelines, Tintoretto watched. He could see that Ira was beyond reason, his eyes fixed on Marco like a lion on a calf, his face bleached with fury. Although Rosella kept calling to him, he ignored her, refusing to look in her direction, Tintoretto moving forward again to try and stop the fight.

"This is madness—"

In reply, Ira pushed him out of the way again, his attention momentarily distracted as Marco managed to get back onto his feet. He was weaving, unsteady, and bleeding heavily from a cut over his left eye, his sight blurred as he lunged forwards. But Ira had already aimed another blow and it landed in Marco's guts so hard that he vomited, bending over and gasping as he tried to get his breath.

"You bastard!" Ira cursed him, "You fucking bastard. You disgraced my family, my name, you made my sister into a puttana!" he lunged out, landing a kick to his opponent stomach, Marco shouting at the top of his voice.

"I didn't mean it!" he gasped, staggering on his feet. "… I didn't mean… for any… of this… to happen…"

"Coward! Liar—"

"Enough!" Tintoretto snapped, stepping between the men again, "Stop it!" he spread his arms, trying to separate them, his voice raised. "Stop it! This will prove nothing."

"I have nothing to prove to you." Ira replied, "Get out of the way, painter, my quarrel is not with you."

Tintoretto held his ground. "Go home, both of you—" But before he could continue he was edged out of the way by Marco who launched himself towards Ira. His face was puffy, his left eye half closed, his mouth bleeding.

"I'm sorry –"

In one swift movement Ira punched him on the face, Marco's head jerking back as he staggered to keep his footing.

"NO!" Rosella screamed, **"No more!"**

She had ducked out of Ferriti's hold and moved between the two men. Without seeing her, Ira aimed a final blow at Marco, his arm curled in a loop, his fist blooded and clenched as it came down – and struck his sister's cheek. Stunned, Rosella faltered on her feet, Tintoretto catching her as she slid to the ground, blood coming from her nose and open mouth as the fog swirled around all of them.

Chapter Forty

Waiting in the doorway, der Witt listened for footsteps. The fog had remained heavy, making vision difficult, but he could hear every sound. In fact it seemed to him that the fog was intensifying noise; that the fluttering wings of a water bird were as loud as a ship's mast battling a night gale. From somewhere close by came the noise of a bucket clanging against stonework, followed by a knife scraping the dirt off the sole of a boot. He could not see the man, but could imagine his posture, one leg bent at the knee, his head lowered as he cleaned off the dirt. Then the satisfied click of the pocket knife closing and a second later, footsteps moving away.

The fog made the city into a chimera. With no horizon, Venice was suspended between earth and air, her watery home merging with the brooding sky. Shadows usually dense were furred with grey, the water a dull, unmoving velvet as der Witt waited patiently. Another ten minutes passed before he finally heard the faint approach of footsteps, followed by the movement through a passageway and then the stepping onto the bridge.

Then a pause.

Der Witt knew that he could not be seen in the fog, but he knew he had been sensed.

"Hello there. *Chi è là?*"

The Dutchman inched forward, the voice now demanding.

"**Chi è là? Speak!** I can't see you. And if you are thinking of attacking me, I wouldn't, I'm armed."

"Why would I attack you, Adamo Baptista?" Der Witt asked, stepping onto the bridge and moving forward until the two men were facing each other, separated by only six feet.

"So it's you, Dutchman." Baptista said, recognising the figure of der Witt. "What brings you outdoors on a night like this? Some girl in trouble? Or perhaps one of our Venetian Contessas needing some medic?"

"I could ask why are you abroad. Are you on an errand for your paymaster?"

"I have no paymaster. Like you, Dutchman, I am my own master." He moved, his feet planted firmly, prepared for any unexpected movement or scuffle. "What do you want with me?"

"I could ask the same of you."

"Ah, but I did not seek you out."

"And I did not look for you..." the Dutchman lied, feeling in his pocket, his hand taking hold of the pistol. "... Fate made our paths cross. As they have done many times before. Here in Venice, in Paris, and The Hague."

"The Hague is your country, der Witt, not mine."

"You do not have to be born in a country to visit it. Especially if you have business there."

"And what business would I have in The Hague?" Baptista asked, his voice emotionless. "Go home, Dutchman, you are getting old and nights like this can be dangerous."

"For me? Or you?"

There was a pause, Baptista stepping forward. "What are you here for? Some midnight assignation? Or perhaps you are gathering some moon dust for your potions. There are rumours of your being involved with the occult, is that true? Do you have séances and dabble with the dead? It's very fashionable, I believe, but not if they catch you. The nobility will escape but the Inquisition will have you hanging by your balls." Der Witt watched as Baptista sat down on the stone wall of the bridge, apparently curious. "Tell me something, Dutchman, have you met the Devil?"

"Perhaps I just have."

"You think I'm the devil?" Baptista replied, amused. "Why would you think that? What have ever done to you?"

"*Were* you in The Hague four years ago?"

"Were you?"

Der Witt changed tack, his hand still clasping the pistol. The Italian firearm was small and inaccurate; at a distance of a few feet he might not kill Baptista, but it would certainly injure him.

"Tita Boldini did not stay long in Venice."

"She's a whore, they travel around."

"Only if someone pays for them to travel," the Dutchman retorted. "I saw you talking with her, Baptista. And she and I ran into each other at the Castilano shop, where she was searching for something."

"Did she find it?"

"How would I know? I didn't even know what she was looking for. But it must have been something of importance, or you wouldn't have hired her." The Dutchman replied, "Strange how much has happened around that shop.

Gabriella Russo murdered and Marina Castilano abandoning her business. And now you – or your hireling – searching for something."

"What if I was to tell you that Marina Castilano owed money? And that Pietro Aretino had sent me to find it?"

"No, you would never have let her leave Venice if she had been in debt to that bastard. And anyway, Marina would have told me."

"You think people confide? Open up their hearts exclusively to you?" Baptista replied, "Don't you realise that they tell what you want to hear? The Contessa whose husband no longer fucks her, the seduction of the shop girl who pleads for you to abort her mistake. The old lady who wants to make contact with her dead husband and ask for his forgiveness from beyond the grave." He sighed. "There is one birth and one death, Dutchman, all else is misplaced hope. You of all people should understand – isn't that what your quackery is all about? Hope is your currency."

"And yours is fear." Der Witt replied, choosing his next words carefully. "I wanted to ask you something. Who are The Wolves of Venice? Gabriella spoke of them, she said there were four. '*...Don't let them tell you less, there are four. Look for the four...*"

Baptista shrugged. "Four 'what'?"

"That's what I don't know."

"But I thought everyone *confided* in you."

"Gabriella died before she could." The Dutchman replied. "And every time I seem to get nearer to the truth – whatever *this* truth actually is – someone warns me about The Wolves of Venice. And I don't understand what it means."

"And I'm supposed to?"

"Oh, I think you know exactly what it means."

"I will tell you one thing," Baptista rose to his feet. "I know about your daughter's murder, but I don't know who the killer was. I don't know who murdered Gabriella Russo either, or the woman in France. You look surprised, der Witt, of course I know about it. Remember, I'm a gambler, it pays me to know the cards a person has in their hand. That knowledge dictates when I should play. Or when I should hold back. You're a gambler too, Dutchman, coming out here tonight to confront me. That took courage."

"But I know only of your reputation, Baptista, not of any examples. They say you're a cheat, a thief, and a killer – but it might all be hearsay. Perhaps Aretino started the rumours to make you seem some kind of demon, employing your reputation to scare his victims. But as to the truth, who knows?" Der Witt shrugged. "I heard that you visited Gabriella Russo in the morgue. Why would you do that if you weren't involved in her death? Or were you making sure the body was hers? Tintoretto identified her, did you know that?"

"*Il Furioso* has many talents." Baptista replied phlegmatically.

"Indeed, even with all the mutilation he recognised her. He had painted Gabriella, you see, he knew all the secrets of her face, even when someone had tried so hard to destroy it."

"So, what of it?"

"'*What of it?*' If Tintoretto hadn't recognised Gabriella she might have gone to her grave without anyone knowing what had happened to her."

Der Witt paused, his hand clasped around the pistol in

his pocket. The fog was building again, along with the rain, the bridge becoming slippery underfoot. He could see the Florentine's face, but it was expressionless and terrifying because of it. In that instant der Witt realised that he could not anticipate Baptista's next move; that even armed with a pistol he felt unexpectedly helpless.

"Dutchman?"

"Yes?"

"I know you have a pistol. And I have a knife. Do you think you could fire that pistol – let alone hit me – before I could ram this blade into your throat?" Baptista asked calmly. "You would bleed out within minutes. The fog is against you, Dutchman. It would aid my escape, and prevent your rescue."

"But you have admitted nothing that could incriminate you, so why would you need to kill me?"

"Do not play games!"

"I am not playing games," der Witt replied, confused. "I am asking you in all honesty, why am I a threat? *What do I know now that I did not know ten minutes ago?*"

"The answer." Baptista replied. "And your safety is in your not being able to see it."

Chapter Forty One

Distraught, Ira and Tintoretto carried Rosella home to the ghetto, where she remained unconscious and unmoving, in an eerie shadow of her late mother. As soon as the blow had landed, the painter had pushed Ira to one side, Ferriti leading a desperate Marco away. He was struggling, his clothes torn, blood pouring down his face, as he tried to shake off the lawyer's grip.

"Let me be! **Rosella! Rosella!**" he shouted, then calling over to Ira. "**You hit her, you bastard, you hit her!**" His face was swollen from the beating, the words muffled as he kept struggling to free himself, his panic audible. "You hit her! Jesus Christ, is she alright?"

But Ira ignored him. With the help of Tintoretto he carried Rosella back to the ghetto, a small group already formed and watching as they passed, Angelo Fasculo running into the street. When he saw Rosella, he ran over to her, his hand grasping hers.

"What happened? Someone tell me, what happened?"

"Ira and Marco Gianetti fought" Tintoretto explained "and Rosella got in the way."

"*They fought?*" Angelo repeated dumbly, "Why were they fighting?"

His mother had already joined him in the street, Gilda turning to her son.

"Why do you think? Ira swore he'd go after Marco Gianetti and now he has." She beckoned to the two men, "Bring Rosella in here, in my house. No, Ira, not in yours, your sister needs care and you can't give her that."

"Rosella should be—"

"Oh, damn you!" Gilda hurled back, interrupting him. "Haven't you done enough to this girl?"

She stood back to let them enter her house, watching as they laid Rosella on a palette bed in the sitting room. In silence, Gilda got a bowl of water and a cloth and wiped the blood off the girl's mouth. When she had finished she wrung out the cloth and laid it over the side of the bowl.

"Rosella's lip is badly cut, and she's unconscious, but she'll be alright." She glanced over to Ira, "Before you say it, I know I'm not a doctor, but you're in no fit state to deal with this." She looked him up and down. "What happened?"

"It was an accident..."

Distracted, he trailed off, Tintoretto finishing the sentence for him. "They were fighting and Rosella came between them. Ira was going to punch Marco and he hit her instead. It was an accident."

Gilda's expression was incredulous. "Why do men always think fighting solves a problem, when all it does it make everything worse?" she glanced over to Ira. "What in God's name did you want to do? Kill Marco Gianetti? To what end? You'd be executed – and for what? Why throw away your life and your career for a worthless man."

"He knew what to expect if he came back to Venice."

"And do you feel better, Ira? Now you've drawn blood

-Marco's *and* Rosella's – do you feel revenged?" her tone was brusque. "I have no love for Marco Gianetti, but if you had wanted to kill the person who had disgraced Rosella, you should have gone after Adamo Baptista—"

"It's not his child she's carrying," Ira said bitterly, "it's Marco's."

Gilda shrugged. "You think you're telling me something I don't know? The whole ghetto knows who fathered that baby. We thought it was Baptista's child at first, but Rosella told us the truth." She studied Ira curiously. "Would you have preferred it to have been Baptista's?"

"Of course not!"

"You're a liar!" she retorted, "it's not the disgrace that matters so much to you, Ira, it's that Marco betrayed you." She nodded. "And yes, he did. But you could have stomached it more if Rosella had been seduced by a creature like Baptista. You could have forgiven her that. Rape is pardonable in your eyes, but not this. Not that she *chose* to go with Marco—"

"You have nothing to do with this!"

"Don't raise your voice to me!" she retorted hotly. "It was us, your neighbours, who comforted your sister when you stayed away, and when you could hardly bear to look at her. You have no inkling of what Rosella has suffered. At first people thought she was going with Baptista willingly – oh, we all gossiped about that – I certainly did. But then she confided in me and I found out the truth."

"The truth is no less shameful." Ira replied, "Make excuses for my sister, say that she was tricked, all that is true, but she still chose to lie with Marco Gianetti—"

"For comfort!" Gilda snapped. "You don't know the

meaning of the word, do you? She did it for *comfort*, because she knew there would be precious little from you."

"So this is my fault?"

"No! It's Pietro Aretino's fault, and Adamo Baptista's. It's Marco Gianetti's fault because he was weak, duped, flattered into obeying his infamous friend. It was my fault too that I once suspected Rosella, and your fault that you couldn't forgive her." She sighed. "But if you ask me who is most to blame I would say Aretino."

His voice was sour. "What do you know?"

"More than you think, Ira. That fat pig has been blackmailing me, he has driven me into a corner from which I have no escape – but I will find one. And I *will* have my revenge on his henchman, Baptista." Her expression was resolute. "I chose my battles with care, because that is the only way to survive in this world. Don't put your whole focus on Marco Gianetti, but on the puppet masters behind him. Why fight a monkey when you are being stalked by wolves?"

Giving one last glance to his sister, Ira left. They could hear his feet pound on the paving outside and the slam of the neighbouring door.

"Are you?"

She turned to Tintoretto. "Am I *what?*"

"Being blackmailed by Aretino?"

"Yes," she replied curtly. "Like many others in this city... You know him, I believe."

"He has commissioned paintings from me. But he is no friend." Tintoretto replied, "His loyalty is to Titian, and as all of Venice knows, Titian dismissed me from his studio when I was his apprentice. For years I have weathered their petty slights, their determination to exclude me from their circle," he laughed, shaking his head. "without their once realising how grateful I was for the exile. I am no courtier."

She smiled. "It is easier when you are not proud."

"But I can be proud" Tintoretto teased her, "it was merely that in the past I could not *afford* pride. It demands a high cost on the character. So much is lost through pride, through fearing humility or rejection, through believing yourself better when we all are little more than a fleck of paint."

"You are a philosopher."

"No, I am a simple man, not as rigid as Ira, nor as foolish as Marco."

Gilda bridled at the name. "Gianetti is hated in the ghetto for what he has done."

Tintoretto clicked his tongue. "Which is understandable – but it was not an act of malice, but of manipulation. Aretino is a very wicked man. People are fooled by his wit *'the best thing for a man to do is to be born and, being born, to die at once.'* They are mesmerised by his clever conversation and his lavish way of life, but he *is* wicked in the way that godless people are, without conscience or remorse."

"And Adamo Baptista?"

Tintoretto blew out his cheeks.

"That is a man I fear… When I was a child my mother told me an old fable about a water devil that lived under Venice. She said that the sprite would come to the quayside and call to the children and when they were close enough, grab at their heels and pull them under. Down under the city, she would tell me, into cages made of coral and old bones, where they were imprisoned forever." He paused, remembering. "The story goes that at night, when Venice was silent, you could hear the children crying and rattling their cages, weeping to be let out."

"You see Baptista as the water devil?"

"Yes, and in all the little cages he keeps his victims. People who are childlike, trusting, foolish—"

"Like Marco Gianetti?"

"Like Marco," Tintoretto agreed.

"You care for him."

"How could I not? His mother committed suicide after his birth and his father blamed him, Marco never knew affection. He knew beauty, abundance, he was promised a legacy and reminded of his importance, but no one protected him, he was first in no one's heart. That was why he enjoyed his friendship with Ira and Rosella, they welcomed him, the ghetto welcomed him—"

"And look how he repaid us." Gilda said scornfully.

"But now he is free from Aretino—"

"You think so?"

Tintoretto shrugged. "I hope so. Marco was ashamed of what he did, bitterly remorseful. I believe he finally realises what kind of man Aretino is and will want no more to do with him..." He leaned towards her. "Give Marco time to prove himself. Give Rosella and Ira time to forgive, let the water settle – and then judge."

"If a man can betray his friends once, he could do so again."

"Yes, he could, but Marco does not want to hurt people. He would never have *planned* to injure Rosella or her brother. Believe me, Gilda, I understand why everyone in the ghetto hates Marco Gianetti, but there are people more worthy of that hatred..." Tintoretto held her gaze. "... people who have dedicated their lives to earning it."

Chapter Forty Two

Unable to kneel because of the pain, Lavinia was leaning forwards in her pew with her head in her hands, her lips moving silently, a black veil covering the white crown of her hair. In her own private chapel she was giving thanks to a God she did not believe in, for the return of a grandson in whom she had no faith. Ever the realist, long ago Lavinia had decided that it was foolish to prematurely dismiss anything in life. Whether that be a god or a grandson.

Crossing herself, Lavinia rose to her feet and made her way out of the chapel and along the private corridor to her apartment. A message had been sent half an hour earlier that Marco was waiting to see her and it was with some trepidation that she approached the door leading to her rooms. Her hand shook as she reached for the door handle and she took in a long, protracted breath to compose herself before entering.

Evidence of the fight with Ira was obvious, his left eye almost closed, bruises along his chin and forehead, his hair matted with blood. If she had expected him to return to the palazzo first, she had been disappointed and yet inwardly proud that at least her foolish and disgraced grandson had not evaded a fight.

"I will call for a servant to prepare your bath," Lavinia

said, examining Marco as he stood before her. Silent, battered, and much changed from how he had been before his flight. "Do you need a doctor to tend to your wounds?"

"They are nothing," Marco replied, his head bowed.

"Where are your possessions?"

"I sent someone to collect them from the quayside," Marco answered, looking at his grandmother. "I… I am sorry…so sorry."

And Lavinia felt his needing her; aware that he craved for her to extend her arms, or at least a hand, in comfort. She could sense the pleading from inside him, the call for affection, and yet she could not respond. Her own emotions had been extinguished by time and neglect, the language forgotten from negligence.

"Arrangements will soon be made for the legal handing over of the Gianetti estates to you as sole heir, Signor Ferriti will organise such matters, and also your marriage to Rosella Tabat—"

"My marriage to Rosella?" Marco repeated blankly. "She is hurt—"

"I know and I have been assured that it is not serious. My own medico has visited her at the ghetto – how strange that it should be that way round, but life is, in itself, stranger ever day. Apparently Rosella was knocked unconscious by her brother's strike—"

"Accidental strike."

"— and although her lip was cut, she is otherwise in perfect health. There is no concern for the baby, but I imagine she is more than a little upset by what took place."

Marco stared at his grandmother, bewildered. "You want me to marry Rosella Tabat?"

"The girl is pregnant and I am too old to consider the judgment of society. If there is a scandal, so be it. There are scandals all the time, but life continues. You will marry her – you are the master of the Gianetti house and free to wed whom you please. And you please to marry a Jewess." Lavinia paused, shrugged. "Perhaps this new blood will be a valuable contribution to our unfortunate line. Your grandfather and father were troubled in the mind, as was your poor mother. This girl seems stable. Even in her unenviable position she was not hysterical when we spoke."

"You spoke with her?"

"Naturally. I needed to meet the mother of my grandchild and see that she was provided for – whether you returned to Venice or not."

"When you spoke... what did she say about the marriage you were proposing?"

"Rosella said nothing. Her brother speaks for her most of the time." Lavinia retorted, "A very proud man, very rigid. We were all due to discuss the matter again when – or if – you finally returned to Venice. Unfortunately you met with Ira Tabat first and so the meeting will no doubt be delayed." She gestured to the fire with her walking stick. "Call the servant, the flames are dying."

Immediately Marco stepped forward and added more wood to the fire, his grandmother watching him.

"You have had to fend for yourself, I see. No servants?"

"No."

"Well, you will have a great many servants now." Lavinia replied. "Far more than when you were a child. You will have people to run your house and your bath, but you – only you – will be responsible for the Gianetti legacy."

"I have to try and explain what I did." Marco said helplessly, "About Aretino—"

"Not another word!" Lavinia snapped, putting up her hands. "We can only pray that devil slips on the Doge's stairs and breaks his abominable head on the marble floor below. Surely his greed will finish him off before too much longer. But then again, the devil looks after his own."

"I was stupid—"

"Marco, you *are* stupid. But I blame your parents and myself for that. Which is why, when you inherit this fortune – and it *is* a great fortune – I would like to attend your discussions with Ferriti. He is a good lawyer and a decent man, but I am your grandmother and I know far more about our wealth than he can ever guess. Jacopo and I were not close, but often he asked for my opinion on financial matters." She leaned forwards, stretching out her hand towards the warmth of the fire. "The fog has gone at last, but the cold remains..."

Marco looked like a dog after taking a whipping. Beaten, still in his bloodied clothes.

"...I will see you for dinner at eight. Please do not be late, Marco, I cannot eat after that time." With an effort Lavinia struggled to her feet and was about to walk past him when she paused. "I am relieved that you returned to your home and your inheritance. But from now on do not confide in fools and sleep with whores, and do not receive any visits or messages from Pietro Aretino. He has brought much grief to this house, as to many others, and must be avoided at all costs." She gripped her grandson's arm tightly. "Let him back in – and you destroy us all."

Chapter Forty Three

He had hoped that the fog would last until evening, but as dusk settled over St Marks the mist melted, the turbulent sea becoming still as a mirror. Weaving in between the crowd of merchants, bankers and nobles idling around the square, Lauret pulled the hat down over his forehead and avoided the gaze of passersby. He was soon out of breath, his lungs straining as intensely as his leg muscles as he hurried towards the quayside. A boat was offloading slaves, a young African woman holding a child and five men, all standing on a plank which had been arranged between the ship and the dock. Frightened, the woman comforted the baby, the men silent, manacled together at the wrists and ankles.

Lauret had a fear of being manacled, thrown into the New Prisons as they were laughably called. He had experienced a week in gaol because of Baptista, a week which could have been shortened to a mere day if he had spoken up for him. Not that he would have done, even for a man who had served him well. Although he had been alone at first Lauret was soon joined by another man, a thief who had exposed his genitals and mocked him relentlessly.

Though not a sodomite, Lauret knew how feminine he

appeared, his round body pigeon-plump, his hands white and ladylike. All his life he had been mocked; ridiculed for his short legs and bald head, his siblings all handsome and lofty. When he married his wife continued the treatment, more gently: her ridicule was more like teasing, but in time she passed it onto their children and Lauret was mocked *en famille*. He grew – if not content – accepting of the mockery. But when he met Gabriella Russo his expectation of ridicule never manifested and her acceptance of him quickly became love.

He never spoke of it, he would not have risked losing the friendship, instead he treasured their meetings and conversations like a miser treasures coins. When she died his body emptied; the ungainly exterior remained, but the interior – the beating heart, the moving organs, the circulating blood – seemed to die with her. He knew it could not be so; his legs were still functioning, he still peed from a full bladder and coughed when he moved too quickly. His tongue was working, words were spoken, and his brain was still operating, but the spark of soul that had recognised an allied soul in her, had been put out.

"Pardon!" Lauret said automatically as someone bumped into him. "Excusez-moi."

His hand tightened over the bag under his arm. If anyone looked inside they would see the usual travelling items, but there was something else. Something Lauret had only just uncovered. The last time he had spoken to Gabriella she had told him about The Wolves of Venice, the Four. She had been scared that night, looking around repeatedly, her head covered by a lace veil, edged with ribbon. He had asked her if she had just been to Mass.

"Yes, I lit a candle for you and for myself."

"I can't leave you here alone. If I had money, I would give it to you, Gabriella, but I am coming back to Venice very soon and I will have money then." She had gripped his hands in hers as he continued. "Come with me tonight—"

Her eyes had widened. "What?"

"I'm leaving, I could sneak you onto the boat, get you away from Venice." Urgently, he had pressed her. "Do it, come with me, you would be safe then."

In answer she had shaken her head, the veil falling away. "It's too late—"

"No!"

"—Shush, shush, be still, Lauret. My good friend, be still." Then reaching into her bag, Gabriella took out a small package wrapped in paper. "Here are some herbs for you, mixed in a tincture. I got them from the Dutchman, he said it would help your sea sickness." She pressed the parcel into Lauret's hands and kissed his cheek. "Remember to take them when you travel. Don't forget. Please, don't forget. It's important."

Lauret had only remembered the herbs when he had packed earlier, picking up the parcel and opening it. The herbs had been there, some mixed into a tincture contained in a small vial. But it hadn't been those which had caught his eye, instead Lauret had noticed another piece of paper used as a lining. On which had been written a list of names.

The names of The Wolves of Venice. The four.

Anxious, Lauret had rewrapped the parcel and hidden it in his case and was now hurrying on, head down, afraid of being spotted by Baptista or one of his infamous spies. Only minutes later Lauret reached the quayside, looking round for the boat on which he had booked passage. The first booking he had made he had cancelled within the hour, instinct warning him against taking the vessel, but this boat had been recommended by a merchant he knew, a Frenchman he trusted.

Moving towards the head of the boarding queue, Lauret found himself suddenly pushed backwards, his hat sliding over one eye as he struggled to hold onto the bag tucked under his arm. But his grip was secure and as he saw the gangplank ahead leading to the vessel, Lauret turned to look anxiously behind him one last time. He was certain that he would be stopped, that the tall form of Adamo Baptista would materialise at any instant, or that some stranger would come out from the crowd and prevent his leaving. But the queue continued to edge forward, person by person, carrying him along.

When Lauret finally stepped onto the boat he was shaking, his sweating hands leaving greasy marks on the leather of his bag. Flopping down onto a bench, he took off his hat and wiped his forehead, his breathing gradually becoming regular. And as the vessel moved away from the squabbling, hustling crowd on the quayside he nearly wept. Over the mirrored sea the boat moved, under a merciful sky, as Lauret was rowed from Venice towards safety.

And only yards away, sitting silently amongst a group of other passengers, was Nikolas Volt.

Caterina stared at the Dutchman in disbelief. "You did what?"

"I challenged Adamo Baptista, I asked him if he had killed my daughter."

"And naturally he admitted it," she replied, exasperated. "Whatever possessed you? Have you no regard for your safety? To meet up with that man" she paused, "don't tell me you were alone?"

"I'm not afraid of him—"

"You are in a majority of one," Caterina replied.

"I had a pistol."

"I wonder if you are as adept with your pistol as he is with his knife?" she said coldly. "What did you expect to discover?"

"I'm not sure," der Witt admitted, "but when I spoke to him about The Wolves of Venice—"

"You did *what!*" she replied, her voice high pitched, trembling. "We were warned to stay silent. That whore Tita Boldini told us that silence was our only safety. You may not care what happens to you, Dutchman, but I do. And I very much care about my own safety." She paced the floor, five steps one way, five the other. "We were told to *never* mention it again. To forget it—"

Der Witt interrupted her.

"I told Baptista that Gabriella had confided about the Wolves of Venice, how she had said *'Don't let them tell you less, there are four. Look for the four.'*" And then his manner changed. I thought he was going to attack me—"

She stopped pacing, her hands clasped together. "Sweet Jesus."

"—but then I asked him *why* he would need to kill me, as I had said nothing which would incriminate him. I was confused, asked him what I had just learned that I did not know before... And do you know what he replied?"

She shook her head.

"*'The answer. And your safety is in your not being able to see it.'*"

The Dutchman sat down with his hat on his lap. Shaking his head, he looked out of the window to the Lagoon below.

"I have walked around this city most of the night trying to decipher what he meant. Repeatedly running over the words Gabriella had said, endlessly reviewing them. Did I forget a word? Did I place them in the wrong order? I am Dutch, did I mispronounce her Italian and give it another meaning? *What* was it that decided Adamo Baptista to stay his hand?"

Caterina stared at him. "Did you find the answer?"

"No... I tell you, he was going to kill me. I saw it in his eyes. He was poised, like an athlete, ready to take the jump." Der Witt took in a long breath. "I have never witnessed it before, that instant where a man sees a threat and decides to remove it. Now I believe every rumour I have ever heard about Adamo Baptista."

"This is madness," Caterina said quietly, sitting by him on the sofa. "Why do you court danger?"

He seemed not to hear her. "What *was* it that I missed?"

"My friend—"

"What *was* it in Gabriella's words?"

"Enough!" she said, uncharacteristically sharp. "Can't you see that you have been let off the hook and thrown back into the river to swim to safety? Dear God, Dutchman, see the situation for what it is. For some reason Adamo

Baptista is relieved. He no longer suspects you of knowing something that endangers him—"

"But what?"

"I don't know! And I don't want to know." Caterina replied, "When Marina Castilano departed Venice and that little whore also left, I was relieved. I thought my life could return to its usual routine. I have Bakita, and a new man, an ex mercenary from Sicily, guarding me. What do I have to fear now?" She smiled, but her charm was forced. "Nothing. At least that is what I wanted to believe. But now you come here and disturb me again... I'm a whore, Dutchman, a courtesan, for sale. I live to give pleasure and to be paid for it. Before much longer my beauty will not be enough and I will rely on my allure instead, but that is what the finest Venetians courtesans do, they survive."

"I do not mean to cause you anxiety—"

"I believe you. You are obsessed, rightly so. I have a son and if anything were to happen to him, I would be unable to rest until I had found his killer. I am not trying to dissuade you, or criticise you, I am trying to protect you." She took the hat out of his hands and smoothed the brim tenderly with the tips of her fingers. The action was slow and sensuous. "If you would just recognise it, you have been given a reprieve. And *I* have been given one also... Listen, Dutchman, what do you hear?"

He paused, turning his head slightly to the window.

"A mumble of voices, a water bird, and someone has just slammed a shutter back against a wall. What am I *supposed* to hear?"

"Venice, going about her day. Life, with all its tedium and sweetness." She leaned towards him, her hand touching his cheek. "You and I must be survivors in this game. We must be judicious. Let Baptista – and by extension, Aretino – believe you doltish. Say no more on the matter of The Wolves. Act as though it is forgotten. Baptista will not expect you to cease looking for your daughter's killer and will think your attention is concentrated there."

The Dutchman nodded. "You are a clever woman. But now he knows I suspect him."

"You said he only appeared to be dangerous when you repeated Gabriella's words about The Wolves..."

Der Witt nodded.

"...so stay silent on that subject. Do not provoke this man." Her voice softened. "Do you think he murdered your daughter?"

"I believe him capable of murder and all manner of brutality, but did he kill my child? I am not sure of that." Der Witt thought for a moment, then glanced back to Caterina. "Baptista is a renowned gambler, a man who has perfected the art of deception and understands the capriciousness of chance. A great card player and a great cheat share the same ability – that of pretence. Adamo Baptista could disguise his feelings with the same ease with which a clock chimes. And like a clock he has many faces – his skill is at showing them only one at a time."

Chapter Forty Four

As Lavinia had predicted, there had been no injury done to the child Rosella was carrying and within days she recovered; but, withdrawn and uncommunicative, she avoided her brother and stayed at the Fasculo house instead. Seeing himself as her protector, Angelo became devoted to the comfort of their guest, Gilda scolding Hyman Golletz when he asked when Rosella would be well enough to work again.

"You have to give her a little more time," Gilda told him, protective of Rosella and curious as to news of Ira. "Have you seen her brother?"

"I saw him early this morning, just after dawn. He tried to avoid me, but I stopped him anyway." Hyman laughed, "He said he had been called out to see a patient at the Doge's palace."

Gilda raised her eyebrows. "His reputation as a doctor is secure, even if there is chaos at home."

"And Marco Gianetti?"

"What about him?"

"They said he disappeared after Rosella was hurt, that he was taken to the Gianetti palazzo." Hyman replied, "I wonder what would have happened if Rosella hadn't got in the way and the fight had continued."

"We'll never know," Gilda replied, trying to terminate the conversation.

But Hyman wasn't finished. "That poor girl. Who'll have her now? Her being pregnant…" he glanced at Gilda slyly out of the corner of his eye. "Of course everyone here thought that Rosella and your son had some kind of agreement before all that trouble…" He trailed off, sensing he was on dangerous ground. "But it's a blessing the girl is with you, Gilda, she needs a mother figure at a time like this."

Rosella might have needed one, but she did not turn to Gilda for guidance. And she avoided Ira, talking with Angelo instead about trivia, trying in some way to haul in a net of comforting, old memories whilst perched on the rim of a leaky boat. When a message came from Lavinia asking for her to visit, Rosella did not respond, a further message – delivered by a servant – forcing her hand. Diffident and inhibited, Rosella listened to the old woman's plans for a future in which she had no say, and found herself unexpectedly ambushed by the arrival of Marco.

At first she was angered: but his manner was not dominant nor flippant. In fact, he was almost timid, reticent around his grandmother and keeping a distance from Rosella. Sitting beside a fire banked high in the grate, the venerable countess talked on, Rosella glancing over to Marco and seeing – with incredulity – a look of helplessness. The bruises and cuts about his face might have suggested the embarrassment of a beaten man, but she soon realised that his mortification was due to indecision. Like her, Marco was swinging between the past and the future; both of them tightrope walkers on a line they could not see, moving towards a conclusion that they could not even imagine.

If they had been alone Rosella would have reached out to him, just as she knew he would have comforted her. Their love making was as nothing. In that instant they were merely remembered friends, grasping for an intimacy whose loss was indescribably painful to both.

Surprised to see a figure in the studio doorway silhouetted against the cold morning, Tintoretto called out to him.

"Ciao, chi è quello?"

The figure entered, taking off the hat he was wearing and passing a large canvas surmounted on an easel beside which two apprentices were hammering a frame together. Their blows were not in unison, but battling with each other like quarrelsome woodpeckers.

"I hope you will excuse my arriving without making an appointment first," the man said "I was wondering if I might speak with you."

Tintoretto wiped his paint smudged hands on his studio apron and nodded. "Of course, please come with me, I have a room back here. *Mind the easel! Take care! Take care!*" he snapped at the apprentices, then smiled and beckoned to the man to follow. "We have too much going on, too many paintings, too many commissions." Opening the door, he ushered his visitor in, then sat down opposite him. "So, do you wish me to paint a portrait for you?"

The man shook his head.

"No, I am here on another matter. My name is Barent

der Witt, I'm a Dutchman come over to Venice for private reasons." As he always did, he began to roll his hat in his hands. "I believe that a few months ago you used a model called Gabriella Russo."

"I did, but she only sat for me a few times." Tintoretto said, his tone guarded. "May I ask what concern that is of yours?"

"I knew Gabriella. She came to me for help, but I was too late to save her." Der Witt paused, glancing around the studio, his gaze settling on a painting of a Madonna and Child. "I have never had the ability to create anything, I envy you your talent, Signor."

"You are very kind, but I'm curious about Gabriella. Were you related to her?"

"No, merely friends. She had no one left in this world." The Dutchman continued. "Perhaps that is why she became embroiled in something that frightened her."

Tintoretto leaned forward in his seat. "She said nothing to me about being afraid."

"I did not think she would have confided on such a short acquaintance. Gabriella was slow to trust people. And yet it was you who identified her corpse. Marina Castilano told me you visited her shop and informed her of Gabriella's death, and that you informed the authorities afterwards. You also paid for her funeral."

"That's true, but why are you asking me all this?"

"Why does a man pay for the funeral of a girl he did not know well?"

"Did you see her corpse, Signor der Witt?"

"No, thank God, I was spared that."

"Well, I *did* see it. I saw what had been done to her,

and I made a drawing of those grievous remains. Because they were *remains*, remains of a young woman who had been beautiful." Tintoretto hurried on. "And I *pitied* her. I pitied that beauty could be reduced to a lump of torn meat... And that was why I paid for Gabriella's funeral, because I wanted her to have the dignity in death that was denied her in life."

The Dutchman nodded. "You have my gratitude for that." He sighed, then continued. "However, the reason I am come here today is to ask if you have any notion as to who killed Gabriella."

"No. I do not. If I did, I would have told the authorities."

"I have been trying to discover her killer for some while."

"Forgive me, but again I must ask the same question – *why?*"

"Because Gabriella was killed in exactly the same manner as my own daughter." Abruptly the waved away Tintoretto's condolences. "And there was another victim in France. What is more, I believe it might be made to look as though I was the murderer—"

"That would make no sense."

"— it makes perfect sense if the true killer wishes to pass the blame onto an innocent man. Which brings me to another question. Do you have any dealings with Adamo Baptista?"

Tintoretto leaned back in his seat. "No. I avoid that particular man... Do you suspect that he killed your daughter and the other women?"

"I don't know, and until I have proof one way or the other, I can do nothing." Der Witt stood up, putting on his hat and then pausing. "Before I leave, I wanted to ask you if '*The Wolves of Venice*' means anything to you?"

Tintoretto shrugged. “No, nothing. I’ve never heard the expression before. Should it mean something to me?”

“I just wondered.” Der Witt replied, moving to the door.

“A moment,” Tintoretto called after him. “You are not unknown to me, Signor. I have heard your name often and people who have benefitted from your treatments have spoken well of you... But others have said you are a dangerous man who uses the occult for his own advancement. A necromancer, a man of poisons... Or so they say.”

“And what do you say?”

“Oh, what I say does not count. I keep away from society and gossip” Tintoretto waved his hand in the direction of the studio. “Paintings are my life, I would be of no use at court, or politicking favours from the Doge. But I would say this – if you believe someone is trying to make you seem the murderer do not continue on your quest alone. You must find yourself some powerful allies – an army of one has no chance of success.” The Dutchman nodded as Tintoretto continued. “The Inquisition has its spies and its informants. If someone betrays to you to them any amount of false claims could be made against what they would regard as a Protestant quack.”

Der Witt smiled wryly.” You are very wise, Signor.”

“No, not wise, merely observant.” Tintoretto replied, pointing to a box in which he had placed a group of his little wax figures. Quickly he fashioned a hat and placed it on the head of one of the bodies, then turned back to the Dutchman, pointing to it. “Here you are, right in the middle, an easy target.” Quickly he moved the figure to the back of the box, behind the others. "But look now. Here you are at the back, able to see everything – and remain unnoticed." Handing Der Witt the wax figure, he said: "Keep to the shadows, Dutchman, and chose your army well."

Chapter Forty Five

Having been refused entry to the Gianetti palazzo, a humiliated Pietro Aretino made his way to his sedan chair and ordered his return home. His bulk made walking difficult, his belly overhang sweaty under the mound of fat, his thighs chafing as they rubbed together. And yet being carried in the sedan chair was uncomfortable too. His great weight forced him to employ four men – where usually there would be only two needed – and even then they would stagger at times, especially if the ground was slippery or uneven underfoot.

So the old bitch Contessa would refuse him admittance, Aretino thought bitterly. She would rue the day.

"Stop here!" he bellowed, the men jerking to a halt, Aretino's fat body lurching forwards as he signalled to someone across the street. "Adamo, where have you been? I've been waiting to see you for two days."

The Florentine shrugged, blithely unconcerned. "I have other calls on my time—"

"And other paymasters, I'll be bound."

Baptista ignored the bait. "You look angry," he said, leaning against the sedan chair.

"Come back with me—"

"There isn't room for more than one in that thing." Baptista replied, mockingly.

"I don't mean *with* me, you fucking moron! Follow me."

"I am awaited at a game of primero." Baptista replied, "I will come along later."

Aretino's fury could not be contained.

"I have been refused admittance at the Gianetti palazzo! I cannot get beyond the door. How dare that old corpse of a woman turn me away. And not just her, I could not get access to her craven grandson either!" he snapped, wiping the sweat from his face. "They will pay for this fucking insult."

"Can you really expect to gain entrance after what we did?"

Throwing his handkerchief to one side, Aretino ignored the comment. "I need to speak to Marco!"

"And you think that by arriving on his doorstep you will achieve your aim?" Baptista leaned down, his voice lowered. "The Contessa will not let you in, she is protecting her grandson. And as for Marco himself, no, he will not meet with you again. If you wish to see him—"

Aretino strained to look up at the Florentine. "Yes?"

"— he needs to be tricked into it."

"Then get on with it!"

"I will. Later."

"I don't pay you to keep me waiting!"

"If the cost of my hire is too high, then I will stay at my card game and we will part company." Baptista retorted, Aretino reluctantly nodding.

"Very well, come when you've finished your cards and cheated everyone. By then you might be a better frame of mind."

"As might you." Baptista replied, tipping his hat and moving on.

Silent, Rosella sat in the Fasculo house looking out of the window onto the square below. In the same room Gilda was holding a long and involved negotiation with a customer, Angelo beckoning for Rosella to follow him.

Once outside, Angelo presented her with a bag of oranges, great ginger orbs, each one almost the size of a hand.

"See what I got from the market. Look and feel the weight! From Naples." he smelt the aroma, one fingernail digging into the peel and releasing more of the scent. "The best in Venice, the man said."

Rosella took the one he offered her, sitting on the back step of the house and peeling it slowly. The juice ran over her fingers, magnifying the pores of her skin underneath. Intrigued, she nudged him.

"Look."

"What is it?"

"My skin... I was only just wondering what kind of skin my baby would have..." Rosella explained, lowering her voice so that he had to strain to hear her. "Angelo, I am telling you this in confidence. The Contessa wishes that I marry Marco—"

"But—"

"Sssh!" she urged him, "You are my only friend, the only person I can talk to. Please listen, and let me speak... She is intent on Marco being held responsible for his actions and asked if I would convert to Catholicism." She looked at him helplessly. "I do not want to deny my faith! But the

Contessa said I should think of the child and act in his best interests."

"And what do you think?"

"What kind of life would a child have if I married someone of another faith, another nationality, another world? How could I live in such wealth when I come from so little? The family and their associates would laugh at me, mock me, and more than that…" she looked into the orange flesh of the orange, split open in her hands. "…such a match would be a scandal in Venice."

"Yet the Contessa suggested it."

"The Gianetti family cannot possibly want it in reality. The whole city would talk about it and I would be taken away from everything I love here."

Angelo was torn between speaking out and keeping silent. He wanted to ask how she could think of marrying Marco Gianetti, the man who had tricked her. Yet at the same time he knew Marco was the child's father and the man who had once been her lover.

"…I wonder if they really want to take control," Rosella continued. "perhaps later get rid of me and keep the baby. After all, Marco's child would be the next Gianetti heir. Maybe that is why the Contessa seems fixed upon the marriage."

"Perhaps she is merely offering the best solution—"

"*You think I should deny my faith?* I am a Jew, Angelo, I was born a Jew and wish to die a Jew."

"Then talk to the rabbi."

"When I am ready. But not yet. First I want to think…" she bowed her head. "Ira wants to marry me to a Jewish widower in another city to avoid the scandal."

"You would not have to go to another city, Rosella, you know how much I feel for you—"

She shook her head. "No, my friend, I cannot ruin your life. You cannot be expected to take on a woman carrying another man's child. Your life would be made miserable here because of me." Gently she touched his arm. "We are friends, and we can never be anything else. But I value your friendship more than you know. Do you understand?..."

Reluctantly he nodded, glancing down.

"...And you are not angry with me?"

"No." he said, taking in a long breath and changing the subject. "If Ira arranged a marriage for you, would you agree to it?"

"It would mean that the baby will grown up amongst its own kind and will never know it's true parentage. I want that for my baby – but by the same token, am I right to deny the child it's inheritance?"

"If it was a girl, it could not inherit."

"I know, but she would still have a good life, full of chances. Girl or boy, they would want for nothing, affluence, opportunity, status... but then I wondered if they would ever be completely accepted. Or if everyone would remember that their mother is a Jewess, a poor Jewess from the ghetto. A woman who – instead of living in a palazzo – was locked up when the curfew bell rang." She flung the orange into the gutter and shook her head. "Ira is so angry with me."

"He was shocked—"

"*Shocked?*" she repeated bitterly. "It was not him that was used, it was me. If his pride is injured, what of mine? Is *he* carrying an illegitimate child? No. Ira said he would stand by me, but where is he now? Not here, Angelo, not here. I have shamed him and he will never forgive me for it." Her voice hardened. "The fight he had with Marco was not for my benefit, Ira has cast Marco as the scapegoat—"

"Is he not?"

"Marco was as used as I was." She replied, "His greatest failing was his weakness, his desperation to please Pietro Aretino. I came second to the writer because Aretino could offer Marco something I could not – a father. That was why he wanted to please him so much. Marco thought that in some way if he could please Aretino he could please his own father, the man who had always despised him." She tapped the back of Angelo's hand. "What Marco did was treacherous, cruel, stupid – but I understand *why* he did it. What I do not understand is Ira's hostility towards me. I think he believes that I have ruined his career, that this scandal has made him a figure of mockery – and he cannot endure that. If I marry Marco Gianetti not just the ghetto will know what happened, but the whole city. Venice thrives on gossip, they will take their fill from this."

Uncertain of how to respond, Angelo stared at the burst orange in the gutter, seeing the sunlight glisten hotly on the split fruit.

"Ira's a proud man, but he loves you."

"He *did* love me," Rosella conceded. "...but now? Now I am so sure."

Nervously waiting outside the artists shop on the Rialto, Marco watched for the approach of Tintoretto. The painter's message had said that it was urgent for them to meet and that Marco should tell no one as the matter concerned Rosella. Hopeful at the thought she might want to see him, Marco studied every passerby for the familiar stocky figure of *Il Furioso* and was surprised when he felt an unexpected grip on his arm.

"What do you want?"

Adam Baptista feigned disappointment. "We are old friends, Marco, are you not happy to see me?"

"I am meeting someone—"

"Ah, well, Signor Tintoretto is not coming. I used him as a ruse to get you here."

Marco tried to shake off his grip. "I want nothing to do with you!"

"Nor Aretino either, I imagine." Baptista replied. His grip had tightened on Marco's arm. "We don't want to cause a disturbance out here, what would people think if Marco Gianetti was involved in *second* fight only days after his return? Let's move on." He steered Marco away, moving towards a moored boat with the initials **P** and **A** emblazoned on its side.

Gesturing for the boatman to leave, Baptista urged Marco into the vessel where Aretino sat shaded under a tasselled canopy. After the storm and the fogs of the previous days the weather had turned itself around, teasing a little late summer from the October air.

"You must try these figs, dear Marco," Aretino said, his tone mellow. "I have never experienced such lushness."

"What you do want with me? I am only here because I was tricked into coming—"

"You *are* easily duped, are you not? But your naivety

makes you all the more adorable." Aretino continued. "We must regain our friendship—"

Marco snorted. "Never!"

"Angry men are blind and foolish, for reason at such time takes flight and, in her absence, wrath plunders all the riches of the intellect while judgement remains the prisoner of its own pride." He gestured to the figs again. "Try one, you will be consumed by its sweet moistness." He looked to the side of the canal and addressed Baptista, who was waiting there. "We will chat for a little time, come back in a while when we have made amends." His small, shrew eyes turned back to Marco. "Please sit down, we have much to talk about."

"I have nothing to say to you—"

"Fucking donkey!" Aretino sneered, his anger suddenly uncorked. "You might have nothing to say to me, but I have plenty to say to you. Your antique grandmother banished me from the Gianetti palazzo, sent me packing like a beggar, but soon we will see just who is the genuine beggar." He wiped his mouth with a napkin, pointing irritably to a seat. "Sit down, little boy, and learn how the real world works."

Hesitating, Marco looked from Aretino to Baptista, the latter standing a little way off on the canal side.

"That flight of yours was pointless, Marco. See how you returned? Some doubted you would, but I knew better, even if you did miss your own father's funeral. Poor Jacopo, we were friends for many years."

"My grandmother said that he hated you and that you blackmailed him."

"Did she say why?"

"No."

"No, she denied knowing when we spoke," Aretino replied. "But you and I, being friends, can speak freely together. The truth is often painful, but we are none of us children forever." He paused, reaching for his wine, sipped at it, and then continued. "Rosella Tabat is pregnant with your child."

"I know."

"And there is gossip that you intend to marry her—"

"How would you know that?"

"My dear Marco, how many servants does your family employ? Thirty? Forty? Oh, and boatmen too. Many are loyal, but there is always someone who finds that loyalty wavers in the face of a purse of coins." He smiled sleekly. "Servants are like mice, unnoticed most of the time, but always in the background, scuttling about and overhearing much with their big, ever open ears."

"Do you have spies everywhere?"

"Everywhere I need them." He replied, reverting to his previous theme. "Are you not curious as to *why* I blackmailed your father?"

"So you admit it?"

"Yes, I admit it."

"And as my father is dead," Marco replied, "it does not matter anymore."

"So you think his secret is without value now?"

"I do not know his secret. I do not want to know his secret," Marco said, understanding that he was – in some way – being cursed. That the bloated man in front of him, still sweating even under a sheltering canopy, was not content to have fed off a dead man, but was now turning his eyes on the living son.

At that instant he marvelled that he could have ever admired Aretino, or thought him amusing. He wondered how he had endured his capriciousness, his casual cruelty, and felt the same sense of entrapment that his father had once felt. A noose of control about to slide over his head and tighten around his throat. And he wondered why he had returned to Venice. If he had stayed away, Rosella would have married a Jewish widower and raised her son in peace, Ira would have prospered in his career and if Marco Gianetti's name had ever been mentioned it would have been with hatred and relief that he had left Venice forever.

But he *had* returned, and Aretino was talking again.

"Your father was quite prepared to pay me for my silence and our deal continued for many years. Of course his death was a matter of grief for us all—"

"What hold did you have over him?"

"— I will tell you in time, Marco. You are impatient."

"And you are like the boy who pulls the wings off a fly to see it suffer and stay earthbound before watching it die." Marco replied. "If you have any mercy, tell me now. Unless you have nothing to tell, and are merely bluffing."

Aretino raised his eyebrows.

"How brave you have become, Marco. Your sojourn away from Venice has matured you. But then again, only a mature man could be the heir to the Gianetti fortune. Only a strong man could handle the many duties and burdens of such wealth." He sighed, his chest wheezing like a pair of bellows. "The fog induced in me a cough, something from which I had not suffered before. I find it irksome..." Marco said nothing and waited for him to continue. "...Your grandmother and I had a long conversation about your welfare."

"My welfare?"

"You have people who care for you, Marco, you must never doubt that. The ghetto rats are of no importance. If they hate you, what does it matter?"

"It matters to me."

"So naïve..." Aretino replied, moving on. "The Contessa was anxious for your return, obviously to see you in good health, but also for you to inherit the legacy which is yours by rights. I believe that as you have no siblings the estate would go to your cousins in the event of your death. Which naturally is not pertinent here."

"What *is* pertinent?"

"As you know, your dear father was affected in the mind before he died, and your mother, God rest her soul, was unstable also."

"I am not afflicted that way."

"No, no, you wouldn't be," Aretino replied, pausing for an instant before he continued. "And why? Because you are **not** Jacopo Gianetti's son—"

Confused, Marco stared at him. "What are you talking about?"

"You are **not** the heir to the fortune for which you long—"

Marco shook his head, his voice wavering. "No, no..."

"—the fortune which would ensure influential friends at court and willing whores." Aretino stared at him, his voice malicious. "There is only one way you will inherit, Marco Gianetti – and that is by paying me to keep your secret."

Chapter Forty Six

I am falling, Marco thought, *I am falling without wings. A fly torn apart. I am sinking through space and through earth, and the breath in my lungs feels like liquid and the blood in my veins like oil. I am falling, alive, to no death. A corpse within a living man.*

"You are lying!" Marco said finally, surprised that the words left his lips, because he could feel no breath, no moving of the tongue.

"No it's the truth, and I have proof. And now I will tell you something of great strangeness. Your father never asked what hold I had over him. *He* never asked for proof. I can only surmise that he had a number of secrets, business dealings from which he profited, some would say, stole. Land sales which were corrupt. His list of misdemeanours was impressive, so much so that he could not afford to question me as to what I was blackmailing him about in case he inadvertently gave himself away by mentioning something of which I had no prior knowledge." He paused, fanning himself with his hand as the light began its slow fade into dusk. "But *I do* have proof that you are not his son."

Marco could barely form the words. "What proof?"

"Your mother wrote a letter to her father in Milan – a

letter which was intercepted. In despair she admitted that she had been unfaithful and that she was carrying another man's child. The man with whom she committed adultery – your real father – sadly died years ago in a boating accident. But your mother's infidelity with this gentleman was the real reason she committed suicide... Have some wine, Marco, you look faint." He passed him a glass, Marco draining the wine, a few drops spilling down his doublet. "When the truth comes out, what a scandal it will be. The Venetian authorities will obviously not allow a bastard to inherit the Gianetti fortune, especially a bastard who would be married to a Jewess."

"I...I..."

"The legacy will be taken from you," Aretino said with triumph. "As well as the Gianetti name, and then the inheritance will be dispersed amongst your many dull male cousins." He leaned back against the cushions, glossy with malice. "Your dreams of riches are over, Marco. When your true parentage is revealed you will be penniless, the lands and monies taken from you as you are turned out of the palazzo and forced onto the streets with your whore."

Marco shook his head helplessly. "I don't believe it. I don't believe you."

Aretino tossed a sheet of paper towards him. "Read it. That is copy of the letter your mother sent to her father. Remember I told you that there is always one servant who will act as a spy? The woman was in my employ at the Gianetti palazzo—"

"Is she still there?" Marco asked bitterly. "Is she still spying for you?"

"No, she retired to the countryside." Aretino smiled. "And

don't fret, it was not your plump Cara, who fucked your virginity out of you." He laughed, his chest booming with a mixture of coughs and laughter. "You look so surprised, Marco! Did you think that you did *anything* about which I did not know? I had a timetable of your testicles and bowels, a calendar of your sleeping, I daresay I can tell you the temperature of your bath water."

Marco struggled to his feet, the wine and the shock had befuddled him. "I will contest it!"

"With whom?" Aretino countered. "The Doge? The Counsel? And if you bring the matter into court be aware that the secret will be exposed. Poor Marco, you cannot win. I have the *proof* that you are a bastard, unable to inherit the Gianetti fortune—"

"It is my birth right!"

"It is not!" Aretino retorted, his black eyes flickering with spite. "One word from me to the Doge and you are a beggar. One word and you are destitute. One word and you are set to fend for yourself in this world and believe me, Marco, you could not do it. Your little escapade was a jaunt. You took money to ease your way, but without money there is nothing – no food, no roof over your head, no friends. Those people who accepted you in the ghetto hate you now, if you went to them they would spit in your face. And who else can you go to?"

"My grandmother—"

"*Your grandmother?* What can she do with the proof I would show her? She is a very old woman, if the shock didn't kill her being made destitute would—"

"What are you saying? Why would it affect her?"

Aretino rolled his eyes.

"You have a handsome face, Marco, but you are so slow... It would affect the noble Contessa because she is residing in the Gianetti palazzo in ignorance. If I expose your secret, she will be penniless like you. You can't save her. All the Gianetti possessions and properties would be tied up by law, to be assessed and then distributed amongst your dreary cousins. And we all know how apathetic litigation can be."

"You can't do that to her!"

"I am not punishing your grandmother, but *you* will be if you refuse an offer to save her." Aretino pushed another cushion into the small of his back, leaning his bulk against it and sighing. "Be reasonable, Marco, you have no one to help you. There is only one person who can save you. Only one person who can ensure that you inherit your fortune and keep your name and status." Aretino paused, looking up to the balmy October sky. "They say it will be foggy again, but I doubt it. The sky looks as clear as a child's eye."

Marco slumped back into his set. "The letter could be a fake—"

"No, I have the original and a signed and dated copy of a letter written by your real father, admitting who he was."

"How did you get that?"

Aretino clicked his tongue. "The same way I obtain everything, little boy, I *bought* it. The man was a drinker, a fool, he was more than willing to oblige." He sighed, shaking his head. "You enjoyed your acceptance at Court, relished the affection with which the Doge treated you as his old friend's son, without realising the level of Jacopo's corruption. The Doge would not appreciate being taken for a fool and would be sure to exile you from court when your true origins are revealed." He sighed again, "But all this can be avoided, Marco, did I not keep your father safe for many years?"

"And how much did it cost him?"

"Greedy boy," Aretino reproached him. "The Gianetti fortune is immense, my fee was no more than a straw dropped from a passing hay wain."

He signalled for Baptista to approach, putting up his hand to signal for him to stop about three yards away. Close enough so The Florentine could see what was going on, but not close enough for him to overhear the conversation.

Then he turned back to Marco. "So, what is your decision?" Aretino asked, his tone impatient. "Penury for yourself and, by extension, your grandmother? Or my little creaming off the top of the Gianetti fortune to keep you safe? Think about it, Marco. When you inherit you will be one of the most powerful men in Venice, the Doge will court you, the nobility fawn over you, and you will have not only the best whores in Venice, but your pick of the most influential and wealthy future wife."

"My grandmother wishes me to marry Rosella Tabat—"

"Pah! A man of the stature you will become necessitates a wife from a powerful family."

"She is carrying my child."

"A matter that can be solved to everyone's agreement. Rosella Tabat will be found a suitable Jewish husband. Naturally the child with remain with you, to be brought up as a Gianetti—"

Marco shook his head. "She will not give up her child, neither would I asked it of her. It would be too cruel—"

"You must think of the future and suppress your kind heartedness. Otherwise years from now your son – if it *is* a boy – will come back from exile to claim his legacy after your demise. And how would that play out with your legitimate heirs? As for Rosella Tabat – be very careful, women can wait and plan for many years to exact their revenge via their offspring."

"Rosella is not like that—"

"All mothers are like that." Aretino corrected him. "Be reasonable, Marco, this is not just one man's future, but the future of the whole Gianetti family." He smiled to himself, thinking of how he had used the same argument with Marco's father, and how Jacopo had reacted. Would his son react in the same way? He wondered. "Think of the lands you will own, the horses, properties, paintings – your father commissioned several Titians, amongst other. No more playing at being an apprentice to Tintoretto – who expects the Gianetti heir to *work* for a living?" his voice took on a lilting tone. "Servants to do you bidding, women to obey every whim. Without your father's sober influence, the Gianetti palazzo could become a pleasure house, famous in Venice and across Europe. You have the charm and the appearance, Marco, you look like the heir to a fortune. If you had been ill tempered, an uncouth, illiterate hunchback no one would have accepted you, but you have been favoured by the gods."

"I do not feel favoured," Marco said hoarsely. "I feel used—"

"It will pass," Aretino said abruptly. "A man feels less used in a palazzo than a hut." His rapped his hand on the arm of the chair in which he was sitting. "I would have your answer, Marco!"

"If I agreed to your terms my whole life would be a lie—"

"Many lives are just that."

"—and how could I hurt Rosella again?" Marco shook his head. "She is innocent in all of this. How could I steal her child from her—"

"*Your* child." Aretino remonstrated. "You are not stealing anything. Besides, if it is a girl, then what harm? Leave the infant with its mother... You have to choose, Marco, a business arrangement with me is all it would take to settle this matter. The choice I offer is simple; poverty and disgrace – or power and acclaim."

"I cannot do this." Marco said hopelessly. "I cannot... I cannot cause such injury—"

"Very well," Aretino beckoned for Baptista to approach. "Signor Gianetti wishes to leave now."

"Is there no other way?" Marco asked desperately. "Dear God, is there no other way?"

Aretino shook his head.

"God has no say in the matter. It is *your* decision as to how to live your life. It is *your* choice and the one with which you will have to live... You look at me as though I were a devil, but you're wrong." Aretino spread his arms out in an expansive gesture. "Behold, your Saviour. From now on money is your Father and secrecy your Holy Ghost."

They say the Devil is a young and handsome man, otherwise why would we be seduced by him?

Yet that is just another old wives tale. The Devil came to me in the bloated form of a man; and his trickery was not wonderful. At first it had appeared seductive, but that had been Aretino's way to get the puppet used to the strings; once the victim is entrapped his charm is gone. What is left is a carapace of wit, hiding a pustuler core.

All my life I had accepted that Jacopo Gianetti was my father. Never once had I questioned it. I believed that his dislike of me had stemmed from my mother's suicide, the 'milk fever' motive that had seemed logical. A child is told what to believe. Only later do we challenge the accepted version with our own judgement. So when Aretino stated that I was illegitimate; unable to inherit the Gianetti fortune; that everything I had been taught to expect would be snatched out of my hands

I burned.

Being disliked and rejected by a father I had sought to please seemed all the more unbearable. Jacopo Gianetti had known I was not his son, and yet for the sake of greed – that organ he had fed so assiduously – he had kept me in ignorance. And he had not even known which of his sins Aretino was holding over his head like Damocles' sword. Which property deal, which false witness, which bastard child – which was it? Jacopo had never known, nor dared to question.

And in all those chilling childhood years I had been cared for like a botanical specimen. Kept in the right conditions for growth; fed plentifully, brought out into the sunlight to flourish, my roots to be dug deep into the Gianetti soil... And yet, in just minutes, Aretino had annihilated my life; my past a lie, my present a charade, and my future – unless I agreed his terms – penury.

The promise of the Gianetti legacy had been an enduring anchor to my wavering life. But Aretino had wrenched the anchor from the sea bed and left the boat adrift. I could say that the shock made up my mind, but that would be a lie, and I never lie. For a while I admit that I pretended I was anxious for my grandmother and how exposure would ruin her. A woman born to plenty could not have endured poverty. But neither could I. It is only when we are threatened with its loss that we appreciate the value of anything.

So, in one way, I was very similar to Jacopo Gianetti. I had his greed, and allied to that I was carrying a grudge, as indelible as a birthmark. Abandoning Rosella was a necessity, I told myself. She would not have been accepted socially as my wife and would have suffered for it. As for the child, if it was a boy, recompense would be made to the mother and he would be raised as a Gianetti. Another bastard, second in a line of bastards that would remain unexposed for as long as I paid a ransom.

Do not doubt, it was a ransom. A bribe by which I could secure myself. Money for status, for a name, for riches, for properties and houses and servants, for power. And it seemed a just revenge, that I, who had felt so demeaned, so disparaged, for so long by my imagined father, would inherit the Gianetti fortune. And its power.

So I agreed to pay the sweaty palmed Aretino for his silence. And in doing so, I knew I would never escape his manipulation. He would remain the puppet master. As he had been with my father, he would be with me. The strings were already set, the movements rehearsed, and besides, I was such a willing puppet.

Chapter Forty Seven

Curious to see what the furore was about, Caterina paused on the bridge, looking down onto the canal side. With Bakita following, she made her way over the bridge and approached the small crowd, all huddled around some unseen object. Impelled to continue, she nudged her way through the first few people and then paused, one hand going over her mouth.

The girl was lying on her back, her clothes wet. Her body had obviously been dredged from the water by the two men on a small boat who had then brought her over to the canal side. They were both looking down at her, one man holding the rope which stopped the boat from drifting, the other bearing the wet imprint of her body where he had carried her. The face of the drowned girl was untouched, but around her neck were red marks already turning a purplish blue. Although fully clothed, her feet were bare, and on her left wrist was a deep cut.

"Oh Dear God," Caterina said, shaken, "has someone sent for the authorities?"

The man holding the rope looked at her. "Someone's already gone."

"When did you find her?"

"About ten minutes ago."

"Was it suicide?" Caterina asked, a large woman behind her jostling to get a better view of the corpse.

"Doesn't look like suicide to me," she replied, "look at her neck."

Caterina pushed the woman away and took off her shawl, covering the dead girl's face with it.

"Does anyone know who she was?"

The big woman shrugged. "Not me, not seen her around. But how can anyone see her now with her face covered?"

"It's a matter of respect—"

"Respect be damned," the woman replied, looking Caterina up and down. "...she was probably one of your sort, only not as successful."

"And if she was, should we not care about her death?" Caterina countered, the woman shrugging and walking away.

The boatmen watched her go, one turning back to Caterina. "I tell you something else about that girl – look in her right hand."

Caterina bend down, taking hold of the girl's hand and gently opening the fingers. Inside, sticking to the flesh of her palm, were number of dark hairs; hairs pulled from her assailant's head as she had fought for her life. Caterina stared at the hairs, then, as the boatman's attention was diverted, slid them into her pocket before replacing the girl's hand back on her unmoving breast.

Waiting impatiently until it was dark, Caterina left her house by the street entrance, leaving Bakita on guard and giving him instructions that if anyone called she was busy and not to be disturbed. Do not, she told him emphatically, let anyone know I am away from the house.

"You need me—"

She touched his arm. "No, not tonight. But you must stay here and pretend I am at home." Her voice dropped. "Do not tell the other guard, or any of the staff. Do you hear me, Bakita?"

He nodded. "Where are you going?"

"Somewhere I need to go alone," she replied, "I am not in danger, but someone I care about may well be. Do as I say, Bakita, I *will* come back."

She took a circuitous route across the Rialto, avoiding the most populated areas where the taverns were filling up with drinkers, gamblers and the whores greeting the soldiers who had come off the boats that morning. Dressed in dark clothes and a hooded cape, Caterina passed unnoticed across bridges and through alleyways where the shops had closed, doors bolted for the night. By a shrine to Our Lady she was accosted by two men, but avoided them, hurrying on with her head bowed.

The bells were ringing out the hour of six when she reached the terrace of low houses and approached the third in the row. The night was comforting, yet the flowers planted in the neat garden shimmered like glow worms in the moonlight. Glancing round to see that no one was watching her, Caterina knocked, then knocked again. She heard movement from inside, but it took several seconds for someone to approach the door and call out.

"Hello, who's there?"

"Caterina. Let me in, Dutchman."

He did at once, standing back as she entered and guiding her into his study. "What are you doing here?"

"There's been another murder. A girl was drowned a little over an hour ago..." He seemed curiously unmoved and she continued. "...don't you hear me? Another girl has been murdered."

"You said she drowned."

"She was found in the water, but she had marks around her neck and a deep cut on her wrist."

"Perhaps she tried to kill herself?"

"With marks around her neck?"

"Maybe she tried to hang herself and then attempted to cut her wrist. It's painful, perhaps she thought drowning might be easier."

Surprised at his unconcern, Caterina persisted. "I thought I would warn you—"

"Of *what?*"

"You told me that someone is trying to make you look like a murderer." She explained hurriedly. "Now there has been another killing, I wanted to tell you what had happened so you could be prepared."

Her voice trailed off, her anxiety replaced by a feeling of unease. She had trusted the Dutchman, had developed a fondness for him, and had sympathised when he had told her about the loss of his daughter. They had become allies. But now she was seeing him differently, wondering if she had been duped: if his involving her with the deaths of his child and that of Gabriella Russo had worked on her sympathies and blunted her senses. She also realised that she was alone.

"What am I supposed to be prepared *for*, Caterina?"

"The… The Inquisition, the authorities. You said they were watching you."

"I was *told* they were watching me, I never said it." He replied, leaning against his desk. "So why did you come here? To tell me about another girl's death?"

She lifted her head imperiously, refusing to show unease. The killer's hairs were in her pocket, but although she had arrived willing to confide in Der Witt, she was now determined to keep the evidence to herself.

"I came here because I was trying to help an old friend."

"But you have told me so little. Surely if you were really trying to help me, you would tell me all the details. Who was this girl?"

"I don't know."

"Was she mutilated?"

"Not that I saw," Caterina replied, her tone cool.

"And she had all her limbs?"

"Yes, Dutchman, the girl had all her limbs. Perhaps her killer was not the same person as the man who murdered your daughter, or Rosella, or the woman in France—"

"Or perhaps he was disturbed."

"*What?*"

"Perhaps he was going to mutilate her and could not go through with his plans because he was about to be caught."

She shrugged, feigning nonchalance. "I do not know what happened, or who he was, or why he did it. As I say, I just wanted to inform you."

"Did you know the girl?"

"No."

"Did I?"

"How would I know?" Caterina replied, "She is in the morgue now, you could look yourself."

"And you say that they found her body an hour ago?"

She nodded. "Yes, just as it was beginning to go dark."

"Which canal?"

"The Merziere."

"The killer chose a public place. All the more reason to suppose that he was disturbed before he could complete his ritual."

"It is not busy the entire distance of the canal." Caterina retorted. "Besides the girl's body could have drifted from where she was originally left."

"Had she been in the water long?"

"The boatmen said no, that she could not have been there for more than a matter of minutes because they had passed by earlier and there had been no body there then."

Faking an interest in the objects around her, Caterina moved around the studio, edging closer to the door. She could sense the Dutchman's gaze on her as she pretended to be intrigued by a drawing on the wall, but in reality her attention was fixed on the exit. All she had to do was to get within a couple of feet of the door, she told herself, then she could make a run for it. Der Witt was a heavily built man in his fifties, she could be out of the house and away from the terrace before he could catch up with her.

"You like the drawing?"

Caterina was momentarily caught off guard, then glanced back to the picture. "Yes. It's beautiful."

"Was she?"

"What?"

"The girl who was just killed," he replied. "Was she beautiful?"

Caterina nodded. "Yes, she was beautiful. Gabriella was beautiful too. Were your daughter and the woman in France also beauties?" He stared at her without answering. And then, for a reason could never explain, she asked. "Where were you an hour ago, Dutchman?"

Angelo pushed aside his plate of food, his brother staring at him. "What's wrong with it?"

"Nothing," Angelo replied, glancing over to his mother. "Where's Rosella?"

"She went home," Gilda replied, her tone brusque. "She had it in mind that she wanted to talk to her brother, although what good it will do remains to be seen." Reaching for some bread she tore off a hunk and then rolled it around in her fingers absent-mindedly. "I tried to convince her to stay, but Rosella was determined. She wants to make things right with Ira. I understand—"

"I don't." Angelo said flatly. "He's made it clear what he thinks. And he's made Rosella feel guilty, even a burden. She told me that Ira thinks she's ruining his career—"

"Really? How can he believe that?" Gilda replied.

"—Rosella being pregnant with Mario Gianetti's child is a disgrace. Ira wants to send her away and marry her to some Jewish widower in another city."

"Maybe that would be for the best—"

"For the best!"

"Angelo, you are in love with Rosella," his mother said

indulgently. "Of course you want her to stay here, but what is there for the girl in Venice now?"

Marco hesitated. He knew what Rosella had told him had been in confidence, but the secret burned on his tongue and would not stay hidden. Leaning across the table he dropped his voice. "You must tell no one – and that means you too, Federico." he warned his brother. "I was told this in confidence by Rosella – the Contessa wants Marco to marry her."

"Nonsense!" Gilda snapped, tossing her bread to one side. "She was teasing you."

"Rosella was **not** teasing me!"

"You think the heir to the Gianetti fortune would marry some Jewess from the ghetto? Be sensible, Marco, this is nonsense. The old Contessa must be losing her mind." She tapped her forehead. "You cannot mix Jew with Catholic—"

"Unless Rosella converts." Gilda stared at her son incredulously as he continued. "It's true, the old lady wants her to become a Catholic, then she will see to it that her grandson owns up to being the child's father, and marries Rosella to secure the baby's inheritance."

"She believes this?"

Marco hesitated. "Rosella has some doubts—"

"*Some* doubts! She should do more than doubt."

"—she wondered if the family might want the marriage so they could get rid of her later and bring up the baby themselves."

"What did she mean – get rid of her?"

Angelo shrugged. "I don't know. Send her away from Venice, get her away from the city to marry someone else or have her baby in some convent."

"And where does Marco Gianetti come in all of this?" Gilda asked curtly. "Does he want the marriage?"

Angelo shrugged. "I don't know – I've told you everything Rosella said."

"I don't imagine that she told you – or maybe she didn't know herself – that Marco Gianetti's father was married twice. Both of his wives died."

He frowned. "I don't know what you mean—"

"I don't *mean* anything, Angelo, I'm just thinking aloud. It would be strange if his son followed in his father's footsteps." Gilda stared at her sons. "Both of you have to keep quiet about this, you hear me? You in particular, Lorenzo, you have a big mouth—"

"So has Marco!" he replied, aggrieved. "Why pick on me, when it was him who broke Rosella's confidence?"

"*None* of us must mention this," Gilda said firmly. "We are not to get involved—"

"*Rosella is living here!*"

"Rosella *was* living here!" his mother countered. "She has now returned home. Only Rosella and Ira can work out what they are going to do about the child and about the future. It is none of our business and we can't interfere – or mention it outside this room." She looked from one son to the other. "Agreed?"

"She shouldn't have gone home," Angelo persisted. "Ira is barely there, he's always away. Here she has us, she had company—"

"Maybe she doesn't want company, Angelo! Rosella needs to think. She has a decision to make which will set the course of not only her life, but that of her child. We *must* leave her in peace." Gilda rose to her feet and began to clear away the plates.

But Angelo persisted. "Can't *you* talk to her?" he pleaded. "She might listen to you—"

"If Rosella had wanted to talk to me, she would have come to me already." Gilda replied. "When Rosella Tabat needs me – or you – she will come back."

"And if she doesn't?" Angelo countered.

"Then that is her choice. And one you will have to live with."

Chapter Forty Eight

Weary, his footsteps dragging, Ira made his way to the ghetto, ringing for admittance. It was three in the morning, the moon incandescent, casting its silk white ribbons on the water of the canals and the rounded roof tiles. He had walked without carrying a lamp, the moonlight enough to illuminate his way, the night stripping the stonework of colour, the bridges and alleyways silent as a graveyard.

He had decided that he would talk to his sister in the morning and allow Rosella to make the choice as to whether she wanted to marry Marco Gianetti or a Jewish man from another city. Ira's own instinct was against any involvement with the Gianetti family; his mistrust of Marco increasing rather than decreasing. Their fight had served no purpose; Ira had hoped it might absolve some of the shame and betrayal he felt, but it had done the opposite. Rosella had been right; he *had* chosen to see Marco as the scapegoat and, to his shame, the destruction of their friendship mattered more to him that his estrangement from Rosella.

Sometimes Ira even wondered if – in the early hours when he found sleep absent – he had struck his sister deliberately. His conscious mind denied it, but his subconscious wondered if the misaimed blow had been intended. Having admitted the truth to himself, Ira was eager to make amends with his sister and as he rang the ghetto bell for the second time he was keen to be admitted. His plan was simple: in the morning he would ask Rosella for forgiveness. They were family, two people alone in the world: she needed his support and blessing and he – reluctant as he was to admit it – needed the same from her.

"Ira." The gatekeeper came to the entrance, unlocking the gates and stepping back to allow him to enter. He said nothing, but kept his gaze averted, his head bowed.

"Did I wake you, Samuel?"

"No, you did not wake me." He looked up, eyes moist. "I am sorry, so sorry..."

What are you sorry for? Why are you crying? If not at this moment, you have been weeping because your eyes are swollen. And you will not look at me... Ira stared at the man, his mouth opening, but not speaking... I know, I know what you will not tell me. I know. But I will ask anyway, because it is not real until I hear the words

"What is it?"

"Rosella..."

Tell me, go on. Go on, tell me. Say it, form your lips into the words and speak them. You will remember them all your life – but not as I will. I will never stop hearing them and know I was too late. That there will never be a morning, there will never be that conversation, that offered choice, my reluctant, arrogant, unfeeling, uncaring surrender.

Suddenly Ira's hand lost its grip and he dropped his medical bag, leaning against the wall for support. Besides him, the gatekeeper was talking gently, holding his arm.

"Your sister was found a little while ago... she is dead, Ira..."

"Dead? How?"

And the gatekeeper paused, scrabbling to make the phrase.

"She was ... she was...found in the Merziere canal."

"Drowned?"

Sliding his arm under Ira's, the man leaned forward, preparing for the weight he would have to bear. "No, she was murdered... Rosella was strangled."

Ira's legs buckled, the gatekeeper taking his weight as he struggled to keep Ira upright. As he did so, two other men came running towards them to help, Ira pushing them away.

"Leave me alone!" he shouted, heaving himself upright. **"Let me be."**

In unison, the men stepped back, watching as Ira Tabat inched his way home. They could see he was struggling to walk, weaving slightly from side to side, one of the men following after him with his medical bag. Agonisingly slowly Ira covered the fifteen yards to the home he had shared with his sister. Finally, his hand shaking, he lifted the latch.

"Ira, take your bag..."

He turned, nodded to the man and took his case, then walked in and closed the door behind him.

Outside the men waited in silence. They saw a candle lighted in an upstairs window and glanced at each other, wondering if they should stay or leave. But Ira Tabat did not make a sound that could be heard outside. There was no wailing, no crying, instead he sat motionless at the window and watched as the moon died away and the dawn came in.

Chapter Forty Nine

Making a gesture for his apprenticeships to be quiet, Tintoretto dismissed two of the men and scolded the third, berating him for under priming the canvas he had wanted to work on that morning.

"How many times do I have to teach you?" he asked, tapping the young man's temple. 'Is it solid in there? Like one of Michelangelo's marble statues?" he picked up a large priming brush and waved it in front of the apprenticeship's face. "Two coats! How many times do I have to tell you – lay on **two** thick coats."

But the apprentice's gaze had moved from Tintoretto's face. Instead he was looking over the artist's shoulder, his expression curious.

Turning to follow his gaze, Tintoretto stared at the figure in the studio doorway. It took him a moment to recognise the man, then he beckoned urgently to him.

"Ira, come, come in."

"Shall I do the second coat now?" the apprentice asked, Tintoretto waving a dismissive hand in his direction. "No, tomorrow. Tomorrow will do."

"I could do—"

"Tomorrow!" Tintoretto repeated, hustling the lad out of the studio and locking the door behind him. When he turned Ira was standing with his hands extended towards the stove for warmth. Colourless, his face drawn, his eyes shadowed, the lips bloodless.

"My friend, are you ill?"

"Do you think she is cold?"

Tintoretto pulled out a seat and gestured for Ira to sit down. "Who?"

"Rosella."

"I don't know, the temperature is falling, that's true." He continued, puzzled. "Where is Rosella?"

"Not at home." Ira replied, staring intently into the artist's face. "You know where she is, you know the place, you have been there often."

"I don't understand—"

Ira looked around him blindly. "I did not know where else to go, but here. Marco *was* my friend, but I couldn't go to him. Not now... Did he do it, do you think?"

Confused, Tintoretto took Ira's arm. "You have to explain, tell me what you are talking about."

"Rosella. She's dead."

Tintoretto blinked, re-running the words in his head before replying. "*She's dead?* How?"

"Murdered. She was strangled and left in the Merziere canal yesterday. Some boatmen found her and they took her to the morgue. I've been talking to the authorities, they've been questioning me, asking me strange things – *'Did I love my sister? Had we fought?'*" his hands reached out towards the stove again. "It will be cold in the morgue. I should take a blanket to cover her..."

"Ira, look at me," Tintoretto said calmly, "and concentrate. You said that the authorities had been asking you questions. Why?"

He ignored his words. "...They don't know she was pregnant, that she was carrying Marco Gianetti's child and that we had argued about it. When they do, it will change everything... He wouldn't have killed her, would he?"

"*Marco?*" Tintoretto replied, incredulously, "No, he wouldn't kill anyone!"

"I didn't kill her."

"I know that."

"*Do you?*" Ira asked, his eyes unreadable, "the authorities thought I was capable."

"Did they say so?"

"No, but I could tell—"

"How do you know what they thought?" the artist replied shortly. He was trying to remain composed, but the conversation was a struggle for him. Rosella was dead; he could hardly believe it. Rosella, murdered. His attention turned back to Ira. "You loved your sister, you provided for her and for your mother for years, everyone knows you were a close family. And besides, you are a respected doctor—"

"I was ashamed of her."

"Tell me that, Ira, but no one else!" Tintoretto snapped. "There are things that should remain private, or they will be misconstrued."

"But it's true," Ira persisted, "I was ashamed of her being pregnant. And now it seems unforgivable—"

Tintoretto's grip on his arm tightened. "You must mind what you say, Ira, the inquisitors will trap you otherwise, make your words seem as though they mean other than what you intended...” He pulled a bench over to the stove and sat down, encouraging Ira to take a seat beside him. The light from the stove illuminated his features and threw umber shadows around his eyes. “Why would anyone want to kill Rosella?” Tintoretto asked, his voice wavering. “She never hurt anyone, who would want her dead?”

“The Gianetti family?”

“Why?”

“Perhaps the Contessa’s idea that Marco should marry Rosella did not find favour with everyone. Maybe someone did not want a Jewess in the family, or the scandal which would be sure to follow. They have the money, power, either Marco or the old woman could have arranged my sister’s death.”

Tintoretto shook his head.

“No, it makes no sense. You said that Rosella had been strangled and abandoned. A public death, a messy death.” He paused, controlling his feelings. “... If the Gianettis had wanted to kill her, they would have organised it to look like an accident. Or that she had died from natural causes. She would have been found in bed, not in a public canal. They would not have risked bringing suspicion on themselves by acting recklessly.”

“Who knows what anyone is capable of?”

“Not murder. Not Marco,” Tintoretto replied firmly, “I do not believe it.”

“It wasn’t me.”

“You have told that already. Have I accused you?”

“Not in words.”

"Not in a look either!" Tintoretto retorted heatedly. "We must be calm and consider all the facts."

"Rosella has been murdered and you say that the Gianettis cannot be responsible... But why would anyone else want her death?"

Tintoretto thought back to something Ira had said earlier. "Rosella is in the morgue now?"

"Yes."

"Several months ago I went to the morgue do an anatomy study." The artist chose his words with care. "There was the body of a girl that I recognised. She was called Gabriella Russo and she had posed for me a few times—"

Ira flinched. *"Here?"*

"Yes."

"Rosella posed for you too! I knew I should never have allowed it—"

"Listen to me, Ira! Please, listen. The girl died in horrible circumstances, her body mutilated." He stared at Ira. "Do you know the Dutchman, Barent der Witt?"

"I know of him. Why?"

"His daughter was murdered in The Hague, and there was another woman killed in France. The Dutchman came to Venice in the hope of finding the killer, but he was too late to help Gabriella. Now Rosella has been killed." Tintoretto leaned towards Ira, hurrying on. "Four murders. Two killings in this city within the last few months. And no one held to account. No one even suspected... So I am wondering if the victims were all murdered by the same man."

Ira frowned. "Why was Gabriella Russo killed?"

"I don't know."

"But if no one is suspected, how can we prove anything? How can we even prove there is a connection? You are grasping at straws." Ira replied, his head in his hands. "Rosella did not know Gabriella Russo, or the women in The Hague and France. *Rosella* is dead and it's her we should be thinking about."

"But if the same man killed all four women—"

"And how will you prove it?" Ira replied desperately. "I *hit* my sister, remember?"

"That was an accident! You were fighting with Marco and Rosella got in the way—"

"What if I *meant* to hurt her?..."

"Did you?"

"...Maybe think I did." Ira admitted.

The painter took in a breath. "Do not repeat what you have just said to anyone. The Doge and the Venetian authorities are draconian on murder. The prisons are always full, but most demeanours are due to whoring and theft. There are few murders in the Republic and the Doge wishes that it remains that way. All the more reason, Ira, that you must take great care. Be judicious, calm, answer any of their questions with equanimity... Where were you when Rosella was killed?"

"You think I did it?"

"No! I am merely asking what *they* will ask you... Where were you?"

"They said that my sister was found about an hour after her death. At that time I would have been between patient visits. There was a long walk between the two locations—"

Tintoretto nodded. "And you were alone?"

"Yes, I was alone."

"No one saw you?"

"I walked past many people, nowhere is empty in Venice, but I doubt they would remember me, or I them." His voice was speeding up. "It was dark, it was cold, people were intent on their own business. No, no one can vouch for me! I spoke to no one, I bought nothing, I was just walking..."

Tintoretto leaned towards him. "Who told you that Rosella had been killed?"

"The gatekeeper at the ghetto."

"And when did the authorities come to see you?"

"They asked me to go to their offices this morning and I have been there all day. I came here as soon as they let me leave." Ira stared at the artist. "What if they don't believe me? What if they really think I killed Rosella? They knew about our arguments, the bad feelings. They will—"

"They will do nothing – unless you give them reason to suspect you." Tintoretto replied, rising to his feet. "I have a friend, a patron who is connected to the Council of Forty."

"I don't understand."

"The Council of Forty deals with crime in Venice. It is made up of counsellors from the nobility – not lawyers – but they act as both jury and judge. They decide and give a ruling on violent crimes like murder." He took off his work apron and tossed it to one side. "Stay here, Ira, I will go and see him."

"But surely if he is a member of the Council he will not see you about this—"

"He is not a member. He is my patron and a friend."

Tintoretto put a hand on Ira's shoulder. "Stay here, speak to no one, and wait for my return. Do you hear me, Ira? Say nothing."

Chapter Fifty

Below he could hear the guards at the water entrance, someone calling out to a passing woman on the bridge. She said something in reply which Marco could not hear and then she laughed. The sound snaked up from the water and up the stone walls, pushing its tongue into the crumbling brickwork and then falling deep amongst the wooden poles on which the city rested.

Silence followed. Behind him, Marco could hear the lowered voice of the lawyer, Ferriti, the squirrel like man bending down to speak to his grandmother. One hand rested on the back of her chair, the other on his leg, a ring on the first finger of his right hand. Perhaps a crest ring, Marco wasn't sure. Perhaps it was the Gianetti crest – but then a lawyer would not be allowed to wear that, only members of the family could.

He would be able to wear it. *He* would be able to use it to impress its design into the wax when he signed and sealed documents. The Gianetti crest, known all over Italy... Looking up, Marco's gaze rested on the stained glass panel of a triumphant bull, the animal treading an armed man underfoot. The Gianetti family, crushing his enemies as easily as a man could crush mosquitoes from the wetlands outside Venice.

As a child he had been taken there once, by Cara. When he was ten and she was twenty. No one ever wished to know where Marco went – as long as he was accompanied, no one worried. And so Cara, plump and full of mischief, took her young charge to the wetlands where the fisherman worked, and where the sand flats extended towards the far horizon into the clouds. They had eaten a meal of bread and salted fish, their company merely a trio of elegant heron and a flock of indignant geese. A sky that had no intention of darkening and a sun that was holding tight to the day, saw them wander amongst the eerie quiet sand flats, the light casting chequered shadows from the fishing nets.

It had been long before Marco had known what the future would bring him, or that his promised legacy wavered on a lie... He glanced over to his grandmother, the pernicky Ferriti still leaning over her like a weather vane and wondered what he was predicting. And if he had ever suspected that the arrangements he was making for Marco's inheritance would be declared null and voice in a court of law.

If Aretino exposed the truth.

If he took the letter from Marco's real father and that of his mother, and waved the catastrophic duo at the Venetian authorities. And all that prevented – and prolonged – the revelation was Aretino's paid silence... Marco knew he was trapped, but had accepted his capture in return for the power. After all, he reasoned, the legacy was plentiful, enough to assuage Aretino's greed... Marco's gaze moved upward to the stained glass window again, fixing on the Gianetti crest. His grandmother did not realise it, but he had no intention of marrying Rosella Tabat. He would not tell her his decision until his legacy was confirmed, but he would never marry the mother of his child. He had some real affection for Rosella, as he had once had affection for Ira, but their relationship had curdled and belonged in his past.

"Marco?"

He turned to his grandmother. "Yes?"

"You have some final papers to sign now and then the documents will be official, as will your legacy, making you Master of the Gianetti household." She gestured to Ferriti, watching as the lawyer set the papers on the table for Marco to sign them. Content, she then waved the lawyer aside, waiting for Ferriti to leave the room before speaking to her grandson again. "Remember what I asked of you – include me in your dealings and I will assist you to the best of my ability. As I did for your father."

And he wanted to say *how?* How did you assist my drunken, treacherous father, a stranger you never knew? But he didn't blame her, because he realised Jacopo Gianetti had deceived his grandmother just as he had deceived him. And now *he* was about to repeat the past in denying the Contessa the truth.

"How does it feel, Marco, to be master?"

"It feels..." he paused, shuffling words. "...comfortable."

Idly he moved about the room, his hand resting on a celestial globe, then touching a marble portrait head of a satyr. The bronze statue in Jacopo's study would be removed, Marco decided, relegated to the storerooms below, and a marble nude put in its place. Smiling to himself, he moved over to the window, looking down into the Lagoon. The servants were lighting the first early lamps as the afternoon closed in, the water throwing back the illumination as it flickered against the stone walls.

His pleasure came as a surprise to him, an intensity beyond eroticism. No woman had ever excited such emotion as the realisation that all Venice would admire him. The handsome, charming Gianetti heir. No longer ignored, or touted as Aretino's protégé. No, he would be a man of influence in his own right, at the head of a prestigious family and fortune. He would provide for his child with Rosella, but in time he would marry and have another son, maybe several sons, consolidating his empire for their eventual inheritance.

And then he remembered Aretino. The fat devil who would always be just behind him. Holding an empty purse towards him, smiling like a wolf with Adamo Baptista in his wake... Marco winced, unsettled. He imagined for an instant that Aretino had died and the secret with him. But he knew that the writer would have made certain he could keep working the puppet strings, even from hell. Adamo Baptista was still young, if not aware of Marco's origins now, he would be in time. Or would he? Marco wondered. After all, how would it profit the dead Aretino if Baptista continued the blackmail? Aretino had no family, no dependents, it would not be in his nature to give Baptista such an opportunity. Perhaps, Marco thought with increasing hope, when the writer died, he *would* be free.

With such a feeling of expectancy, Marco left the room, the Contessa having fallen into a doze in her chair. His steps were quick down the corridor, his mood exhilarated, when Ferriti suddenly approached him.

"You have a visitor, Signor Gianetti."

"I am not expecting anyone."

"The gentleman says it is of great importance that he speaks with you."

"Tell him I will see him tomorrow. Ask for his name—"

"I have his name, signor. It is Aretino, Pietro Aretino."

'Let him back in – and you destroy us all.'

His grandmother's words came back to Marco as he shook his head. "No, Signor Ferriti, I cannot see him. Tell him I am not at home."

"But you are," a voice boomed down the corridor, "you are standing here in front of me, very much at home." Aretino said, walking, flat footed, towards him. "You must not bar me, friend, today of all days."

Marco stared at him. How had the writer known he had just signed the documents which secured the Gianetti inheritance? Barely before the ink was dry on the paper he had appeared, magicked himself into a house which should have denied him admittance. And now he was standing, wrapped in a voluminous red cape, his feet swollen in their embroidered shoes, and behind him stood Adamo Baptista.

"Should I call the guards, signor?" Ferriti asked.

"No," Marco replied shortly, "I will attend to this."

"Would you like me to remain?"

"You don't need a nanny," Aretino said, "I won't hurt you. We are merely talking." He looked at the lawyer. "You may leave us."

Ferriti glanced over to Marco, then nodded as he was dismissed.

His light mood vanished, Marco retraced his steps down the passageway past the room where his grandmother was sleeping, moving into a reception room at the front of the palazzo. The chamber was decorated in a soft, limpid green, the cornice and ceiling gilded, curtains drawn back and looped with corded silk. In the fireplace a blaze had been lit, tempering the chill of the October evening. In silence, Marco moved over to an armchair, gesturing for Aretino to take the one opposite him across the fireplace, six feet between them.

And leaning against the wall by the door, Baptista stood with his arms folded, his face expressionless.

"Such a tragedy."

Marco stared at him, the words meaning nothing. "I don't know to what you refer."

"The poor girl. Who would have expected such a dreadful event?"

"Which poor girl?"

Aretino glanced over to Baptista then leaned forward in his seat. His voice was hushed, thick with sympathy.

"Rosella Tabat. She has been found murdered."

"Rosella murdered?" Marco shook his head. "No, that can't be true."

"But it is," Aretino insisted, "her body was discovered yesterday evening. I had thought you would have heard, that was why I came to offer my condolences."

"Rosella?" Marco repeated dully. "She is having my child—"

"No, my friend, she is dead."

"But why would she be dead?" Marco looked from Aretino to Baptista, his confusion obvious. "She was well yesterday. I sent word to the ghetto and was told Rosella was recovered—"

"From her brother's attack?"

"Ira did not attack her!" Marco replied hotly. "It was a mistake, he was aiming for me and hit Rosella instead."

"Of course you would say that—"

"I would say that because it is the truth!" Marco snapped, staring at the massive figure facing him, the red cape flashing crimson as the firelight illuminated it. "Rosella came between us, that was all. It was a mistake."

"She had come between you and Ira for some while, hadn't she?" Aretino said, "Her pregnancy had caused her brother much humiliation. I heard he was not speaking to her and that the poor girl was living with neighbours."

"No, no, it wasn't like that." Marco corrected him. "Rosella just wanted to be with the Fasculos. She found a mother figure in Gilda—"

"The usurer?" Aretino raised his eyebrows. "The Tabats keep bad company. You know the Fasculo woman is a money lender, a thief, a fugitive from her native Florence? Why would Rosella consort with such people?"

"They were friends. Gilda is not a thief, she helps the poorest in the ghetto, people who cannot obtain a loan from elsewhere. The Venetian law—"

"You are questioning the law of the Republic?" Aretino asked, exchanging a glance with Baptista. "You are an Italian, now the Master of a great family, you would do well to choose your friends with more care." He sighed expansively. "People will try to take advantage of you now, Marco, you must beware."

The atmosphere in the chamber had shifted; Aretino falling silent, Baptista still standing by the door as Marco hesitated. His breath seemed to strain from his lungs, his ribs barely moving as he felt the full force of his visitor's ominous presence. Should he believe him? He wondered. Was Rosella truly dead, or was it another trick? Another lie? ... A threat hung in the air between them; it was heavy, choked with malice, Marco struggling to clear his thoughts.

"Why would anyone kill Rosella?"

"Why do you think, Marco?"

And he wanted to say – *Was it you? No, it would not be you, it would be the man standing by the door. The man saying nothing, his expression unreadable. Adamo Baptista... Had he killed Rosella?...* Marco struggled to inhale, touching his breast, his fingers bruising the beaded velvet.

"I don't understand. Who killed Rosella?"

"You know who killed her," Aretino said, with a frisson of impatience. "You are the head of the Gianetti household, you must take charge and speak up. You cannot demand respect unless you earn it."

"I don't believe she's dead or murdered!" Marco said defiantly. "How did she die?"

"She was strangled."

He could feel the blood fizz in his ears, the fire's flames making darts up the chimney, the padded doublet crushing his chest. Urgently his hands gripped the velvet and tore the waistcoat apart as he gasped for air.

And Aretino watched him, in silence, waiting until Marco had steadied himself. "I am heartbroken to be the bearer of such sorrowful news. Poor Rosella, it was a poor death" the writer continued, "but she will have justice."

"Yes." Marco nodded, avoiding Baptista's gaze, wondering what to say.

Wondering which was the murderer in the room, or if he was floundering in some great pool where the water was black underneath him and the ghouls were reaching up to take hold of his feet. For some inexplicable reason, he thought of the flatlands, the acres of water and solitude.

"It was not me."

"I know that. You are not capable of such horror. But" Aretino said, his voice compassionate, "we must be very careful, or you will be blamed."

Marco's head jerked up. "*How can I be blamed?* I did nothing."

"But there are rumours. People have been talking about the suggested marriage of you and poor Rosella Tabat, horrified that that a Jewess – a *pregnant* Jewess – would become mistress of the Gianetti family—"

"How would anyone know?" Mario asked, baffled. "We spoke of it in private."

"How many times do I have to tell you there are spies everywhere in Venice? Everything is heard and anything of importance is reported back to me. There has been talk..." he pulled his chair closer to Marco, his voice low. "... that you were unwilling to marry Rosella Tabat, that you were being coerced by your grandmother."

"My grandmother wanted it," Marco agreed, "but I was not against it—"

"Yet when we spoke the other day you were musing about finding your own wife, someone more suited to your position, were you not?"

Outmanoeuvred, Marco shook his head. "I... I... I cannot think clearly—"

"No, you cannot, and that is why you must let your friends think for you at this sad time," Aretino said smoothly. "We must not let any suspicion fall on you. There must be no hint of guilt on your part."

"There can be none, because I did *nothing!*"

"We know that," Aretino gestured to the man by the door, Baptista barely nodding. "but people believe rumours. You had tricked Rosella and then seduced her. She was carrying your child. Actions which are not the behaviour of a gentleman—"

"You forced me into tricking her!"

"— but *you* complied," Aretino retorted coldly. "You went along with it, and then you were ashamed and ran away from Venice. Only the guilty run, Marco, did your tutor never tell you that? And you *stayed* away, whilst your lover faced disgrace alone. People might think that on your return Rosella confronted you, you argued, and there was an accident that ended in tragedy—"

"No!" Marco replied heatedly. "There was no argument. I did not even know she was carrying my child. I would not have left Venice had I known."

"A guilty man denies everything—"

"I am not guilty!" Marco replied, "I did nothing. I did not kill her, I would not hurt her, I cared for Rosella, every one knows that."

"As everyone knows you fought with her brother on your return." Aretino said calmly. "The brother who had been so ashamed of his sister's behaviour. The same brother who was angry with her, who wouldn't talk to her, who blamed her for bringing disgrace to the family. The respected doctor with the brilliant future who is now a laughing stock." Aretino leaned closer. "How he must have hated her—"

"He loved Rosella!"

"— she was strangled. They say that is a very personal

crime, committed by someone who wants to look their victim in the eyes as they kill them."

"Enough!" Marco shouted, jumping to his feet. "Ira would not kill his sister."

"Your loyalty does you justice, but you must consider the facts. Ira Tabat is a doctor, a man who deals with life and death every day. He is also a very proud man—"

"Because he stood up to you?" Marco countered, immediately regretting his words. "Pride does not make a man a murderer."

"Sit down, Marco," the writer said, gesturing to the seat he had vacated. "You are in shock, you do not know what you are saying. I understand – you were a friend of Ira Tabat's, and close to Rosella – but suspicious as it looks for Ira, it also looks dangerous for *you*." He glanced away, then paused to listen. There were voices outside, people talking and laughing, then silence. "You hear that? Venice is a chattering city. Hear how they gossip, every bit of news fought over like crows fighting for a scrap of meat. People love scandal, murder, punishment..."

Almost hypnotised, Marco watched him as he continued to speak.

"... I do not wish anything to happen to you, Marco. I am most fond of you and wish to protect you."

No, you wish only to protect your *investment*, Marco thought to himself. You are not concerned about me, but about your prosperity, the possibility that you might loose out on the Gianetti fortune. You do not care if I am the killer, but you care that I am saved in order to remain your hostage.

"I did not kill Rosella Tabat."

"I know that, Marco. We both know that, don't we?" he glanced over to Baptista who nodded. "We are your protectors, we will keep you safe. But only if you do as we say. Otherwise, you put yourself in great peril. I have friends amongst the Council of Forty, but no influence. You must understand that the Doge is intolerant of murder, and I can only protect you if you work with me, and are guided by me."

"But we should find the real killer—"

"We *know* the real killer," Aretino said patiently, "I realise how difficult it to accept that Ira has murdered his sister—"

"We do not know that!" Marco replied hotly. "It could have been someone else—"

"Who?" Aretino asked. "In whose interests would it be to murder Rosella Tabat? She had no money, nothing of interest to anyone – except her brother. And *you*." He shook his head as though exasperated. "The motive is obvious – passion. The girl's killing was spontaneous—"

"How would you know that?"

Stepping forward, Adamo Baptista answered.

"A planned murder would have been committed in private. Not a violent act in a public place, where anyone could have come across them fighting or seen the killer. The girl was murdered in the heat of the moment, in an argument probably, but it was not planned."

"And you're an authority on this subject?" Marco asked defiantly.

His courage shocked him. That he would bait a man of whom so many were afraid – a running mate of Aretino's, a known villain, gambler, spy – and yet he felt compelled to make some resistance, some show of defiance. The outcome was predictable, Marco already knew that. He would be manipulated into place, Aretino making all his gestures and speaking all his words as his puppet performed the set piece written for him. The mannequin was not to be allowed to resist; his strings were not to be cut whilst his pockets could be so profitably picked.

Afraid for his own life, desperate to retain the Gianetti name and fortune, Marco turned away from Aretino's gaze, passing Baptista as he moved to the window. Instinct told him that Ira had not killed his sister; however much his pride had been injured, however much he had believed himself wronged, he would not have killed Rosella...

But neither had he.

He was innocent. If the authorities suspected him his life would be ruined. And if he was imprisoned and put on trial – or if he tried to protect Ira – Marco knew that Aretino would desert him. Pretend that he too had been duped, deny all accusations of blackmail as he exposed Marco's origins; holding him up for all of Venice to see – a liar, a bastard, the kind of man who might well commit murder to protect his status and his legacy.

Baptista's voice was even when he spoke again. "You would do well not to provoke me, Marco. I can be a valuable ally, but a ruthless enemy."

"I do not doubt it."

"Come now," Aretino said smoothly, "let us not talk of enemies, we must work together, for the good of all of us. Believe me, Marco, you would not survive a week in the Doge's New Prisons. They have as many as ten men in a cell and the conditions are brutal. Especially for the nobility." He sighed. "I could not help you if it went so far, my friend.

If you lost your status you would not even have the money to pay friends to bring food into you."

If you lost your status... He was making it clear, Marco thought to himself. Spelling it out like letters to a child. If you refuse to do as I say, I will ruin you.

Chapter Fifty One

Bakita was standing at the entrance to Caterina's house when the Dutchman approached and requested admittance.

"I will ask Signora Zucca," the guard replied, gesturing to a maid in the hallway. "Tell Signora Zucca that Signora der Witt wishes to see her."

The maid nodded and ran upstairs, the Dutchman smiling. "Your Italian is improving quickly." He remarked.

"My mistress is a good tutor."

"And a friend?"

"I hope I may say so." Bakita replied, "in time."

"And yet she bars old friends," der Witt replied, taking off his hat and rolling it in his hands. "Do you know why I am in exile?" when he realised that the man did not understand him, he repeated the question more simply. "Why does she not let me in?"

The guard, resplendent in his striped silk uniform, his cropped hair covered by a silk turban, fixed his dark eyes on the Dutchman. "I do not know."

"And if you did, you would not admit it," der Witt replied, seeing the maid over the guard's shoulder beckon to him.

"I am allowed admittance," he said pleasantly, Bakita stepping back to let him enter.

In her sitting room above, Caterina was preparing herself. Lying back against a cushioned sofa, her dress displayed to its full advantage, she turned her face slightly to the light and smiled as the Dutchman entered.

"I was worried you would not see me."

She nodded to Bakita, knowing he would close the door and then stand on guard. "Why would I not see you, old friend?"

"I believe I frightened you."

"*Yes, you did!*" she retorted sharply. "You acted so oddly, what were you meaning? I came to you with news that I thought would be of interest and you acted like a stranger." She smoothed her hair. "A sinister stranger at that."

"I was testing you."

She threw up her hands. "Testing me! For what?"

"You came telling me about another girl being killed. And wondered how you knew about it so quickly—"

"Because I saw her!" Caterina replied, "I saw the murdered girl when they brought her out of the water. I told you that when we met, I explained. Why did you doubt me?" her tone was angry. "How often have we spoken of the murders? Worried about your being made to seem the killer? Of course I told you! Why would I *not* warn you?"

"You sounded as though you suspected me."

"No, you *acted* as though I suspected you," Caterina countered. "If I had truly thought you a murderer would I have gone to your house alone? I left Bakita here. I didn't want him to overhear our conversation, I was trying to protect you, in case anyone came after you." She paused, shaking her head. "You and I share secrets. We *must* trust and protect each other."

"I have become suspicious of everyone. Even you." He said uncertainly. "Do they know who the dead girl was?"

"Rosella Tabat, from the Jewish ghetto," Caterina replied, "that is all I know so far, but my maid hears every morsel of gossip and will no doubt have more to tell me... You worried me, old friend. You were not yourself."

"I'm sorry..." He replied, then added "...but I don't want you to suspect me. I did not kill the girl."

A silence fell between them, Caterina reaching for his hand and holding it for an instant against her cheek. It was true that she had been afraid of him, and although he had explained his behaviour she was still wary. Not for a moment did she truly suspect him the Dutchman of murder, but there had been a darkness about him that she had not expected and it had left her uneasy. They shared too much for her to banish him, but as der Witt continued to talk Caterina thought of the clump of hair she had taken from the dead girl's hand. The hair now hidden in her desk, behind lock and key.

She had studied the hair many times. Short in length, with only a slight wave. Very dark hairs, one of them grey – and she had considered from whose head they might have come. From the Dutchman? She knew his hair well, had touched it when they had made love; it was short and dark, but his grey hairs were plentiful. Even in a small sample there would have been more white hairs than just the one. Her thoughts had then moved onto Aretino, who was dismissed immediately. A killer in his fantasies, but not in life. Which left Adamo Baptista. Caterina remembered his hair too. She had been forbidden to touch it when they had had sex, but she had noted its thickness and the way it grew long at the base of his neck. Hair with a slight wave, but densely, uniformly black.

Often she had thought of showing the hair to der Witt, but had resisted, withholding the evidence for a reason she did not fully understand.

She would.

In time.

Chapter Fifty Two

Despite Tintoretto's efforts, the following day he was told by his patron that the matter had been handed over to the Council of Forty and on 12th October 1548 Ira Tabat was arrested. Angrily, the painter demanded to see Ira at the prison, but was told that no visitors were allowed, unless they were members of the prisoner's family. Thwarted, the painter headed for the Gianetti palazzo and asking to see Marco. There also he was refused admittance.

"Give him my name!" Tintoretto shouted to the guards. "He knows me well."

"Signor Gianetti is seeing no one," was the reply. "No one is to be admitted."

"I am Tintoretto, *Il Furioso*, I demand to see him." The painter shouted, calling up at the window. "Marco! Marco! Let me in!"

But the windows remained closed, the doors locked against him, the old Contessa ducking back from the balcony of her sitting room, watching as *Il Furioso* stormed away, muttering under his breath. The death of Rosella had affected her more than she would ever have thought. Perhaps, Lavinia wondered, she had imagined some family life in the Gianetti palazzo. A mother and father with a child, brought up within the sumptuous walls; some form of blessing to overpower a tragic heritage.

It had not been meant. Death walked the hallways and the kitchens below. Suicide, madness, murder, all breeding amongst the Titian and Bellini paintings and the Cellini sculptures. Where once she had come as a young bride expecting love and ready to bear a flock of children, Lavinia had aged amongst coldness, separation, rooms and hearts segregated. The rebellious desire to see her grandson marry Rosella Tabat had been her swansong.

But the dark had overpowered her.

"You should speak with him." Lavinia said, turning to her grandson. "Tintoretto was a friend of yours, as well as your mentor. This tragedy must not destroy all friendships. The painter knew the Tabats well—"

"Can no one talk of anything else?" Marco replied, "it is news in all the taverns and in the streets, the pamphlets are full of it. Tintoretto has allowed his drawing of Rosella to be reproduced in print, alongside that of Ira Tabat—"

"How strange you now refer to him as *Ira Tabat.*"

"That is his name."

"Before you would have said just Ira." The old woman replied, "do you believe that he killed his sister?"

"No..."

"But you do not speak up for him." The Contessa replied sharply.

"How can I be *certain* Ira did not kill Rosella? The evidence is against him." Marco turned away from his grandmother, unwilling for her to see his face. "Everyone knows he has a fierce temper. Look how we fought..." Marco let the inference hang, then hurried on. "Ira Tabat was ashamed of Rosella, everyone knew he was angry with her."

"Siblings quarrel, it does not usually result in murder."

"Ira would barely speak to Rosella, and he hit her—"

"**Marco!**" Lavinia snapped. "You told me that was an accident. Tintoretto told me the same. Were you both lying, or is it just you who wants to make Ira seem guilty? Why is that? What have you against him? You were friends once."

"That was the past—"

"Yesterday is the past. We live through the past to get to the present. So what changed in your relationship with Ira?" Marco shrugged, longing to change the subject, Lavinia continuing. "He disapproved of Aretino, didn't he? Ira thought you were wasting your life, mixing with the wrong people—"

"We grew apart, with different interests. I moved into a different social circle."

"You moved into a circle of hell," she replied, cupping her chin in her hand and looking ahead thoughtfully. "Like Tintoretto, I imagine Ira tried to advise you, warn you about the writer—"

"He was jealous." Marco said, on the defensive. "Envious of my new life."

"Maybe he was, a little. Maybe Ira saw you living without responsibility, flattered and petted, a great legacy waiting for you when your father died. Yes, I imagine Ira *was* a little jealous as he worked daily to provide for a dying mother and his sister." her voice hardened. "But is that reason enough to abandon him when he most needs you?"

"I can do nothing to help Ira Tabat," Marco replied. "The evidence damns him."

"The evidence also serves you poorly." She gave her grandson a sidelong glance. "I do not doubt that some will suggest you might have been the killer."

"*Dear God, how can you say that!* I was here when Rosella was killed."

"In the palazzo? You say you were here, but how would I know? How would anyone know? This place has dozens of rooms, corridors, passageways, the cellars themselves reach like tentacles into the Lagoon." She smiled wryly. "No, I do not suspect you, Marco. I know you did not kill Rosella, but I am not convinced that Ira did."

"He had a reason to kill her. He was ashamed of her."

"An honour killing? Rosella had brought disgrace on her family and he was obliged to make restitution? If that is so, why did he not kill *you*? You seduced her, Marco, she was carrying *your* child. *You* were the reason she was disgraced—"

Cornered, Marco moved to the door. The arrest of Ira had become a scandal once it was known that Marco Gianetti had been due to marry Rosella Tabat. The Jewess from the ghetto, the woman who had been carrying his child. And when Ira was charged with the murder of his sister the city clamoured for news. On the rare occasions Marco left the palazzo he was approached and followed, the Doge requesting a meeting – Aretino's intervention ensuring that any suspicion concerning Marco was summarily crushed. In the shadow of the malignant Behemoth, Marco was shielded and whilst Ira was imprisoned he walked Venice a free man.

Having been about to leave, Marco paused at the door

and turned back to his grandmother. "What do you want from me? What do you want me to say? I did wrong, I know that. But I cannot change anything. Why do you have to torment me? Rosella is dead, the baby is dead, and Ira Tabat will pay for it."

"No," she said simply. "If he is found guilty, he will be executed – but *you* will pay."

Gilda Tabat pushed away the ledger she had been working on, her attention wandering. Around her she could hear the usual noises of the ghetto; voices, dogs barking, plates clattered one against the other, and occasionally someone playing a piano. Hyman Golletz, she thought, the old man making tunes into the night. Rising to her feet, she walked to the door and stood, looking out. The curfew was long over, the ghetto inhabitants gathered in, two children swinging from a lantern hook in the wall.

"Ira never killed his sister."Angelo said suddenly.

Gilda nodded. "I know."

"Do you think it was Marco Gianetti?"

Giada glanced at her son. "No, he didn't kill Rosella, not with his own hands. But he was responsible. I don't know how, but he was. And he's going to let Ira die for a murder he didn't commit."

"He can't do that—"

"He *can*. And he will. Marco Gianetti's involvement can be traced through all of this. It was him that tricked Rosella into meeting with Adamo Baptista; it was him who seduced her and made her pregnant; and now it's him – Marco

Gianetti – who will not say one word in his friend's defence." She shivered at the doorway. "With his power and money he could have found the real killer."

"Unless it *was* Marco Gianetti."

"No, I've told you, Gianetti's not man enough to murder anyone." Gilda replied, "Someone else will have done the killing. Someone like Adamo Baptista. Perhaps on Aretino's orders. After all, Marco and the writer are old allies. They have the power, the money... These are the people who rule this city. How long has Aretino terrorised his victims? How long has Baptista come to houses like ours and threatened us with the galleys? Oh, I remember every word he said to me – and so do many others." Her voice cut like a blade. "Gianetti will not get away with this, I swear it. The wolves – Aretino, Baptista and Gianetti – will suffer. If it takes me a day, a month, a year or a decade, I will have revenge on all three of them. Gianetti in particular. And I will not be alone."

She moved indoors, closing the door behind her, Angelo following. "What are you going to do?"

"Rosella was one of us, a Jew who belonged in the ghetto with us. As did Ira. If he is found guilty tomorrow – which he will be – he will be put to death. Then, despite the scandal, everyone will forget. It may take a little time, but it will happen. And Marco Gianetti will prosper and marry and have a family; Aretino will bribe and charm his soiled body further into the Doge's court; and Baptista will move about Venice unchallenged, his reputation as feared as that of the devil himself." She drew in her breath. "But we have something they do not – the ghetto. There is power in numbers, in a group banded together in a common cause. Believe me, as they have sought to destroy us, we will destroy *them*."

"How?" Angelo asked, "how can we?"

"By waiting." His mother replied, "we wait and wait, and if necessary we wait a little longer. We are patient for the perfect time, the precise moment..." She picked up a kitchen knife, driving the blade into the wooden table "...and then we strike."

Chapter Fifty Three

Through the intercession of his patron, Tintoretto was allowed to visit Ira in prison. The trial had been a debacle, the involvement of Marco Gianetti making what would have been a quiet affair into a circus. In an attempt to curtail public interest, the Council of Forty had held the trail in secret, but details had filtered out and gossip was rife. Watching from the sidelines, der Witt hoped that there might be an investigation into there being another killer, but there was none. And he, together with Caterina Zucca, witnessed the disastrous proceedings in silence. Ira Tabat was beaten, but The Wolves of Venice were not.

In court, Ira's natural reserve did not serve him well, he seemed to be indifferent, removed from the case. A man without feelings could easily be regarded as a murderer, people thought, and even when details of Rosella's death were discussed Ira expressed no emotion.

"You must fight back!" Tintoretto told him, sitting on a bench in a cramped prison cell. One of a row of single, narrow cells with a connecting corridor. "You must rebut their accusations."

"They have already made their judgement, I am guilty in their eyes." Ira replied, "Witnesses have spoken of my anger towards my sister, my hurt pride, my sense of shame that she was unmarried and pregnant, and the fact that I struck her—"

"*Which you do not do on purpose!*" The artist retorted. "I have gone to the authorities and given a statement to that effect. I expect them to call me as a witness at any time. No one must be unaware of the truth."

"The truth? The absolute truth is an instrument that can only be played by an expert."

Tintoretto sighed. "My application to the Council that consider another person to be the murderer was dismissed. There was no evidence to support it. When I informed them about der Witt's daughter, the death of Gabriella Russo and the woman in France, they almost laughed in my face. Told me I was weaving fairy tales. They even said that I should not endanger my own status by supporting a suspected killer."

"They are right, you should not." Ira replied. "You should not even be here. But I am grateful that you are."

"They will not allow anyone from the ghetto to visit you."

"No, I thought not. I am not even allowed the comfort of my own people." Ira replied, adding bitterly. "Marco Gianetti did this."

"The murder? No, no, he is not capable. You cannot truly think he killed your sister."

Ira stared ahead.

"He *caused* her death. If he did not murder her with his own hands, he caused it to happen. The night he arranged for Adamo Baptista to walk my sister home – that was when it all began. *That* was Marco's doing. Marco, obeying Aretino's orders." Ira lowered his head. After a month's imprisonment he had lost weight, his collar bones protruding, his face gaunt. Food had been brought in for him, but had been ignored, wine also had been sent from the ghetto, but little was touched. "If he chose, Marco could speak up for me, he could tell them how I loved my sister, how I could never have killed Rosella." His voice wavered. "He knew us, we were friends. How *could* he let them believe I'm her killer?"

"You have to speak up for yourself—"

"To what end!" Ira snapped, his temper rising. "I am as nothing to the likes of Gianetti, Aretino and the Council of Forty. I have no say in this city, no power. This is all planned."

"Planned?" Tintoretto leaned towards him. "*What* is planned?"

"Marco needs a scapegoat, and I serve that purpose." Ira replied, glancing at the artist. "Consider this. Marco has just inherited a vast legacy and the honourable name of Gianetti. Perhaps he decided that marriage to my sister would not serve him – even if it had been his grandmother's wish. Suddenly he wanted to be rid of Rosella, to free himself."

"Not by murder—"

"Marco was always foolish, lead by the nose by charlatans... I see the hand of Pietro Aretino in this."

Tintoretto clicked his tongue. "That bloated pig has been quiet, not seen at court since the trail began."

"He will be watching, mark my words." Ira replied, "He used Marco as a puppet before and he will be using him again. Marco has a great fortune and status now, but no true friends. He will be feeling adrift, his sudden prominence unnerving – what better time for the bastard Aretino to offer support? "

"Surely even Marco would not be that stupid?"

"He's lost, he always was, and people like Pietro Aretino always attack the weakest lamb, the one trailing behind the flock."

"Then we most expose him!"

"Aretino?" Ira countered wretchedly. "'The Scourge of Kings,' the blackmailer royal? Better and richer men than I have tried and failed. Aretino has the favour of the Doge, he has the powerful eating from his hand like snakes taking milk from a saucer."

"Then I will talk to Marco, force my way in if I have to."

"He will not see you!" Ira snapped. "He *cannot* see you, *cannot* face you. Do you *still* not understand?" his voice dropped, all anger gone. "Please, will you make me a promise?"

"Anything."

"Discover who killed Rosella and the other women about whom you told me. Find the murderer and stop him. Get justice for his victims, and clear my name... Will you do that for me?"

"You have my word."

Ira nodded. "You have been an unexpected friend and a great comfort to me, Tintoretto, I thank you for that."

"You speak as if it were over—"

"It *is* over for me," Ira replied, composed. "But time will tell when it is truly over. Marco Gianetti has much on his conscience and the likes of Aretino and Baptista should beware. One man might be overpowered, but justice will not be so easily trodden underfoot. This murderous game is merely beginning."

Chapter Fifty Four

On 25th October 1548 Ira Tabat was hanged, a rabbi from the ghetto staying with him throughout his final hours and at his end. In a square courtyard away from sight, Ira was lead to the scaffold calmly claiming his innocence and making a wish that the true murderer of his sister be found and punished. The Council of Forty, despite Tintoretto's many and desperate entreaties, refused to reconsider their verdict and all mention of another person being responsible for Rosella Tabat's murder was expunged from the record.

It was a grieving Tintoretto that returned to his studio, letting his apprentices leave early and bolting the double doors. Cold to the marrow, he threw kindling on the stove and sat beside it, remembering when he had talked with Ira there. How he had warned him, advised him, to no avail. Ira Tabat, rigid to the last, had refused to pander to the court and had paid the highest cost known to man. Without lighting any candles, the artist continued to sit in front of the stove, its meagre illumination making ghouls out of draped paintings and imps out of the little wax figures.

He did not have to concentrate to remember Rosella's face, or Gabriella's. Rosella's mass of black hair and the chip on Gabriella's front tooth; details of faces he knew would accompany him for the remainder of his life. And he thought of Ira, grown thin in prison, his direct gaze just short of arrogance. Their ghosts seemed to gather around him as he sat watching the flames through the glass door of the stove, and for one instant he imagined that he heard the studio door open and a voice call out to him.

Marco as he had been. Young, laughing, bringing wooden crates from the market stained with tomato juice, the colour of blood. Marco, watching Pietro Aretino as he visited, impressed, fascinated, entrapped. Marco, the lad with meagre artistic talent who had played tricks on him, encouraging Rosella in their practical jokes. Marco, now the head of the Gianetti legacy: once affectionate and amusing, now corrupted, a scorpion in silks.

"You are late, why are you always so late?"

"I was looking at the oils in the market—"

"You are a liar, Marco, you were watching the jugglers in the Rialto, someone saw you there. And now you are late. Again."

And he wanted to say that it was of no account any longer. That time meant nothing. Early or late, fate was mapped out, the future moving in rhythm to the clock of the spheres.

Tintoretto glanced over to the painting he had put to one side. Tomorrow he would have to concentrate, he was behind with his work and soon Titian would return from Augsburg and their rivalry would reignite. The contest for commissions would begin again, Aretino his rival's slinking agent, the Doge dispensing largesse to Titian, as *Il Furioso's* triumph threatens Venice's premier painter.

He tried to find some excitement in the idea, thinking of the new painter come to Venice – Veronese, apparently a genius in his youth. Another rival, Tintoretto thought. Well, he would take him on. Like the alley pugilists, he knew how to fight… But grief was not ready to let go and for hours Tintoretto sat by the stove, feeding the listless fire with kindling, seeing faces in amongst the flames of the people he had loved and lost.

Whilst Tintoretto remembered, Marco stood by the window of the Gianetti palazzo and looked out over the night Lagoon. He told himself that his choice had been unavoidable, that his life had been under threat, that his grandmother had been in danger also. But his mind rejected the thoughts. Spitting them out like bad oysters, his memory mocking him. The isolation he had felt as a child seemed to intensify, the ballast of his fortune inadequate, the vacuum inside him expanding until he was sick with distress.

And then he noticed a group of people below, looking up to the windows of the palazzo and staring at him. They did not move and they did not speak, they just accused him. Without court or jury, evidence or rebuttal, they fixed their gaze on him and he knew. He knew they had come from the ghetto; that they had come to revenge Ira Tabat.

Stepping back from the window, Marco nearly stumbled, turning as he heard a servant enter.

"What is it?"

"You called out, signor, do you need something?"

"I made no sound."

"Forgive me, I thought I heard you cry out."

"No, it was not me." Marco replied, gesturing to the window. "Look out and tell me what you see."

Surprised, the servant did as he was told, opening the casement and glancing down.

"I see the Lagoon, Signor, and a gondola."

"What about the people?"

"There are no people, Signor Gianetti. There is no one there."

"The group! Are you blind, can you not see the group looking up at the window?"

"There is no group, no people, signor—"

"But I saw them!"

"If you did, they are not there now." the man replied, "Perhaps they will return later. Are you expecting someone?"

I am expecting ghosts, I wanted to say to him.

I am expecting my mother to come to me and choke and dangle her feet above the floor, looking for purchase. I am expecting Rosella to shake her head at me, and Ira – oh, yes, I am expecting Ira Tabat. Wrathful, like a wronged saint, his eyes burning with revenge. Yes, I wanted to say, I am expecting someone.

For the first weeks after Ira was executed I barely slept. I could tell the shape and depth of every shadow, each corner was measured for any unexpected sound or movement. I had guards, but could I trust them? Sent from Aretino, were they loyal to me? Or to him? My inheritance had given me a status I could never have expected. Invitations poured into my home like melted honey, the Doge courted me and the most influential people in Venice sought my company. I was handsome, amusing, charming, I was everything a great man should have been, and every moment I remembered what I had done.

My conscience thwarted my sleep, my pleasure, my peace.

I told myself that it would fade, that time would blunt the intensity. But the planets worked in reverse, the universe making my conscience defy logic. If I was haunted those first nights after Ira's death, I was ridden by demons in the weeks and months that followed. My grandmother died soon after and the palazzo became entirely mine. A massive colony of majestic rooms and staircases leading upwards and downwards towards more rooms. All filled with sculptures, paintings, silver in cabinets, medals on velvet pads and a myriad of marble pillars like the cold branches of a dying tree.

Wherever I walked, an echo accompanied me. As did my shadow, it followed, one more servant at my bidding. Tintoretto asked to see me, but I refused, I could not have borne the look in his eyes. The accusation, the same look I saw whenever I walked about the streets of Venice. If I crossed people on bridges spanning the canals, or in the churches, or in St Marks Square, there was always that look. I sat in the church pew inherited from my father, with the Gianetti crest branded into the polished wood, and in my direct line of sight was Pietro Aretino. Sometimes with Adamo Baptista, sometimes not.

The writer's girth increased as mine diminished. His greed seemed to pour out of his skin like oil, the great bristle of his beard piebald with age. I paid him and he kept my secret; no one knew of the bastard sitting in the Gianetti pew, or occupying the Gianetti palazzo. And, like Jacopo before me, I lived with the threat of exposure. It became a disease, always present in the blood, but at times virulent, at others, in remission. When Aretino ignored me, the sickness flared up, when he was amicable, my body restored itself.

So the first year passed. Unlike Ira, I lived on. And I knew that ever day I was watched. I could sense it, that unending scrutiny, and remembered how often Aretino had spoken of spies. Spies in the palazzo, spies on the streets, spies from the ghetto. Oh yes, I knew where they came from. I had betrayed the Tabats and my wealth was no protection. At first I thought they would strike, but time passed and they did not. Together with Aretino's threat I lived with the threat from the ghetto, and I changed. My conscience began to waver. I was rich, of high status, who was I to be judged?

In the second year that followed Ira's death I gave myself over to pleasure. Wine was the ideal solution for a guilty conscience and I was glutted with it. Women also, of every race and creed, the Venetian whores always skilful and inventive. With them came the card players, the acrobats, the jesters and tumblers that once I had watched in the park with Ira. In a smear of wine and sex I lunged on, always knowing that the ghetto would one day punish me.

Ghetto, yes, that was the place from which I expected judgement, and I was right. But before they made their move another came into my life. A woman, offering love to a man who had long since ceased to deserve it. A woman who would set in motion the next part of this tale.

Her name was Tita Boldini...

I am writing this forty years on from these events. At the beginning I promised you honesty – and I have kept my word. What follows next in my story you will discover in due course; it is enough to state that Marina Castilano returned to Venice; the Dutchman was betrayed to the Inquisition; and Caterina Zucca came more and more under the protection of her guard, Bakita. As for the others

– Nikolas Volt, that ally of the feared Adamo Baptista – followed the hapless Lauret to his native France; and Aretino kept collecting secrets and filling his pockets.

I had been an innocent once, but had chosen to be corrupted. So I stood by as the Wolves of Venice gathered from all corners of the city to feed off the new arrivals.

And I waited for the ghetto to claim their revenge.

About the Author

ALEX CONNOR also known as Alexandra Connor, has written several historical novels. She is an artist and has worked in the art world for many years and is also a motivational speaker who is regularly featured on television and BBC radio. She has had a variety of careers including photographic model, journalist and working in a Bond Street art gallery. Alex's articles appeared in The Times, The Telegraph, Observer, The Daily Mail, and Le Figaro. She published with Newton Compton Cospirazione Caravaggio (2016) and Il dipinto maledetto (2017) and was awarded the Premio Roma 2017 for foreign fiction.

Hello from Aria

We hope you enjoyed this book! If you did let us know, we'd love to hear from you.

We are Aria, a dynamic digital-first fiction imprint from award-winning independent publishers Head of Zeus. At heart, we're committed to publishing fantastic commercial fiction – from romance and sagas to crime, thrillers and historical fiction. Visit us online and discover a community of like-minded fiction fans!

We're also on the look out for tomorrow's superstar authors. So, if you're a budding writer looking for a publisher, we'd love to hear from you.
You can submit your book online at ariafiction.com/we-want-read-your-book

You can find us at:
Email: aria@headofzeus.com
Website: www.ariafiction.com
Submissions: www.ariafiction.com/we-want-read-your-book

@ariafiction
@Aria_Fiction
@ariafiction